ACCUSED

Also by Lisa Scottoline

Rosato & Associates Novels
Think Twice
Lady Killer
Killer Smile
Dead Ringer
Courting Trouble
The Vendetta Defense
Moment of Truth
Mistaken Identity
Rough Justice
Legal Tender
Everywhere That Mary Went

Don't Go
Come Home
Save Me
Look Again
Daddy's Girl
Dirty Blonde
Devil's Corner
Running from the Law
Final Appeal

Nonfiction (with Francesca Serritella)
Meet Me at Emotional Baggage Claim
Best Friends, Occasional Enemies
My Nest Isn't Empty, It Just Has More Closet Space
Why My Third Husband Will Be a Dog

ACCUSED

A Rosato & Associates Novel

Lisa Scottoline

ST. MARTIN'S PRESS ✠ NEW YORK

ACCUSED. Copyright © 2013 by Smart Blonde, LLC. All rights reserved. Printed in the United States of America. For information, address St. Martin's Press, 175 Fifth Avenue, New York, N.Y. 10010.

www.stmartins.com

The Library of Congress Cataloging-in-Publication Data is available upon request.

ISBN 978-1-250-02765-8 (hardcover)
ISBN 978-1-250-02766-5 (e-book)

St. Martin's Press books may be purchased for educational, business, or promotional use. For information on bulk purchases, please contact Macmillan Corporate and Premium Sales Department at 1-800-221-7945, extension 5442, or write specialmarkets@macmillan .com.

First Edition: November 2013

10 9 8 7 6 5 4 3 2 1

To my amazing daughter, Francesca

Fiat justitia, ruat caelum.
Let justice be done, though the heavens may fall.

—William Murray, Somersett's Case, 1772

ACCUSED

Chapter One

CONGRATULATIONS! read the banner, but Mary DiNunzio still couldn't believe she'd made partner, even at her own party. She felt stunned, happy, and hopeful, ready to leave behind her doubts, insecurities, and guilt. Okay, maybe not her guilt. Guilt was like her handbag, occasionally heavy, but something she just felt better carrying around. Same with her insecurities, with which she had grown secure. As for her doubts, she remained doubtful. On second thought, it remained to be seen whether becoming a partner would change Mary DiNunzio at all.

Everyone she loved stood around her smiling, filling the small conference room at Rosato & Associates, and Mary smiled back, trying to find her emotional footing now that she was no longer on the terra firma of associatehood. Bennie Rosato, the superlawyer who was her former boss, had just become her alleged equal, and if that wasn't confusing enough, her friends Judy Carrier, Anne Murphy, and Marshall Trow also worked at the firm. Mary didn't know how she'd morph her friends into her employees, or if she could double their salary.

Her boyfriend, Anthony Rotunno, was standing to the right, the proverbial tall, dark, and academic, with thick wavy hair, a gorgeous smile, and eyes the dark brown of a double shot. He was a history professor who had just moved in with her, and they were still working out the closet situation and those little hairs he left in the bathroom sink. He had his arms around her parents, Mariano "Matty" and Vita DiNunzio, who had grown shorter and rounder, resting on either side of him like meatballs on a plate of spaghetti.

Mary's father was bald and chubby in his white short-sleeved shirt and Bermuda-shorts-with-black-socks-and-sandals combination, dressed-down as usual, since the DiNunzios reserved fancy clothes for weddings or funerals. Her mother was in her best flowery housedress, with her white hair freshly teased into a cumulus cloud meant to hide her growing bald spot. Still her eyes retained their warm brown hue, doubtless the color of fertile Abruzzese soil, and the gray rimming her irises didn't obscure the love in her gaze. Beside them stood The Three Tonys—her father's friends "Pigeon" Tony Lucia, Tony "From-Down-The-Block" LoMonaco, and Tony "Two Feet" Pensiera—a trifecta of octogenarians who served as traveling uncles for Mary, occasionally helping on cases and generally clinging to her like cigar smoke.

"DiNunzio?" Bennie frowned, her eyes a concerned blue. She was six feet tall, of Amazonian strength and proportions, and had only gotten fitter since she was rowing again. Her unruly blonde hair was up in its topknot, and she had on her trademark khaki suit, so retro it had become hipster. "You don't look happy."

"I am, no, really, very happy." Mary was still afraid of Bennie, but she expected that would change, in twenty years. "It's just so overwhelming. I mean, thanks, all of you."

"Awww," Judy, Anne, and Marshall said, smiling in unison. The phone started ringing at the reception desk, and Marshall scooted out to pick it up.

"We love you, Mary!" Anthony winked at her.

"*Maria, ti amo.*" Her mother's eyes misted behind her thick glasses, and her father sniffled, wrinkling his largish nose. It was the Di-

Nunzio nose, which guaranteed its wearer more oxygen than anybody in the room.

"MARE, YOU DESERVE IT!" her father hollered, speaking in
capital letters by habit, though his hearing aid sat behind his ear,
more an earplug than a help. "WE'RE SO PROUD A YOU!"

The Tonys nodded, being good-natured in general, especially
when the cannolis were free.

Bennie raised a styrofoam cup of champagne. "Then let's toast to
DiNunzio. I mean, Mary. And we have to change our letterhead.
Here's to Rosato & DiNunzio."

"Wait, call me DiNunzio," Mary blurted out. "I'm used to it, and
let's hold off on the letterhead, for now. I'm not ready yet. Let it
sink in."

"Mare, that's silly." Judy looked at her like she was nuts. She had
superintelligent blue eyes in a round face, framed by yellow-blonde
hair cut short and raggedy, so she looked like the beaming sun in a
crayoned picture.

"Mary, really?" Anne frowned in a meaningful way. She was a
model-pretty redhead in a dress that fit like Spanx. "Don't give away
your power. Remember your affirmations."

Mary tried not to laugh. She didn't have any power to give away,
and she always skipped her morning affirmations, since I DESERVE
ALL MY SUCCESS AND HAPPINESS made her late for the bus.
"Let's stick with DiNunzio and the old letterhead for now, okay?"

"Congratulations, DiNunzio!" Bennie grinned, and everybody
raised their cups and took a sip, then hugged and kissed her, each
one in turn, an aromatic blend of flowery perfume, CVS aftershave,
and mothballs.

Marshall returned, leaning in the doorway, her face flushed with
excitement. "Bennie, the desk just called from downstairs. Allegra
Gardner is on the way up, and she's looking for representation."

"A Gardner, from the Gardner family?" Bennie's face lit up, and
nobody had to tell Mary the party was over. She was a partner now

and knew that money trumped fun. The firm could use new business, and the Gardners were a wealthy family, like the Kennedys with a Philadelphia accent.

"Which one's Allegra?" Mary asked, setting down her cup.

"I don't know, she didn't say, but she's a real Gardner." Marshall nodded, excited. "She just interviewed Morgan Lewis, but isn't hiring them. She wants to see us about a new matter."

"Great!" Bennie turned to Mary. "DiNunzio, we'd love to get business from that family. Do you mind if we cut your party short?"

"No, I agree," Mary said, making her first partner-y decision. She wanted to start on the right foot, and agreeing was always good. Even partners sucked up, this being America.

"Good." Bennie turned back to Marshall. "Set up the big conference room. Make sure there's laptops, fresh pads, and pencils."

Anne blinked her lovely green eyes. "I know the Gardners are super-rich, but how did they make their money?"

"It's so old they forget," Mary answered. "It's just there, like oxygen. Or carbohydrates."

Judy lifted an eyebrow. "Balzac said behind every fortune is a great crime."

Bennie scoffed. "Balzac didn't have a payroll to meet, and let's not prejudge our clients. The Gardner family interests are run by three brothers, and they own banks, reinsurance concerns, and real estate development companies." She turned to Mary's parents, Anthony, and The Tonys. "Folks, please excuse us. I know you're having dinner with Mary tonight, and you're welcome to stay here until the meeting's over. It won't take more than an hour."

"Alla good, Benedetta. We know you gotta work, we wait." Mary's mother waddled over and gave Bennie a big hug, except that Bennie was six feet tall and Vita DiNunzio was a foot shorter, so her face landed between Bennie's breasts. When Bennie released her, she looked vaguely asphyxiated. "Benedetta, take cookies, cannol', *sflogiatelle*."

"SHE'S RIGHT, BENNIE, TAKE THE COOKIES AND PAS-

TRY TO THE MEETING. WE'LL SIT AND HAVE ANOTHER CUPPA COFFEE." Her father gestured at Pigeon Tony, who was already pouring another round of black. Tony-From-Down-The-Block was settling down with the sports page, and Feet was tugging over a chair to put up his feet, which, oddly, had nothing to do with his nickname.

"Thanks." Bennie turned to Judy and Anne. "Ladies, we need as many people on our side of the table as she has on hers. Everybody to the big conference room for a dog-and-pony show."

Judy set down her cake. "I'll be the dog."

Anne set down her Diet Coke. "I'll be the pony."

"I'll be the partner." Mary brought up the rear, because she had to hug and kiss everybody good-bye, as was customary in South Philly, where hugs and kisses were like passports, required for all comings and goings. She hurried to the big conference room, which had one wall completely of glass, with an impressive view of the metallic ziggurat of One Liberty Place, the sharp spike of the Mellon Center, and the quaint figure of William Penn in his Quaker hat, atop City Hall. They all got busy setting up laptops, pads, and coffee, then Mary, Judy, and Anne arranged themselves on one side of the table with Bennie at the head, because it went without saying that she would run the meeting. She wasn't the only partner anymore, but she was still the Office Mom.

Which, as it turned out, was exactly what Allegra Gardner needed, because Allegra Gardner was only thirteen years old.

Chapter Two

Allegra Gardner was a slight young girl, only five feet tall, with bright blue eyes behind round plastic glasses. She had a small, straight nose, fair skin, and thin lips pressed over major orthodonture. Her hair was a nondescript brown, gathered in a loose double ponytail under a white cap that read, APIARIST. Mary didn't know the word but she gathered it had something to do with bees, since Allegra also had on a white hoodie with a smiling bumblebee that said BEE HAPPY, which she wore with baggy jeans and low-profile Converse sneakers. Allegra had arrived alone, carrying a blue backpack on her narrow shoulders, apparently unfazed by the fact that she was outnumbered by legal firepower as well as estrogen levels.

Everybody took her seat after Bennie made the introductions, and Mary grabbed a legal pad to write notes to Judy. She was pretty sure that even partners wrote notes to each other, especially when they took meetings with children. It was confusing, and Mary couldn't fight the feeling that Allegra needed a babysitter, not a lawyer.

Bennie smiled at Allegra, in an official way. "Before we start, are your parents coming?"

"No, but they know I'm here." Allegra's voice was as firm as a tweener's could be, which was not at all. "I'm on my own."

Mary wrote to Judy, ISN'T ALLEGRA SO CUTE? I DON'T KNOW WHETHER TO REPRESENT HER OR BREASTFEED HER.

Judy wrote back, TOTALLY, BUT WHAT'S WITH THE BEES?

Bennie frowned, slightly. "How did you get here, Allegra?"

"I took the train."

"By yourself?"

"Sure. I do it, all the time."

Mary's heart went out to Allegra, but then again, her heart went out to everybody. She was more surprised when it stayed in her chest. She wrote, TIME FOR THE BIG GIRL PANTIES!

Judy wrote back, DON'T BEE SILLY!

Bennie paused. "Allegra, how old are you?"

"Thirteen, yesterday, June tenth."

"Happy Belated Birthday!" Mary smiled at Allegra, seeing in her face the baby that Allegra used to be, as well as the woman she would become. She was a pretty young girl under her goofy hat, but gave the impression that she didn't care about how she looked, which would make her the only teen on the planet who felt that way, or maybe an alien.

"Yes, Happy Belated Birthday," Judy and Anne said in cheery unison.

"Thank you." Allegra smiled, showing braces with pink rubber bands.

Bennie cleared her throat. "Yes, well, to stay on track, tell me, Allegra, who are your parents?"

"Does that really matter?" Allegra's eyes flickered, a suddenly sharp blue. "I'm here, they're not."

"Understood, but you're a minor. If you're looking for legal representation, you're not of the age of contract."

"Then we won't make a contract. Would that work?"

Mary admired Allegra for not being intimidated by Bennie. She wrote, WHEN I GROW UP, I WANT TO BE ALLEGRA.

Judy wrote back, NO, BEE YOURSELF.

Bennie blinked. "Let's set it aside for now."

"Ms. Rosato, if you're worried about whether I can pay you, I can and I will, I have my own money now. I've been planning this since I found out I get a distribution from my grandfather's trust at thirteen."

"It's not about money. It's common courtesy. We don't get a lot of walk-ins, and we like to know with whom we're meeting."

"Okay, my parents are John and Jane Gardner." Allegra reached for her backpack and slid out a silvery MacBook Pro, which sported a yellow bumper sticker that read, MIND YOUR OWN BEESWAX. "They live in West Whiteland, and my dad is the oldest of the three brothers who run the family businesses. My parents won't stop me from hiring a lawyer. They know what I'm doing, I told them. If they try to stop me, I told them I'll file to be declared legally emancipated."

Bennie frowned. "Do you get along with your parents?"

"Yes," Allegra answered matter-of-factly, opening the laptop.

"Then legal emancipation would be odd. It's like divorcing your parents."

Mary wrote, I WOULD NEVER DIVORCE MY PARENTS. IN FACT, I WISH I COULD MARRY THEM. THEY DON'T LEAVE LITTLE HAIRS IN THE SINK.

Judy wrote, DON'T BEE GROSS.

Allegra hit a key on her laptop. "I don't think emancipation will be necessary. My parents said they won't help me, but they won't oppose me."

"Where do you go to school?"

"I board at Milton Academy in Massachusetts, but I'm going to register in the public school for ninth grade. I want to be here during this case, not out of state."

"Where will you live?"

"At home. I interviewed several of the big law firms, but I didn't like them, so I thought I'd come see you. I researched you and the firm."

Mary couldn't believe how serious-minded Allegra was. She thought back to what she'd been doing at thirteen, which was lightening her hair with bottled lemon juice and picking a confirmation name, even though Theresa was a shoe-in. She loved St. Theresa, one of the few saints who had the mojo to go up against Mary, the biggest brand name in the religion.

Bennie nodded. "So tell us, Allegra, what's the case? Why do you need a lawyer?"

"I'm here about my sister." Allegra's face fell. "Her name was Fiona, and she was murdered six years ago, at a party at my father's new offices."

"Our condolences. I seem to recall reading about the case."

Mary set down her pen, having lost her sense of humor. The murder case was coming back to her, too. She'd seen it in the news, a girl stabbed to death, at sixteen years old. Suddenly Mary realized why she felt for Allegra in the first place. Despite her funny decals and bumper stickers, Allegra Gardner was a sad girl, and it seemed to travel with her, like a backpack.

"Thanks," Allegra said quietly. "The thing is, I believe they sent the wrong man to jail. His name is Lonnie Stall and he's in Graterford Prison. I think he's innocent. He said he was at trial, and I believe him. I want to find out who really murdered my sister and punish him. I need somebody to look at the case and start over."

Bennie frowned. "Wait a minute. I seem to remember that the defendant in that case pleaded guilty."

"I know he did, right before the jury came back, but I'm sure he didn't do it."

Bennie paused. "What makes you say he's innocent, even though he pled guilty?"

"I don't want to go into it now. I'm not sure if I'm hiring your firm."

"Fair enough." Bennie eased back in the chair. "So we're clear, you'd want us to evaluate the evidence and record to see if the decision was correct or incorrect?"

"No, I want you to solve my sister's murder." Allegra's request had a weight of its own, hanging in the air.

"So you want an investigation after the fact."

"Right. Exactly."

"We're not investigators, we're lawyers."

"That never stopped you before. I saw online. And you have a firm investigator, right? Lou Jacobs. His photo is on the website."

"Yes, but he's on vacation. He's not back until next week."

"Okay, so add him in, whatever it takes, I can pay. I want this to be done right. I want to know the truth." Allegra pressed her lips together again. "I was there when Fiona was murdered, at this big office party. It was supposed to be a grand opening, and well, it was so, so horrible."

Mary shuddered, but said nothing. Her biggest nightmare was something terrible happening to her twin sister Angie, a former nun who was in Tanzania on yet another mission, saving a world that refused to be saved.

Allegra frowned deeply under her little cap. "I kept thinking and talking about Fiona, and what happened to her, and my parents worried I was getting obsessed. They sent me to a therapist, then to boarding school, but I wasn't obsessed or depressed, and I'm still not."

Bennie leaned over to Allegra. "So your parents believe Stall is guilty?"

"Yes."

"Why?"

"Because of the evidence at the trial and because he pleaded guilty himself, in the end. They want the case to be over, but I want it to be right."

"Allegra, you have to be realistic. It's harder to find out what happened now than it was then." Bennie opened her palms in appeal. "The case is six years old. Evidence may be lost or thrown away, and memories have faded."

"I understand that, but I want to try. I can't do it myself because I'm a kid." Allegra met Bennie's gaze behind her big glasses. "Ms. Rosato, you have a reputation as one of the best trial lawyers in the city, if not the country. You've defended many people who were wrongly accused. I want a do-over."

"There's no backsies in murder cases, Allegra." Bennie seemed momentarily nonplussed, but Mary felt as if she could help out, since Bennie wasn't good with kids or human beings, in general.

"Allegra, what she means is, this is a lot for a thirteen-year-old to deal—"

"That's why I need a lawyer, and I'm not your typical thirteen-year-old, anyway. I'm a genius."

"Pardon?" Mary smiled at the matter-of-fact way she said it, without a trace of arrogance.

"Really, I am, but being that smart only makes things worse." Allegra's lips flattened. "I know I'm weird, different. Kids make fun of me for everything, of my grades, the way I look, or my bees. They call me Allergy, Allergan, Bee Girl, Bee Geek, brainiac, whatever, I don't care."

"What is it, with the bees?" Mary couldn't help but ask.

"I keep bees."

"For fun?"

"Yes." Allegra smiled.

"Don't you get stung?"

"No, they're in hives and I know how to handle them. I wear a veil and I have a smoker, which calms them down. The smoke blocks their pheromones that send out a distress signal, so you can work in the hive." Allegra warmed to her topic. "It's a very old hobby, beekeeping. It dates back to the Egyptians. And mine are very docile and nice, and they're used to me, and they all get along and help each other. Did you know that each hive holds thirty thousand bees? That's more friends than anybody in my class has, even counting their fake Facebook friends. I'm fine with it."

Mary felt for her. No kid was fine with being different, and it wasn't easy being green. "But I'm thinking that you can't be so legalistic in your approach to this problem. There's too much emotion involved."

"There's emotion because it matters. What should I spend my time on, stuff that doesn't matter?"

Mary had to admit it was a good point. "But it won't be easy for you, living at home, going forward with this investigation. Your parents will be upset, I'm sure. They had closure, but now they won't. You want to prove that a man they believe killed their daughter really didn't do it."

"I know that, too, but I have to know the truth, no matter who likes it and who doesn't." Allegra's forehead buckled again. "If I do what makes them happy, then I'm unhappy, and that's not very grown-up, is it?"

Mary felt momentarily stumped. She wouldn't hurt her parents for all the truth in the world. She hadn't, in her life. She'd die with her secret.

"And anyway, I owe it to Fiona." Allegra reached under her collar and showed them a delicate necklace, with a heart-shaped pendant. "This was hers, and I wear it all the time. She looked out for me in everything. She was my sister."

Mary swallowed hard. "I understand."

"I'm giving up everything to do this. I had to leave my hives at school. Luckily the headmaster keeps bees, too, so he knows what to do."

"Why didn't you bring them with you?"

"You can't. Bees get to know their territory. They consider it their home. They'd be upset if I tried to move them."

Mary didn't know bees had emotions, but maybe they did. The way Allegra talked about her bees reminded her of the way Pigeon Tony talked about his homing pigeons.

Judy frowned. "To get back to the investigation, Allegra, I'm surprised the other firms would represent you, given that your parents will be unhappy if you get any traction."

"Why?" Allegra flushed, and Mary realized that intelligence and sophistication were two separate things.

Judy answered, "You're essentially opposing the Gardner interests. The big firms will want more business from the family, so they'll choose them over you."

Allegra shook her head. "No, I disagree. They'll represent me if I choose them, I'm sure of it. I met with them. They said they'll get back to me with a proposal."

Mary and Judy looked over at Anne and Bennie, and they all knew what Allegra Gardner had yet to learn. Money talks, and justice doesn't pay. If Allegra were taking on the Gardner family, she'd be radioactive to the big firms. Only the women at Rosato & Associates would take her on, because they were a bunch of mavericks who never would have gotten business from the Gardners anyway. And Allegra was an underdog, which was their weakness.

Bennie leaned over. "Regardless of what the others do, we'd be happy to represent you."

"Cool beans." Allegra grinned, in a newly relaxed way. "How does it work? Do you all work together, or can I choose which lawyer I want?"

"Of course you can choose. We work separately or together, depending on our availability. When would you want to get started?"

"Right away. Who's available?"

"I'm not and neither is Anne." Bennie gestured at Anne, who made a cartoony sad face, like an emoticon with perfect makeup. "We're starting a trial, but Mary and Judy are free. They're a great team."

Allegra grinned. "I can tell. They've been writing each other notes this entire meeting."

"What?" Bennie frowned.

Mary grimaced, busted. "Sorry, it's a bad habit."

Judy's eyes flared. "I'm really sorry, too."

Allegra shrugged happily. "It's okay, and I can read upside down, too. I like that you think I'm cute, but please don't try and breastfeed me."

Mary laughed, feeling a rush of warmth for the young girl, who had the very mature ability to laugh at herself.

"We'd love to represent you," Judy said, then added with a grin, "Bee our client."

"Good one!" Allegra laughed.

"We could get started right away." Mary leaned forward. She

wanted the case and she needed the business. Her caseload was light because her client base was in South Philly, and Italians didn't like to fight when it was hot. "I'm free right now. I could drop everything."

"Just like that?" Allegra turned back to Bennie. "No proposals?"

"It's a lawsuit, not a marriage. I can email you a fee-and-costs schedule. Our retainer is five thousand dollars. Is that a problem?"

"Not at all. The trustee of my trust will send you a check. I'll speak with him and give him your information."

Mary blinked. "Can you get a distribution from a trust, when you're only thirteen?"

"Yes, if the trustee says it's okay, and mine did. He's not even supposed to tell my father. The trust is from my grandfather, and one of his old banker friends is the trustee. He told me he has a duty of undivided loyalty to me."

Bennie looked over at Mary. "Trustees have some discretion about when to make a distribution, unless there's restrictions in the trust. If it's set up that distributions are to be made for her care, support, and welfare, which is typical, then the trustee can exercise his discretion to make the distribution. It's probably a generation-skipping trust or a dynasty trust."

Mary figured her trust skipped her generation, too. She turned to Allegra. "You're a really impressive young woman, and I'm happy to represent you."

"Thanks!" Allegra beamed. "You guys are so different from the other law firms. This is the firm, right? Four women, no drones?"

Mary laughed. "I'm the drone."

"No, you're not. Drones are male. People think drones are worker bees, but they're two different things. Worker bees do all the work, collecting pollen, nectar, and water, but a drone doesn't work. He exists to mate with the queen and he dies after, with his genitals still in her."

"Yuck." Mary recoiled.

"Nice," Judy said, then, "I mean, yuck."

Allegra smiled. "The way I see it, if this law firm were a hive, Ms.

Rosato would be the queen bee and everybody else would be a worker bee."

"Bingo!" Mary burst into laughter, and so did Judy and Anne.

Bennie shot them a sly smile. "Not exactly, Allegra. Mary is my partner, so at the very least, we have two queen bees."

"You can't have two queens in the same hive. It's not possible." Allegra lifted an eyebrow. "A new queen starts to emerge, laying superscedure cells, getting ready to take over. Then the new queen will fight the old queen to the death. I've seen it happen."

Suddenly there was a commotion at the threshold, and Mary looked over, vaguely horrified. Her mother chugged into the conference room, bearing the platter of pastries and cookies, with her father right behind her, and Mary jumped up to head them off. "Ma, Pop! Thanks, but we're kind of busy."

"*Maria,* you no bring the *sfogiatelle,* the cannol'. Here, have!"

"MARE, I TOLD HER YOU WERE IN A MEETING, BUT YOU KNOW HOW SHE GETS."

"Psssh!" Her mother waved her off, set the pastries down, then did a double-take when she spotted Allegra. "*Deo, che carina!*"

"She says you're cute," Mary translated, uncomfortably. She loved her mother, but this wasn't good for client development. "Ma, thanks, but you should go—"

Her father shouted, "IS THIS KID THE RICH ONE?"

Her mother was already engulfing Allegra in a big hug. "*Che carina! Si carina!*"

"Whoa, hi." Allegra giggled as she righted her cap, which had come askew in the love attack.

"Ma, please don't hug the clients!" Mary hurried over to extricate Allegra. "Sorry, this is my mother and father."

Judy jumped up to help. "Mrs. D—"

"So skinny, so skinny!" Mary's mother let go of Allegra only long enough to pick up the pastry dish. "Have *sfogiatelle, cara.* Amaretti cookie, imbutitti cookie, musticiolli cookie."

"Have what?"

"Ma, please, no force-feeding." Mary touched her mother's shoulder. "Sorry, Allegra, really. *Sfogiatelle* is a pastry stuffed with ricotta and orange pieces, and the cookies have pine nuts, hazelnuts, or honey. My mother thinks the world needs more saturated fats."

"Sweet!" Allegra beamed. "Which cookie has the honey?"

"*Cara, prego!*" Mary's mother thrust a brown musticiolli cookie at Allegra, who popped it in her mouth.

"This tastes awesome! I make my own honey, but this is almost as good!"

Mary caught Bennie's eye, and the queen bee didn't look happy. "Uh, Ma, Dad, you should go, we're trying to—"

"No, Mary, it's okay." Allegra grinned, and brown flecks of cookie filled her braces. "It's better than my birthday cake."

Mary's mother's hooded eyes flew open behind her thick glasses. "Is you birthday? *Tanti auguri!*"

Her father's face lit up. "HAPPY BIRTHDAY, DOLL! WHAT'S YOUR NAME?"

"Allegra," she answered, between bites, and Mary's mother started singing her the birthday song, clapping her gnarled little hands.

"*Tanti auguri a te, tanti auguri a te . . .*"

Then her father joined in, "*TANTI AUGURI, ALLEGRA, TANTI AUGURI A TE!*" The Tonys came up from behind with Anthony, singing, clapping, and transforming the conference room into an Olive Garden.

"*Bravissima,* Allegra!" Mary's mother gave Allegra another hug. "*Tanti auguri!*"

"Please, Mrs. DiNunzio—" Bennie blanched, but Allegra jumped to her sneakers with a big grin.

"Mary, can I hire your parents, too?"

Chapter Three

Mary, Judy, Anthony, The Tonys, and her father crowded around the tiny kitchen table, eating, drinking, chattering away, and sitting hip-to-replacement-hip in the cramped DiNunzio kitchen. Fresh basil and garlic scented the air, and steam rose from hot plates of home-made ravioli and peppery sausage. Everyone sweated into his food, but it would never occur to Mary's parents to eat anything cooler, even in a Philadelphia summer, and Mary wouldn't have it any other way. Whoever said you can't go home again wasn't Italian.

She tuned out the merry chatter and let her loving eyes travel around the kitchen. The cabinets and counter were clean, white, and simple, and on the walls hung an ancient church calendar with Jesus Christ, next to faded newspaper photos of John F. Kennedy and Pope John, the three Lifetime MVPs in the DiNunzio Hall-of-Fame. Nothing ever changed at her parents', who were like the Amish, but with better food. They still drank perked coffee, from a dented cof-feepot always brewing on the stove, while they read an actual news-paper, a quaint custom from the days of colonial America. The kitchen didn't have a TV or radio, much less an automatic coffeemaker or a dishwasher; her mother was the coffeemaker, and her father was the dishwasher. There was no air conditioner, only an oscillating counter fan, which distributed the humidity evenly. Her parents didn't own a computer, and they thought a laptop was something children sat upon.

Mary's gaze went to the cast-iron switch plate, which had tucked behind it a frond of dried Easter palm and a collection of Mass cards. A Mass card was given when someone died, and she remembered when there were only a few, then ten, and now it looked like practically a full deck. More of their relatives and friends were passing, and her parents were in their eighties. Her father could see fine with his trifocals, but he was almost deaf and his back ached from a working life of setting tile. Her mother's hearing was surprisingly good, but her eyes had only worsened, from macular degeneration and sewing piecework in the basement of this very rowhouse. Still she hovered happily over the kitchen table, topping off water, fetching second helpings, and ladling extra gravy onto pasta and sausage, like the CEO of the DiNunzio family—or maybe the queen bee.

"Ma, sit, and I'll help," Mary said, though she knew her mother would wave her off, which she did. Vita DiNunzio would never give up her wooden spoon to anyone, like a regent with a scepter, if you could stir gravy with a scepter.

"*Maria,* you eat, alla eat! Alla good?"

"VEET, THAT WAS GREAT!" her father boomed, rubbing his tummy in his white short-sleeve shirt. "I'M GONNA BUST A GUT!"

"Great, Mrs. D!" Judy twirled her spaghetti against her tablespoon like an expert, having been taught by Mary's father. Judy was their honorary daughter, and Mary could remember the first time she brought Judy home and her mother had fallen in love with her, the same way she had with Allegra today.

"Good, *grazie.*" Mary's mother came up from behind and touched Mary's hair, a gesture that always made her feel warm and cozy, like an adored kitten. "We so proud, *Maria,* you work so hard alla year. You deserve alla good dings inna world."

"Thanks, Ma." Mary didn't need affirmations if she had a mother.

"Here, here," Judy said, raising a thick glass.

"I second that emotion." Anthony smiled, and so did The Tonys, adding a chorus of *salud* and *cent anni,* and it struck Mary how lucky she was in this cobbled-together collective of best friend, lover, family, and random senior citizens. She smiled up at her mother.

"So Ma, what did you think of our new client? Why did you like her so much?"

"So young, so serious like you." Her mother shrugged happily and pushed her heavy glasses up onto her nose.

"SHE'S *TOO* SERIOUS," her father added. "SHE PROLLY READS TOO MUCH."

"Prolly." Mary smiled. Her parents never pushed her to work hard in school, but she went to Goretti, where she got straight A's and became Most Likely to Achieve Sainthood. They wanted her to go and play outside, but she buried herself in Nancy Drew books, which worried them no end. They believed that reading ruined your eyes and they could have been right. She was nearsighted by the time she graduated from Penn and Penn Law. Mary said to her father, "Dad, guess what, she keeps bees."

"FOR REAL? WHY?"

Mary smiled. "She likes it. She's really smart, a genius."

"She good at numbers?" Tony-From-Down-The-Block interrupted, fork in mid-air. He was single again, having broken up with his girlfriend Marlene, which meant he was dyeing his remaining hair a shade of orange that looked better on orangutans.

Tony Two Feet looked over, his hooded eyes blinking behind his Mr. Potatohead glasses. "Yeah, Mare, can she count cards, like the movie?"

Tony-From-Down-The-Block elbowed him, frowning. "Feet, that's not why I was axin'."

"The hell it ain't." Feet turned to Mary, squinting in thought. "What's'a name a that movie, Mare? With the '49 Buick? Boy oh boy, I was, like, twenny years old when they came out with those babies. I wanted one so bad. Came in green, like a new C-note."

Tony-From-Down-The-Block snorted. "When's the last time you saw a new C-note?"

Feet kept his head turned away and ignored the question, which may have been rhetorical. "You know that movie, Mare. What's the name again? With the guys?"

Tony-From-Down-The-Block chuckled. "The movie with the guys. How's she supposed ta know?"

Feet stiffened. "Everybody knows."

"Everybody but you."

"*Rain Man,*" Mary told him, to end the conversation before fisticuffs. Feet and Tony-From-Down-The-Block were bickering so much lately, but it wasn't the time or place to press the point. She turned to Pigeon Tony, who was generally the quiet one because he spoke only broken English. "Pigeon Tony, our new client keeps bees. That's like keeping pigeons, right?"

"*Si, si.*" Pigeon Tony shook his head, slurping his coffee. He was only five feet tall and bird-thin, with a nose curved like a beak and round quick eyes that would have looked fine on any one of his homing pigeons.

"They say bees know their territory, too."

"*Si.*" Pigeon Tony shook his bald head, which was tan and spotted as a hen's egg, from him being outside at his loft. "Pigeon racing, bees, alla old. Egiziano."

"From the Egyptians?" Mary translated, surprised. "So is beekeeping."

"I 'ave bees, in Abruzzo, alla time." Pigeon Tony gestured with his gnarled hands. "I make 'oney, for Silvana, she love."

"Aw." Mary could see his eyes tear up at the mention of his late wife, so she let the topic alone. They all finished dinner, after which her father and The Tonys retired to the living room to watch the Phillies game, her mother went upstairs to bed, and Mary, Judy, and Anthony stayed at the table, talking over pignoli nut cookies and coffee strong enough to melt teeth.

The sun had set outside, the kitchen had cooled, and the play-by-play from the Phillies game blared from the living room, a half-step behind the play-by-play blaring from a neighbor's TV, which wafted through the screen like an electronic echo. Mary felt her mood depressing, and it wasn't a sugar crash. "I have to tell you," she said, picking pignoli nuts off a cookie, "I'm worried about this case."

Anthony put a gentle arm around her. "You shouldn't be worried about anything tonight, babe. This is your day to celebrate. You're a partner now."

Mary forced a smile. "But we partners are responsible people, especially when there's a kid involved."

Judy nodded. "I'm having buyer's remorse, too. You go first, Mare. Tell me what worries you."

"It's so emotional. If Allegra goes forward, it's so difficult for her and her family. It's hard enough to get over a murder the first time, much less to reopen it." Mary didn't need to remind anyone that she had lost her husband Mike Lassiter to violent crime, many years ago. He had been struck and killed when he was riding his bike, and though it had looked like an accident, it had turned out to be murder. They had been married so young, only a year, and Mary felt haunted by the loss, still. She hadn't dated anyone seriously until Anthony, who had been so patient with the aftershocks of her grief. "And part of me thinks, what if her parents were right, and she is obsessed with her sister's murder?"

"I know. Who wouldn't be?" Judy shuddered. "Also she seems like the obsessive type, right? We get it, with the bees."

Mary winced, on Allegra's behalf. "She just likes bees. Why, didn't you get into anything at that age? Buy all the stuff, wear all the gear? Like me, with Catholicism."

Judy smiled because she was agnostic, and as such, incapable of disillusionment. "Do Brownies count? I was majorly into Brownies."

"It would be the last time you wore brown."

"Or matched." Judy smiled with her, then it faded. "Anyway, I think Allegra's wound too tight, for a kid."

Anthony nodded, listening. Mary and Judy had briefed him on the way home, and he was a good listener. He had to be, in this crowd. "I think lots of kids are, these days. There's too much pressure on them, and life is more complex than it ever was before. I see it in my students. Some of them, they break by the time they get to college."

Mary sipped her coffee, which tasted like distilled caffeine. "And the fact that she's a minor poses a lot of questions. Should we be talking with her parents before we go forward? We don't have to legally, but it might make sense to meet with them, just to get them on board."

Judy shook her head. "I don't agree. She can hire us, and there's nothing unethical about representing her. It's like a custody case, where a guardian ad litem is appointed. Allegra may be a minor, but she's entitled to an advocate."

Mary met her eye. "I know, but I'm just saying we might want to meet with the parents. I'd like to hear why they think Stall did it, and they're a good source of information until we get the police file."

"Why give them the chance to discourage us, or worse, block us?"

"We can deal with that, I just think it's respectful. Fiona was their daughter, and it's her murder."

"But Allegra is our client, and they gave her the go-ahead. We don't need their permission to proceed, and neither does Allegra."

"It's more respectful."

Judy snorted, and Mary didn't need her to elaborate. She had to stop asking permission for everything, because she was a partner now. She had to be more badass, get a tattoo or a nose ring.

"Let's both sleep on it."

"Okay." Judy wiped her mouth on a crumpled napkin. "You know what worries me? That this is a no-win situation. The way Allegra posed it today, she combined two questions that need to be separated. One, did Lonnie Stall commit the murder? That's hard enough to answer, but the second issue is even harder. Two, if Stall didn't do it, who did? It's completely possible that we could find exculpatory evidence on Stall, but still not figure out the answer to question two. In other words, who-dun-it."

Mary took an emergency sip of wine, which tasted dry and bitter. "Then Allegra and her family are left with no answer at all, like the rug was pulled out from under them. I don't want to break that kid's heart."

"Don't worry, sweetie, it'll be okay." Anthony put an arm around Mary and kissed her on the cheek. "Let's go home, okay? You're tired, I can see it."

"He's right, Mare." Judy looked over at Mary, with a sympathetic smile. "You're going into your pre-case funk. You think we're going to screw this up. You think we're not going to be able to figure it out. You can't believe we got ourselves into this in the first place. Stop now."

"I can't."

"You must. Go home, crazy. It's Monday, we'll deal tomorrow."

"Wait, let's do one thing before we leave." Mary jumped up, fetched her messenger bag from the floor, and slid out her laptop. "When you're nervous about work, the best thing to do is work."

"Now, babe?" Anthony groaned. "Can't we go home?"

"Soon, I swear, it won't take long. I want to Google Fiona's murder and get all the facts I can." Mary checked the oven clock as she put the laptop on the table and opened the lid. "It's only nine o'clock."

Judy clucked. "Boyfriend's right. Let's call it a day."

"Jude, you're going to do this when you go home and so am I, so why not do it together?" Mary woke up the computer and navigated to Google. "I just want to read a few articles about the case. This will take half an hour, tops, and I'll feel better if I can scope it out, so we can hit the ground running in the morning."

Anthony rose with a good-natured sigh. "Okay, I'll go watch the game with the boys."

"We'll be an hour." Mary started typing.

"We'll keep it short," Judy said, pulling over a chair.

And the two lawyers got busy.

Chapter Four

"Thanks for hanging in," Mary told Anthony, as he steered the Prius onto Twentieth Street, looking for a parking space near the house.

"No, I get it. I knew it would take longer than an hour."

"But not by much."

"Easy for you to say. You ever watch a game with Feet? He never shuts up. They should call him Mouth."

"Sorry." Mary's head was swimming with details of Fiona Gardner's murder, though the media seemed more concerned with the wealth of the family than the details of the case. "I learned a lot from the articles, though."

"How so?"

"The headline is that Lonnie Stall was a waiter hired by the catering company that the family used all the time for their parties."

"Okay." Anthony steered smoothly around the corner. There was almost no traffic and nobody was out on the street.

"They were going to make a presentation and somebody at the party realized Fiona was missing. They found her dead on the second floor, in the corporate library, which had been cordoned off, and Lonnie was fleeing the scene. She had been stabbed once, through the heart, but they caught him."

"Sounds like he did it."

"Also he's black."

"Who represented him?"

"A guy I never heard of. I can't wait to see that file." Mary bit her lip, looking out the window into the night. It was dark and muggy outside, and she felt encased in the air-conditioned car, insulated from the grit of the city. They turned onto Twentieth Street again, and she realized they were on their fifth drive around the block. They lived in the Rittenhouse Square neighborhood, which meant that they circled for a parking space like a spaceship in orbit, praying for a docking station. "Babe, now that I'm partner, we should rent a parking space."

"We're gonna luck out."

Mary sighed inwardly. "It would be so much easier if we were in the garage. We could just pull in and be done with it."

"It's not that hard to find a space."

"It would save time. They have a guy there twenty-four hours."

"Nah, we're fine without one." Anthony fed the car gas. "We don't need everything easy, do we?"

"Honestly, yes, we do. Why not?"

"There are $780 worth of reasons why not."

Mary closed her eyes, frustrated with herself. She really needed to be more of a badass. She had the money to get them a space in the garage, and she shouldn't have to ask Anthony's permission to spend her own money. They'd had the same issue with the house, which she could afford but he couldn't, and they'd almost broken up when she paid the down-payment. They'd worked it out, so he'd moved in, paying half the mortgage and expenses, but she felt like she was always asking him to spend her money or to do her job, like after dinner. Other than that, she was blissfully happy and in love, for the past several years.

"Don't be that way," Anthony said, softly.

"Sorry, but it bugs me."

"I know. Gimme one more lap, then we'll put it in the pay lot for the night."

"I won't have time to move it in the morning."

"I'll do it, no worries."

"Thanks." Mary knew it was a concession, since he had to be at school early, and her mood lifted when she looked over to see him smiling. He had a great smile, which came easily to him, and always dressed well, in a sport jacket and white oxford shirt, like a man instead of a boy, and kept his dark wavy hair neat, with long sideburns.

"Hey, look, a space right in front!" Anthony hit the brakes, flipped on the emergency lights, and grinned. Their street was tree-lined, and one of the most quaint in town. "Told you."

"You live right."

Anthony steered their car into the space, parked it like an expert, and turned off the ignition. "You say that every time."

"Because it's true." Mary gathered her bag and messenger bag, got out of the car, and walked to the steps of their old colonial townhouse. It was three stories tall, with black shutters and a brick façade, replete with historic details that Mary adored, like mullioned windows with bubbled glass and windowsills a foot deep. Every time she came home, she couldn't believe how lucky she was to live here.

"After you, partner." Anthony unlocked the front door, and Mary flicked on the hall light and dumped her stuff on the chair, while he closed the door, turned the deadbolt, and picked up the mail. Their division of labor was that he sorted mail and she watered plants, then they had decaf tea, went to bed, and watched Jimmy Fallon. Anthony looked up from the thick stack of bills and catalogs. "What's the deal? We having tea or are you working?"

"I was going to." Mary met his eye, feeling a new tension between them, as if his question were a test. She felt torn between wanting to make him happy and wanting to work. The Gardner case gnawed at the edges of her brain, and she hadn't finished reading the Google articles yet.

"But it's a special occasion." Anthony set down the mail without sorting it, and Mary couldn't help but smile.

"Is that code for partnership sex?"

"Ha!" Anthony laughed. "I'd settle for tea with the love of my life."

"Aw, have one with me instead."

"I'll take it." Anthony shed his jacket and hung it up, and Mary kicked off her heels, then they headed down the hallway past the empty living room to the kitchen, to which they gravitated, both by nature and necessity. The house didn't need work, but it needed furniture. They'd ordered a couch, coffee table, and chairs, but were waiting the requisite forever to get it delivered, which bugged Mary no end.

"When are we going to get our living room furniture?"

"You know the answer to that question. After they grow the tree, they cut it down, then mill it, and they have to plant the cotton seeds, pick the cotton, and make it into our dumb fabric, whatever it was called."

"Bargelle."

"Gesundheit."

Mary smiled, padding into the kitchen, which was typically small for the city, but lovely and grown-up, with black granite counters, windowed cabinets, and stainless steel appliances. She could feel her worries about the Gardner case recede as she went to the sink, her favorite spot. During the daytime, a mullioned window over the basin flooded with sunlight, because of its southern exposure, and she was pretty sure she could get tan off the reflection of the refrigerator.

"You having normal or chamomile?" Anthony picked up the tea kettle, then put it on the stove and turned on the burner.

"Normal." Mary grabbed two mugs from the cabinet, then a box of Lipton Tea.

"Nothing but the best, eh?"

"Damn right. An old-school, flow-through tea bag." Mary went to the drawer, pulled out two napkins, and set them on the round cherrywood table, then crossed to the refrigerator to fetch the Half & Half. Anthony was getting two teaspoons and setting them on the napkins, but she didn't even have to turn around to know that, their domestic routine was so familiar. "You want anything to eat?"

"God, no."

"Me, neither."

"How's your fig tree doing?"

"Lemme check." Mary picked up the pitcher next to the sink, filled it with water, and sprinkled some gently on the fig tree she was starting in a container on the windowsill, next to smaller clay pots of basil, rosemary, and bay leaves, which made her feel as if she actually gardened. Anthony had given her the fig tree, and its young leaves sprouted a fresh yellow-green, too floppy yet to be strong. The figs were still green, too, shaped like miniature hot air balloons.

"Is it your paradise?" Anthony asked, because the tree grew Paradiso, or Genova, figs, allegedly named for an old man in Genova, who used to say, "this is my paradise," when he sat under his fig tree, eating its fruit with bread. Mary had no idea if the story was true, but she loved it just the same.

"Yes, it is my paradise," she answered him, as part of their call and response. "Someday I'm going to be a farmer and have a grove of figs, or an orchard, or whatever you call the whole bunch of fig trees. How great would that be?"

"Great. How are the figs? Can we eat any yet?"

"No, not for a month or so." Mary watered the basil, but happened to glance back and see something bright on a fig leaf at the base of the tree, near the soil. She set down the pitcher, reached out, and plucked it off, only to see that it was a diamond ring. For a minute, she didn't understand, then she gasped and turned around, astounded to find Anthony behind her on his bended knee, looking up at her.

"Hi, honey," he said, with a shaky smile.

"*What?*" Mary felt stunned. She held a gold ring with a round, sparkling diamond, but she couldn't believe her eyes. "What *is* this?"

"Mary, I love you. You're my best friend, and you really are the love of my life." Anthony's deep voice wavered. "More than that, I feel that we are so good together, so close, that we're somehow, *of* each other. And that we have, over the years, become each other's *family.*"

Mary swallowed hard, trying to process what he was saying. Trying to understand how she should react. Trying to figure out what to say. Because what Anthony was saying was so right, and so true, and she loved him to the marrow, but she didn't know if she was ready to get married.

"You know what I'm saying? You know what I mean? You're in me, you're inside, a part of me." Anthony's hand went to his heart. "In here, and I love who you are and everything you are. You're sweet, funny, smart, and you're stronger than you think. And you're beautiful, too, but you don't know that, either. You're my best friend. I understand you and appreciate you, and can make you happy the rest of your life, I promise you that."

Mary felt her eyes fill with tears. It was such a lovely thing to say, and she thought he could, too, but she still didn't know how to answer him.

"I hope you like the ring, and it's your size. That's why I've been so cheap lately, I've been saving for it."

Mary felt a terrible pang of guilt for the nagging she'd been doing lately about money, the parking situation, and the furniture. She hadn't realized that he'd been saving for a ring, and the diamond must have cost a fortune. It sparkled like a flashlight and looked gorgeous, about a carat and a half, as big as a meatball.

"I know we didn't talk about this, but we always said that when you make partner, we'd talk about getting engaged, and now you made partner. In case you're wondering, I did ask your father and mother for your hand, and they said yes. So did The Tonys."

Mary smiled, touched. She could imagine the scene. There would be tears and hugs, like opera.

"Mary, I would be honored if you would wear that ring and be my wife." Anthony's dark eyes filmed, and he swallowed hard, his Adam's apple going up and down above his open collar. "So I have a question to ask you, from my heart. Mary, will you marry me? Because *you* are my paradise."

Mary held tears in her eyes. She didn't know what to say. She looked at his expression, so full of hope. She could see his love, too, and felt the truth of his words resonate within her chest. She loved him, too, with all her heart.

"What do you say, honey?" Anthony smiled nervously. "Because my knee can't take it much longer."

Mary swallowed hard. There was only one answer, whether it was wrong or right.

Chapter Five

Mary turned over in bed, shifting onto her left side, away from Anthony. The bedroom was dark and still, quiet except for some laughter from the street below, probably people returning from a restaurant or a night out, maybe a married couple, like she and Anthony were about to be. She knew she should be happy, but she wasn't, then she felt guilty for not being happy, making a club sandwich of guilt.

Mary glanced at the clock, and its glowing red numerals read 3:05, big enough to read without her glasses or contacts. She shifted upward on the pillow, trying to clear her mind. She listened for Anthony's soft breathing behind her, the sweet rhythm of human respiration, and though she appreciated the fact that he was alive and breathing, it didn't help her sleep in the least. In fact, it only reminded her of what a jerk she was for not being over the moon at a proposal from the sweetest guy on the planet. He had been so happy she had accepted, and they had made love, then he had fallen asleep, but she wasn't going to sleep anytime soon.

She eased the covers off, slid out of bed, and padded naked to the back of the door, where she got her beloved pink chenille bathrobe, slipped it on, and left the bedroom. She went down the hall to her home office, closed the door quietly behind her, and flicked on the

light, glancing around with satisfaction. Her home office was a converted bedroom, lined with white bookshelves that held law books,
legal treatises, files from her active cases, and dumb stuff from her
old room at home, which she couldn't put anywhere else, like a bulletin board that had her medals from citywide Latin Club competi-
tion, and next to that were some old photos from high school, one in
particular which she went over to see, close-up.

It was a photograph of Mary and her twin sister Angie, the two of
them smiling their identical smiles, with identical braces, and even
matching glasses, of hideous paint acetate in an oversize shape that
was considered fashionable at the time, especially if you were a hoot
owl. They both had on their navy uniforms, complete with old-
school black-and-white saddle shoes, an outfit more recently found
in amateur porn videos. They were grinning ear-to-ear, their faces
pressed together, cheek-to-cheek, and their arms were wrapped
around each other as if they were trying to merge one into the other,
which was their problem, after all.

Mary scanned the photo, thinking about Angie, who had become
a nun in order to find herself, or to differentiate herself from her
identical twin, or maybe merely to escape from her entirely. Mary
and Angie looked identical, but their personalities couldn't be more
different, with Angie the quiet, contemplative version of Mary's
yappy and outgoing nature. In time, Angie had embraced quietness
more and more, turning ever inward, so that it seemed not only natural, but inevitable, that she would end up in a cloistered convent, as
hard as they were to find after the Renaissance.

Mary swallowed hard, bitter still. She and Angie had been so
close for so long, amazingly, for as long as they had been alive, but it
had proved too close for Angie, and even when she'd left the convent, had embarked on one faraway mission after the next, the latest
in Tanzania, where she couldn't be reached by phone or email to be
told that her twin had just become engaged to be married. As long as
Angie was away, Mary would always feel like half of her was missing,
but unfortunately, Angie felt whole only when they were apart.

Mary turned away from the photos, went to the desk, sat down, and woke up the computer, squinting against the sudden brightness. She rolled the chair toward the screen because she'd come in without her glasses, but she was nearsighted and didn't need them for close reading anyway. She logged onto her email, clicked Compose Mail, and typed in Angie's name, then stopped. It was an old email address, and she doubted it would work, but that wasn't what stopped her. In the old days, when they had been close, they told each other everything and were each other's best friends, even having their own language, the kind of twins that people read about but don't realize really exist. Mary wondered if Angie remembered any of their special language now, or if they could even talk to each other at all, in any language.

She confronted the blank email, wondering what to say. She wished she could tell Angie how she really felt about getting engaged, how she was happy and terrified both, and that the old Angie was gone and would never come back again, but the lawyer in Mary worried about writing that down anyway. If Anthony happened to use her computer, he would see it.

Mary blinked at the super-bright screen, and the cursor blinked back at her. Then she typed: **Dear Angie, I love you and miss you. Me.** She stared at the sentence, the black letters so stark against the white screen, until her eyes blurred a little and she sniffled. She had no idea if Angie would get the email, because she'd sent emails before and had only rarely gotten a response, since the village Angie lived in had no electricity, much less Internet, and Mary told herself that was the reason Angie never wrote back. Still she hit Send with a prayer to St. Jude, Patron Saint of Lost Causes.

Mary's thoughts turned to Allegra, and her brain shifted gears to work. She navigated onto the Internet, went to Google, plugged in Fiona Gardner, and hit Go. A line of newspaper articles filled the screen, and she clicked on the first one. GARDNER HEIRESS FOUND SLAIN, read the headline, on the *Philly News,* which was the city's tabloid newspaper, and the photo under the headline broke

Mary's heart. It was what she'd heard reporters call the "money shot," which was a photo of a body bag being carried on a litter from the Gardner offices and loaded into the open doors of the coroner's black Econoline Van. Behind the van was a police sawhorse and a crowd, and Mary spotted a much younger Allegra, in her round glasses, long hair, and a party dress, hugging the waist of a woman who must have been her mother.

Mary palmed her computer mouse, drew a blinking square around Allegra's little face, and enlarged it, without really knowing why. But the magnification only intensified the graininess in the photograph, because its focus was the body bag in the foreground, and Mary found herself searching the black, blurry circles that were Allegra's eyes, indistinct and bottomless behind her glasses. She knew exactly how Allegra felt in that moment, because she had lived that moment herself. The sudden, shocking loss of her husband had hit Mary with the stunning force of a blow to the skull. She would never forget when she'd gotten the news, from the police. Incredulity had both paralyzed and saved her sanity, creating an awful sort of waking unconsciousness; she had lived the next few minutes after she'd heard in the interstices between believing and not-believing that her beloved husband was gone forever.

Mary shook her head to break the spell, clicked Print, and scrolled through the article, which also contained a photo of Fiona Gardner, obviously taken for school, and the sight caught Mary by the throat. She realized she'd had no idea what Fiona looked like, even though the murdered girl was at the center of the case. Fiona was an adorable brunette, with long, wavy hair that looked unstyled, heavy eyebrows that were natural and pretty, and dark, wide-set eyes, which were probably brown, but Mary couldn't tell the shade from the photo, which was black-and-white. Fiona wasn't a small, delicate girl like Allegra, and her cheekbones and forehead were large, and her shoulders broad and strong, which gave her a wholesome, athletic appearance. The slight tilt to her head seemed to prove what Allegra had told them, that she had a funny side.

Mary felt heartsick. Seeing Fiona alive only made her more real, and her murder more obscene. Suddenly she wanted to read, copy, and bring into the office every article about the murder. She had four hours before she had to be at work, and she knew it was more than her job that was driving her tonight.

What it was, however, she wasn't exactly sure.

Chapter Six

Mary was running late the next morning, after a long and sleepless night, and stepped off the elevator carrying her coffee, purse, briefcase, and an old-school newspaper. She walked through the modern reception area with a blue patterned couch, chairs, and a glass coffee table with a fan of fresh magazines. Judy and Anne were hanging with Marshall at the front desk, and Mary crossed to them, hiding her ring and trying to figure out a way to tell them that she was somebody's fiancée. "Good morning, ladies."

Marshall smiled. "Back at you. How come you're late, you usually beat us all in."

Anne smiled, too, her lipstick freshly pink. "Those days are over, Marshall. She's our boss now. We might get fired."

"Ha!" Judy looked over. "Mare, want to know how great I am? I went over to Common Pleas Court and ordered us a copy of the Gardner file. It's being copied."

"Great, thanks." Mary realized that she didn't want to tell them the news because that would make it real, even though she knew it was real. She hadn't even called her parents yet, telling herself they wouldn't be up, which wasn't true. Her father would be hosing off the front steps, and her mother would be getting home from Mass, where she'd have said novenas for grandchildren.

Judy sipped her coffee from a styrofoam cup. "Ask me why I'm wearing this dumb outfit."

Mary smiled. Judy had on a white tank, a cropped navy blazer, jeans, and blue clogs, which was fifty colors less than her usual get-up. "Why?"

"Because of where we're going today."

"Where are we going?" Mary set down her cup, hiding her right hand, with the ring. The diamond looked so showy, and the band felt loose. She had already turned it around so the stone faced her palm, because she didn't want to get ring-jacked as she walked to work. She'd felt so conspicuous with the big diamond, blinding passers-by like a driver with high beams.

"I have a plan of action for us. I was reading the case file, and they had a mountain of evidence against Stall—"

"OH MY GOD!" Anne squealed suddenly, finding the ring with time-warp speed. "Mary, seriously? Are you? Is it? What? A ring!"

"Mare, really?" Judy did a double-take, then her blue eyes flew open. "Are you engaged? Oh my God!"

"Oh my God!" Marshall leapt to her feet squealing, and Anne was jumping up and down, a neat trick in mules.

"Mary!" Anne shrieked, grabbing Mary's hand. "Let me see that ring! It's huge!"

"Mary, it's so pretty!" Judy burst into happy laughter, then all hell broke loose and they went nuts, jumping up and down and screaming, which brought Bennie running into reception in alarm.

"What is it? What's the matter?"

"Ask Mary!" Anne yelped, and they all parted for Bennie to rush over, her khaki jacket flying open, her stride powerful, and her expression concerned under her curly topknot.

"Are you okay, DiNunzio?"

Mary realized she had to say it out loud. "I'm getting married?"

"Wow!" Bennie threw open her arms, grabbed Mary, and swept her into a big hug, then Judy, Anne, and Marshall joined in, and they were all swirling around like a girl hurricane, and Mary surrendered to their happiness, going along with the atmospheric pressure.

"Mare, Jeez!" Judy brushed her bangs off her face with a palm. "What a surprise!"

"Right?" Mary met her eye. "Did you know?"

"No way, not at all!" Judy grinned. "Jeez, you're a partner *and* you're engaged! Woohoo!"

"I know, right?" Mary smiled, knowing that her best friend would be happy for her, not in the least jealous. Judy had a great boyfriend in Frank Lucia, Pigeon Tony's grandson, and they were happily living in sin.

"How did he propose?" Judy asked, astonished. "When? What did he do?"

Marshall nodded, excitedly. "Tell us! And when's the date, and what's your dress gonna look like?"

"Yeah, tell us everything!" Anne's eyes lit up, and Marshall sat on the desk and even Bennie formed a little semicircle around Mary, so she began the story and told them every detail.

Everything except how she really felt.

Later, Judy caught up with her in the coffee room, after Bennie and Anne had gone off to trial, and Marshall was back at her desk. The room was small and cozy, ringed by pine cabinets with white countertops, like an office kitchen, which was why Mary gravitated there. Judy popped a Keurig cup into the coffeemaker, hit the Brew button, and turned to Mary, lifting an eyebrow. "Well?"

"Well what?" Mary asked, her, but she knew. Judy could read her at a glance, and they'd talked about getting married a zillion times.

"He asked, huh?"

"Yes."

"You said yes."

"I did." Mary sighed, then felt guilty for even having the conversation. "I do love him."

"I know that. So what's up? It's a good thing. You love each other."

"We really do."

"It's love love, right? Not roommate love or like buddies."

"No, it's love love." Mary thought back to last night, when they had made love. Anthony was wonderful, sweet, and strong, and he'd made her toes curl. Twice. "He's great."

"He is great." Judy smiled, nodding. "I love him, too. He's a great guy and he's great for you. So then what?"

"I'm not sure." Mary felt oddly flustered. "For starters, the ring."

"What?" Judy frowned at the ring. "I like it. What's the problem? Is it a conflict diamond?"

"No."

"But it's conflicting you." Judy smiled, trying to cheer her up. "Is it about Mike?"

"No, I don't think so." Mary had asked herself that question last night, because she had felt sad after meeting with Allegra, thinking about the Gardner case. Murder wasn't something anybody ever got over, and it was the double-whammy of grief, not only do you have to deal with the fact that someone you love was murdered, but you also have to deal with the fact that they are gone for good. It was impossible for anyone, least of all Mary, who should have been voted Least Likely To Get Over Anything.

Judy sipped her coffee, black. "Do you want to marry him?"

Mary hesitated. "Let me put it this way. If I wanted to marry anybody, it would be Anthony."

"I have an idea. Close your eyes. Imagine yourself walking down the aisle in a white dress, plastic hair, false eyelashes, the whole thing. How do you feel?"

Mary squeezed her eyes shut. "Nervous."

"How nervous?"

"Very." Mary opened her eyes. "Wrong answer, right?"

"No, truthful. So you're just not sure."

"Right." Mary brightened. It was good to be understood even

when you were crazy, which is why there were best friends and psychiatrists. "I'm not sure. I feel unsure."

"It's natural to be unsure before such a big decision. I'm sure nobody walks down the aisle a hundred percent sure."

"I did, with Mike."

"You did?"

"Totally." Mary could remember the day she married Mike. She had been so happy and excited, a sunny sky of a person. Her family had cried like babies, which was how she knew they were really happy, the line between joy and agony being hair-thin with the DiNunzio family. The Tonys, Mike's family, and the entire neighborhood had been there, since Mary was the Girl Who Made Good. Mike had been an elementary school teacher, and his third-grade class had come to the church, giggling and fidgeting. She'd felt blessed and happy, and thinking about it now, she fell silent, mulling it over.

"Okay, well, that aside, how unsure are you now? Quantify it."

"Like a percentage?"

Yep." Judy nodded, sipping her coffee, and Mary felt oddly as if she were describing symptoms to a doctor.

"I'm 50 percent sure, and 50 percent unsure."

"Yikes." Judy grimaced.

"I know. I can't help it." Mary rubbed her forehead. "I couldn't say no."

"I get that. So what now?"

"I said yes, and I'm hoping my feelings will catch up, like my nervousness will go away."

"You didn't set a date, did you?"

"No." Mary had avoided doing that, and as soon as the possibility of sex came up, Anthony forgot about wedding plans. "Honestly, that would feel like a deadline. A trial date."

"Ugh. That's not good."

"I know."

"All right, don't worry. You want to hear what I think?" Judy eyed her with a sympathetic smile.

"Tell me, doc. What's your diagnosis?"

"The fact is, you're a baby-steps kind of girl. You take things slow, you *process.* I've known you forever, and you've always been that way. And coming right after becoming a partner, getting engaged is too much. You overloaded."

"You think?" Mary straightened up.

"I know."

"That's sounds right." Mary felt her heart ease, just a little. "Maybe you're right."

"I am. If you don't start to feel more sure, as time goes on, you shouldn't go through with it."

"No?"

"No."

Mary sensed she was asking permission, even from Judy, but it was nice to have the assist. "When do I make the call?"

"Not yet. Take your time."

"Do I tell him?"

"Don't, no. Let it cool. Chill."

"Right, agree."

"Trust yourself. You haven't made any wrong moves yet." Judy reached out and squeezed her arm. "Okay?"

"Okay." Mary went to the sink, turned on the faucet, and poured some water into a styrofoam cup. She sipped it, and it tasted like styrofoam, but it wasn't the cup. Philadelphia water tasted like styrofoam when it came out of the tap. In fact, styrofoam improved the taste of Philadelphia water.

"Also, I thought about that meeting with the Gardners, and I think you were right. We should meet the parents before we go forward."

"Good." Mary had thought about it, too, and decided she was right. "It's good to play nice."

"So I hear. That's why I dressed so boring, in case we can see them today." Judy gestured in disgust at her perfect outfit. "Look at me, in white and blue. I'm so nautical, I'm practically a yacht."

Mary smiled. "They're probably too busy to see us, him being a captain of industry."

"A mogul's work is never done."

"We'll have to call Allegra, to make sure she's okay with it." Mary's phone started ringing. "This will be my parents, screaming with joy."

"Put it on speaker." Judy grinned. "I love to hear them happy. It adds years to my life."

Mary slid her phone from her blazer pocket and hit the speaker button.

But it wasn't her parents at all.

Chapter Seven

"Ms. DiNunzio?" said a man's voice, which was too stern and authoritative to be anything but a bill collector.

"If you're calling again about the Verizon bill, I told you, I paid it."

"Am I speaking with Mary DiNunzio?"

"You guys always pull this. I never give any information over the phone, and I'm supposed to be on a do-not-call list." Mary set the phone down on the counter to show Judy what a badass she had become overnight, coincidentally the same night she said yes to a marriage proposal when she really meant to say maybe. "You're just bullies, and you picked on the wrong girl."

Judy shot her a thumbs-up.

"Ms. DiNunzio, excuse me, this is John Gardner, Allegra's father."

Gulp. "Oh, sorry." Mary cringed, and Judy's eyes flared. "I didn't realize, here, I have you on speaker. Mr. Gardner, I'm here with Judy—"

"Call me John. I understand your law firm is representing Allegra."

"Yes, and we were about to call to set up a meeting with you."

"Excellent. How about today? I'm at the house, and you can come here. I'd like to keep this away from my offices in town, which as you probably know, are at the Delaware River Complex."

Mary did know. That was where Fiona was murdered, which was why the Philadelphia police had jurisdiction and the trial was in Common Pleas Court, here. She caught Judy's eye. "Perfect, when are you free? We'd like to meet with your wife as well."

"Of course, she'll be there."

"And Allegra?"

"Yes. We live in Townsend. When can you get here?"

Mary looked at Judy, who nodded, so she answered, "We can leave now. How long does it take from the city?"

"An hour and a half, at this time of day."

Mary would have to get her car, too. "We'll leave right away, and be there in two hours. We'll talk with Allegra first to ascertain that she's okay with our meeting with you."

"Of course she is. She's our daughter."

"I understand that, but she's our client."

John paused. "Frankly, we'd like to meet you without Allegra."

"Why?" Mary asked, and Judy shook her head, no.

"We feel that we can speak more freely. We don't want to upset her any more than she already is."

Mary didn't like the sound of it. "She didn't seem upset to us."

"Allow me to suggest that her mother and I know her slightly better than you do."

Mary didn't like the new edge to his tone, either. "We'll meet with her first and discuss this with her. It will be her decision."

"We'll sort this out when you get here. Our address is 947 Springhill Lane. Buzz at the gate and look for the sign that says Houyhnhnm Farm."

Mary thought the word sounded familiar, then realized it was from *Gulliver's Travels.* She couldn't begin to spell it. She'd recognize the sign because it would look like Greek.

"Call if you get lost, which is very easy to do. My cell number is 610-555-0363, but I may be on a conference call. If you can't reach me, my wife Jane's cell is 555-0364 and Allegra's is 555-0365."

"Will do. Thanks so much, see you soon. Good-bye, now." Mary pressed End Call, troubled. "Tell you something interesting."

"What?"

"The cell number that he gave us for Allegra is different from the one she gave me yesterday. Hold on, let me see if I'm right." Mary scrolled to her address book to double-check, and confirmed what she remembered. "I am. So Allegra has two cell phones."

"She's baller, for a middle-schooler." Judy set down her coffee. "Let's go. I'll get my notes on the file. I made some when I copied it."

"Good idea. We'll take my car. It's cleaner."

"You got that right."

Half an hour later, Mary had called Allegra but hadn't been able to reach her, so she'd left a message, picked up the car, and hopped on the expressway heading west, speeding out of the city in Mary's blue BMW 325, which replaced Mike's ancient green BMW 2002. She stopped driving the green one only after it turned 100,000 miles, and even so, she couldn't junk it, but left it parked on the street, moving it occasionally so the Parking Authority didn't tag it as abandoned. Sometimes she found notes on the car windshield, offering to buy it, but she never responded. Mike had loved that car, and she couldn't bring herself to sell it. She wasn't the most insightful woman on the planet, but even she knew Mike's old BMW was all bollixed up with Anthony, the proposal, and the meatball ring.

"Okay, I'll brief you on the way, since you're a partner now."

"Sounds good," Mary told her, coming out of her reverie. The expressway was clear and sunny, the sky a bold blue over the Schuylkill River to their right, and on its far bank stood a line of brightly-painted Victorian boathouses, flying bright pennants that flapped in the gusts. Crews rowed past in sculls as long and skinny as toothpicks, and Mary couldn't understand why Bennie loved to row, when you could so easily drown.

"I'll take you through the trial, it's cut short by the guilty plea, when the jury was dismissed. Prosecution calls nine witnesses, defense calls two."

Mary hit the gas. "Who was Stall's lawyer? Was he a public defender?"

"No, a private lawyer. I never heard of him. Bob Brandt."

"Never heard of him either. Was he court-appointed?"

"No."

"So they went out of the system. Too bad." Mary knew that Philadelphia had a fairly decent system for representing indigent murder defendants, in that 80 percent would get a well-qualified lawyer appointed by the court, and the remainder went to the Public Defender's Office, which was staffed with experienced and committed criminal defense lawyers.

"His firm is the Law Offices of Bob Brandt." Judy slid her iPhone from her purse and hit a few keys on the touch screen. "Here's Brandt's website. It doesn't say he practices criminal law except DUI." She pinched the screen to enlarge it. "He looks young, even now. Five years ago, he must have been very young. Went to Temple Law and Penn State. Okay, so he graduated law school three years before he tried Stall's case. Wanna bet it was practically his first murder case?"

Mary was already thinking they could attack the conviction based on ineffective assistance of counsel. It was a tough argument to win, but the law was that if trial counsel was incompetent and his incompetence made the difference between conviction and acquittal, Stall could get a new trial. Mary asked, "Who was in for the D.A.?"

"The district attorney himself. Mean Mel Bount."

"For real?" Mary looked over.

"Of course. It's so high-profile, a résumé case. I read that Mel's about to run for governor. Bet it helps to have a check from the Gardner clan. Okay, here we go." Judy scanned the legal pad on her lap. "Day one of the trial. The Commonwealth's opening is that Stall was seen by three witnesses running from the building and was caught by the guests with blood on his shirt and hands. He was distraught and scared. He had to be tackled and tried to get away. He had a cut on his hand consistent with a knife that's slick with blood, common in knife murders. His blood, hair, and skin cells are found on Fiona's body. When the cops come, he asks immediately for a lawyer."

Mary kept her eyes on the road. She wasn't Pollyanna enough to think that race didn't matter, but she wasn't jumping to any conclusions. "You know that Philadelphia juries tend to be mostly African-American."

"True, and blacks can be racists, too."

Mary let it go.

"First Commonwealth witness is the arresting cop who testifies that Stall is five foot ten and right-handed, and that he asks for a lawyer, even before his interview."

"Did they videotape the interview?"

"Such as it was, yes. The cop testifies about the knife wound found on Stall's right hand, and he is right-handed. After the cop, the second witness is the coroner, who testifies that Fiona's death occurred from a single stab wound through the heart, from a slight downward angle, as if from a taller person, probably right-handed."

"Uh-oh."

"Right. Also he testifies that the wound looks like it was made by a common kitchen knife, though the weapon was never recovered. He also says that the knife wound on Stall's hand was made by the same knife, and here's where he also says it's common in knife murders for the killer to get cut. Gruesome."

"Really."

"Yep, and hold that thought. The third witness is a blood expert who says that the blood found on Stall's shirt, hands, and under his nails was Fiona's blood type, which is Type O. By the way, Stall's type is A, so by process of deduction it's not his."

Mary switched to the fast lane, bypassing the traffic backing up at the Montgomery Drive exit.

"Blood expert also says that it's Stall's blood on Fiona's shirt, presumably from the cut on his hand. Still day one, fourth witness is a DNA expert, who says he has a match on the blood on Stall's shirt, and it is Fiona's."

"So they got her blood on him, and his blood on her."

"Yep. Plus, DNA expert also testifies that they find Stall's DNA on Fiona's clothes, in the form of skin cells and hair."

"Hair ID's not that reliable."

"It's just icing. The cake? They find his saliva in her mouth, identified by DNA."

Mary groaned. "No sexual assault though."

"No."

"Thank God. Did you see whether Brandt scored any points on cross?"

"No, I didn't have time to read the trial transcripts." Judy flipped to the next page of her pad. "Second day. Three witnesses testified that they saw Stall hurry up a back stair to the small conference room where she was killed, minutes before she was killed, and one saw him come back down again. They pick him out of a lineup, which appears to be properly conducted."

"They're not really eyewitnesses. They didn't see the crime."

"True, and still, even properly conducted eyewitness IDs are suspect. And also, keep in mind, that this one is cross-racial."

"What does that matter?" Mary glanced over, intrigued.

"There's cases that say that cross-racial IDs are especially unreliable. White people can't tell black people apart, and black people can't tell white people apart."

"Bodes well for the City of Brotherly Love."

Judy consulted her notes. "Final fact witness is the catering manager, Stall's boss, who testifies that one of the kitchen knives went missing. Obvious implication, that's the murder weapon, and he also testifies that Stall would have had access to it, all night."

"Maybe they lost it or misplaced it."

"Possible. Lastly, of course, both John and Jane Gardner take the stand and talk about how Fiona went missing that night. They were supposed to make a speech about the new offices' dedication at nine o'clock, but she wasn't around, so they went looking for her. They found Stall running before they found her."

Mary could imagine the horror of that night, for Allegra. "So what was the defense?"

"Brandt argued in his opening that there was no evidence of motive, and reasonable doubt that Stall was the doer, and Stall testified himself."

"That's practically malpractice. What's his side of the story?"

"He said he ran up to the conference room because he heard a shout. He saw Fiona on the floor, got blood on his hands when he covered the wound to try and stop her bleeding, and got his saliva in her mouth when he tried to resuscitate her."

"That's not CPR procedure anymore, is it?"

"No. And he says the cut on his hand happened in the kitchen that night when he cut limes."

"Did the chef testify?"

"Yes, but for the Commonwealth. He said that he didn't ask Stall to cut any limes."

Mary mulled it over as she drove. "So when Stall hears a shout, he goes to see what it is himself? He doesn't tell anyone? He doesn't call security? It does sound fishy. Why doesn't Allegra think that's fishy?" She hit the gas, heading west toward Valley Forge. "How did they prove motive?"

"Mel's opening argued Stall must have tried to push himself on her, and when she resisted, he killed her. If you have blood, skin, hair, saliva, and positive IDs, that's enough evidence of motive." Judy closed her legal pad. "Plus maybe they made something of it on cross. We'll have to see the transcript or talk to him, and in any event, remember, it didn't go to the jury. Stall pled guilty after he testified."

Mary nodded. It was hard to believe Stall was innocent if he had pled guilty, but she knew that it happened, having had a false confession case before, in which a man pled guilty to protect someone else. "So the day he testified he was innocent, he pled guilty?"

"Yes, and we can both guess it didn't go well for him on the stand. That's probably why."

"I wonder how often that happens, that someone takes a plea deal after trial has commenced?"

"It happens."

"But why does the Commonwealth offer it, after they'd been put to the trouble of a trial, and especially after his testimony went south?"

"A deal is still better than the risk of an acquittal. They get a guarantee, and no appeals."

Mary thought of another angle, too. "It probably looks better for the D.A. if Stall pleads out, instead of being convicted, in a case with racial overtones, and class, too. Then there's less question of his guilt in the press."

"Excellent point, and the case did get a lot of press." Judy looked over, nodding. "How did you figure that out?"

"I'm an expert on guilt. I have enough for every felon in the Commonwealth." Mary managed a smile. "Who was his other witness?"

"His mom." Judy paused.

"So what was his deal, in the end?"

"Let me take you through it. He was charged with first degree murder, which carries only two possible penalties, death or life without parole. LWOP, as they say."

Mary snorted, never having liked the acronym. "Italians don't like the WOP part."

Judy smiled. "It's not a death case, he has no record and no aggravators."

"Right, and second degree murder doesn't apply, since that's murder in the course of a felony."

"Yep, so the Commonwealth reduced the killing to third degree, which has a statutory maximum of twenty to forty. He pled guilty to twenty-five to fifty."

"So they increased it during trial."

"Because he didn't take it the first time. At twenty-four, he's in Graterford until he's fifty, at least."

Mary felt a twinge. "Did he appeal the guilty plea for any reason?"

"No."

"Did he file for post-conviction relief, based on ineffective assistance of counsel, in connection with the plea?"

"No."

Mary steered the car past the City Line exit, at speed. "So if he's innocent, all he has is us."

"No, he doesn't even have us. Allegra has us. Don't mix your clients, remember?"

"Okay." Mary thought a minute. "Remember that Allegra told us she had a reason for thinking Stall was innocent, but she didn't want to tell us in the meeting?"

"Sure. Wonder what it was."

"We'll ask her." Mary glanced over to see Judy deep in thought. "We're not gonna let her parents close her out of our meeting, are we?"

"Hell, no." Judy grinned. "Nobody grounds our clients but us."

Mary laughed, then accelerated, heading for open road.

But for a second, she wasn't sure if she was speeding from something, or to something.

Chapter Eight

Houyhnhnm Farm, read the sign, and Mary turned into the driveway, her car tires rumbling over gray cobblestones until they reached
a tall iron gate covered with English ivy. Beside it were stanchions of
gray stone, with a silvery call box on the left, discreetly hidden in
evergreens that flanked the driveway.

"Can you believe this place?" Mary lowered the window to press
the call button. They had arrived after driving through the prettiest
countryside she had ever seen, and they weren't in South Philly anymore. "Think they'll adopt me?"

"Just because they have money, doesn't mean you want to be in
this family."

"It doesn't mean I don't, either." Mary pressed the buzzer, which
crackled instantly. "Hello, it's Mary DiNunzio and Judy Carrier, here
to meet with the Gardners."

"Welcome," said a woman's voice, warmly. "Come in and follow
the road. Take a left, then turn right, toward the house."

"Thank you." Mary raised the window while the iron gates swung
open. "The mom sounds nice."

"It's the maid."

Mary smiled and turned onto the road, which switched to a gray-ish gravel. "I'm intimidated."

"Don't be. Remember, they're just people and we're lawyers. We can sue them to death."

Mary steered the car past groupings of specimen bushes and trees, each with little brass nameplates. "The farm has a name, the trees have a name, everybody has a name."

"Birds." Judy pointed at a white aviary on the right, housing color-ful finches that darted about, and a white chicken coop with a long run, where black-and-white hens clustered in the shade. "Look at that. Birds of a feather really do flock together."

"This isn't a house, it's a theme park."

"It's a petting zoo, but you can't pet anything. There's the stables." Judy nodded at a large hill on the left, and at its crest sat a large white stable, surrounded by fenced pastures where dark horses grazed, the graceful heads bent toward the grass and their tails flicking.

"Aw, I like horses."

"Evidently, so do they. Except that in *Gulliver's Travels*, the Houyhnhnm weren't very nice. They were stern and imperious, like John Gardner on the phone."

"Keep an open mind. Rich people can't help it if they sound like bill collectors. They kind of are."

"There's the house."

"Jesus, Mary, and Joseph." Mary steered the car toward a huge mansion of gray stone, which had three wings, Palladian windows, and a bright white portico over the front door, under which stood an attractive, middle-aged couple.

"There's Barbie and Ken."

Mary smiled. "I don't see Allegra."

"She's in shackles in the basement."

Mary steered closer, then parked in a cobblestone lot that held a black Escalade, a white Mercedes sedan, and a silver Prius, the same model as Anthony's. "See, a Prius. That shows they're good people."

"It's the maid's."

"Do people really live like this?"

"Let's find out. You take the lead in our meeting."

"Me?" Mary turned off the ignition. She and Judy always ran meetings together as equals, which meant that they constantly interrupted each other.

"Yes, you. You're a partner now, and you have a better feel for Allegra than I do."

"No, I don't."

"Yes, you do." Judy's eyes narrowed as she looked through the windshield at the Gardners, who were approaching. "They're coming. Game face."

"Got it." Mary cut the ignition, and she and Judy got out of the car as the Gardners approached, walking in matching stride, which lent an unfortunate uniformity to their appearance, since they were both dressed in white polo shirts, pressed khaki shorts, and boy-and-girl patterns of Teva sandals.

"Welcome, I'm John Gardner." John extended a large hand, and Mary shook it, trying to give good handshake. He was tall, fit, and handsome, with blue eyes and crow's-feet that made him look reliable and reddish-brown hair that was turning sterling silver at the temples. His teeth were predictably straight and even, but his smile had a genuine warmth of a suburban dad.

"I'm Mary DiNunzio and this is Judy Carrier." Mary stole a glance at Allegra's mother while introductions were being made. Jane Gardner was also tall and thin, with wide-set hazel eyes and highlighted blonde hair scissored into a straight bob, curling obediently at her delicate chinline. Remarkably, however, a four-inch scar marred her right cheek, adding a badass touch to her wholesome American beauty.

"Call me Jane, and we're happy you could make it today. Did you have much trouble finding us, Mary?"

"No, not at all, thanks." Mary smiled to show they came in peace. "It's great to meet you both, after meeting Allegra and hearing all the wonderful things she said about you. She's a really remarkable young girl, and you must be proud of her."

"We are, thank you so much." John touched Mary's arm and steered her toward the house. "Come on in. We'll get you both something to drink and we can hash this out. Jane made us some fresh cookies and lemonade."

"Where's Allegra?" Mary asked, letting him guide them, and John gestured vaguely to the left, toward some evergreens.

"She's setting up her new hives."

"Does she know we're here? I called her and left a message, but I'm not sure she got it." Mary didn't add that she had called Allegra on both of her telephone numbers, not knowing which one Allegra used more often.

"We didn't tell her that we were expecting you, so unless you told her, she doesn't know. As I said, we'd much prefer to meet with you alone."

Mary was kicking herself. It was her own damn fault for not making sure she reached Allegra before they left the office. "Well, we'd like to see her."

"You can, after we meet."

"We'd like to see her first, if you don't mind." Mary hadn't realized that the Gardners would try to game them out of meeting Allegra. She and Judy stopped walking at the same time, and so did the Gardners.

"In point of fact, we do mind."

"Then let's discuss this." Mary hated to confront them as if they were opposing counsel in commercial litigation, instead of parents trying to deal with a painful family matter. She knew that their hearts had to be hurting under their well-dressed veneer. "We know this situation is difficult for you, and you have our condolences on the passing of your daughter Fiona. But Allegra has retained us, and as her counsel, we have an obligation that runs to her first and everybody else second, even her parents."

Judy stood beside Mary, nodding. "John, you probably know that as lawyers we act only as an agent of a principal, and the scope of our authority is narrow. Frankly, we lack authority to meet with you on Allegra's behalf without Allegra's consent. So we have no choice but to meet with Allegra first, or we cannot meet with you at all."

An awkward silence fell as John and Jane Gardner stood opposite Mary and Judy, the four of them squinting at each other in the sun, like rival teams in the most polite face-off ever. Suddenly they all looked over as the front door of the house opened and three older men in pinstriped suits emerged and strode toward them at a clip so purposeful that it could only be billable, like a legal cavalry. The Gardners had lawyered up, but Mary could have told them it wouldn't work. The more outgunned she and Judy were, the more they liked it. You didn't choose to be a lawyer unless you relished a good fight.

John Gardner gestured at the three attorneys, who reached them wearing professional smiles. "Mary, Judy, meet Steve Korn, Vincent Copperton, and Neil Patel, who work in our in-house legal department."

"Hello, gentlemen." Mary smiled back, in an equally professional manner.

"Yes, hi." Judy smiled more aggressively, if she were baring her teeth. She always said that a litigator's smile didn't count unless her incisors showed.

"Excuse me." Neil Patel stepped forward, his expression grim behind his thick glasses, and he buttoned his dark suit over a substantial waistline. "Mary, to come directly to the point, you're well aware that Allegra Gardner is thirteen years old, a minor. Her parents are her legal guardians, and you may not meet with her, absent their consent."

"We were engaged by Allegra to represent her, and as her counsel, we can meet with her at any time."

"Allegra is legally unable to make any form of contract."

"No, that's not precisely true." Mary bore down. "As a minor, Allegra can make any or all contracts she chooses, whether written or oral, but the law is that contracts made by minors will not be enforced in court, should there be a problem. We do not anticipate needing to go to court to enforce our representation agreement, which, by the way, was oral."

Judy nodded. "Of course, we could ask a court to appoint a guardian ad litem for Allegra, and the guardian would have the ability to make enforceable contracts for her and to assure that her wishes are carried out. But if we do that, this matter would become public."

John scowled, and Patel lifted a bushy eyebrow. "Obviously, we wish to avoid that. Perhaps there is a way to compromise. We would agree that you could meet with Allegra, with her parents being present."

Mary shook her head. "I'm sorry, but no. Our conversation with Allegra is confidential and privileged."

"Allegra can waive that."

"I won't ask her to, at this juncture." Mary glanced at Judy, who looked like she was ready to bite. "It's our understanding that Allegra's parents were aware that she was seeking counsel, so I'm at a loss to understand why we're conducting litigation on the driveway." Mary faced John. "You did know she was interviewing law firms, correct?"

"Admittedly, yes," he answered, and Jane looked upset, pursing her lips. "But we didn't believe she would really go through with it, and it's gone too far. We don't want outsiders poking their nose into our family, and we'll put a stop to it, here and now."

"We're not here to interfere with your family."

John stiffened. "Yet you are, and my counsel are prepared to file an injunction against you, if you persist."

"On what basis?" Mary recoiled. "There's no grounds for an injunction."

"Invasion of privacy. Harassment."

Judy scoffed, stepping forward. "None of those grounds would prevail, and your counsel has probably told you as much. Again, we will defend in court, and all that would accomplish is to make this public."

Mary wanted to reason with him. "John, you can't solve a problem legally unless you have a legal problem. You can't stop your daughter from asking questions, whether you tell her not to, or a judge does. Allegra hired us to look into the conviction of Lonnie Stall, and we intend to confine our investigation to the court case—"

"Investigation?" Jane frowned, deeply, and Mary turned to her.

"Jane, we can explain this to you, calmly. Why don't you let us see Allegra, then we'll all sit down, okay? There's no reason for this to be adversarial. It's difficult enough for you."

There was a happy shout from the evergreens, and they all turned to see Allegra hustling toward them, waving. She was wearing a white T-shirt that read DON'T WORRY, BEE HAPPY with white shorts and sneakers, and her long, wavy hair flew out behind her. "Mary! Judy! Hi!"

"Hi!" Mary waved back, and so did Judy, before they could be enjoined not to.

"What are you guys doing here?" Allegra's smile faded as she reached the tense group, and Mary felt for her.

"Sorry to surprise you, Allegra. We thought we'd come by, see you, and talk with your parents about the case, to keep them in the loop. I called you and told you we were on the way. Did you get the message?"

"No, sorry, I didn't have my phone on me."

"Is it okay with you if we talk to your parents, with you present?"

"Sure."

"And can we meet with you alone first, before we do that?"

"Yes."

"No," John answered, at the same time. Neil Patel opened his mouth to say something, but John waved him into silence. "No, no, no."

"Daddy?" Allegra looked over at her parents, her expression anxious, but not completely surprised. "Why can't they? They can't talk to me?"

"Allegra." John placed a hand on his daughter's knobby shoulder. "Your mother and I wish you would stop right now. We've been over and over this, but you're taking it to a new level. Getting lawyers involved is very extreme. It's not good for you, and it's too intrusive to us, to have outsiders in our family life."

Jane came around Allegra's other side, her expression pained. "Honey, Daddy's right. Why don't you tell Mary and Judy to go back to their office, and we'll go inside, have some lemonade and cookies, and talk this over. You know we love Fiona, and if you still have questions about her, well, what happened to her, I promise you we can find a way to answer them."

Neil Patel turned to Allegra. "Legally, your parents are right, and we don't believe that you have the capacity to engage outside counsel with respect to your sister's murder."

Allegra squinted against the sunlight, looking up at her father. "Is that why you were mad when I came home early from Home Depot? And that's why the lawyers are here?"

"Honey, we can explain that."

Allegra frowned. "Daddy, if I can't see them here, I'll see them at their office. You can't stop me from talking to them, or anyone."

"Yes, we can." John's tone remained firm. "You're our daughter."

"Right. I'm your daughter, not your property," Allegra shot back, equally firmly. "Now let me go talk to my lawyers."

Chapter Nine

Mary and Judy followed Allegra across the immense, dappled lawn of the backyard, leaving the Gardners and their lawyers on the driveway. They passed a swimming pool with a flagstone surround and headed for an out-of-the-way, weedy patch near a wooden-sided compost pile, and Mary noticed that Allegra was walking with her head down.

"Allegra, you okay?" she asked, with a sympathetic pang.

"I guess so." Allegra kept her head down. "That weirded me out, sorry."

"No need to apologize." Mary glanced back to see that the Gardners and their lawyers were still on the driveway. She gathered they were going to stay and glare at them from across the lawn. "I should have kept trying to get you on the phone."

"No, it's my dad. He's freaking out."

"It's understandable."

"Not to me." Allegra pressed her lips over her braces. "I guess my parents made a secret plan to get me out of the house while you guys came over. They knew I wanted to get some things for the hives, and that must be why they had the driver take me. They said they couldn't because they had work to do."

Mary exchanged a quick glance with Judy. "Well, try not to blame them. They're trying to deal with a hard situation, and it will take some time to sort it all out. It's new for them, and it's topsy-turvy, a daughter calling the shots. Most parents would feel the same way."

"I'm not giving up." Allegra faced forward, brightening as she motioned to some wooden boxes ahead. "Check out my new hives. What do you think?"

"That's a beehive?" Mary eyed the boxes, which looked like night-stands, with three drawers.

Judy looked over with a crooked grin. "Mare, what did you think it would look like?"

"A hive, you know like a big curved thing that's wider at the bottom and comes to a point at the top, like in the cartoons."

Allegra smiled. "This is a Langstroth hive, which was invented by a man from Philadelphia, Lorenzo Langstroth. It's the best-selling hive in the world, but it's sad, he never got royalties from the patent. That bugs me."

"No pun."

"No. Bees aren't bugs *per se*. I prefer to call them insects."

"Oh." Mary stepped to the hive, then stopped herself. "Wait a minute, there's no bees here, right?"

"No, they come in the mail this week."

Judy turned. "You can mail bees? No wonder the Postal Service is so cranky."

Allegra smiled. "It took me all morning to assemble this, and I'll paint it tomorrow."

"How does it work?"

"The trays slide out so you can keep them clean, like this." Allegra pulled one out. "Langstroth discovered the concept of bee space, which means that the trays are only as far apart as a single bee, so the honeycombs don't get gummed up with propolis."

Mary didn't ask her what that meant, because she wanted to get the conversation back on track. Between *Houyhnhnm* and *propolis*, the place was a vocabulary nightmare, and the Gardners and the lawyers were still watching them from the driveway. "Allegra, remember in our meeting when you said that there was a reason you think Lonnie Stall is innocent? What was the reason?"

"I think Fiona knew Lonnie." Allegra straightened up, brushing brownish hair from her glasses, where a few strands had gotten caught in the hinge. "Everybody believes he was a total stranger to her, like he was just one of the waiters hired by the catering service, but my parents used that catering service all the time and they entertained a lot. There were always parties. Even I got to know those guys."

"Okay, so why does that matter? Would Lonnie hurt Fiona? Do you think there was a problem between them?"

"No." Allegra's faced changed, her eyebrows slanting unhappily down. "I think Lonnie didn't kill Fiona. I think he loved her. I think they were in love. I even think they were having sex."

"What makes you say that?" Mary gathered the birds-and-the-bees lecture was a moot point, especially for a bee expert.

"Because when Fiona babysat me, Lonnie came over to visit."

"You mean, at the house?"

"Yes."

"Didn't you have a nanny or a sitter?"

"We have a housekeeper, but Fiona sat me, too."

"Did your parents know that Lonnie was coming over?"

"No."

"You're sure it was him?"

"I am, I remember, and he was such a nice guy."

"How do you know it was him? You were so young at the time."

"I remember him. He was nice to me, he talked to me, and introduced himself. He didn't treat me like a baby. I remember his voice, even."

Mary was confused. "How many times would you say you saw him, when she babysat?"

"Maybe five times, when she babysat, but more at my parents' parties." Allegra glanced over at her parents, but they were well out of earshot. "My Mom and Dad like to entertain at the house and the office. It's a Gardner thing, because it's a family business, so everything's kind of together."

"I get that," Mary said, though her experience had been the opposite, growing up. The DiNunzios barely socialized, except with blood relatives or neighbors in the same parish, which was Epiphany. In fact, Mary had an epiphany when she realized there was an outside world.

"So I think that Fiona and Lonnie were, you know, together, when she was babysitting me."

"How many times? Five? Ten?"

"Five. I think she volunteered to babysit me so he could come over. And she knew him, they hugged and kissed. The night she was murdered, I think he went into the small conference room to meet her, to be together. He wouldn't kill her. He had a major crush on her."

Mary tried to process the information. "She was sixteen, right?"

"Right, and Lonnie was eighteen."

"Where did she go to high school?"

"Shipwyn, in Bryn Mawr. It's a private school. She didn't board."

Mary didn't understand why Allegra boarded when Fiona didn't, but she let that go for now. "Did she have a boyfriend at school? Was she popular?"

"Fiona was super popular." Allegra brightened. "She was smart and funny and she was nice to everybody, not only the cool kids. Her school was very cliquey but she was never a mean girl, ever. All the boys were crazy about her, but she didn't date anyone there except for Tim Gage."

Mary made a mental note of his name. "Do you think Tim or the kids at school knew about Lonnie?"

"No." Allegra shook her head, emphatically. "I don't think anybody knows about Lonnie. Lonnie was Fiona's secret."

Judy, who had been listening quietly, stepped over. "Allegra, fast-forward to after your sister's murder. Did you tell your parents that you thought Lonnie and Fiona were seeing each other?"

"Yes, but they didn't believe me, and they still don't. They think Lonnie was just one of the waiters. They don't know that he knew Fiona."

"When did you tell them?"

"After I heard that Lonnie was arrested. I knew his name, not his last name, but his first. I remember I even told the detectives, when they came to the house. I told my parents' lawyers, too."

"Your parents had lawyers, then?" Judy caught herself. "Of course, they would have."

"Yes, totally. Mr. Patel." Allegra permitted herself a tight smile. "My Dad is a really careful guy, and the lawyers are always around. That's the weird thing about a family business. Like I remember when I was having a problem with one of the mean kids at school, Mr. Patel wanted to sue the parents."

Judy paused. "So you don't know what happened after that, if the police investigated whether Lonnie knew Fiona."

"No, I don't."

Judy nodded. "The fact that Lonnie knew Fiona doesn't mean that he didn't kill her. In fact, it cuts both ways."

Mary didn't say what Judy was thinking, which was that, if anything, it gave Lonnie evidence of motive, making him look guiltier.

Allegra frowned. "I know, but I just don't think it was him. He's a quiet, shy guy. It's just not him. He didn't do it."

"You didn't go to the trial, did you?"

"No. My parents didn't think I should. I was eight by then, but they thought I was too young."

"Lonnie took the stand in his own defense and he didn't say anything about knowing Fiona, or that they were meeting that night. He said he heard a noise and that's why he went into the small conference room."

Allegra pursed her lips. "I remember my parents telling me that, but I don't understand that."

"Maybe it was the truth."

"Maybe not. That's what I want you guys to figure out."

Judy turned to Mary, her eyes narrowing against the bright sun. "Sounds like we have our work cut out with that for us."

"Right." Mary nodded, turning to Allegra. "To switch gears a moment, I have a question for you. Before I ask you, you understand that anything we talk about is confidential, right? That means we won't tell your parents anything we discussed, without your approval."

Allegra nodded. "Yes, I understand that."

"You gave me a cell-phone number at our office that was different from the one your father gave me. Do you have two cell phones?"

Allegra flushed under her fair skin, and her eyes flared slightly. "Uh, yes. I have a cell phone that my parents don't know about."

"Why?"

"So I could set up the interviews with law firms and make the phone calls I wanted to make without my parents' seeing. I'm still on the family plan with them on the phone they gave me, and I even think that comes from the company."

"Okay, I get that. Obviously, I won't say anything, and Judy and I will use your private cell phone to reach you. Does that make sense?"

"Yes. I'll keep it with me more. I guess I'm just not used to getting calls."

Mary patted her on the shoulder, on impulse. "Now, we do want to meet with your parents. It's clear they're not happy about your hiring us, or your going forward with your questions, but we think the best way to deal with this is to be as respectful as possible. That's why we'd like to meet with them today and get their view of the case. You're sure you're fine with that?"

"Yes, totally."

"Your parents want us to have this meeting without you, but I think you should be present."

"Me, too."

"Good." Mary loved the kid's strength. "Ready to go?"

"Sure."

"Then let's rejoin them." Mary touched Allegra's arm, and they all turned toward the driveway, trooped past the pool, and reached the Gardners and their lawyers, hoping to defuse the situation. "Thanks so much for waiting for us to finish. Now, maybe we can all go inside and talk a little further."

John stepped forward, his mouth a grim line, his eyes flinty in the sun. "We would be happy to meet with you and Judy, but we don't think that Allegra should be present."

Mary was about to respond, but Allegra spoke first. "Daddy, why not? We can try to figure this out together. It's about Fiona, not us or the lawyers. Mary and Judy are just trying to help us."

John shook his head. "Allegra, this is getting out of hand. Your grandfather's money may be giving you the power to hire these lawyers, and they can do with you whatever they have the legal power to do. But I'm still your father, she's still your mother, and this is still my home." He gestured at Jane, whose expression was equally grim. "We still have some say in this house and on this property, and you are not permitted to be at this meeting, as long as it's here."

"Daddy, really?" Allegra sounded disappointed, but John ignored her, turning to Mary and Judy.

"Ladies, if you want to meet with my wife and me on this property, you will do so without my daughter present. Otherwise, we can set the meeting for another day at your office, and my wife and I will consider whether we want to attend."

Mary read between the lines. If she insisted on having the meeting here with Allegra, she'd never get the meeting at all. She had no legal grounds to compel the Gardners to meet with her, especially if they were going to go with the my-house-my-rules routine, which had served fathers from the beginning of time, even her own, when she really wanted a pony for Christmas.

Neil Patel stood next to John Gardner. "From now on, I am representing John and Jane Gardner, and all of your communications regarding any putative meetings should be addressed to me." Patel slid his hand inside his jacket pocket, extracted a leather wallet, flipped it open, and took out a business card, which he handed to Mary. "Am I making myself clear? You may no longer communicate with Allegra's parents except through me."

"Daddy," Allegra said, her tone softer. "It's more important to me that you and Mom meet with Mary and Judy, than I be there. So go have your meeting without me. I'll go set up my hives." She turned and walked away without another word, and Mary looked at Judy, both of them thinking the same thing:

Who's supposed to be the adult again?

Chapter Ten

Mary and Judy sat on a forest-green leather couch across from a mahogany coffee table from Jane and John Gardner, with Neil Patel sitting off to the side, in a matching leather club chair. They met in a large, paneled room with a separate entrance around the back of the house, like a home conference room, lined with bookshelves of leather-bound books that looked collected, if not read. Brocade curtains framed the Palladian windows, but wooden blinds forced the sun to struggle through bare slats, darkening the room. The other two company lawyers had scurried off, and there was no lemonade or cookies in sight, since Mary and Judy had behaved too badly for treats.

"Let's begin." John crossed his legs in his khaki shorts, his manner relaxed and in control. "You came here to meet with us, so perhaps you would like to tell us why."

"Yes, well, first let me reiterate that we know the situation is difficult for you." Mary slid a fresh legal pad and pen from her oversized purse, while Judy did the same. "We extend to you our sympathies on the loss of your daughter Fiona."

"Thank you," John answered, and the firmness of his tone suggested that he was going to be doing the talking for his wife. "By the way, we are recording this meeting. I'm sure you have no problem with that."

"Feel free." Mary glanced at Judy, then she paused, confused. "Do you want us to wait while you get your handheld or tape recorder?"

"There's no need to."

"Oh." Mary guessed he meant the room was wired, which was straight-up freaky. She wondered where the microphones were, and if they had them outside too, strapped to the chickens. "As I was saying, Allegra came to us because she does not believe that Lonnie Stall killed Fiona. She asked us to investigate the case, and you should understand that we do not intend to interfere in your personal family business."

"And how precisely do you intend to avoid doing that?"

"An easy way to think about this is to think of us as appellate counsel—"

"That's not so easy for us, because we don't wish to see this matter appealed, in any way, shape, or form. We know that Lonnie Stall is guilty of murdering our daughter in cold blood, in my very own offices. He's in prison, which is exactly where he belongs." John lifted an eyebrow. "Now what were you saying is easy?"

"Forgive me if I seem glib, because I don't feel that way." Mary swallowed hard. "We are charged with investigating the murder and the trial, to determine if the result was correct. While that may not be what you wish, it is what our client wishes, and my point is that it should not involve your family at all. We have already begun to review the trial transcript and the evidence in the case—"

"Let me interrupt you. Allegra told you that Fiona was having a relationship with Lonnie Stall, correct?"

"I'm not at liberty to discuss with you what she told me, because that's privileged."

John sighed audibly. "There's a lot about Allegra you don't know, and none of it should be your business, except that she has made it so by hiring you."

Mary couldn't miss the angry edge to his tone.

Jane cleared her throat quietly, and John glanced at his wife, then continued. "We love our daughter, both of our daughters, very deeply, and except for this issue, we get along very well. I'm not the big, bad, scary businessman that you imagine me to be, and my wife is a wonderful mother. But you cannot begin to understand the repercussions that a violent crime like murder has on a family."

"Yes, I can." Mary hesitated, then went ahead. "My husband was murdered many years ago, and I will never be the same, nor will my family."

"I'm sorry, and I stand corrected." John's cool gaze shifted sideways to Neil Patel, and Mary could read his look. Patel should have briefed him before the meeting and he'd get no lemonade or cookies, either.

Jane interjected, "My condolences. That must have been very difficult for you."

John nodded. "Then you will know exactly how painful this is for us, to relive the murder of our daughter. Like you, we will never be over it, nor will we be the same as a family. But the conviction did give us some closure, which is now in question."

Mary wanted to reason with him. "But you don't want Stall in jail if he's an innocent man."

"Of course not, but he's guilty. Let me give you some background, which may provide you some additional perspective." John cleared his throat. "Allegra was a wonderful surprise to us, coming along late in our life. She was a sweet, quiet child and showed an amazing intellectual ability even at a young age." John smiled slightly, looking over at his wife. "Jane could tell you the stories as a loving mother, but suffice it to say that at an early age, Allegra tested at a genius level. Her IQ is confidential, but I will tell you that she required all manner of gifted courses and excelled at them. She has unique reasoning abilities and uncanny powers of observation. She is lucky in many, many ways. Blessed, really."

Mary listened, taking only a few notes, knowing that Judy would pick up what she didn't.

"You may remember seeing a news item about Allegra, right before the murder. She was at recess in first grade, and she happened to notice that the mulch on the playground was lifting slightly upward."

Mary didn't know where he was going with the story.

"She couldn't have known the scientific principles, but she deduced correctly that a vacuum was being created in the sky. She looked up but it was cloudy, so she ran to the teacher's aide and told her there was something wrong with the sky and that the children had to leave the playground. The aide panicked and got everybody inside. Only a few minutes later, a helicopter and a small plane fell through the cloud cover onto the playground, crashing and burning."

Mary gasped. "My God."

"The pilots and passengers of both aircraft were killed, but no students were, because of Allegra. Of course, the media got involved, and they dubbed her the Girl Genius."

Mary began to remember reading something about it in the newspaper.

Judy looked up from her notes, wide-eyed. "That's amazing, but what created the vacuum? Why did the mulch lift upward?"

"The helicopter and the small plane had flown close to each other, because the helicopter was examining the landing gear of the plane, which was evidently stuck, not coming down when the plane had tried to land at the airstrip. I'm no scientist, but from what I understand, a vacuum was created that pulled the two aircraft into each other and also caused a mild disturbance on the ground, which Allegra spotted, as she would. Even as a toddler, she didn't miss a trick." John glanced over at his wife and patted her leg with a smile. "We could tell them stories, right, honey?"

"We sure could." Jane smiled back, placing her hand over her husband's, with a little pat.

John continued, "You would think the attention at school would be positive, but kids aren't like that. It turned to bullying and teasing. Her genius-level IQ became a target for some very cruel behavior.

We date Allegra's emotional troubles from then, and they were only compounded two months later, when Fiona was murdered. Allegra was in mourning, but she began to exhibit behaviors that we felt would benefit from a therapist. She was diagnosed with situational depression, and the therapist thought she would recover more easily in a different school, out of the area. We enrolled her in boarding school, where we hoped she would recover, in time, under the care of a private therapist."

Jane nodded. "We didn't want her to go, we loved having her with us, but the bullying was too intense. We couldn't move because of John's businesses, so it made sense to send her away. Still, we missed her."

Mary's heart went out to them both. It's sounded like a nightmare, as if they'd lost both of their daughters in one fell swoop.

John continued, "However, Allegra's grief over her sister's murder seemed to migrate to a preoccupation with the murder case itself, the testimony, and the witnesses, even the exhibits."

Mary shuddered. She had seen that before, sometimes in medical malpractice cases, when a client found it easier to transfer their anger at losing a loved one onto a lawsuit.

"Allegra is simply obsessed with the case. For example, she has studied the trial transcripts and can recite entire passages to you, by memory."

Mary tried not to show her alarm. "I didn't know she had the file."

"She does, it's public record, and she obtained it herself. Over the years, and despite various types of medication, Allegra has only become more convinced that she and she alone knows the truth about Fiona's murder. She believes the delusion that Fiona and Lonnie Stall engaged in a love relationship, which if you read the trial transcript, he himself did not claim on the stand, and we know to be untrue."

Mary tried to process the information. "How do you know that's delusional? Why don't you think it's true?"

"She undoubtedly told you that Lonnie and Fiona met when Fiona was babysitting, but we never asked Fiona to babysit her baby sister. Not once, ever."

Mary didn't get it, but John wouldn't have any reason to lie. "So if she told me that, you believe she made that up?"

"Not consciously. She believes it, but it's not true. Professionals whom we have consulted have suggested that her native ability to focus and concentrate are part-and-parcel with an obsessiveness that you have already seen with her, whether it's her beekeeping or any of her other interests, about which I'm sure you will hear."

Mary tried to keep an open mind, but she didn't know if he was being fair to Allegra.

"We believe, and Allegra has been diagnosed more recently as having a form of obsessive-compulsive disorder that relates to thought processes, like ruminative thinking. She thinks obsessively about the murder trial, and one therapist has even identified it as a justice obsession syndrome, with cases observed in Sweden, Germany, and other places around the world. I can send you the article if you like."

"Please do," Mary said, shaken.

"So, you understand, that while Allegra is blessed with preternatural intelligence, she also suffers as well. The proverbial blessing and curse."

Mary's heart broke for Allegra, and for all of them.

"We don't know the details of her fixation on the murder case, because like you, her therapist is governed by confidentiality and will share nothing with us other than her diagnosis and treatment plan. So we find ourselves, as loving parents, kept in the dark about our own daughter. And by the way, we pay for that privilege." Anger resurfaced in John's voice, controlled yet unmistakable. "What makes this situation so singular is, of course, money. Any average thirteen-year-old wouldn't have the means to indulge this obsession, but Allegra is lucky, or unlucky, in that regard, too. The distribution from her trust fund has empowered her to hire you, and though we disagree with what she is doing, we are powerless to stop it. Unless you can be prevailed upon, to exercise your common sense and decline to enable her."

Mary didn't realize that he'd finished the sentence. "You mean drop the case?"

"Exactly." John eyed her, tilting his head back. "I've given you a great deal of information about Allegra, and I gather much of this is news to you, isn't it?"

"Yes, it is."

"Well, then, if you are as qualified an attorney as your reputation would suggest, I would think that you would go no further with this matter. I know that some lawyers will do anything for a fee, but I had Rosato & Associates pegged as a cut above. Perhaps I was incorrect."

Mary took it on the chin. "We're not in the habit of dropping a client, once engaged."

"Even though you know Allegra is having emotional difficulties and the lawsuit is only the expression of that?"

Mary glanced at Judy, but she could read her mind. "We appreciate your input, but Allegra isn't an incompetent, that is, she isn't mentally unable to engage a lawyer."

"I see." John sucked in his cheeks as if he'd eaten something sour. "So you can be bought."

"No, but we can be hired. And we were."

"Then this meeting is over." John rose abruptly, with Jane after him, then Neil Patel.

"Oh." Mary realized they were being thrown out, albeit in the classiest possible way, so she gathered her stuff hastily, and so did Judy.

"This will be the last time we meet, because we don't wish to be involved in Allegra's delusion, nor do we think it's good or healthy for her. We cannot stop her from going forward, but we won't enable it." John paused. "We hope and pray that some good will come of this, when you find that Lonnie Stall is properly in jail. Perhaps then Allegra will put this matter behind her, once and for all."

Mary wasn't about to give him any reassurance. "Thank you for your time."

"Yes, thanks," Judy said, and they let themselves be escorted out by Neil Patel, who walked them in silence to a brick walkway lined with red rosebushes, which led back to the lot where they'd parked.

"Safe travels, ladies." Patel waved to them, then folded his arms and watched them walk toward the car.

Mary fell into step with Judy. "Say nothing. The flowers have videocameras."

Judy smiled, then gestured to the lawn. "Here comes Allegra."

Mary turned to see Allegra hurrying across the lawn toward them, half-walking and half-skipping, looking every inch a carefree young girl, except that she wasn't. Her thoughts were obsessive and dark, preoccupied with murder and death. Mary resisted the urge not to see her with new eyes. Allegra had a sweetness that was impossible to miss, and what Mary had heard about her only made her feel more sympathetic and protective. More than anything, Allegra needed a friend, and Mary wasn't about to abandon her.

"Allegra!" she called out, shielding her eyes from the sun.

"Hi, guys!" Allegra came over, still smiling.

"How are you?" Mary smiled back at her. "You get your hives done?"

"Not yet." Allegra's smile faded, and her sharp gaze shifted from Mary to Judy and back again. "He told you I'm crazy, right?"

Mary felt a pang, caught off-guard. "He also told us you were a genius."

"Same thing," Allegra said, flatly.

Chapter Eleven

"Well?" Mary steered the car on roads that wound through the sunny countryside, her fingers tight on the wheel and her diamond ring blinding her.

"Well, what?" Judy looked over with a crooked grin. "Another fine mess, obviously."

"What do you think? Is she crazy?"

"Is batshit a medical term?"

Mary felt another pang. "Aw, that's not a nice thing to say."

"Then why ask me?"

"I didn't think you would say that. She's sweet."

"And nutty."

"Stop." Mary whizzed past a dairy with a herd of cows, a black-and-white blur. She couldn't wait to get back to the city, where all the milk came in plastic containers and none of the rooms was wired. "Do you think Stall is guilty?"

"Yep."

"Why?"

"Little thing called evidence."

"And you think Allegra's obsessed and delusional?"

"Yes." Judy kicked off her clogs and put her bare feet up on the dash, and Mary almost stopped the car.

"No feet on the dash."

Judy rolled her eyes and moved her feet. "Partner attack."

Mary smiled. "Now tell me why you think she's delusional."

"Because I've seen that before, when I clerked for the judge. We had case after case filed by the same litigants, and we even got to know their names. There's a lot of sad people in this world, and they file a lot of abusive lawsuits, gumming up the courts." Judy's tone turned disgusted, because nobody loved the law more than she did. "It prevents legitimate cases from being heard timely, clogs the court's dockets, and costs a fortune. Most courts have a staff attorney, whose sole job it is to handle all the *pro se* complaints. It's a waste of taxpayer dollars."

"Unless they have merit."

"The abusive ones don't. We know those litigants. They're crazy."

"But politics aside—"

"It's not politics. One of the great things about this country is that we let everyone have his day in court, and one of the worst things about this country is that we let everyone have his day in court." Judy turned to the window, running fingers through her raggedy blonde hair. "Anybody with a filing fee can file a frivolous lawsuit, and I've seen them for a ton of wacky reasons—a belief that injustice occurred, or for attention, or for something to do, or to feel important and lawyer-y, even for the drama of it."

"But you think Allegra is one of those?"

"She could be, like a conspiracy theorist with no conspiracy. I get what her father is saying, I see that in her. She's all over the bee thing."

Mary couldn't buy in, so quickly. "But isn't every teenager like that? I was obsessed with the Backstreet Boys and Boys II Men. I went to every concert and had every album, shirt, and poster."

"This is a murder, not a boy band." Judy shuddered. "It's a ghoulish preoccupation."

"It was her sister."

"All the more ghoulish."

"But when Mike was killed, I was overly involved with that case. I thought about it, and him, all the time. It's part of grieving." Mary glanced at her hand on the steering wheel, where her diamond ring blazed in the sunlight, searing her eyes.

"She's in treatment. She's diagnosed."

"So what? Maybe I would have been, too, if I had gotten to a shrink. I just didn't have the money."

"She's not you."

"I know that."

"But you're already too emotional about her."

"Of course I am. Have we met?"

Judy laughed. "It's a difference of degree, and we can't say for sure when an avid interest in something, whether it's murder or bees, shades into obsession."

"You sound checked out." Mary turned onto a two-lane road, which was as many lanes as she was going to get out here. "Where's your loyalty?"

"I'm still on board, but I have my doubts about her now."

"Her own father slandered her."

"He told us the truth."

"He told us his view."

"And a professional's."

"Please." Mary hit the gas, switching lanes. "Everything isn't a disease. Allegra wants to find her sister's killer, so we call that 'justice obsession syndrome'? If there is such a thing, then Bennie has it, and so do we all."

"You totally have it. You got it from a toilet seat."

"I'm lousy with it." Mary smiled. "In fact, I'm addicted to justice. I'm a justice junkie. Treat me. Send me to rehab."

Judy chuckled. "No, but here's the thing. I didn't think it was a wild-goose chase when she came in, or us playing out some fantasy for a very confused kid. Now, I do."

"We don't know that it is."

"We don't know that it's not."

"You're judging her because she has emotional issues. That's not right."

Judy paused. "Okay, point taken. Maybe I'm wrong. I table my objections."

"Thank you." Mary checked the clock, which read 12:15. "I want to read the file and plan our next move."

"Our next move is obvious."

"But we can't go until after we've read the file."

"Why read it? We could just ask our genius client what it says, since she memorized it."

Mary didn't smile, worried.

"I'm hungry."

"Because they didn't give us the cookies."

"I know. Daddy punished us."

"We need to go back to the office, set up a war room, and order lo mein for dinner, like we always do."

"Can we still, now that you're a partner?"

"Yes, only now, I pay for the dinner that we charge to the firm. So, no appetizers." Mary's phone started ringing on the console. "Can you grab that?"

"Will do." Judy picked up the phone and read the screen. "It's your mom and dad. I'll put it on speaker."

"Damn, I forgot to call them." Mary braced herself while Judy hit the button, and screams of excitement came from her mother, her father, and a third voice.

"MARE! YOU AND ANT'NY ARE GETTIN' MARRIED! CONGRADULATIONS! WHY'N'T YOU CALL US?"

Mary flushed. "Sorry, I got busy at work, I was going to call you."

"S'ALLRIGHT! YOUR MOTHER AND I ARE SO HAPPY AND ANT'NY'S MOTHER IS HERE, TOO!"

"Thanks." Mary smiled to hear her mother talking in frenzied Italian, which was redundant. "Ma, don't have a heart attack."

"*Maria, Maria,* I'm a so happ' for you, so happ'!"

Judy beamed. "It's Judy, Mrs. D! How about this? Our baby grew up! We need grandchildren!"

Mary smiled. "Don't encourage her. Hi, Ma!"

Anthony's mother joined in, her voice raspy from years of smoking, "Mary, my new daughter! God bless you both! He's the luckiest man in the world, and you're the luckiest woman!"

"Thanks, Elvira."

"No more with the Elvira! Call me Mom!"

Mary liked Elvira, even though she could be annoying, but it would be weird to call her mother, especially since she'd secretly nicknamed her El Virus. Mary didn't need another mother. She already had the best mother in the world.

"Mare?" Elvira asked, froggy. "You there? Did we get cut off? Oh, no, Matty, we got disconnected—"

"Elvira, I'm here," Mary rushed to say, because any disconnection in a cell-phone call panicked her parents, requiring endless discussion about why the call dropped, who had been cut off first, what it sounded like when they were cut off, and how the old days used to be better, when phones were two cans and a string.

"Mare, call me Mom!" Elvira croaked. "You gotta call me Mom! We're *family.*"

Judy shot Mary a meaningful look, so Mary bit the bullet. "Hi, Mom."

"Ha!" They all dissolved into applause and laughter, and Mary had to switch lanes not to run into the back of a construction truck.

"Okay, I have to go! I'm in the car! I love you guys! Talk to you later!"

"BYE, MARE! CALL US! LOVE YOU!"

"Good-bye Mr. and Mrs. D, Mrs. Rotunno!" Judy pressed the button to end the call. "That was fun."

"Was it?" Mary rolled her eyes. "I have to call her Mom now?"

"Go with it. What's in a name?"

"But she's not my mother, for God's sake. I love my mother. El Virus isn't in my mother's league."

"You're really negative about this, aren't you?"

"No, I just feel, well, maybe, negative about calling El Virus my *mom*. Sheesh."

"Mary, you should go home tonight."

"Why? We have to work. You're working late, aren't you?"

"Yes, but you don't have to."

"I have to read the file. You read it, and so did our client."

Judy clucked. "But they want to see you and celebrate with you."

"They just saw me. We just celebrated."

"That was business, and this is personal. Plus Anthony might want to see you. What if he wants to talk about it? Maybe it will help clarify your feelings."

Mary felt her stomach tense. She hit the gas and spotted the highway on-ramp, up ahead. "He'll understand that I have to work late."

"Will he?"

"He'll have to." Mary steered the BMW onto the highway and accelerated smoothly into the fast lane.

"Mare, are you avoiding going home?"

"No, but I won't drop Allegra because I'm getting married."

"You sure that's it?"

"Yes." Mary gestured at the phone. "Do me a favor and press A on my phone, to speed-dial Anthony. I'll call and give him the heads-up. He doesn't have class until this afternoon."

"Okay if I talk to him first?" Judy pressed A.

"Sure."

"Anthony!" Judy said into the phone, when the call connected. "It's me, on Mary's phone. You're betrothed! Congratulations!"

Mary kept the car at speed, in light traffic. She could hear Anthony laughing, but she couldn't make out what he was saying.

"Yes, she's showing everyone that big rock you got her! You selling crack now? Ha!"

Mary smiled. It was so touching that he'd been saving for the ring. She should wear it with pride, not guilt. He was a great guy. "Tell him I love him."

"She loves you, but she's driving. We left the client's and we're going back to the office."

Mary reached for the phone. "Gimme."

"Not while you're driving. Where's your earphone?"

"I forgot it. It'll be two seconds." Mary reached for the phone, but Judy pulled it away.

"She's grabbing the phone, but I want you to know that I'm happy for you both. Love you. Bye, here's the love of your life." Judy handed Mary the phone.

"Hi, babe. How are you?"

"Fine, sweetheart." Anthony's voice sounded soft and warm. "I hear my mother just called you."

"Right, they're all going nuts."

"Tell me about it. Your mother already talked to the priest about booking the church. She got busy at morning Mass."

Mary cringed. "No flies on her, right?"

"She says you need to, a year in advance."

Mary scoffed. "Who's she kidding? The parish is all old people. Who's getting married?"

"There's funerals." Anthony chuckled. "We'll have to talk dates later anyway, because I have to tell them at school when I want time off for our honeymoon."

"A honeymoon!" Mary kept her eyes on the road. Traffic was picking up, and she couldn't begin to think about a honeymoon. "Okay, we'll have to deal."

"How are you? You sound busy."

"Honestly, we are." Mary felt her gut tense in a way that was uncomfortably familiar. "Can you live with it if I'm not home for dinner tonight? I have a file to read."

Anthony didn't hesitate. "Do what you need to. What time will you be home?"

"Nine, or so?" Mary didn't even want to commit to a time. She wished she could just see how it went. Even if she finished the Gardner file, she had to work her other cases. They were on the back burner, but still simmering. Now that she'd made partner, she felt more pressure to perform up than ever. After all, Bennie was a woman with a coffee mug that read, I CAN SMELL FEAR.

"How about I wait dinner?"

"No, don't." Mary hated when he waited, which added guilt on top of guilt, like a double layer cake of guilt.

"Okay, see you around nine."

"I'll call if I'll be later."

"No worries. Drive carefully. I love you."

"I love you, too." Mary pressed End and set the phone down on the console.

"So he's talking honeymoon?"

"Yes."

"Is that good or bad?"

"Both."

Judy paused. "Mare. Just so you know, don't worry about the maid-of-honor thing. You can wait to make a decision. See how you feel about getting married, in general. And if you want to have your sister be maid of honor instead of me, I'd totally understand."

"Aw, honey." Mary glanced over, touched. She hadn't thought about choosing a maid of honor, but Judy must have been, because her blue eyes were filming.

"I mean it, really. I know I'm your bestie. Or you can have two maids of honor. Angie and I can be co-maids of honor, like co-counsel with bad dresses."

Mary's throat caught. "I would want it to be you, maybe with Angie, but we can't talk about it now or I'll crash the car."

"Yay!" Judy clapped her hands, squealing with excitement, and Mary managed a smile.

Wishing she could feel half as happy as everyone around her.

Chapter Twelve

The offices of Rosato & Associates were empty, quiet, and still, and the air smelled of stale coffee, cold lo mein, and sugary Bubblicious gum, which both Mary and Judy chewed with the intensity of hamsters on a flywheel, as if they were generating an alternative source of energy, powering themselves. They had transformed the small conference room into a war room, with the Stall trial record, exhibits, and stacks of daily transcripts cluttering the conference table, and the articles Mary had found online about Fiona's murder tacked up on a bulletin board that rested on two easels.

Mary was reading the trial record, but had finished only with the first day and knew she was running out of time. The windows showed the bright lights of the office buildings, and the wall clock, which she checked every five minutes, read 8:35. She resented that she had to hurry up and get home by nine, which would never happen, and she was kicking herself for not telling Anthony later. She pulled over the thick transcript of the second day of trial, looking up at Judy. "How are you doing?"

"Fine, plowing through." Judy raised her bleary gaze from the pleadings index, which would show everything that had been filed in the case. She loved the academic side of the legal analysis and was a born appellate lawyer, which was considered the *crème de la crème* of lawyerdom. In contrast, Mary was a trial-court kind of gal, because she liked the nitty-gritty of courtroom battle and preferred tomato sauce to *crème*.

"Learning anything?"

"His lawyer wasn't terrible, just inexperienced. But he cited the right cases, even current ones. His papers were very good."

Mary smiled. That "papers were good" was the highest compliment Judy could give someone. "So he did a good job."

"Yes, but he lost, because as we know, you can do a good job and still lose." Judy nodded curling her upper lip. She had taken off her blue jacket and left it crumpled on the seat next to her, whereas Mary had hung hers on a hanger behind the door. They were the Goofus and Gallant of the law, and liked it that way, especially Mary, who got to be Gallant.

"I admire Stall for not taking the deal at the outset," she said.

"I don't. That's why he was sentenced to the maximum. They were making him pay. Not only didn't he plead out, he asked for a jury trial." Judy didn't have to elaborate. They both knew the dirty little secret of the criminal justice system, that it rested on a shaky foundation of plea bargains in which defendants could be cajoled, manipulated, and sometimes pressured into pleading guilty. Mary knew that many of them would be guilty, but some wouldn't, and she wondered if Lonnie Stall could be one of them, actually innocent.

Suddenly, they both turned to the pinging sound of the elevator and the commotion in the hallway that told them that Bennie and Anne were back.

Judy set down the pleading index. "The hunter is home from the hill."

"Wonder if they won," Mary said, as Bennie popped her head in the doorway, with a grin. Her suit was wrinkled and her blonde curls looked even more unruly, but her blue eyes flashed with animation.

Bennie came alive on trial. When she wasn't around a jury, she was like an attack dog with time on his hands.

"Hey, ladies!"

"How'd you do?"

"Good. Got another day left." Bennie entered the room and picked up the take-out container of lo mein, which happened to have two ballpoints stuck inside. "What's this?"

Judy smiled. "They forgot the chopsticks. It works. Have some."

"That's okay, I ate."

"Where's Anne?" Mary asked.

"She went home. I came by to pick up some papers. The Natick case is rearing its ugly head, and I'll be up all night. What's happening on Gardner?"

Mary and Judy exchanged glances. "We're of two different minds," Mary answered.

"You want to talk it out?"

"Sure." Mary had an eye on the wall clock. "We'll tell it quick."

"DiNunzio, you go first." Bennie eased onto the conference table.

Mary brought her up to date, and Bennie listened carefully, asking only a few questions, her expression impassive, then Judy gave her point of view, after which they both waited nervously, like opposing counsel before a hanging judge.

"I don't like what I'm hearing." Bennie folded her arms, and her lower lip puckered with dissatisfaction. "I'm worried about Allegra Gardner and her emotional stability. I agree with Judy that we're being led around by this kid, and the qualms I had before are only worse. We could actually be doing her harm by indulging her in a fantasy."

Mary could see that Judge Rosato wasn't ruling in her favor. "But we don't know that, and Allegra is our client. We've never been in the business of evaluating or judging our own clients."

Bennie shook her head. "That's true, but we've never represented a minor before, particularly one under psychiatric care."

"What if Allegra is right about Stall's innocence? I think she is." Mary turned to Judy. "Don't you agree?"

"Yes." Judy nodded. "But to me, it's a broken-clock problem. It's right twice a day."

Bennie eased off the table and headed for the door. "Tread carefully with the family. Her parents obviously love her and they're trying to do the right thing by her. The question is what is the right thing, and the father is correct, the balance of power is warped because she has money."

Mary couldn't agree. "But her having money isn't a bad thing, it's a good thing. If Lonnie Stall is innocent, then that money will set him free."

Bennie paused in the threshold. "Either way, resolve this quickly. Get Lou involved as soon as possible. Send him an email on his vacation. He's only in Jersey, he can come back early. You guys could use the extra hand, and that could bring it to a close more quickly."

"What's the rush?" Mary checked the time, and it was almost ten o'clock. She needed to work all night, too, and Bennie was only turning up the heat.

"The Gardner family has resources, and they're only starting to flex. They didn't get successful by rolling over, and John Gardner isn't about to be pushed around by his teenage daughter, much less by the lawyers she hired."

"So what are you saying?" Mary asked, with dismay. "We're not dropping the case."

"Of course not, but this representation shouldn't last much longer. I don't want to bill her for any more than the five grand. Nor do I want the Gardner case to be a priority for this firm."

"I do," Mary blurted out, and for a second, the partners looked at each other from opposite sides of the conference table. Judy's blonde head swiveled back and forth, as if she were watching a tennis match.

Bennie's expression softened. "That probably came out wrong. You have an equal vote, DiNunzio, I know that."

"Thanks." Mary felt her heart beat a little quicker, but told herself to calm down. "We'll work the case and keep you in the loop. Thanks for your help."

"Anytime. Good night." Bennie left the conference room.

Judy looked over at Mary, then burst into a sly grin. "I think the queen bees just crossed stingers."

"Bzzz," Mary said, reaching for her cell phone.

Chapter Thirteen

"Honey, I'm home," Mary said, coming through the door. She dropped her purse and messenger bag on the floor beside the console table, exhausted and worried. She hadn't finished reading the trial record, but she hadn't seen anything in it so far that looked shaky or worth exploring. She'd emailed their firm investigator, Lou Jacobs, but he hadn't written back yet. She hadn't even gotten to catch up with her other cases or answer her email. It was almost midnight, but she had called Anthony to tell him she'd be late.

"In the kitchen, honey!" he called out, his tone warm and friendly, which only made her feel more guilty.

"Sorry I was so late," Mary called back, ignoring the mail, sliding out of her jacket, and walking through the living room to the kitchen, where Anthony sat at the table, grading papers.

"It's okay, I understand. I figured I'd get the jump, too." Anthony rose and held out his arms, and Mary walked over and fell into his embrace. He had on his Ramones T-shirt, which felt soft against her cheek, and he smelled vaguely of pencil lead, which made her smile. Anthony Rotunno was one of the few people who still used pencils.

"I love you," Mary told him, meaning it. She was lucky to have him here, waiting for her.

"I love you, too." Anthony squeezed her tight, then rocked her in his arms. "You're going to be my wife, and I'm going to be your husband, you realize that?"

Mary stiffened, but hoped he couldn't feel it. She pulled away, managing a smile. "Whoa, husband."

"Whoa, wife." Anthony grinned down at her, his eyes a soft brown. He reached out and moved a strand of hair from Mary's face. "You look stressed out, babe."

"I am, kind of, and this Gardner case is a tough one. Bennie's not really on board with it, I found out tonight, so we'll have to see how that goes." Mary let him go, rubbing her eyes.

"What happened?"

"Nothing really, but it'll be interesting to see what results when we disagree." Mary wandered over to the refrigerator, even though she wasn't hungry. She was a classic emotional eater, though she couldn't think of a better reason to eat. "What did you do for dinner?"

"I had a cheese sandwich. There's some leftover provolone, and I got fresh olives on the way home."

"Yum." Mary spotted the plastic container of green Ceregnola olives, which Anthony knew were her favorite. "What a nice thing to do."

"I'm trying to show you what a good husband I'll be."

"I know that." Mary set the olives on the counter, then noticed that her fig tree was looking a little dry, so she picked up the watering can, twisted on the faucet, and filled it. "So how was your day?"

"Very exciting. I told everybody in the department, which was quite a scene." Anthony chuckled. "So they're all happy. Jim, Ravi, and Celine want to take us out tomorrow night. Can you go? It's the one night they're all free."

"Not sure yet, but I doubt it." Mary cringed. "This new case, you know?"

"Can we leave it open? Call me if you can't? They can make it late, even after dinner, like around nine o'clock. They all live near school."

"How about I call you if I can, instead?" Mary knew he didn't mean to pressure her, but it felt that way.

"Okay," Anthony said, and if he was disappointed, he didn't let it show. "Of course, they're planning a bachelor party, but a bunch of academics, don't worry, we'll behave. Also don't forget, my mom's birthday is Thursday night, six o'clock. Your parents will be there, too."

"Oh, right." Mary saw more of her family since she moved out. If she moved back in, she'd never see them. "What did you get her?"

"A silver photo frame, well, silverplate. I figure she'll need a nice one for our wedding photo."

"Good idea, thanks for taking care of that." Mary watered her fig tree, thinking that it was just last night she had spotted her engagement ring, and now they were talking about honeymoons and bachelor parties.

"Did Judy really like the ring? It sounded like she did on the phone."

"She loved it, they all did."

"What did everybody else say?" Anthony shifted forward on his seat.

"When I walked in, they all clucked and cooed, and jumped up and down, even Bennie." Mary finished watering the plant, then set the pitcher down. "Lawyers gone berserk."

"Good!" Anthony beamed. "That was the desired effect. I was so nervous trying to pick it out. I wish we had done even a flyby once or twice to get an idea of what you like. But I know you generally keep it simple, so that's why I went with the solitaire."

"Good call." Mary opened a container of olives, then did a double-take. "It's almost as big as an olive pit."

"Ha! The saleslady gave me the clarity-and-cut speech, but I ended up going for the better stone instead of the bigger ones."

"But it's a big stone." Mary didn't add, *too big*.

"Most importantly, it's high-quality, just like you."

"Aw. Just one thing, I was wondering if we need to get the band sized down." Mary walked over, swiveling the ring back and forth on her finger, which she'd been doing most of the cab ride home. "I'm kind of worried that it could fall off."

"Let me see." Anthony held out his hand, and Mary placed her hand in his palm, an unintended replay of last night that made her feel a warm rush of love for him, so strong that it almost sent her ambivalence scattering. Anthony bent over the ring, moving it this way and that slowly, frowning with a concentration that was characteristic of everything he did. He wanted everything to be perfect for her, and Mary thought she must be crazy to have doubts about marrying him.

Anthony looked up. "It looks just a little bit big. I thought you were a size seven, but maybe they can make it down to a six and a half."

"They should. I worried the whole day about it falling off." Mary slid the ring off her finger and handed it back to him. "You think you can take it back?"

"You should come with me, don't you think?"

"Oh, right, of course." Mary picked up a napkin from the holder on the table, wrapped the ring inside, and put it in her skirt pocket. When she lifted her head, Anthony was looking at her funny. She asked, "What is it?"

"I feel like that's an accident waiting to happen. Don't forget it's in there and take the skirt to the dry cleaner's or something."

"I won't."

Anthony's expression darkened. "Listen, there's something important I need to ask you about, though. You need to be sitting down. It's a hard question."

"For real?" Mary's heart sank. "Didn't we just do this last night?"

Anthony blinked, frowning in confusion. "No, last night I asked you to marry me. That wasn't a hard question, was it?"

"No, of course not, I didn't mean it that way." Mary flushed, busted. "I was just tired. Sorry." She sat down opposite him. "What is it you wanted to ask me?"

"Well, it's about your dress."

"What dress?"

"Your wedding dress. I'm giving you the heads-up. I think my mother wants to go with you and your mother when you try them on. Is that okay?"

"Of course," Mary answered, relieved. She hadn't pictured anyone but her mother, Judy, and maybe even Angie coming along when she tried on wedding dresses, but she hadn't really imagined trying on wedding dresses yet, at all. "Sure, she's welcome. It'll be fun."

"Thanks." Anthony broke into a grateful smile. "She was asking me about when you and your mom are going for your dress. She knows you and your mother are really close and she won't ask. She wouldn't want you to think she was overstepping her bounds."

"Not at all," Mary said, rising. Her face felt warm, and her mouth had gone dry, but she was telling herself it was the salty olives. "I called her Mom today."

"She told me." Anthony rose, coming over and slipping an arm around Mary's shoulders. "That was so sweet of you. She called me afterwards, crying."

"Really?" Mary felt touched.

"She always wanted a daughter, and who wouldn't want a daughter like you?"

"Aw, thanks," Mary said, her heart lighter as they turned off the lights and left the kitchen. She felt relieved not to have the ring on her finger any longer, as if a weight had been lifted off her mind, or she was back to being herself again.

Maybe it would take her a while to get to the jeweler.

Later, after Anthony had gone to sleep, Mary awoke, sneaked in to her home office, and closed the door quietly behind her, flicking on the light. She padded in her pink bathrobe and bare feet to her desk, sat down, and moved the computer mouse to wake up the laptop.

She navigated to the Internet, went to Google, and plugged in **girl genius helicopter**, and a line of articles popped onto the page, just like last night. She clicked on the first article, again from the city's tabloid, with a headline, **FIERY FATAL CRASH ON PLAY-GROUND**, above a horrific scene of orange-red flames blazing skyward from the blackened carcasses of a helicopter and an airplane.

Mary swallowed hard, scrolling down to read the article, which showed a school picture of Allegra in first grade, her eyes preternaturally serious behind her glasses, with just the barest hint of a smile, and her long hair tied back too severely to be cool or pretty. The caption read, **ALLEGRA GARDNER, who predicted the crash only minutes before, from watching wind currents on the playground.**

Mary cringed, knowing what that kind of notoriety could cause, and she read on, but the article provided no new details beyond what John Gardner had told her today. Still she clicked Print, then Close, and went to the next article. She'd read that, too, printed it like the others, and would bring them into the office, where she could put them up on their own easel in the war room, next to the articles about the murder. She knew that it wasn't necessarily relevant, but the more Mary knew about Allegra, the more she wanted to know.

She worked the rest of the night that way, in silence and solitude, a woman sitting in front of a computer, reading until the blackness outside had lifted and ceded the sky not to sun, but to the thickest of cloud covers, impenetrable. And when she realized it was dawn, Mary found herself looking out the window, wondering what it was like to be able to see through the clouds like Allegra, to be able to sense disaster in the very wind, before it struck.

Saving everyone, but sacrificing yourself.

Chapter Fourteen

The sky was incongruously clear and sunny over SCI Graterford, which was Pennsylvania's largest maximum-security prison, located in Collegeville, about thirty miles west of Philadelphia. Presently, it housed an all-time high of 3,700 adult male felons on 1,700 acres, which made it sound positively bucolic, if you'd never seen the place.

"Honey, we're home." Mary cut the ignition, and Judy regarded the prison in somber silence. It was a massive concrete structure, the oldest part of which dated from 1929, with brick additions built in the intervening years. Much of the prison remained hidden behind a grimy fifty-foot-high wall of stained concrete, topped by barbed concertina wire and old-school turrets with armed guards, like ominous black shadows behind windows of bulletproof glass.

"Remind me never to do anything bad, ever." Judy chuckled, nervously. "How do I look? Undesirable? Gender-free? No fun in general?"

Mary glanced over, and Judy was dressed in their agreed-upon outfit of jeans, flats, and a white shirt with a dark blazer. "Are you trying to make me laugh, because it won't work. Maximum security always puts me in a bad mood."

"Occupational hazard for a criminal lawyer."

"Let's go." Mary knew they wouldn't be allowed to bring their phones or handbags, so she pocketed her keys, slid her ID from her wallet, grabbed a legal pad and pen, while Judy did the same, and they got out of the car, walking through the large parking lot to the entrance, which had a concrete overhang.

"Hey, where's your engagement ring?" Judy asked, as they passed a black van that read Coroner's Office, Montgomery County. "Did you leave it home so the bad guys don't steal it?"

"No, it needs to be resized."

"Why?" Judy smiled slyly. "It fit you perfectly."

"It was big, and I didn't want to lose it."

"God forbid." Judy chuckled, and Mary tried not to notice the long Pennsylvania D.O.C. bus with grates over the smoked windows, idling noisily at the curb.

"I *don't* want to lose my ring."

"But if it fell down the drain, or disappeared down the sewer, or got flushed down the toilet, or spontaneously combusted, you might not mind."

"Stop." Mary couldn't smile because the prison was giving her the heebie-jeebies. She couldn't imagine spending the next fifty years behind these thick concrete walls.

"Anything could happen to it, accidentally on purpose. Unfortunately, it's carbon, the most indestructible substance known to man, so unless you wander into an atomic blast, you have to deal with that ring, sooner or later."

"Enough. Get your head in the game." Mary climbed the concrete steps to the entrance and walked through the smudged glass doors, with Judy falling into step behind her.

They entered a waiting room that looked ancient enough to have been part of the original building. It was a long rectangle, only dimly lit by small windows at the end of the room and panels of fluorescent lighting, in the ceiling of peeling white paint. The floor was of a grimy tan linoleum, apparently inadvertently matching the tan, battered lockers that ringed the far side of the room, behind rows of old-fashioned wooden benches. Visitors filled the benches, under a sign that read NO SPANDEX, NO HOODIES. There was a large wooden reception desk across the room, staffed by a slim female corrections officer, wearing a black uniform with the yellow patch of the Department of Corrections.

They made a beeline for the reception desk, and Mary took the lead, placing her driver's license across the counter. "We're here to see Lonnie Stall. We're attorneys, and we called ahead to be put on his visitors' list."

"That's fine. Sign in, please." The corrections officer slid an old-school sign-in log across the counter, and Mary signed them both in while Judy handed in her driver's license, the corrections officer examined them, then handed them back. She gestured at the benches. "Take a seat, and we'll call you in a minute. He's been approved for legal mail."

Mary didn't understand. "We don't have any for him."

"No, he has some for you."

"Oh, okay." Mary was nonplussed, but she didn't want to let it show in front of the corrections officer, because she had implied on the phone call that she was Lonnie Stall's lawyer, referred by one Allegra Gardner. It was the only way to get the visit on such short notice, since lawyers and clergymen generally had unlimited visits in state prisons.

"Here we go." Judy led them over to the first long bench, which reminded Mary of a pew and turned out to be just as comfortable, when Mary sat down and looked around. There were roughly ten benches full of all kinds of people, all ages and ethnicities; an older African-American man reading a discarded newspaper, a heavyset white woman who was pregnant, a pretty young Asian woman applying lip gloss, and a middle-aged Hispanic woman with a toddler on her lap.

Mary's heart went out to each of them, and what struck her mostly was the very mundaneness of their manner, even the way they talked among themselves or to each other. None of these visitors felt nervous or edgy, but they were here to visit someone they loved and had been visiting undoubtedly for years, since all of the inmates at Graterford had been sentenced for major crimes. For their families, the horror of the setting had become routine, and Mary wondered if the fact of the crimes themselves had become routine, as well. She prayed not.

"Lonnie Stall!" a corrections officer called out, motioning them forward, and Mary and Judy rose together and walked toward a grimy metal door, which the corrections officer opened with a loud metallic *ca-chunk*. "Take off your belts, shoes, and jewelry, and put them in the bins, ladies."

"Thank you," Mary said, as they passed through the door together and entered a narrow room that held an old wooden table with wooden bins, in front of a metal detector. The air felt warmer and closer, but that could've been her imagination. She couldn't deny that it felt strange to be admitted to the secured part of a maximum-security prison, full of murderers, rapists, and other violent offenders, with the proverbial door clanging closed behind them. She had read on the website that Graterford housed a significant proportion of inmates serving life without parole and it had one of the two Death Rows in Pennsylvania.

Mary and Judy went through the metal detector, collected their belongings, had the back of their right hands stamped and read by an ultraviolet light, and were led through one locked door, then the next, being watched by prison guards behind a smoked glass panel. They were admitted into an old narrow staircase with painted cinderblock on either side and traveled down the nonskid steps, where the air grew hot enough to make it difficult to breathe.

The stairwell bottomed in a large visiting room the shape of an L, with vending machines on the right and rows of faded red, blue, and tan chairs, filled with people visiting inmates in brown jumpsuits, without handcuffs. The sound of conversation, laughter, and tears filled the room, and the air conditioners were no match for the collective body heat, strong perfumes, and stale cigarette smoke that clung to many of the visitors. A large sign read, **Inmates and Visitors**

May Embrace When Meeting And Departing Only. An elevated wooden chair against the wall held a brawny young lieutenant, wearing a white short-sleeved shirt and black pants with a gray line down the side. His eyes scanned the room under the black bill of his white cap, a walkie-talkie crackling in its belt holster.

"Ladies, this way to the attorney booths," the female corrections officer said over her shoulder, leading Mary and Judy through the rows of visitors and inmates, with no more concern then someone going down the aisle in a movie theater. "You've never been here before, have you?"

"No," Mary answered for the both of them. She gestured at an area beyond the chairs to the right, enclosed by thick, scratched glass. "What's that?"

"That's for inmates who can only have no-contact visits."

"Who would that be? Inmates from Death Row?"

"No, capital-case inmates have a visiting room upstairs, all to themselves. What you're looking at is the visiting area for J-block and L-block, which are our restricted units, for inmates who got written up for misconduct. Things like that."

Judy looked at a line of paintings that covered the cinderblock wall, as if she were at a nightmare art show. "Is that inmate art?"

"Yes it is," answered the corrections officer, and they passed scenes of moonlit oceans, a pastoral landscape, a portrait of Elvis, an Eagles logo, and a still life of red wine with several hunks of cheese, which would've been at home in a fine Italian restaurant. The correctional officer pointed to the left. "Outside is a pretty mural the Mural Arts Program did for us."

Mary looked to her left, where there was a long line of tall windows that overlooked a grassy outdoor area with picnic tables and blue-and-white umbrellas. On one end was a cheery children's playground with a bright yellow slide and blue monkey bars, and beyond that a colorful mural depicting children at play, which read CHERISH THIS CHILD. But even the mural couldn't dispel the grimness of the gray concrete wall that bordered the yard, topped with spiky concertina wire. Mary realized it was the inside of the wall they had seen from outside the prison.

"And there is another mural the program made for us." The corrections officer gestured, and Mary looked over. Hanging on a wooden rack was a mural depicting a stone archway with a cobalt blue river winding into the distance. She knew that prisons often provided idyllic backdrops for inmates to use in photographs, on days when family picture-taking was authorized.

"Here's where you get off." The corrections officer stopped outside three battered doors at the end of the room, painted a bizarre turquoise color, and unlocked the door. "Wait here and he'll be brought down."

Mary and Judy thanked her, and they squeezed into the attorney booth, which described exactly its size. It held only three old wooden chairs, and a small Formica shelf mounted in the corner. The air smelled close and dirty, like a hot box.

"Yikes," Judy said, which just about summed it up.

Chapter Fifteen

Lonnie Stall was of average height, about five-ten with almond-shaped eyes, of a soft brown color. He wore his hair natural, shaved close to his head, and a brown jumpsuit, with dull yellow trim around its short sleeves. His arms were muscular, and his right biceps had a script tattoo that Mary couldn't read, though she was sitting right across from him.

"My name is Mary DiNunzio, and this is my colleague Judy Carrier. We both work at Rosato & Associates, a law firm in town, and we were hired to look into this case by Allegra Gardner, the younger sister of Fiona."

Lonnie nodded slowly. His brown eyes remained steady and his manner subdued. "Okay."

"Allegra believes that you're innocent of killing Fiona and we've been hired to investigate the crime."

"I know that," Lonnie said calmly. "I've been waiting for you."

"I don't understand."

"I'll show you." Lonnie set a manila envelope on the counter and pulled out a piece of folded white paper. "That's from Allegra Gardner."

Mary opened the paper, and Judy leaned over to see a letter written in small, cramped handwriting, dated three years ago.

DEAR LONNIE, DON'T WORRY. I KNOW YOU ARE INNOCENT AND SOME-DAY I WILL GET YOU OUT OF JAIL. YOUR FRIEND, ALLEGRA GARDNER.

"That's just one of the letters."

Mary looked up, surprised. "There are more?"

"Yes. Plenty."

"How many?"

"I'll show you the first batch." Lonnie pulled a thick packet of letters from the envelope, wrapped in a rubber band. "You can have them. I don't want them. I stopped opening them after the first few years."

"Years?" Mary asked, aghast.

"I probably have one hundred letters from that little girl."

"What do they say?"

"The same thing, over and over again." Lonnie shrugged. "She knows I'm innocent and when she gets some money, she's going to get me out. She must've gotten her money, and here you are."

Mary set the letters aside, trying to get back on track. "Do you have the other letters?"

"Sure, I saved some." Lonnie glanced at the door, which was closed. "The guys in my block think they're from a girlfriend, which isn't the worst thing for my reputation."

"May I have the other letters? I'll send you a stamped envelope for them."

"Sure, no problem."

Mary caught Judy's questioning eye and moved on. "To get to the point, you're telling us you're innocent of Fiona Gardner's murder."

"I am," Lonnie answered, his tone genuine. "I didn't kill Fiona. I'm completely innocent."

"So why did you plead guilty?"

"Because I was going to get convicted and my lawyer told me it was a good deal and I should take it."

"Did you know Fiona?"

"Not that well. Just to be polite, nod to her at the parties, s'up, that's all."

"You didn't know her better than that?"

"No." Lonnie shrugged again. "I worked for Cricket Catering, and they did the parties for the Gardner family. I worked for them nights and weekends while I was in high school and kept it up when I went to college. I was a freshman at Temple, working for my degree in business."

"It's our understanding that you had a romantic relationship with Fiona. Is that right?"

Lonnie frowned. "No. Not at all."

Mary scanned his face, trying to see if he was telling the truth, but she couldn't tell. "Did you meet Fiona when she was babysitting Allegra?"

"No."

"You didn't hug and kiss Fiona?"

"No."

"You didn't have a relationship at all?"

"No."

"That's the main reason Allegra thinks you didn't kill her sister. What do you have to say to that?"

"I never was alone with Fiona when she was babysitting, or any other time."

Mary couldn't figure out how to reconcile the conflicting information from Allegra and her father. "You really never did that?"

"No, I never did."

"You weren't in love with Fiona?"

"No."

Mary avoided Judy's eye. She didn't want to conclude that Allegra was delusional. "I read your testimony at trial, but could you just tell me what happened the night Fiona was murdered?"

"What's the difference?" Lonnie's tone was flat, without affect. "It's not going to get me free. Nothing's going to get me free."

"Just tell me what happened that night."

"It's like I said at trial. I was working the party, serving. I was walking past the back stair when I heard a shout, faint, so I ran upstairs."

"Let me stop you there. What did the noise sound like?"

"Like a woman's shout. Not a scream, but a shout."

"Why didn't you ignore it?"

"I just reacted. I thought I could help."

"Why didn't you tell anyone?"

"I was right there, walking past the stairwell, so I just reacted. I figured somebody maybe got lost and fell, so I handled it."

"What happened then?"

"I went down the hall and the door was open. I saw Fiona lying on her back, on the floor, next to the table. I didn't understand what I was seeing. I couldn't believe my eyes. There was blood in the center of her shirt, she had on a white shirt, and I didn't understand."

"What didn't you understand?"

"It was like there was a wound, but I couldn't see what made the wound, and I went over to her and put my hand in the shirt with the blood. I guess I was just feeling for what caused it, like what was it?"

Mary could visualize it. She would have done the same thing.

"I got blood on me, that came out later at the trial, but I didn't notice. I wasn't worried about it, I was thinking about her." Lonnie's cadence quickened, though he told the story without the drama it deserved. "I put my head to her mouth, like my ear, to see if she was breathing. I couldn't hear anything, so I pressed on her chest and tried to give her mouth-to-mouth, but it didn't work. Then I started to think, I got to get out of here. This doesn't look good, not for me. So I ran out."

"Why didn't you yell or call for help?"

"I don't know. I was just dealing with it."

"You didn't make any noise when you saw her? Like a scream?"

"I'm a man." Lonnie smiled slightly.

Mary didn't understand something. "What was Fiona doing up there anyway?"

"I know the family was up and down during the night, and they took some VIPs up there, to show off the offices."

"Then, when you saw you couldn't deal with it, why didn't you run and tell your boss, or any of the guests or even security?"

"I don't know. I should have, but I panicked. I felt like I was in the wrong place at the wrong time. Like I should'nt've gone into the small conference room, I didn't belong up there." Lonnie's gaze shifted somewhere on the scuffed and dingy wall. "I used to think about it over and over, when I first got here. Why didn't I just keep walking down the hall? I should've just kept going."

"Tell me about the cut on your hand."

"I cut it when chef asked me to cut a lime, because we ran out. Anyway, somehow the blood from my cut got on her. I didn't cut it stabbing her, like they said. I didn't stab her."

"They never found the murder weapon but they think it was a common knife. At trial they think you got it from the kitchen."

"I didn't take any knife from the kitchen. Chef testified that none of his knives were missing, but he didn't know what knives were in the kitchen when we got there. Chef keeps an eye on his own knives, because they're expensive."

Mary made a note. "Let me ask you this. What do you think happened that night?"

"I think somebody stabbed Fiona and got out through the other stairway, door, just before I came in and found her."

Mary brightened, glancing at Judy. "So there's another stairway to the floor?"

"Yes, there's two. One was in the reception area and they had a velvet rope on that. But the one I used was near the cafeteria. No guests went back there but us."

Mary took rapid notes. "Do they have a sign-in at the door, like with security?"

"I don't know."

"Did you mention any of that to your lawyer?"

Lonnie frowned, scratching his head. "I think so, but I don't know what he found out. He wasn't really looking at who did the murder, just trying to show that I didn't."

Mary thought back to his trial lawyer's opening argument. "His basic defense was that they had no murder weapon and no proof of motive by you."

"Right."

"But the prosecutor suggested it was a sexual assault that turned deadly when Fiona said no."

"That didn't happen."

Judy gestured to get Lonnie's attention. "Who was the security company that night? Do you remember, was it in-house or did they contract that out?"

"I don't know. We used the delivery entrances at the loading dock, and we set up in the kitchen, like the company dining room."

"Did you notice anything or anyone unusual around Fiona that night?"

"No, I wouldn't know. I was working."

"Did you see Fiona that night, before you found her on the floor?"

"Yes."

"Did you talk to her?" Judy asked, jumping in.

"No, just smiled, and she smiled back."

"Do you know if she had a date that night?"

"No idea."

"Do you remember who you saw her with?"

"No."

"Does the name Tim Gage mean anything to you?"

"No."

Judy looked over at Mary. "Okay, back to you."

Mary nodded, turning to Lonnie. "How well did you know John and Jane Gardner?"

"Not very well. My boss dealt with the clients."

Mary thought about the Gardners' house. "They entertained at that house out in Townsend?"

Lonnie thought a minute. "Yes, sure."

"So you were out there, working at their parties?"

"Yes."

"How many times?"

"About ten."

Mary made a note. "Did you meet anybody from the Gardner companies?"

"Not really met them, but I saw them. I knew some of their names. I don't remember them anymore."

"Did you have a criminal record before this?"

"No."

"Any drug or drinking problems?"

"No."

"Where did you go to high school?"

"University City High."

"Do you have any sisters or brothers?"

"No."

"Are your mother and father alive?"

"My mother is, my father isn't."

"What's your mother's name?"

"What difference does that make?"

"I'm just curious."

"Rita."

"Rita Stall?"

"No, Henley. Gerold Henley was my stepfather, he died when I was in high school. Don't know where my real father is. Never met the man. I was an infant when he left. Gerold raised me. Worked for the post office."

"Where does she live, your mother?"

"West Philly."

Mary tried another tack. "Tell us about your lawyer. How did you find him? How did you pay for him? Why did you use him and not a public defender?"

"I still don't see why this matters."

"I'm interested in your view of his competence, so that we can see if there's grounds for collateral attack on your conviction, like for ineffective assistance of counsel."

Lonnie pursed his lips. "Okay, his name is Bob Brandt. I had some money and so did my mom, and we figured we had a better shot with a private lawyer instead of the public defender."

"Do you think Brandt did a good job?"

"He did his best."

"How frequently did he meet with you? Did he meet with you enough?"

"He met with me whenever I wanted."

"Did he explain his defense to you?"

"Yes." Lonnie nodded.

"And he told you to take the deal?"

"Yes, right away, but I didn't in the beginning. I knew I was innocent and I wanted my chance to say it in court. That's why I got on the stand. I was going on the truth, but he thought the jury wasn't going my way and the D.A.'s case was going good, so I took the deal in the end."

Mary felt any appellate argument slipping away. "Did your lawyer advise you that it was risky for a defendant, even an innocent man, to take the stand in his own defense?"

"Yes, he did. He told me that the prosecutor was going to tussle with me. He told me to tell the truth and only answer the questions they asked me. I was the one who messed up on the stand, I got flustered." Lonnie pursed his lips. "But I also knew that if I didn't testify, I had no case at all."

"Why didn't you appeal?"

"We ran out of money. I had no grounds."

"Is there any reason you can think of that would give you grounds for a collateral appeal?"

"No." Lonnie shook his head. "If I did, I would've tried to file one. I spend a lot of time in the prison library and I'm pretty good with the law books."

"Do you have any other information at all about that night that you can tell us?"

"No."

Mary couldn't hide her frustration. "It's like you've given up."

Lonnie shrugged, yet again. "I don't think of it that way. I think of it like, I accept what happened. I'm here now, and this is where I live. I made a life for myself here."

"How?"

"I do my job in the garment shop here, I make uniforms, boots for Correctional Industries. They pay bonuses. Everybody on B-block wants that job, I was lucky to get it. Most of the guys in the garment shop are lifers, they got hundreds of lifers here, and there's no job opening in the shop unless they die." Lonnie permitted himself a chuckle. "Also I take courses, trying to get enough for my college degree. I study, read, work out."

"Do you have friends here?"

"Some, I stay out of gangs, out of trouble."

"Don't you get lonely?"

"Nah. My mom visits every Wednesday and prays with me. We're allowed four visits a month by the same person. She comes even though it's not easy to get here from the city. She helps me to accept my life's path."

Mary still didn't understand. "How can you accept it? If you're innocent and you didn't kill her, doesn't it drive you crazy that you're in here paying for a crime you didn't commit?"

Lonnie met her eye, then shook his head again. "No. No. I will not go there. I will not let myself go there."

Mary swallowed hard, taking another tack. "Did you know Allegra at all?"

"No."

"Did you ever speak to her at the parties?'

"No, not at all. She was a little kid. I couldn't even tell you what she looks like. Long hair, glasses, that's it."

Mary felt dumbfounded. "She thinks you were very nice and quiet."

"I am." Lonnie smiled slightly. "You can see that."

"Think you ever talked to her, like maybe just made an offhand comment at a party, and you don't remember it? You know, the kind of thing that might mean a lot to a little kid, but an adult just doesn't even remember?"

Lonnie shook his head. "No. I was the help at those parties. We were told not to talk to the guests or the clients. We were supposed to be as invisible as possible, not speak unless we were spoken to, and make sure the drinks and food kept coming."

Mary let it go for now. "Did you have a girlfriend at the time Fiona was murdered?"

"No, not really. I went out, but I mostly went to school and worked."

"When you went out, who did you go out with?"

Lonnie hesitated. "Why you want to know that?"

"Just curious."

"Girl named Linda Wall. She's married now."

"Who were your friends at school?"

"Didn't really have very many."

"Can you give me a name or two?" Mary paused, reading his eyes. "Again, I'm just curious. I'm trying to get as full a picture as I can of your life. Maybe I'll be able to figure out something, just the littlest thing, that can prove you weren't the one who committed the murder."

"Okay. My friends were Dave Jackson, DeQuan Merry, that's about it. They went to my church, we were in the choir."

"Are you religious?"

"I am." Lonnie's expression relaxed, and for a moment he looked like a much younger man. "I feel blessed to walk in God's light, and he guides me every step I take in here, every minute of every day."

Mary's ears pricked up at a new strength in his voice. "Have you always been religious?"

"Yes. My mom was in the choir and she took me as soon as she could, yes she did. I accept the world the way it is, and I accept my role in the world. God has a plan for me, and I'm here to fulfill His plan."

Mary struggled to understand him. "What's His plan for you? What plan are you fulfilling by staying in prison for a crime you didn't commit?"

Lonnie hesitated. "I don't know God's plan, only God does. I work in the garment shop, so my clothes keep people warm. I help out in the library, and maybe something I tell somebody helps them. That is God, working through me. I don't know the reason yet."

"What about, 'God helps those who help themselves'? What about justice?"

"I am helping myself. I help myself to be a better person, every day."

Mary couldn't let it go. "Then help us to get you out of here. If you think of anything that we could use, let us know."

Lonnie blinked, and his eyes shone. "I don't want to hope."

Mary swallowed hard. She had never felt so confused about a case, or a client. "Still, we're going to try."

"I wish you luck, but you know what this says?" Lonnie pointed to the dark green script on his forearm. "It says, 'Only God can judge me.'"

Mary didn't remark on the irony, to a man behind bars.

Chapter Sixteen

"Are you thinking what I'm thinking?" Mary asked Judy, as they walked through the prison parking lot to their car.

"What?" Judy looked over.

"Call me crazy, but I don't think he did it. I believe him."

Judy fell into step beside her, nodding. "I agree with you. I don't think he did it, either."

"It's ironic, right? There's a record full of evidence against him. Like you say, he didn't have a chance on appeal. Why do you think he's innocent?"

"Just by what he said, and the way he said it. He gave a completely plausible explanation for how Fiona could have been murdered. If he hadn't gotten so flustered on the stand and he had a better lawyer, he would've had an excellent chance of raising reasonable doubt."

"That's why I think it. He's either the best liar on earth or he's really telling the truth. Or we're projecting wildly and being insanely naïve."

"There's also the facts of record, not just us being naïve." Judy shook her head, musing as they walked in the same stride. "He didn't take the plea deal initially. That intrigues me. Also he has no criminal record, and lastly, he testified in his own defense. You can watch *Law & Order* and know that's suicide, especially if you're guilty."

"Good point," Mary said, as they reached the car and she chirped it unlocked.

"What a difference a day makes."

"What do you mean?"

"Yesterday, I believed in our client, but not Stall. Now I believe in Stall, but not our client."

"I still believe in both." Mary got into the car, so did Judy, and they closed the doors behind them. "Will you read me those letters he gave us while I drive?"

"If you promise not to drive off the road in despair."

"Go, girl." Mary started the engine, they both put on their shoulder harnesses, and Judy dug into the manila envelope, taking out the packet of letters and opening the second one.

"You want me to read to you? It's all on one line." Judy cleared her throat. "Dear Mr. Stall, I hope you are doing well. I know you are innocent and you will be free soon. Your friend, Allegra Gardner.' "

"Doesn't that sound like the first letter?" Mary steered out of the parking lot and down the long road to Route 29.

"Yes. Let me see the third one. Lonnie was nice enough to put them in chronological order." Judy put the second letter away and opened up the third one, while Mary looked over nervously, seeing that it was only one line.

"Please tell me it doesn't say the same exact thing."

"It says the exact same thing, which would be the obsessive part."

"Oh no." Mary bit her lip, hitting the gas in light traffic, on the two-lane road. "I can't wait to read the other ones, and try to understand what was going on with her. What's the next one say?"

"Let's see." Judy opened the fourth letter while Mary held her breath. "Mare. Remember in *The Shining*, when Jack Nicholson writes, 'all work and no play makes Jack a dull dull boy,' over and over and over again?"

"Yes," Mary answered, dismayed.

"Well, it's like that, only less entertaining."

Mary groaned, hitting the gas and heading for their next appointment.

An hour later, Mary and Judy were sitting across the neat desk of Bob Brandt, who turned out to be an up-and-coming sports agent and lawyer. He was African-American, six foot three and powerfully built, a former running back at Temple, whose broad shoulders strained against the seams of his tailored gray suit with a sharp tie of melon silk. His jovial air belied his size, and his brown eyes were deep-set, earnest, and even playful, under a prominent forehead. He wore his hair natural, cut medium-short, and he had a close-cropped beard. He must have recently turned thirty years old, because there was an array of birthday cards open on a cherrywood credenza, next to framed family photographs of a pretty wife and two adorable little boys.

Mary introduced herself and Judy, then got to the point. "We've just come from Graterford, where we met with Lonnie Stall. We know you represented him in the Fiona Gardner murder case about six years ago, and we need to just ask you a few questions."

"Go right ahead." Bob leaned forward on his desk, linking his immense hands together. His desk was neat, holding only a silvery MacPro laptop, a stack of neat papers, and a tiny Eagles football. Sports memorabilia shared shelf space with law books behind him, and framed football and baseball jerseys lined the wall of his large, modern office, which occupied an entire floor of a building on Locust Street, one of the nicest streets in Center City. "As I said when you called, I will do anything I can to help Lonnie Stall, and if you are trying to find grounds for ineffective assistance, may God be with you. I was just out of law school when I took that case, but I did everything humanly possible for Lonnie and I believe any court in the land would agree with me. In fact, I wish it weren't so, because I know he is innocent of killing Fiona Gardner."

"How do you know that?"

"I know Lonnie, I watched him grow up, I know his mother. He's worked his butt off, in school and at work, from day one, and he never got anywhere near trouble." Bob's eyes burned with conviction. "He was Honor Roll at University City High and Dean's List at Temple. It's impossible that he killed her, or anybody."

Mary brightened, feeling validated. "How did he come to hire you, if you didn't have much experience in murder cases?"

"As I say, we've known each other forever, and we go to the same church, United Bible. Lonnie and his mother thought they would get better representation with a private lawyer than they would with the public defender." Bob paused, pursing his lips. "Sadly, that's not always the case. The public defenders are more experienced and smarter than anybody gives them credit for. I tried to tell Lonnie and his mother that, but they really wanted to go with somebody they knew. That's why it kills me that I lost. They put their faith in me, and I didn't come through."

Mary felt terrible for him. "It wasn't an easy case to have for your first murder trial. There was a lot of evidence to deal with."

"Thanks. It was my first murder case, and my last. I still think about what I could've done differently, or better, but I also know I worked my butt off, met with Lonnie more than anyone else would have, and gave him good, practical legal advice. I really wanted him to take the plea deal, and I was glad when he did. The jury would've convicted him for sure. He'd be there for life."

"Why do you think he didn't take the deal, at first?"

"I know why, and I don't think it's breaching any privilege to tell you. He was innocent and he wanted his day in court. He's that kind of kid." Bob looked like he was about to say something, then fell silent.

"What?"

"It brings me down." Bob paused, his dark gaze restlessly scanning his desk. "From the get-go, the cops had their man. From when he ran. Then her blood was on him, his blood was on her, and his saliva in her mouth. I begged Lonnie not to take the stand, but God bless him, he went up against Mel Bount, the District Attorney *himself,* one of the best practitioners of cross-examination anywhere. It kills me. I firmly believe that if Lonnie hadn't taken the stand, he'd be walking around today." Bob gestured to a row of colorful baseball caps on his bookshelf. "You see the kind of guy I am. I love to work for players and fight with management, but the only stakes I like are money. I don't practice criminal defense anymore, I'm not cut out for it. I can't move on to the next case, like those dudes." Bob frowned deeply, raking his hand through his hair. "Lonnie haunts me, and can you imagine what it's like to know he's doing hard time, then to see his mother every Sunday, praying for him? She sits where they used to sit together, with his cousins. He should be with her, with them."

Mary felt moved. "We've all lost cases that we wish we had won, but I feel for you, when an innocent man ends up in jail. That's what we're hoping to correct."

"Okay then, I'll stop. My wife says I love to talk about myself, and she might be right." Bob permitted himself a slight smile. "How can I help you?"

Mary knew this would be the difficult part, because she could see a major error that Bob had made, which no experienced criminal lawyer would have. She didn't know how to broach it tactfully, so she started slowly. "Well, we think the best way to go about it is to try to understand who else was on the suspect list. What other suspects were there, in your mind?"

"I didn't have any. I didn't think that was my job, that was the police's job, and they had their man. This was the highest-profile case you can imagine, and I had my hands full, just trying to deal with the evidence they had against Lonnie." Bob's tone turned defensive. "Also Lonnie answered a lot of questions when they picked him up, so I had to file a suppression motion, which I ended up losing anyway. They went by the book, they didn't play. They weren't about to make any mistakes with him, except the biggest one, they got the wrong guy."

Mary remembered reading the motions in the file. They were

well-written, but they lost because Lonnie had been properly Miran-dized and had nevertheless gone on to answer questions, the actions of someone who felt confident in his own innocence.

"I'm no detective, and I certainly wasn't then. I didn't know the victim, Fiona, and I had no information on who murdered her or why."

"Did you have a firm investigator?"

"You're kidding, right? I didn't even have a firm." Bob laughed, without mirth. "I had a desk in a room that I rented with three other frat brothers, and we pooled for a reception service."

"You've come far." Mary smiled.

"Thanks." Bob smiled back, but it faded quickly. "I handle myself better now and I'm tougher in negotiations, but then, I let myself get pushed around, and they threw everything they had at Lonnie. They rushed him to trial, they gave us no extensions, and it was a fast-track to hell."

Mary could hear the anguish in his tone. He was blaming himself, over and over, like the boy version of herself.

"I'm not making excuses, believe me, but you have no idea of the kind of media attention and the sheer *heat* this case got." Bob hunched over the desk, eager to elaborate. "The Gardner family was as major a family as Philadelphia has, they still are, and when the D.A. himself tries the case, there's no way he's going to lose. They won't *let* him lose. Everybody falls in line, from law enforcement on down. It was David and Goliath, and Goliath is on deck to be the next governor. Governor Goliath!"

Mary could imagine the pressure. "Let's go back to this idea of a suspect list."

"Okay, but why?"

"You know, I've only worked on a few murder cases, but my part-ner, Bennie Rosato says—"

"*Bennie Rosato* is your partner?" Bob's eyebrows flew upward in surprise. "She spoke at our Young Lawyers luncheon last year and she was awesome. She's impressive."

"I know, I'm as impressed as you are." Mary smiled. "Anyway, she always says that, in murder cases, it helps raise reasonable doubt if you can point to another person who might have committed the murder. She doesn't think it's enough to just say anybody could've done it, but it really helps the jury visualize it if you give them a name. They find it easier to go your way."

"Oh, no." Bob grimaced, rubbing his face, then his beard, with strong hands. "I didn't do that, not at all. Like I say, I didn't have a chance. I was *so* over my head."

"The purpose of this isn't to make you feel worse." Mary felt like the guilt fairy, flitting from Lonnie Stall to Bob Brandt, raising false hopes and lowering self-esteem. "You couldn't be expected to know that, and I didn't know it myself until Bennie explained it to me. Some people think it's a lawyer's trick, and maybe it is with other lawyers, but in this case it can serve us well. We have the luxury of representing someone who is innocent."

Judy interjected, "Mare, we represent Allegra Gardner, not Lonnie Stall."

"Right, sorry." Mary faced Bob. "So back to the suspect list. The murder occurred at a party, and I'm assuming that this was essentially a closed system."

"Sure." Bob leaned forward eagerly, putting his hands on the desk. "It's a huge system though, two hundred people. Caterers, two bands, a DJ, sound equipment dudes, and other equipment rental guys, like chairs or a dance floor, all at a party spread to show off the new offices."

Mary made notes. It was more than she had thought. "So let's reason together. It was a private party, of about two hundred guests, and God-knows-how-many service people. Any one of the guests or staff could be the killer, and I'm going to assume that one of them was, because I don't think a private party given to celebrate the Gardners' new offices would be easy to get into. They had to have some kind of guest list and security to check them in."

"I bet, and as I recall, the Gardner family companies owned the building, but they subcontracted the security to Brockmore, so the security must have been Brockmore people."

Mary made a note. "I didn't see any guest list in the file. Do you know if you were given anything like that?"

"Not that I recall." Bob gestured vaguely to his right. "I sent for the file when you called today, I had it stored in business archives. When I get it, I'll have it messengered to you."

"Thanks. Did you know if Fiona had a date at the party?"

"No, I don't know."

"Do you know if she was there with any of her girlfriends?"

"No I don't know that, either. I'm sure the Gardner family could give you that information, though."

"They're not exactly cooperating. We went to their house and sat in a home conference room that was wired for—" Mary caught herself, then glanced at Judy. "Wait a minute. They taped our meeting. I wonder if they had a videotape going the night of the party."

Judy's eyes lit up. "I'm sure they'd have one. If they do it at home, for sure they're going to do it at work. There are security cameras and videotapes everywhere, these days."

Bob frowned. "I didn't get a security videotape from the D.A. and I don't believe there was one introduced into evidence by the Commonwealth. So I don't know if the police got one from the family, or they got one but didn't turn it over. They have to turn evidence over only if it shows a defendant is innocent, right?"

"Right. They have a duty to turn over only exculpatory evidence, and there can be prosecutorial misconduct issues, where the D.A. has exculpatory evidence but hides it."

"It would be such a risk for the D.A. to do that, in Lonnie's case."

"But it happens." Mary's thoughts raced ahead. "I would love to see the videotape of that party. It could show us Fiona, who she was with, who she talked to, everything about her that night."

Judy looked over. "I don't remember seeing security videotapes listed on the exhibit list, do you?"

"No, but I didn't get as far as the exhibit list." Mary was kicking herself for not staying up to work last night. "But even if it wasn't turned over to the police, I assume the Gardner family company has a videotape, or the very least, they'd certainly have a guest list, in addition to a list of the service people."

Bob nodded. "I'm sure they would. They would turn over copies of those things to the police, not the originals. Who would part with the original videotape taken at a party the night your daughter was murdered? That's what I'm talking about." Bob threw up his hands. "Nobody was looking to cast the net wide, because they thought they had their man. The only person who believes Lonnie was innocent was Lonnie and his family, and all of us, at church."

"Why did he take the plea, in the end?"

"I begged him to, and after he testified, he saw the light. He talked to his mom, then Linda, who he saw from time to time, she had a crush on him anyway. Then he gave me the word, take the deal."

"Why did they still offer it?" Mary wanted to verify her theory. "They'd gone all through the trial."

"There was still a risk they would lose, or hang the jury, and they didn't want to risk anything. They increased it, added five more years." Bob's voice turned bitter. "It was payback for Lonnie's turning down the deal when it was first offered. I do the same thing when I negotiate, but a man's liberty and life aren't involved."

"Was race a factor, at all?" Mary was wondering if it was grounds for collateral attack.

"No." Bob's tone was firm. "There were twelve people on the jury, and ten of them were black. But you know what *was* a factor? *Gender.*"

"How so?"

"There were eight men and four women, and even I knew that was bad news, as soon as they were empaneled." Bob shook his head. "It was the first jury I ever picked, but even a rookie could tell that a young, good-looking black kid, Dean's List in college, who had a steady part-time job, also sang solos in two church choirs, was going to appeal to women, especially the older ones we had to choose from.

I struck every middle-aged white man I could, to try to get more women, but it was just luck of the draw."

Mary made a note. "How about Judge Vander, was he a factor? He sounded fair and reasonable in the transcript, but I know a judge can sway a jury in a way that doesn't show in print."

"Nothing there. Vander was completely down the middle. He wasn't prejudiced either way." Bob's gaze traveled to the window, but Mary knew there was nothing to see, except for the blinds. "That's the thing about this case. We had so much right, but so much wrong, from the jump."

Mary recognized the resignation in his tone, and he sounded uncannily like Lonnie at Graterford this morning. "You know, when we went to see Lonnie, he wished us luck, but he said he doesn't have any hope. He doesn't even want to hope."

Bob turned to Mary, locking eyes with her over his desk. "I didn't want to hope either, until you two walked in."

His words stayed with Mary, worrying her as they left Bob's office and walked back to Rosato & Associates, where hope had arrived, or at least help, in one of its many forms.

Chapter Seventeen

"Lou, you came back!" Mary cried out, when she and Judy stepped off the elevator to find Lou Jacobs, their firm investigator, standing at the reception desk, talking to Marshall. He was in his mid-sixties, but hardly looked it, trim and fit in his white polo shirt and khaki pants, which he always called slacks. He had a year-round tan that he earned fishing on his boat, but he made a sunburn look outdoorsy, rather than carcinogenic.

"Hiya, girls!" Lou turned with a broad smile, throwing open his brawny arms. His hair was a slicked-back white-gray, his eyes a lively black-brown, and his nose curved like a seagull above thin lips. His cheekbones were high and slanting in a weathered face creased by deep crow's-feet and even deeper laugh lines. "Mare, you gettin' married? Marshall just told me! Congratulations!"

"Thanks!" Mary dropped her gear and hugged him, breathing in his smells of salt air, Drakkar Noir, and the liverwurst and onion sandwich he'd undoubtedly had for lunch, because he was a walking deli. She released him, happily. "That was so nice of you, to come back from your vacation. I feel guilty."

"Don't. I woulda felt guilty if I stayed. Jewish guilt trumps Catholic, every time. We've been at it longer than you guys. Experience shows." Lou grinned down at her. He was only of average height, but had been a beat cop and later a homicide detective, so he had a naturally commanding presence. "And you, kiddo? I turn my back five minutes, and you become a partner *and* get engaged? I'm happy for you, and I love Anthony, but if he does you wrong, I'll break his face."

"Now, that's love." Mary smiled.

"Only kidding, anyway, I got you something, to say congratulations on your partnership." Lou reached into his back pocket, produced a long skinny box wrapped in newspaper, and handed it to Mary. "Sorry, I didn't have any gift wrap on the boat. But at least I didn't use this for the fish."

"Lou, you didn't have to do that. We said no presents."

"I don't listen to you ladies, and we know I'm special."

"You are." Mary tore off the paper to reveal a dark blue box, which she opened. Inside was a silvery Cross pen, and she held it up to the light, where it gleamed. "Oh, you're too nice. What a great gift, thank you so much!"

"Happy to." Lou nodded, pleased. "I know you're on the computer, but every lawyer should have a nice pen, don't you think? At least to sign those nice big checks that'll be coming in."

"True! Or those big bills that will be going out." Mary put the pen back, closed the box, and gave him another hug. "Thanks again."

Marshall stood up, frowning. "Mary, where's your engagement ring, to show Lou?"

Mary reddened. "It's being resized."

"To nothing," Judy added, and Mary shot her a look.

Lou was oblivious, having learned to disregard their girl talk. "So what do you ladies got for me? That case in the conference room? I glanced through the file already."

"Good, then let's go. We need you." Mary took Lou's arm, and she and Judy led him to the war room, where they settled in around the conference table, and Mary and Judy took turns bringing him up-to-date, which included showing him the stack of letters that Allegra had written to Lonnie Stall, which were all basically identical, except that Allegra's handwriting got better as she got older, then turned to typing, on laser-printed computer paper. When Mary was finished, she eased back in the chair and asked Lou what he thought, because she respected his judgment.

"You wanna know what I think?" Lou rubbed his eyes, leaving a little redness under his fresh tan. "I feel sorry for this kid, Allegra, for lots of reasons, but that's not the point."

Mary felt comforted. "It's not the point legally, but I feel it, too."

Judy sipped a fresh coffee. The late-day sun beamed through the windows and flooded the conference room with a warm golden hue, as it began to dip over West Philly. "Me, too. Do you think Stall did it, Lou?"

"Too soon to say. I'm reserving judgment, and we all know I'm not the bleeding heart that you ladies are." Lou's expression settled into grave lines. "They had a boatload of evidence on him, and I agree you want to look at that videotape."

"The security company they use is Blackmore."

"Good, I know a few guys at Blackmore. I can make some calls. Unofficially."

"That would be great." Mary brightened. Lou had been their security guard when Bennie had hired him, and he was totally plugged into the retired-cop network, most of whom were bored to tears working as security guards.

Judy straightened up. "But what's our next move? Ideally, we'd try to get information about that night from the family, but that isn't happening anytime soon. Should we try to talk to some of the trial witnesses? Does that make any sense?"

"No." Mary leaned forward, trying not to look at the letters from Allegra that littered the table. "I don't think we should be talking to the trial witnesses. Allegra asked us to solve her sister's murder, and so far, what we've done is retraced the steps of the police. I get it, because we needed the background, but if we do only that, we're just going to end up in the same place that the police did, without testing their conclusion."

Lou nodded. "That's right. I looked at the file and I can tell you that they had only the best personnel on this case. Not just with Mel trying it himself, but I know Mort Ledbetter, the lead detective and his partner. They've been around a long time and they're some of the best in the department, even now."

Judy looked over. "What's your point? That they're right?"

Lou shook his head. "No, but given the circumstances, I see why they liked Stall."

Listening, Mary reminded herself that Lou, as an ex-cop, still used cop jargon, so when he said the cops *liked* somebody, it meant that they suspected him. It was probably why Mary couldn't have been a cop, because she liked everybody and suspected no one.

Lou continued, "And I know that confirmation bias affects even the best guys. It's not really a rush to judgment, but more, we like this guy, and then you start to see only the facts that support your theory. That could be what happened here, but you won't find that out, or challenge it, by following what they did."

"Right." Mary found herself rising, as it was a little-known fact that though Italians needed their hands to talk, they needed their feet to think. "We have to start fresh and not continue on the track we were starting with. We have to talk to Tim Gage."

Lou nodded. "That's right, the boyfriend. I'd like to know if he was there that night."

Judy sipped her coffee, her eyes narrowing. "I see, and we should also look into whether Fiona had any friends there. Girlfriends. Allegra may be a loner, but I get the impression that Fiona wasn't. She was pretty and popular, and she probably had lots of friends. Maybe Allegra could give us some of their names. If Tim Gage wasn't there, she could've been there with her girlfriends, any guy friends, or all of them."

Mary felt her heart beat a little faster. "This should take about thirty seconds on Facebook. Start with Gage."

Judy was already pulling over her laptop. "Right, he's the only name we have, and boys are so dumb, they keep everything in their profiles public."

Lou rolled his chair next to Judy, to see her laptop. "I remember when your profile was how you looked from the side."

"Lou, don't start." Mary smiled, then pushed her laptop across the table, to work next to Judy. "You're hipper than you think. You're a hep cat. Or for this case, you're the bee's knees."

Judy looked over as she typed. "Mary's right, Lou. You're hot for an olds. You're hot enough to be on a Cialis commercial."

Lou laughed. "Never touch the stuff. Ask Michelle."

Mary sat down next to Judy, logged onto the Internet, and started typing. "Judy, while you do that, I'll email Allegra and ask her who Fiona was with that night, and even if she wasn't there with her girl-friends, to give me the name of her three closest girlfriends." She logged into her email account and started typing. "I'd call, but I don't want to risk her parents' catching her on the phone."

Lou looked from Mary to Judy and back again. "You guys slay me. Since when did detectives become typists?"

"Yay!" Suddenly Judy threw her arms up in the air. "Tim Gage attends Wharton grad school at the University of Pennsylvania. Ladies and gentlemen, we have a winner."

"Penn is my alma mater." Mary hit Send on her email to Allegra and shifted over to see Judy's laptop screen. "That means we can run down and see him. What's he look like?"

"What's his story?" Lou picked up his black reading glasses from the letter pile, came over to stand behind Judy, and slipped them on. "Looks like a nice kid."

"Hardly." Mary pointed to Gage's Relationship Status, which read, **Random Play.**

Lou frowned. "What does that mean?"

Judy snorted. "It means he's a jerk."

Mary smiled up at Lou, explaining, "It means he doesn't want a steady girlfriend."

Lou frowned. "So he plays the field?"

Judy snorted. "No, he screws the field."

Lou burst into laughter, gesturing at the laptop. "A guy can just say that straight out? That he only wants to fool around? What girl would say yes to that?"

"Exactly." Mary eyed the photo of Tim Gage, who was handsome, with big brown eyes, a patrician nose, and a broad, confident smile. Straight brown hair flopped casually onto his forehead, and Mary was already hating on him, which she knew was probably her residual class-warfare impulse. She knew she had to get over that, now that she was an adult partner and everything. She hoped someday her inside would catch up with her outside.

"Let's look at his Spring Fling album." Judy opened one of Gage's many photo albums and clicked through an array of beautiful young men and women at a party, holding Solo cups. "Did you ever notice how everybody's photo albums look alike?"

"I know, right? College kids keep Solo cups in business. Go back to his Wall." Mary read Gage's Wall, after Judy clicked back. "He likes Coldplay and Maroon 5, he was an Econ major at Wharton, and he played varsity lacrosse. Classic profile for a murderer."

Lou laughed. "Or the CEO of any Fortune 500 company."

Mary sniffed. "Also he lives at St. A's, the preppy frat. Why am I not surprised?"

Judy looked over. "So when do you want to go, or do you want to wait until Allegra gets back to us about Fiona's girlfriends?"

"No, we can do that on the fly. Let's go as soon as I'm finished here."

"Okay. Let me take a second to see what else I can find out about Gage." Judy started typing, and Mary logged on to Facebook and searched under Allegra Gardner, scanning her page when it popped onto the screen. Allegra had most of her profile settings on private, but she named her interests as beekeeping and criminalistics. She had ten friends, whose names were not public, but they were all in the Milton School network.

Mary groaned. "Poor kid."

"What?" Lou asked, reading over her shoulder. "Is that the client? Why are you looking up the client?"

"I just want to know more about her." Mary navigated to the menu and sent Allegra a friend request. "She hardly has any friends. I feel so bad for her."

Lou placed a warm hand on her shoulder. "While you guys are doing that, let me step outside and make a few phone calls to my buddy at Blackmore."

"Thanks," Mary said, as Lou left the room. She started searching Facebook for Jane Gardner, which returned hundreds of names. She scanned the pictures to see if any of them were Allegra's mother.

"What are you doing?" Judy asked, puzzled.

"Just seeing what the mother's really like, who her friends are. You never know what you might turn up." Mary clicked to the next page, but didn't see any thumbnails of her. Many of the profile pictures weren't of the person, but of a dog, a flower, or a cartoon, which didn't help. "Something could lead to something else. That's the way we always do it, right?"

"Mare, we have to keep our eye on the ball on this case." Judy gestured at the bulletin boards that Mary had made and set up on easels on the other side of the table. "I understand why you searched for articles about Fiona's murder, but I'm not sure I follow why articles about Allegra being a girl genius are relevant to finding out who killed Fiona."

"They're not, I guess. But they're interesting and they might be helpful."

"And sending her a friend request? Is that helpful?" Judy gestured at the massive pile of letters that Allegra had written to Lonnie Stall. "And the letters, you told Lonnie you wanted to get the rest, and you said something about wanting to go through them. What did you mean by that?"

"Just what I said. I want to go through them."

"Why?"

"I want to read them, try to understand her thought processes about her sister's murder."

"They all say the same thing."

"So I'll reread them." Mary blinked. "I'd like to try to pinpoint when it turned from interest to obsession, and try to determine what caused it. To try and see why she's so alone, on her own."

"But—" Judy caught herself, and Mary knew her well enough to know that she was choosing her words carefully.

"What? Say it. I won't be mad. And I won't fire you."

Judy didn't smile. "I just don't want you to take on this kid's problems. I know why you would, and I love you for it, but you can't make her happy, or healthy, or cool. You can't give her friends, or make up for the friends she doesn't have. I don't know much more about her than you do, but I don't see her as a victim."

"Why not?" Mary asked, surprised. "She is one. She's been a victim of bullies, she told us as much, and so did her parents. And we know she's a victim of crime, because we both know how much a family's affected when there's a murder. I even think she's a victim of her parents, the way they push her around."

Judy frowned, in thought, if not disagreement. "I don't think her parents push her around, necessarily. They're doing what they think is right for her."

"They're chilly."

"Not every family is like yours. You have a really special, loving family. She doesn't have that, even I don't have that."

Mary agreed with that much. "So I can't account for the disadvantages of the upper class, like extraordinary wealth, private schooling, and trees with names."

"Exactly." Judy smiled. "I see what you mean about her being a victim, and maybe you're right. But as for her lack of friends, or her aloneness, I think that's her choice. She isolates herself, don't you think?"

Mary shook her head. "Nobody her age isolates themselves."

"They do when they surround themselves with thirty thousand bees." Judy looked behind her as Lou entered the conference room, slipping his cell phone into his slacks pocket with an unhappy frown.

"Ladies, bad news."

"What?" Mary and Judy asked, in unison.

"It's radio silence." Lou folded his arms, standing with his feet apart. "My buddy, Ray Morley, is now the head of security at Blackmore."

Mary didn't understand. "Isn't that good for us?"

Lou shook his head. "Only insofar as he told me, confidentially, that he's already been given my name and both of yours, with express instructions not to talk to us or permit us at the corporate offices of the Gardner Group. He was told that if anybody from Rosato & Associates comes knocking, calling, or asking questions, to notify him immediately and he's supposed to call one of the Gardner lawyers, I forget his name, Patel."

Judy nodded. "Neil Patel."

"That's the one. They're shutting us out, and they're not wasting any time. I didn't even ask him about the videotape or the guest lists, because I didn't want him to know we'd be looking for it." Lou permitted himself a brief smile. "In fact, I told him that you guys were driving me crazy, tracking down all the trial experts in the case. That will give them something to chew on."

Judy's eyes lit up. "Love that. We're waging our first disinformation campaign. Do you think he believed you? Nobody would believe that we would drive a man crazy."

Lou laughed, and Mary smiled, but her thoughts clicked away. "So that means we should tell Allegra not to tell her parents that we were asking about the names of Fiona's girlfriends."

"Correctamundo."

"Damn." Mary could have texted Allegra, but chose not to. "It doesn't feel right, telling a thirteen-year-old to keep secrets from her parents."

Judy nodded. "Agreed, but it's inevitable in this case, which is why

I'm already hating it, and why Bennie was, too. If we represent a minor, we automatically get issues like that. The case is intertwined with the family. You can't separate the two."

Mary met her troubled eye, then turned to Lou. "So what should we do now, gang?"

"I have a few ideas I can try," Lou folded his arms. "But if you want to see that Gage boy or any of the girlfriends, I suggest you hit the road."

Chapter Eighteen

Having grown up in South Philadelphia, on Mercy and 9th Streets, Mary had gone to college at Penn at 38th and Spruce Streets, and then to the University of Pennsylvania Law School at 34th and Walnut Streets. So as soon as she stepped off the Route 42 bus with Judy and set foot on the corner of 38th and Walnut Streets, she felt her life conflate on the spot, her present collapsing into her past, and her past crashing her present like a house party. There were advantages and disadvantages to living your entire life in a three-mile radius, and the advantage was that you never got lost, but the disadvantage was that you could be disoriented in other ways.

So when Mary looked around at the intersection, she knew she had been here before, heard the hydraulic case of the very same bus, as well as the metallic slap of its doors folding closed, but for a moment, she felt confused. Her physical location was clear, but her temporal location less so, and she was back in college with Angie beside her, because Angie had gone to Penn, too. The twins had been in every grade together, even in the same class, and they'd gotten identical scholarships here, and Mary felt bewildered because the best part of her college life was missing, in the form of her other half, which, she suspected, also included her heart.

"Mary, are you okay?"

"What?" Mary looked over at Judy, seeing Angie's face, then it vanished. "Oh, sorry. I'm a little tired."

"We didn't eat anything. Maybe we should get something from one of the food trucks."

"Good idea." Mary tried to shake it off, watching the traffic speed in three lanes down the street, heedless of the crowded sidewalks, the drivers trying to make the lights, which were badly timed. It was almost the end of the day, and they were all tear-assing out of the city, heading for the expressway ramps at 30th Street. The college branch of her and Angie's bank was on the left, and opposite was the modern building that housed Annenberg Center, the theater where she and Angie had worked part-time as ushers in their work-study program.

"That falafel truck looks good." Judy stepped off the curb as soon as the light changed. "Let's get a nice, thick falafel. It's too hard to get hummus breath otherwise."

Mary tried to pick up the pace, not to get lost in the crowds crossing the street. Students were heading home after their last classes, heavy knapsacks and purses hanging over one shoulder as they yapped away on cell phones or laughed together in groups, a bobbing mass of double ponytails and backwards baseball caps. Mary and Angie used to travel in groups, but always together, the quieter Angie tagging along with Mary's friends, she realized now, with a pang. She hadn't seen it then, but she saw it now. She wondered if Angie had to go so far, merely because they had been so close. After all, if you'd started life sharing the same womb, maybe you'd have to live it on different continents. Mary never felt that way, but she knew Angie did, and she wondered if Angie would come home even if she got married. She didn't really know if Angie was estranged, or merely away, but she had a feeling she was going to find out, sooner rather than later.

"Rats, this is kind of a long line," Judy said, when they reached the other side of the street and joined the line at the falafel truck. It was yellow and red, with a whirring bulb of a fan on top, scenting the air with frying grease. "Let's see if it moves quickly or not."

"Okay." Mary had smelled that fried odor more times than she could count, and it always made her mouth water. Angie loved the Chinese food truck that used to park two blocks up, and its owner was named Ruben, which they always thought was funny. She found herself looking down the street, but Ruben's truck was gone, replaced by a gourmet ice cream van.

Judy followed her eye. "If you'd rather, we can get ice cream. It might be quicker."

"No, that's okay."

"I don't know if we have time for this. It makes me grumpy." Judy checked her watch. "What do you think?"

"Whatever you want."

Judy frowned, her eyes searching Mary's. "You sure you're okay? You want to do this? Should we just go interview the guy and forget about food?"

"Maybe we should skip the food and go see the kid, before the Gardners close in." Mary didn't want to worry Judy, nor did she want to tell her all her amazing new insights about how much life sucked without Angie. It wouldn't serve any purpose, and it would only make Judy feel bad, which was the last thing she wanted. "What do you say?"

"Agree." Judy clapped her on the arm. "You lead. You know where the frat house is."

"I do, but I was only inside once. This way." Mary turned, Judy fell in step beside her, and they joined the swarm of undergrads, grad students, and university staff, wearing laminated IDs around their necks. They passed the Faculty Club and the Christian Association, and Mary tried not to remember anything that involved Angie, or indeed anything at all. It was time to rejoin the present and investigate a murder case. "The frat is St. Andrew's or St. A's. They used to have casino nights with real money and real waiters, in uniform."

"Sounds like jerks," Judy said, as she covered ground with her big stride. She was almost as tall as Bennie, and when Mary walked with Judy, she felt like the stumpy mommy to a child on growth hormones. Obviously, she had been the exact same height as Angie, both were five foot three inches, but she put that out of her mind. She slipped her BlackBerry out of her blazer pocket and checked for Allegra's email, but it wasn't there.

"Allegra still hasn't written me back about Fiona's girlfriends."

"She's probably outside, playing with the bees."

"We'll have to tell her to check her email more often. If she doesn't get back to us by the time we can meet Gage, let's ask him."

"Good idea."

"What do we do if he's at class or something? Wait?"

"Eat falafel," Judy answered with a grin, and Mary led them right up Locust Walk, the pedestrian walkway that bisected the campus, lined with tall leafy oaks that cast dappled shadows on the cobblestones and Gothic buildings with authentic Victorian details, like stone gargoyles and bats. The university housed offices like Student Affairs, Alumni Affairs, and the yearbook in some of the buildings, but a few of the homes were owned by fraternities, and Mary halted when they reached St. Anthony's, an incongruously modern brick building on the right.

"This is it." Mary gestured at the building, which seemed oddly impenetrable, with white curtains covering its windows and no activity out front, unlike all the other buildings, which buzzed with students hanging out, talking, or drinking sodas on the front steps. St. A's was the super-exclusive, rich-boy fraternity, the last bastion of old-school preppies and Eurotrash with world-class trust funds. Angie hadn't liked St. A's because she didn't like anything that smacked of materialism, which was why she became a nun. And Mary, who was generally in favor of money, if not an outright money fan, became a lawyer.

"What are we waiting for?" Judy asked, puzzled.

"Nothing," Mary answered, shooing the ghosts away and heading for the door.

Chapter Nineteen

Mary and Judy were let into St. A's by a uniformed maid, who'd showed them into a waiting room with cracked leather stuffed chairs and floor-length curtains. On the wall hung framed maps of Philadelphia from the days of Ben Franklin, before Italians moved in and brought the flavor. It was so classy, Mary couldn't believe it was a real frat house. She muttered to Judy, "What kind of frat house has a *maid*? I don't have a maid and I'm a partner."

Judy looked over. "You should have a cleaning person. You can afford one. We have someone come in, every two weeks."

"You *do*? Don't you feel guilty?"

"No, why? It's an honest job, and it's the best money we spend." Judy stood up, restless, and wandered over to a Penn's emblem, on the wall. "Mary, what's the motto mean? You're the Latin jock and alumna."

"*Leges sine moribus vanae.* 'Laws without morals are useless.' Now sit down and tell me about your cleaning person. I'd feel so guilty. What do you do, put your feet up while she vacuums underneath? Sheesh!"

Suddenly the doors rolled apart, and Tim Gage stepped out with a smile that he flashed at Mary and Judy like it was beamed from a lighthouse. "I'm Tim, sorry to keep you waiting. Linda gave me your business card and told me you were here, but I had to finish, and I'll be right with you." Gage turned slightly, and out of the living room bopped a little kid with red hair, freckles, and missing front teeth. "Say hello to William, who's in third grade at Drew Elementary." Gage rested a hand on William's shoulder, in its little white polo shirt. "William is starting his own business and learning to be an entrepreneur. He's got his own startup. Isn't that great?"

"It sure is," Judy answered. "What's your business, William?"

William ducked behind Gage, who smiled indulgently. "William is a little bashful with new people, so I'll tell you for him. William wanted his class to have a pet hamster, like he read about in one of his books, so he borrowed the money for the hamster and its cage, and formed a syndicate of other third-graders who hold shares to own the hamster and pay their share in its upkeep. They're going to hold a bake sale to pay back the bank."

Judy smiled. "That's wonderful, William."

Mary couldn't help but be touched, and she was guessing that Gage was the bank and not necessarily a murderer, though that remained to be seen.

"Today, William learned how to make a balance sheet, because the syndicate has some expenses, like hamster pellets and wooden shavings, and he also learned to put a value on his time and labor. Right, William?" Gage bent down and managed to gentle the boy out. "Another day we'll work on meeting new people, because that's something business leaders have to do, too, but not today. Ladies, if you wait a sec, his mom should be waiting for him, and I'll walk him out, then be right back."

"Thanks so much. Bye, William." Judy waved at the boy, who averted his eyes.

"Good-bye, William." Mary tried to process the information while Gage and the boy left, closing the door behind them. "Was that for real or for show?"

Judy laughed. "Mare. He might be a nice guy, even though he has a maid."

"Not possible. He's a stone cold killer."

"Now who has confirmation bias, huh? The kid obviously likes him, so how bad can he be?"

"Kids liked Ted Bundy, too."

"You're making that up. What a guy, huh? He must be in some kind of community outreach program, from Wharton."

"You call it outreach, I call it *noblesse oblige.*"

"Call it what you want, at least he's doing it." Judy paused. "I should take the lead with him. I did literacy outreach in school, and I like him better than you do. Also he's superhot and you're engaged."

"But you're living with someone who has a maid."

"Stop. Here he comes." They both fell silent as the door opened, Gage came in, strolled toward them, and sat down in one of the cushy chairs, crossing his long legs and raking back his glossy bangs.

"Sorry to make you wait, but that hour is sacred to me."

Mary wished for a notepad, so she could write, OH PLEASE.

Gage slid her business card from the pocket of his white oxford shirt, which he wore tucked into his jeans. "So you're from the law firm of Rosato & Associates, and you said you were here on a personal matter. What would that be?"

Judy cleared her throat. "My name is Judy Carrier and this is my colleague Mary DiNunzio, and we're looking into the murder of Fiona Gardner."

Gage frowned slightly. "You know that there's a man in prison for that, right?"

"Yes."

"Were you hired by him, to get him out or something?"

"No, we were hired by Allegra, Fiona's sister, because she thinks that Lonnie Stall, who was convicted of the crime, is in fact innocent."

Gage's eyebrows flew upward, disappearing under his hair. "Allegra thinks that? Little Allegra?"

"She's not so little anymore, and we just thought we'd ask you a question or two, because I'm sure you feel, as Allegra does, that justice should be done." Judy gestured at the wall plaque. "Laws without morals are useless, right?"

"Okay," Gage said uncertainly. "I have some time, so shoot. What's your question?"

"We understand that you dated Fiona in high school, is that correct?"

"Yes." Gage blinked, his mouth falling into a sad line. "We dated for two years, we were boyfriend and girlfriend, you'd say."

"So you knew her well?"

"Yes, absolutely."

"Can you tell me what she was like?" Judy kept her tone light, and Mary knew that she was trying to ease him into the questioning, and it was working because Gage's expression softened.

"Sure, Fiona was a great girl. She was funny and smart and really lively. She was just fun, fun to be around. Everybody adored Fiona."

"Who were her closest girlfriends, do you know?"

"Sure, who doesn't? Sue Winston, Mary Weiss, Honor Jason, and Hannah Wicker."

Judy wrote down the names. "Why did you say, 'who doesn't?' Were you close to them, because you dated her?"

Gage frowned. "Oh, you don't know. Three of those girls were killed in a car crash, a few months after Fiona was murdered."

Judy gasped. "Really? How horrible."

"Yes, it was. It is." Gage sighed, barely audibly. "It was on a stretch of Route 1 near Chadds Ford, and people get killed there all the time. The paper said that drinking was involved, but you should understand it wasn't a coincidence."

"What do you mean?"

"Fiona wasn't a big partier, and she was a civilizing influence for her friends. You know, the field hockey team could get rowdy, but not when Fiona was around. You can imagine how hard they took her death, and once they lost her, they acted out, got wilder." Gage pursed his lips. "She was the center of that group, and as they say, the center couldn't hold, once she was gone."

"That's such a shame," Judy said, and Mary could tell the revelation derailed her line of questioning, so she jumped in.

"Tim, you said that three of the girls were killed. Which one wasn't?"

"Hannah Wicker. She survived the crash, the only survivor."

"Do you know where she is, these days?"

"No idea."

Mary nodded to Judy to take over, and Judy asked, "Do you know if any of those girls were at the party, the night Fiona was killed?"

"I don't know for sure, but I believe they were. They were like a pack, they did everything together. It was basically the forward line of the hockey team. Fiona was the center, in more ways than one."

"So I take it you weren't there, the night she was murdered?"

"No." Gage shook his head. "We had broken up about two weeks earlier, so I was out of the picture."

"Where were you that night?"

"Home."

Mary wished she had a way to check his alibi, but Judy didn't bat an eye.

"Did the police contact you at all, in connection with her death?"

"No." Gage scoffed. "Why would they?"

"Just checking on their procedure. Did they contact her friends?"

"I don't know."

"Also, can I ask, why did you break up? Or, who broke up with whom?"

"Yes, of course you can ask. High school was a long time ago, and whenever I think of Fiona, the sad part isn't that we broke up, but that she was murdered."

"So did you break up with her, or the other way around?" Judy asked again, and Mary made a mental note that she had to ask him twice.

"She broke up with me."

"Do you know why? Did she say?"

"Not really, but I could tell she lost interest in me."

Judy made a note. "When you say lost interest, what do you mean?"

"You know, she was more distant, not as available. Didn't return calls or texts. She used to do office work for her father, filing and such, and all of a sudden, there seemed to be a lot more of that, even on the weekend."

"Did she work at home or in town?"

"At home. With practice, games, and homework, she didn't have time to go into the city. They have a home office complex at their farm. They call it the cottage."

Judy nodded. "Yes, we've seen it."

"Right, well, she used to help out on some project with her father and uncle, and I got the idea that she wasn't that into me anymore." Gage managed a rueful smile. "She had to spell it out, though. I was slow on the uptake."

"You were hurt."

"Yes," Gage admitted, with the slightest of winces. "Puppy love, all that."

Judy nodded. "By the way, which uncle was the project for?"

"Edward, he was a nice one. He was the youngest of the three brothers. The other one, Richard, was a little stiffer."

"Did she break up with you because she became interested in someone else?"

"No, she didn't say, and she didn't start dating anyone afterwards." Gage frowned. "I'm not the jealous type, and this was high school. I mean, really."

"How would you know if she dated anyone or not?"

"We went to the same school. She stayed single, until she was murdered."

"Right." Judy smiled, and Mary knew they were both thinking that maybe Fiona had broken up with Gage for Lonnie, and if that were so, Gage would have no way of knowing it. Judy continued, "This is going to sound off-the-wall, but is there anyone you think would've had a motive to murder Fiona?"

Gage recoiled. "No, not at all. Fiona was just a nice, cute girl. She wasn't nasty or mean, and she didn't have an enemy in the world. As far as I'm concerned, they got the right guy in jail, whoever he is. I heard it was one of the waiters."

Judy hesitated. "Let me ask you something else, off-the-wall. What do you know about Allegra?"

Mary didn't know why Judy was asking him, but kept her own counsel.

"Allegra Gardner, girl genius? Look, I know she's your client, but she is one weird kid."

"Did you ever know Fiona to babysit for Allegra?"

Gage cocked his head, thinking. "You mean like babysit for Allegra when her parents went out?"

"Yes, or any other time. When you were dating Fiona, did she ever babysit for Allegra?"

"No, not at all."

Mary didn't say anything, dismayed.

Judy asked, "You never went over to visit Fiona when she was babysitting for Allegra?"

"No, I never did. I don't remember her babysitting for Allegra, and they had a housekeeper, so I assume she'd do it, if Allegra needed to be babysat."

Mary remembered Allegra had mentioned that. "What's the housekeeper's name?"

"Janet Wolsey. She still works for them."

Judy slid her pad into her leather satchel. "That's all the questions we have." She looked over at Mary. "Unless you have anything else."

"No," Mary said, rising. "Thank you for your time."

Tim stood, brushing down his jeans. "You're welcome, it was a pleasure to meet you both. I'll walk you out."

"Great, thanks," Judy said, and they walked with Gage to the door, where they bade him good-bye again, then left and stood blinking in the sun on Locust Walk, which was more crowded, now that the school and work day was over. Judy turned to Mary, squinting against the sun. "Is he crossed off the suspect list? I say yes."

"Yes, but I wish we could check out his alibi. He said she broke up with him, and you had to ask him twice."

"There's only one friend left to go see. It's so sad about that crash, isn't it?"

"Yes, and as far as Hannah Wicker, we'll have to find out where she lives." Mary eyed Judy. "I can't help but wonder if it's connected, can you?"

"Don't know how, or why, except that Fiona was the leader and they were all a little lost without her."

"We'll see, I guess." Mary slid her BlackBerry from her pocket to see if Allegra had emailed her back, but she hadn't. "Still no email from our girl. Let's call her."

"Okay."

Mary made a beeline for the nearest bench, where they sat down, and she called Allegra on her secret cell phone. The call was answered in the middle of the first ring, but Allegra sounded hysterical.

"Mary? Mary, thank God, is that you?"

"What's the matter?" Mary felt fear going through her like an electrical bolt.

"My parents! They're taking me to a hospital! They're going to commit me! Mary? Mary!"

"Allegra!" Mary shouted in anguish, as the line went dead.

Chapter Twenty

"Do you *believe* the Gardners?" Mary asked Judy, as they hustled toward Walnut Street. The crowd flowed around them, students heading for the Quad, runners in red-and-blue singlets jogging toward Franklin Field, and Penn and Drexel employees burdened with briefcases and messenger bags, heading for trains and buses out of the city. "They'd commit their own daughter? The poor kid! She sounded so scared."

"Not going to lie, I didn't see this coming." Judy raised her hand to hail a cab before they'd even reached the curb, and the few in the congested lanes of traffic all looked full. "Damn."

"What do we even do?" Mary pumped her hand wildly, even though she knew it was useless. She felt overwhelmed with guilt, and not even the funny kind. "We go out there, right? We see where they took her and why?"

"Not yet."

"Why not?" Mary looked at her, surprised. Her heart was pounding under her blouse, and she'd broken a sweat. "Don't you want to see what's going on?"

"Of course, but we have to stay calm, and by we, I mean you." Judy frowned at the traffic, keeping her hand in the air.

"There's a cab!" Mary waved to the driver, and they both hustled toward the Yellow cab as it pulled over.

"Right behind you," Judy said, and the women flung open the door, jumped inside, and yanked their purses and bags onto their laps. Judy leaned forward and said to the driver, "1815 Locust Street, please."

"You really want to go back to the office?" Mary frowned as the cab lurched off, then stopped again in traffic. The backseat smelled like Marlboros and Armor-All, which was par for Philly. "Why don't we just go get my car?"

"I want to know the law, I'm not sure I can figure it out on the fly."

"The law? The law is clear, isn't it? Allegra has constitutional rights, doesn't she?" Mary was trying to control her outrage, but it wasn't easy. "You just can't take somebody and put them in a mental hospital because you disagree with what they're doing."

"Maybe you can, if she's a minor."

"If that's true, then this is one of the times that the law is an ass."

"Mare, chill." Judy raised a palm. "These are her parents, and they love her. They think they're doing the right thing for their kid, who has a history of depression."

"But *committing* her? That's kind of extreme."

"If she needs the help, it isn't. We don't have all the facts."

"Then ask yourself this—why now? She's been home for almost a month, but *now* they decided to put her away?" Mary felt a new wave of anger. The cab wasn't making forward progress, which didn't help, and she heard honking behind them. "We didn't drop the case, so they pulled out the trump card. It's like a chess game, and they just took the queen."

"You're mixing metaphors."

"Sue me." Mary thought a minute, simmering. "Generally the law is that you can't be civilly committed unless you're a danger to yourself or others. Allegra is neither."

"But mental health law is a specialized field, I know. I edited an article on it for our law review."

"What was the gist?"

"That was ages ago and under California law, I'm not sure what Pennsylvania law is. There has to be a statute. Stand by." Judy reached into her purse, pulled out her iPhone, and started tapping the touch screen. "Look at me, reduced to Googling 'Mental Health Act and minors in Pennsylvania.' Legal research isn't supposed to be this easy."

"Whatever works." Mary slid her hand in her blazer pocket, pulled out her BlackBerry, and scrolled through the phone log until she reached John Gardner, then pressed Call. "I'm calling her father. He called me, and his cell number is still in the phone. I want to know what's going on and tell him we're not going to let him do this to her."

"Mary, hang on a sec." Judy kept pressing buttons on her iPhone, frowning at the small screen. "We don't know her legal rights yet."

"Then I'll just yell at him, like Bennie would have." Mary cheered at the very notion. She was turning into a badass before her own eyes. Maybe it had been in her all along, if she had somebody like Allegra to fight for. "You know what they say, 'When you have the law, argue the law. When you have the facts, argue the facts. When you don't have either, pound the table.'"

Judy laughed, surprised. "You're on fire, girl."

"You're damn right I am. John Gardner is a bully, and he's bullying his own daughter." Mary listened to the call ringing in her ear. "I bet he doesn't pick up, the coward."

"Hey, he's represented by Patel. We're supposed to call Patel."

"Ask me if I care. Allegra is our client. Did he pick up a phone to call us?" Mary felt her blood pounding in her temples. "What did they do to that poor kid, anyway? Did they handcuff her? Put her in a straitjacket? That's appalling."

Judy didn't look up. "If he doesn't answer, leave a nice message. Remember, you're a professional."

"What were they thinking?" Mary gritted her teeth as the call kept ringing. "She's trying to get answers to some questions she's been wondering about for a long time, her own sister's murder. Isn't she entitled to that?"

"Evidently, no." Judy looked up from her iPhone screen with a frown. "Something called Act 147 establishes the statutory rights for minors and parents to mental health treatment in Pennsylvania."

"Okay. Wait. Hold on, I'll put it on speaker." Mary pressed the button for the speakerphone, and they both listened as the call stopped ringing and John Gardner's voice came on saying curtly, "John Gardner, Gardner Group, please leave a message."

Judy's eyes flared, a calming blue. "Be nice," she whispered.

Mary cleared her throat when she heard the click, then said, "John, this is Mary DiNunzio and Judy Carrier, calling about Allegra's whereabouts. She's our client, and she has a right to speak with us. Please give me a call immediately at this number. Thanks so much."

"Nice job, because the law is not on our side." Judy read from her screen while Mary hung up. "Under Section1.1(b), the parent of a minor under 18 may consent to inpatient treatment on the recommendation of a physician who has examined the minor. The minor's consent is not necessary."

"Really?" Mary asked, aghast. She was about to put her phone away when she noticed that she had missed two calls and a text from Anthony. She didn't have time to listen to the messages, but scrolled automatically to the text, which read, **can you come for drinks tonight with my colleagues?** She groaned. "Oh, no."

"What is it?"

"Anthony wants me to celebrate tonight with his friends."

"Oh how horrible. What a pain. Who does he think he is, your future husband?"

"Very funny." Mary felt a guilty twinge, but texted quickly, **sorry, have to work. Will explain later.** She hit Send. "Now what were you saying about the statute?"

"It's evidently a change in the law. The parent can consent for the minor, which defines 'consent' out of existence as far as a minor is concerned, if you ask me. The parents have all the cards."

Mary's thoughts raced ahead. "So what rights does Allegra have? She has to have some."

"Under Section 1.1(b)(7), at the time of admission, they have to explain the nature of her treatment and the right to object to treatment, by filing a petition with the court." Judy's tone took on her characteristic professorial bent. "If the minor wishes to object, the director of the hospital has to give her a form to provide notice for the request for withdrawal from treatment."

"Who does she have to file it with?"

"The Court of Common Pleas."

Mary thought a minute, because like many legal issues, it only raised more issues. Lawyers loved to argue about everything, even the argument itself. "But which Court of Common Pleas? I assume where the hospital is located, right?"

Judy nodded. "Probably, so we have to figure out where the hospital is."

"When does she have to file it?"

"Forthwith."

"Terrific." Mary looked outside the cab, where traffic was bumper to bumper. "Somebody needs to tell that to rush hour. Forthwith isn't happening."

"It's Wednesday, so I think we have to do it tomorrow or Friday, at least." Judy's eyes darted back and forth as she read her the screen. "This is interesting. It says that minors from fourteen to seventeen years old have the right to object to treatment, but Allegra's thirteen." She looked up, cocking her head. "The statute doesn't seem to address what rights thirteen-year-olds have, if any."

"We'll find out when we file an objection to treatment."

"Hold your horses, partner." Judy returned to her reading. "Under Section 8, the court will appoint an attorney for the minor, assuming she doesn't have one." She looked up, her eyes narrowing in thought. "I remember most of these commitment issues involve people who are homeless or wards of the state. Allegra is an unusual case, because she's neither of those things, and it cuts against her."

"How?" Mary's phone chimed to signal a text coming in, and she scrolled to check it. It was from Anthony, saying, **can you do Friday night? They say they can all do Friday night.**

"Your pesky fiancé again? Sext him back."

"And record my cellulite forever?" Mary texted back, **I don't know for sure. Can I tell you tomorrow?** She hit Send and slipped the phone back into her blazer pocket, so she could concentrate. Every time she tried to multitask, she messed up all the tasks, and she had learned she wasn't good at multi.

"Anyway, it's easy to see how this would work in Allegra's case."

"How would that work?" Mary was trying to get back on track.

"I mean, I can see how it wouldn't be hard to have Allegra committed, given the resources of the family. The Gardners have the means to get her to a first-rate, really expensive therapist, who diagnoses her, and is very willing to please her wealthy and powerful parents."

"Like an expert witness."

"Exactly, but a reputable one. One who's unbiased, not a whore."

"Nice talk." Mary couldn't help but smile. Judy was always more free talking about sex, but Mary had been raised better and she knew sex was dirty.

"Allegra essentially gets railroaded, probably to one of the nicest mental hospitals around, but it's greased just the same."

"So what happens under the statute, is there a hearing? She should have some modicum of constitutional rights."

"Yes, a hearing."

"When?"

"Within seventy-two hours of filing the petition."

"Lock and load, Gardners." Mary felt her juices flowing, and she didn't even know she had juices to flow. "At the hearing, what do we have to prove?"

"Let me see." Judy's attention returned to her screen. "For treatment to continue against the minor's wishes, the court has to find that she has a diagnosed mental disorder, that it's treatable in the facility, and that the facility is the least restrictive environment."

Mary thought fast. "So the argument we should attack is the last, the least restrictive environment. I bet we can show that she could be treated on an outpatient basis, seeing a psychiatrist every day if she has to. There's no reason for her to be in any kind of hospital, full-time."

"Right, but we can't do any of this without more facts." Judy nodded, mulling it over. "We have to find her a shrink who will treat her, and do a lot more homework before going to court."

"Whatever it takes, we'll do it."

Judy returned to reading and scrolling. "I see here she does have some rights, once admitted, at least an adult admitted under Act 302 would."

"Like what?"

"The right to three completed phone calls, and she can give to the facility the names of three people who should be kept informed of her progress." Judy frowned as she read. "And if she were an adult, under the Patient's Bill of Rights, she'd have the right to see a lawyer in private at any time and also the right to be assisted by any advocate of her choice in the assertion of her rights."

"Thank God. So we're going in."

"That's only if the Patient's Bill of Rights applies to a thirteen-year-old."

"It should, she's a patient, isn't she?"

"Hmm." Judy consulted her iPhone again, tapping away. "I wonder which hospital she is in. You know they must have her in a super-nice place, but there can't be that many of those on the East Coast, can there?"

"It may not be on the East Coast. If I know them, they stashed her as far away as they can."

Judy frowned at the screen as she kept scrolling. "It looks like there's a bunch of really nice places, and now that I think of it, it's not like we can just go knocking on doors. The patients at any particular hospital will be confidential, so we have no way of knowing where she was taken unless we find out from the Gardners, or we subpoena them."

"Now you're talking." Mary met Judy's gaze directly, but saw an undercurrent of ambivalence. "What?"

"I'm concerned that we're venturing into an area of the law we don't know, and also, it's not what she hired us for."

"We have an emergency, don't you think? She got committed because she hired us. They think she has this ridiculous justice obsession syndrome."

"I hear you, but slow down." Judy lowered the iPhone and eased back into the seat. "It's a huge question whether Act 147 applies to thirteen-year-olds, much less the Patient's Bill of Rights designed for adults. Obviously, Allegra loses rights the younger she is. I'd have to study the case law."

"If you study the case law, we don't have time to act. If the statute's new, maybe the cases haven't been decided yet." Mary didn't get it. "Let's just make the argument and let them come back. Rock and roll, run and gun, and several other lawyery clichés, like Bennie."

"Who *are* you?" Judy grinned crookedly.

"A new me!" Mary glanced outside the window at the traffic, which hadn't moved an inch. The cab wasn't cutting it, and she wanted to get on the road. "Did you ever take a subway in Philly?"

"No."

"Then let's do it. Forthwith."

Chapter Twenty-one

It wasn't until late afternoon that Mary and Judy reached Houyhnhnm Farm, where they sat at the iron gate, waiting for the buzzer to be answered. They had pressed it three times, with no reply, which only set Mary's teeth more on edge. "I didn't drive all the way out here to not even be seen."

"Agree."

"Come on, somebody has to be home. This is a huge property with a home office building. They're ditching us and hoping we'll give up."

"Good luck with that. We never give up. We're lawyers."

"Right. We make pests of ourselves for a living."

Judy smiled. "And now we know there's a maid. Remember, Tim Gage told us she still works for them? Janet Wolsey."

"Right again. You wanna snoop around? You love that."

"Totally." Judy smiled, and they both got out of the car and walked up to the gate. Lush green ivy covered the wrought iron, and they gripped the bars, on the outside looking in, like felons with J.D. degrees.

"Hello, anybody home?" Mary called out, but nobody answered. All she could see were the grassy pastures in the distance and the tree-lined gravel road, which she knew led to the right. A hazy sun shone on the quiet, lovely property, and the only sound was the buzzing of an errant fly.

"Do you see what I see?" Judy gestured at the stone stanchions flanking the gate, next to tall evergreens and smaller yellow-green bushes that clustered together, overgrown in a cultivated manner. "They planted this stuff for privacy, not security. It's a man-made forest, there's no bars or fence."

"So?"

"We could leave the car and walk right through. How do you feel about hiking?" Judy grinned slyly, and Mary didn't hesitate, for the first time in her life.

"I'd give it a try."

"Why not? What's the worst they can do? Throw us out?"

"Shoot us."

"Then they'll have to answer to your mother."

Mary smiled. "They have a gun, but she has a wooden spoon."

"So they're dead."

"Exactly."

"Follow me, hiking virgin." Judy left the driveway for the evergreens, moved a few branches aside, and wedged her way into the trees. "I love to hike. We used to do it all the time, in the Sierra Madres and the Grand Tetons."

"Good for you." Mary pressed a branch away from her face, trying not to get scratched. Unlike her, Judy had grown up in Northern California, where she climbed mountains, on purpose. "Think there's snakes here?"

"No, silly," Judy called back. "Only bears."

"Very funny." Mary made her way through the trees and over the underbrush. Twigs snapped under her pumps, and the air smelled like Pine-Sol. She could lose her way without graffiti to guide her. "Remember those pictures you used to have in your office, of your whole family covered with cables? The first time I saw them, I thought you worked for Comcast."

"Ha!" Judy plunged ahead, her lemony blonde hair a bright spot among the dense green needles. "The Carriers are trailblazers from way back."

"The DiNunzios are followers from way back."

"Now we're having fun!" Judy called out, from somewhere inside the forest.

"Yay?" Mary called back, trying to sound positive.

"Here we go!" Judy vanished into a sunny clearing, and Mary popped out of the woods behind her, brushing leaves from her suit.

"Look at me, I'm The Nature Channel."

"You did well." Judy turned toward the house and the aviary, up ahead. "Let's get going. How far do you think we'll make it down this road before they come out?"

"It won't be long." Mary fell into step beside her, glancing behind when she thought she heard something, but there were no bears about.

"Wonder who will meet us and start yelling."

"Patel." Mary kept walking, feeling like a gunslinger heading into town for a lawyer showdown.

"Disagree. I say Gardner." Judy held her head high, and if she was concerned, it didn't show. "Gardner doesn't strike me as the kind of man who hides behind his lawyer."

"Bet me."

"Okay, let's bet your engagement ring. Then you'll have an excuse when you lose it."

"Ouch, that's harsh." Mary looked left and spotted Allegra's beehives in the distance, abandoned. "How sad. She didn't even get to paint them."

"That *is* sad, "Judy said, her tone softening. "I like her, I do. I think she's sweet."

"Bastards."

"That's the spirit. Get your hate on, would you?"

"On it. Look." Judy gestured at the house, and Mary's anger flickered when she saw a commotion at the portico. Men were gathering, but it was too far away to make out their faces, but it looked like Gardner and Patel were among them.

"It's the girls vs. the boys. Maybe we both win."

"Gimme the ring anyway. I'll wear it through my nose."

"Remember your last piercing? Enough said." Mary tried to get calm when a gleaming white Escalade approached the house, stopped at the portico, then Gardner and Patel climbed inside the backseat, closing the doors. "Here they come. Ready?"

"If they don't run us over."

"Let's stop and stand our ground." Mary halted and watched the car come, driving faster then she would've liked. Chickens fluttered panicky in the aviary when the big Escalade barreled past. "I'll take the lead."

"Okay, but keep your temper. All we need is to find out where she is. If we get that, mission accomplished." Judy straightened to her full height, almost five ten, which always made Mary feel like she was standing with a sequoia. She braced herself as the Escalade braked ten feet from them, spraying gravel and chalky white dust. The big engine idled, and the driver made a brawny shadow behind the smoked window glass. The back two doors opened, and John Gardner got out of the closer one, with Patel emerging on the far side.

"Hello, John." Mary suppressed her anger and took a few steps in their direction. "Perhaps you didn't get my phone message, but we're looking for Allegra."

"Allegra is not available at this time." Gardner's tone was cold and firm. Patel came up from behind him, saying nothing. "You're trespassing on this property. I'll ask you to leave immediately."

"John, Allegra has the right to consult with a lawyer under Pennsylvania law. Please tell us where she is, so that she can exercise that right."

"It's none of your business where my daughter is."

"It's exactly my business where your daughter is. Judy and I intend to meet with her, file an objection to treatment with the Court of Common Pleas, and get her out of there."

"Really." John scoffed. "If you don't know where she is, how do you know it's not the best place for her?"

"Because she doesn't need to be in a residential facility." Mary didn't bat an eye. "She's hardly a danger to herself or anyone else."

"How can you be so sure? Do you know my daughter better than I do? She was mentally incompetent when she hired you, and any contract she had with you, whether oral or written, is null and void."

"We'd be here whether we had a contract or not. More importantly, we care about your daughter and we want to help her get what she wants."

"Why don't we test that proposition?" John glowered at Mary, flinty in the waning sunlight. "For your information, payment on the check she wrote for your retainer has already been stopped. I'm taking steps to remove the trustee of her trust, and no other trustee will make any further distributions because of her incompetency. So if you're not getting paid, I assume this is good-bye."

"You assume wrong." Mary couldn't keep the bitterness from her voice. "So I guess we passed your test. Or maybe flunked it, I don't know which."

"You intend to represent her without being compensated?"

"Yes, absolutely." Mary's mouth went dry, though she meant what she said. "We will prove to the court that inpatient treatment is not the least restrictive environment to treat whatever mental illness Allegra has, if indeed she has any at all, other than disagreeing with her controlling father."

"Leave my property this minute." John raised his voice, and behind him, Patel stirred on the gravel.

"Please tell us where she is, and we'll be happy to leave." Mary gestured at Patel. "Ask Neil. He'll tell you that it won't look good in court that you stonewalled us on basic information like this. On the contrary, it helps to prove our point."

"So you're refusing to leave my property when requested to do so?" John folded his arms in his pressed oxford shirt. "That's trespassing, plain and simple, Counselor."

"Please." Mary made a last-ditch effort to reason with him. "We're on the opposite sides of the fence, but the least you can do is play fair. If you think you're right, fight us, but don't hide the ball. Tell us where you sent your daughter."

"I don't need to do that, and I'm about to have you escorted off my property. If you resist, you'll be arrested." John tilted his chin upward, and as if on cue, the sounds of police sirens blared on the street beyond the trees. "We at The Gardner Group find the occasional intruder or disgruntled employee on the grounds, and the West Whiteland Township police are kind enough to come by, to prevent trouble."

"You should be ashamed of yourself," Mary shot back, angry, mostly at herself. She'd have to step up her game if she wanted to go toe-to-toe with John Gardner. He played hardball, and she'd been underestimating him at every turn, to her disadvantage, and worse, to Allegra's. The police siren screamed as it came closer, the cruiser probably pulling in front of the gate.

Judy touched her arm. "Mary, let's go back to the car. We're wasting our time and we'll see them in court."

"No, I'm not finished," Mary said, through gritted teeth. Tears that she couldn't explain came to her eyes. "John, what are you thinking? You're ruining your daughter's life, don't you see that?"

"How dare you!" John's eyes flared in anger, and Patel took a protective step closer to him.

"Mare, we should go." Judy squeezed Mary's arm, but she pulled it away and stepped closer to John, barely in control.

"You're making her crazy, John!" Mary shouted, though a black police cruiser with gold stripes was already driving down the gravel road toward them, its siren drowning out her words. "Taking her from her home, from the things she loves, like those bees! Why, for asking questions? For caring about her sister? A good father would be proud of her!"

"I *am* a good father! I love my daughter!" John shouted back, heedless of Patel at his side.

"You treat her like property, she said it herself!" Mary felt Judy's hand on her arm, but ignored it. "You put her away to shut her up!"

"I put her away to *save her life!*" John yelled, his face flushing and every vein in his neck bulging. "She tried to kill herself, did she tell you that? No, of course not! That's why she came home! That's why she left school!"

"*What?*" Mary said, stunned. She thought she heard him wrong, the siren was so loud.

"Allegra tried to kill herself, a month ago, and I don't want her to try it again!" John seemed suddenly to falter, stepping backwards, and Patel tugged him away by the elbow.

"Mare, please, let's go." Judy pulled a stricken Mary away as the cruiser stopped and cut its sirens, plunging them all into merciful silence. Two officers in black uniforms sprung from the front seat, a skinny one and the heavyset driver, who waved at John in an official way.

"Mr. Gardner, Mr. Patel, we'll take it from here!"

"Thanks, Will!" Patel called back, hustling John back to the Escalade. "Escort them off the property, if you would. We won't press charges, this time."

"Will do, Mr. Patel. We'll be in afterwards to take a statement. Ladies, come with us, please." The heavyset officer gestured, John and Patel disappeared inside the white Escalade, and a shaken Mary and Judy found themselves hustled into the backseat of a squad car, where they were driven out through the gate, and after producing ID and given a stern lecture, were returned to their car, where they finally spoke to each other.

"My God, she tried to commit *suicide*?" Mary turned to Judy, sickened and confused.

"It's awful, but look what I found." Judy's lips parted in surprise, and she held out a crumpled piece of scrap paper about the size of a business card. "This was on my seat, just now. Somebody must've put it in the car while we were gone."

Mary looked down in astonishment. On the paper was scribbled in crude handwriting.

Allegra at Churchill Institute, Sinking Spring

Judy sighed sadly. "I know what you're thinking, but do me a favor. Drive up the road and park. We need to talk."

Chapter Twenty-two

Mary leaned against the BMW, folding her arms across her chest. They'd driven deeper into the countryside and parked along a quiet road. Rows of low, leafy green crops blanketed the surrounding fields, and the humidity had increased, bringing up the oddly chemical odor of fertilizer. The sun burned low, dipping behind the mounded treeline and streaking the sky a hazy orange, like the top of an over-cooked lasagna.

"You want to go to the Churchill Institute, correct?" Judy asked, but didn't wait for an answer, gesturing as she paced at the side of the road, in professor mode. "I don't know if I want to do that, not yet. First, it's so late, almost six o'clock."

"Sinking Spring is only an hour away," Mary said, though in truth, she felt confused after what happened and was grateful for the chance to talk with Judy. "We can be there after dinner."

"How do you know that?"

"I grew up in Pennsylvania, even if I've never been beyond 45th Street."

"Have you heard of the Churchill Institute?"

"No, but I assume it's a private psychiatric hospital, but you could look that up with your trusty iPhone."

"What if they don't have visiting hours that late?"

"That's also knowable, but I bet they do. This isn't a normal visit, anyway. They'd let her see her attorneys in an emergency. Didn't you say she has that as one of her rights?"

"Only if the Patient's Bill of Rights applies to her, and if the Churchill Institute allows it, I assume." Judy shook her head, pacing. "That's what I mean. We have to get our act together, and after what John told us about Allegra's attempting suicide, I'm not so sure we're in the right anymore. Hear me out."

"Okay." Mary had known Judy long enough to expect her to react this way and she couldn't say that Judy was wrong.

"Before, we probably had a winning argument on whether Allegra should be in an inpatient facility. Now it's clear that we need more facts before we make that argument, much less win it."

Mary counted herself lucky in having a best friend like Judy, who didn't say I-told-you-so when she could have.

"If Allegra attempted suicide a month ago, she clearly qualifies as being a danger to herself, even under the adult standard for involuntary commitment." Judy frowned, her head down as she paced. The short strands of hair at her crown blew in the soft breeze, waving like a pale yellow fan. "I don't want to risk that girl's life by removing her from residential care that she might need, and I know you don't, either. The suicide attempt changes everything."

Mary didn't know if she could agree, but her feelings were mixed. "I understand why you say that, and we do need to know more. But part of me still wonders why, if she attempted suicide a month ago, he's committing her now. It's because of us, not the attempt."

"I'm not saying her hiring us wasn't the precipitating factor." Judy stopped pacing and turned to Mary, pursing her lips. "I think it could've been, but the Gardners view this differently than we do, obviously because of her suicide attempt. They see her going to a law-yer as an escalation of her obsession and they worry that if it keeps increasing, she might try to commit suicide again. Do you understand that?"

"Yes," Mary answered.

"I worry about that, too. Do you?"

"Yes, I do." Mary exhaled, gathering her thoughts. "But we have an obligation to her, as her lawyers. You're not suggesting we drop the case, are you?"

"Not sure yet. Maybe."

"Uh-oh." Mary hated disagreeing with Judy, because Judy had such good judgment, and they agreed on everything except wardrobe. "There's no way in the world I want to drop her, and I don't think we could even do that, ethically."

"Why not?" Judy put her hands on her hips, cocking her head. "If she's so depressed or mentally ill that she's incompetent to hire counsel, that releases any ethical obligation we have to continue. To me, it also releases any moral obligation, because continuing to represent her only harms her further, rather than helping her."

"We don't know that yet."

"True, we don't. But it's certainly possible." Judy's blue eyes flashed with concern. "Also, I know it's not about the money, but if we're not getting paid at all, is this really the case you want to take on, right after you make partner? Think about how Bennie would feel about it. We're looking at a long, complicated legal process, which isn't even in our practice field, for free. How will you sell it to her? Do you want to?"

"I do," Mary answered with certainty. "Bennie might throw a fit, but I'm entitled to have a passion project. She has plenty. And in my opinion, part of being a partner is making that assessment yourself."

"Okay." Judy's expression softened. "You might be right about that. It *is* your choice, but here's what you have to ask yourself— what's going on with you and this case?"

Mary's mouth went dry, knowing that Judy was cutting close to the bone.

"Mare, I've never, in all the time I've known you, seen you lose your temper like you did back there. Mind you, you always get emotionally involved with cases, you get emotionally involved with everything." Judy threw up her hands, with a crooked smile. "That's one of the things I love about you. But this time, something is going on I don't understand. You want to talk about it?"

"Honestly, I just feel for that kid. I feel for her relationship to her sister, too. Maybe it has to do with Angie, or Mike, maybe it doesn't." Mary wiped her brow, which was slightly sweaty. "I'm not sure exactly what it's about yet, but I don't think it's the worst thing in the world to identify with the client, especially when no one else around her seems to, in her own family."

Judy fell silent a minute. "So what do you want to do?"

"You know what I want to do. I want to go over to the Churchill Institute tonight and see if we can meet with Allegra, no matter how late it is. It doesn't mean were rushing into court, but I want her to know that we care about her and we're here for her." Mary felt her words resonate in her chest. "I want to look at her and hear her talk, and know she's okay."

"You don't see this as riding to the rescue? Because Allegra may not need rescuing. In fact, it might be that she's exactly where she needs to be right now."

"I agree, but doesn't this note make a difference to you?" Mary waved the little piece of scrap paper like a flag. "Somebody wants us to help Allegra, don't you think?"

"I know, that's weird." Judy nodded. "Do you have any idea who put it in the car?"

"No, and if everything's so hunky-dory at the Gardners', why would somebody slip us this note?"

"You said you heard a noise, but did you see anything or anybody?"

"No, not at all." Mary felt mystified. "It could be anybody who lives or works there. I don't know the cast of characters well enough. All I know is that somebody on the inside is really on our side."

"There's no sides."

"Oh no?" Mary managed a smile. "That's funny, because John Gardner almost got us *arrested*. Me, everybody's favorite good girl, was sitting in the backseat of a *squad car*."

Judy laughed, and Mary could see her forehead ease a bit.

"Look, Jude, I promise not to go off half-cocked. I just want to go to the hospital, sit down, talk to her, and see for myself what's going on. Maybe even talk to her doctor, to understand why she tried to commit suicide."

"Yikes." Judy cringed. "That's so scary, honey. And it's so personal. It's privileged information, anyway."

"Not if she waives it, it isn't." Mary caught herself. "Let's not worry about that now. I want to see Allegra and find out what she wants from us, if anything. If she wants us to proceed, then I want to proceed. If she doesn't, I want to know that too."

Judy nodded, slowly. "But you haven't addressed the open question."

"What?" Mary heard her phone chime in her pocket, signaling an incoming text, but she ignored it. "Go ahead."

"Check the text. You never know, it might be Allegra or Lou."

"I bet it's Anthony." Mary slid out her phone and checked the text, which was from Anthony, reading, **Can you let me know now? Sanchez leaves for weekend if we're not on.** She felt a guilty pang. "It's Anthony, about the drinks."

"Feel free to answer him."

"Sorry." Mary texted back, **okay to Friday, love u but don't wait up tonight.** She hit Send and stuck the phone back into her pocket. "Now what were you saying?"

"What if Allegra wants us to proceed, but after we meet with her or her doctor, we don't think that's in her best interests?"

Mary looked at her best friend and swallowed hard.

Chapter Twenty-three

"We're Mary DiNunzio and Judy Carrier, attorneys for Allegra Gardner," Mary told the older receptionist, who if she was surprised, didn't let it show. "I believe she was admitted earlier today. We'd like to meet with our client."

"Welcome to our campus, ladies," the receptionist said, her tone professionally pleasant. It must've been the end of her shift, because she looked weary, with kind brown eyes that sloped down at the corners, a freckled nose, and a wrinkled smile that seemed forced, at this hour. "Does she have you on her visitors' list?"

"I'm not sure, I expect so." Mary didn't elaborate, keeping the drama to a minimum. She and Judy had decided that their goal was to see Allegra, and it wouldn't help to complicate the situation.

"Let me just check our records a moment." The receptionist swiveled her ergonomic chair to the computer and started hitting keys.

Mary and Judy killed time by taking in the so-called Pavilion, a large, modern circular building with glass on all sides. It looked like a ritzy corporate center, with walls painted a warm golden hue, soft sectional chairs in a brown tweed, and a sisal floor covering. Mary remembered from the website that the Pavilion housed administrative offices, a dining room, a common living room, a cozy library, and ten bedrooms that served as temporary residences for new patients, after intake. It seemed quiet, still, and empty, probably because it was after business hours.

"Here she is." The receptionist read the monitor, running her fingers through her short, graying hair. "And yes, I see both of your names on her visitors' list, so you may visit with her tonight."

"Terrific, thanks." Mary breathed an inward sigh of relief.

"That's funny," the receptionist said, half to herself, frowning at the screen. "You're the only two people on her list."

"We're her only two lawyers."

"It's just that usually, there's family—" The receptionist stopped herself from finishing the sentence, and Mary didn't have to look at Judy to know that they were both thinking the same thing. Allegra hadn't specified her family on her visitors' list, so maybe there were sides, after all, but Mary wasn't the kind of girlfriend to say I-told-you-so, either.

The receptionist cleared her throat. "As I was saying, I see that Ms. Gardner was admitted to our Adolescent Diagnostic and Treatment Unit, and visiting hours for ADTU end at eight o'clock." The receptionist's gaze shifted to the institutional clock on the wall, which read seven thirty. "So you have about half an hour."

"No problem. Where do we meet with her? Do we go to her room, or how does that work?"

"Oh, no." The receptionist gestured behind her. "I'll have her brought up, and if she wants to meet with you, we have private rooms off of the sitting area which we reserve for that purpose."

"Okay, thank you."

"Excuse me a sec while I call." The receptionist picked up the receiver of her beige desk phone and pressed a few buttons. "Morty? I have a Ms. DiNunzio and a Ms. Carrier to see Ms. Gardner. She's the new one, in Room Seven. If she's available and wants to visit, could you bring her up? Thanks." The receptionist hung up the phone and glanced up at Mary and Judy. "I'll get a call back, if she's not coming. In the meantime, may I have your IDs, such as a driver's license?"

"Of course." Mary dug in her purse for her wallet and fished out her ID, while Judy did the same, then they passed them across the counter, which was a glistening curve of butterscotch granite topping a modern desk of blondish wood. The receptionist began to enter Mary's information in the computer, and Judy leaned over the counter.

"Can you tell us a little about the hospital?"

"Certainly. I've been here since it opened, twenty-eight years ago, so I know just about everything."

"I saw the plaque coming in, which shows that it's ranked in the top ten freestanding psychiatric hospitals in the country, by *U.S. News & World Report.*"

Listening, Mary knew that Judy was already lobbying for leaving Allegra, but she didn't mind hearing a sales pitch, either.

"Here at Churchill Institute, we provide twenty-four-hour care, seven days a week, unlocked, on seventy-eight wooded acres, with trails and the like." The receptionist moved on to Judy's driver's license. "We have twenty-five psychiatrists for two hundred patients, and eight separate buildings, excluding the pool and gym, which is in its own building."

Judy nodded politely. "What sort of therapy do you offer someone like Allegra, in ADTU? Does she have a specific psychiatrist and who would that be?"

"We're not permitted to give out information like that with respect to any particular patient, however in general, our patients have a team that includes doctors, nurses, mental health specialists, and a clinical case manager." The receptionist finished entering their information and hit a button to print two visitors' stickers. "We have an array of therapies in our arsenal, individual, cognitive behavioral, and dialectical behavioral therapy or DBT, which helps our adolescents identify triggers to stress and aids them in developing methods to cope with self-destructive behaviors. Of course, we offer family therapy and psychopharmacology, which is administered after a thorough evaluation by a team of child psychiatrists."

"I read on the website that patients are evaluated upon intake." Judy had read aloud to Mary, on the way over. "Would an adolescent patient have a diagnosis, this early in the game?"

"Generally, yes, but it's not a given. It depends on whether the appropriate staff members are available to do the evaluation upon intake, but every adolescent will be seen in the first seventy-two hours, without exception, and they will receive a psychiatric and psychosocial assessment and an individualized treatment plan is established." The receptionist handed Mary and Judy adhesive name tags in gold-and-white, evidently the school colors. "Many of our adolescents deal with depression and anxiety, peer victimization, self injury, suicidal ideation, school avoidance, obsessive-compulsive disorders and the like, and we also have separate units which treat eating disorders and substance abuse."

"I see, thanks." Judy and Mary stickered themselves, just as a delighted shout came from down the hallway.

"Mary, Judy!"

Mary turned to see Allegra leaving her escort behind in the hallway and running toward them in her new bee T-shirt, baggy jeans, and Converse sneakers, with a wan smile, her skinny arms outstretched, and her hair flying out behind her.

"Allegra!" Mary called back, her heart lifting at the sight, and on impulse, she ran to Allegra, scooped her up in her arms, and swung her around. It was then that she spotted Judy.

And her best friend wasn't smiling.

Chapter Twenty-four

They were shown into a small, private sitting room that contained more brownish sectional furniture, a glass coffee table, and air that smelled vaguely lemony. The room had a paneled door that closed, but a window in the top half revealed the escort in scrubs, who sat just outside the door, lingering discreetly. Mary couldn't help but think back to interviewing Lonnie Stall at the prison, with the guard who remained stationed outside the door. She knew as an intellectual matter that the two institutions were very different, but at heart, it felt like the differences were a matter of style, not substance.

"You guys have to get me out of here, as soon as you can," Allegra said, before they'd even sat down. She perched on the edge of her chair, kneading her long fingers in her lap. "This is ridiculous. I don't need to be here. What can you do to get me out of here?"

Mary avoided Judy's eye. "I know it's hard, but try to stay calm. There are things we can do, if that's what's best for you and—"

"Of course that's what's best for me! What are the things you can do? This is like a nightmare! I don't need to be here, they tricked me to get me here." Allegra spoke more quickly then she did normally, and her forehead knotted with anxiety. "They told me we were going to Shadwell Apiary, a really big bee operation near here, so we could see it and use it as a model to set up my hives, then all of a sudden, they pulled into this driveway. It's a good thing I had my phone with me, or you wouldn't have even known!"

Mary felt terrible for Allegra, to be betrayed by her own parents, but she had to keep her eyes on the legal ball. "Let me ask you a few questions first. Did they evaluate you when you came in, like did you receive some kind of diagnosis?"

"No, they said the main guy wasn't here. Dr. Argenti, he's like a specialist, but it doesn't matter. I want to get out of here. Thank God for you guys." Allegra brightened, and her forehead eased. "I knew you'd come, that's why I put you on the visitor sheet. I really appreciate you're trying to help me."

"You didn't put your family on the visitors' list, we heard."

"Why would I? They're the *last* people I want to see! I can't believe they did this to me." Allegra's eyebrows sloped down, and her voice broke. "I mean, I'm used to being away from home and all, but this is so *weird*. It's not a school, it's a *mental hospital*."

"They're just trying to help people, honey. All illness needs treatment."

"I know, I just never knew they really thought I was crazy, not really." Allegra's eyes filmed, and her bottom lip trembled. "It just makes me sad, like they think I'm not even worth having at home."

"I understand." Mary got up and gave her a quick hug, unable to restrain herself anymore. "This is the thing you have to understand, honey. Your parents believe that they're helping you. They just go about it in a way you won't always agree with, or understand. People make mistakes, and you have to forgive them that. That's part of being a human being. Okay?"

"Yes." Allegra hung her head, so Mary gave her a final squeeze and sat down next to Judy, whose expression remained impassive. Allegra sniffled, just the slightest. "You remind me so much of Fiona.

She always tried to see the best in people. She used to fight with my parents a lot, especially my mom, but she was always like, they're trying to do the right thing they're just idiots."

"There you go. That's one way to think about it." Mary smiled, touched by the comparison to Fiona.

"So how do we get me out of here? And I know that money is important, so don't worry, we'll just add onto the bill from the trust."

Mary hesitated. "We're not worried about money, but you should know your father spoke to the trustee of your grandfather's trust, and they stopped payment on your retainer."

Allegra frowned. "I don't have a retainer. I don't get my braces off for another year."

Mary avoided Judy's eye. "I mean the $5,000 check you wrote us. The trustee stopped payment on it."

"Oh no, I'm so sorry." Allegra's expression darkened. "My dad, he must've done this, so I couldn't hire you. I promise you guys, when I get out, I'll make sure you get paid, don't worry about it."

"We're not worried about it." Mary thought a minute. "Allegra, we're here for you and we want to help you. I wish I could get you out of here tonight, but we have to be responsible and think about what's in your best interests."

"What do you mean by that?" Allegra asked, wounded, and Mary tried a more diplomatic tack.

"There is a legal procedure by which you can object to your treatment, and to do that, we have to file a petition with the court and prove that being here isn't the least restrictive alternative for you. In other words, we would have to prove that you could be treated as effectively on an outpatient basis."

"Okay, let's do that."

"We don't have all the facts we need, though. For example, how long have you been home?"

"About a month."

"Were you seeing a therapist at home, at all?"

"No, not yet. My parents wanted me to see someone in the city, but I haven't gone yet."

"Did you see a therapist at school?"

"Yes, in the beginning, I went twice a week, but now we're down to once a week."

"Who was the therapist and what do you think of him or her?"

"It was a woman and her name was Lydia Bright, and I liked her. It was nice to go and talk to her, but I was ready to phase it out anyway." Allegra perched forward in the chair. "Like I told you guys, I know I was depressed by Fiona's murder, but the more I started to think about doing something about it, like hiring somebody to solve it, I started to feel better."

Mary paused, not knowing if she should bring up the issue. "Allegra, we did go to your house to talk to your parents before we came here, and they told us that they brought you here because they were afraid for your life, that you would be a danger to yourself. They told us you had tried to commit suicide."

Allegra flushed. "Oh. That's embarrassing."

"There's no reason in the world you should be embarrassed by that. It's okay to have whatever emotion you have, even the darkest." Mary paused. "You know, I didn't mention this to you, but one of the reasons I understand you as well as I do is that my husband, my first husband, was murdered, a long time ago."

Allegra's eyes flared slightly, and Judy stirred, but didn't interrupt.

"Afterwards, I was very sad, I felt awful. Couldn't sleep, couldn't eat, was having dark thoughts. I didn't try to kill myself, but there were one or two nights when it didn't seem like the worst idea in the world." Mary had never told anyone that, not even Judy. "So you shouldn't be ashamed that you felt that way. It just shows that we have a heart, and sometimes things are harder than we can bear."

"That's true." Allegra swallowed visibly, her little Adam's apple going up and down in her skinny neck.

"The reason I tell you the story is to tell you that I understand. And under the law, if someone is a danger to themselves, they meet the standard for involuntary civil commitment, particularly if there has been a suicide attempt in the past month, as there was with you."

Allegra emitted a tiny sigh, like the last air deflating from a birthday balloon.

"So you understand. If we went into court now, on these facts, to try and get you released, we would lose"—Mary could see she was upset, so she added—"and both of us want what's best for you, not only as your lawyers, as a personal matter. If they didn't have a chance to give you a diagnosis yet, then we both think the better course is for you to stay here, get your diagnosis and treatment plan, then we can all take it from there."

Allegra's eyes filmed again. "It's like I'm being punished."

"No, you're not being punished. But a judge looks at the case objectively, and because you're a minor, and so young, they're really going to look out for you. They are going to do what they think is right for you, even if you don't agree."

"But I don't really want to kill myself. I didn't really think I would die." Allegra's tone dropped suddenly, so hushed that Mary almost couldn't hear her.

"What made you do it, honey? Can I ask, or does that upset you?"

"You can ask, and it doesn't upset me." Allegra's tone strengthened. "I had a really big fight on the phone with my dad, because I told him that when I turned thirteen, I was going to hire a lawyer with my trust money, and he freaked out. He said a lot of things, bad things that hurt my feelings." Allegra's bottom lip trembled again, but she kept it together.

Mary wondered what Allegra's father had said, wishing she'd decked him on the driveway.

"My mom didn't say anything, she didn't even get on the phone, but that's nothing new. Ever since Fiona died, my mom has been, like, a wreck. She started drinking, and now she stopped, but still, she's just, I don't know." Allegra faltered. "It's like she checked out, like I don't have a mom anymore. He runs the show."

Mary didn't say anything, because Allegra needed no encouragement to talk, speaking directly from a heart that sounded broken.

"So after the fight, that night, I just didn't think that even if I had the money it would make any difference, that I would never know what really happened to Fiona, and that I didn't really have anybody who understood me, or got me, or even wanted me." Allegra swallowed again. "It just seemed like nothing was ever going to change, so I guess, I just, well, I took the pills that Dr. Bright gave me, all of them."

"Were you on meds?" Mary asked, gently.

"I was already weaning off of them, which is why they think it happened. Me, too. The drugs are whack." Allegra pursed her lips. "They're such a pain, the meds, getting the right one and the dosages. And sometimes they make you sleepy or not think straight, or more depressed than you were before."

"I bet," Mary said, sympathetically. "So what did you take?"

"It was only Wellbutrin, and all they did was make me sick, and the assistant headmaster found me and got me to the hospital, where they pumped my stomach. It was a pretty big deal, I guess, and my parents fired Dr. Bright and flew up and brought me home." Allegra straightened up, seemingly an act of will, to cheer up. "Then I started to feel a lot better, when I was home. I was in my room, I had my hives, and I saw that I could do what I wanted to with the trust money and I started to feel better. I would never try to kill myself, not really, not ever again. I swear it. If they let me out of here, I will tell the court that. I could explain everything in a way that a judge could understand. You could put me on the witness stand, and I know I could convince him."

Mary patted her hand. "I'm sure you could and I'd bet on you in a minute. But the question is, as lawyers, when is the best time to go to court, and now is not the best time."

"No?" Allegra asked, but it came out like a moan.

"No, I'm sorry." Mary couldn't stand seeing her so forlorn. "But we all want the same thing, which is you happy and healthy, and back home. And in the meantime, Judy and I don't have to be idle.

We can go forward like we were before. We could still keep going on our investigation of Fiona's murder. We met today with Lonnie Stall and with his lawyer Bill Brandt."

"You did?" Allegra asked, surprised. "That's so cool, what did they say?"

Mary thought about Allegra's letters to Lonnie Stall, but this wasn't the time to bring that up. "Bottom line, Lonnie Stall says he's innocent, and his lawyer concedes that he may have not given him the best representation."

"Is that good?"

"Yes." Mary didn't go into the legal niceties of ineffectiveness of counsel. They didn't have that much time, and she could already see the guard at the door. "But Lonnie also says that he didn't have a relationship with Fiona at all."

"Just what he said in court."

"Right."

"Why is he lying?"

"I don't know." Mary let it go. "We also met with Tim Gage, who didn't tell us much, because he wasn't at the party that night and—"

"Tim was at the party. I saw him."

"What?"

Allegra blinked. "Tim was at the party the night Fiona was killed. I know, I saw them together."

Mary and Judy exchanged glances, equally mystified. "Where did you see them, do you remember?"

"Not very well, but I think they were outside, out back, by the back exit. If you knew the offices, you'd understand. I could draw you a picture."

"Not now, we don't have time. Just tell me what you remember."

"Okay." Allegra frowned in thought. "I remember because my mom and I went looking for Fiona and I found her friends, and not her, and they said she was outside."

"So your mom saw Fiona?"

"I don't know. I just know I did, and she told me they broke up, or something." Allegra scratched her head. "I don't know how much I remember. I just know I saw Tim, and that I got the idea that I wasn't supposed to be there, like she waved me away, or something. Whatever, I saw him there."

"Were they fighting?"

"I don't know."

"Do you know why he would lie to us about that?"

"No." Allegra looked stumped. "Why is everybody lying?"

"Could you remember wrong?"

"No."

Mary didn't dare look over at Judy, who was undoubtedly thinking that it was more likely that an almost seven-year-old Allegra was remembering wrong or imagining things, than that everybody was lying. "Were the friends Sue Winston, Mary Weiss, and Honor Jason, and Hannah Wicker?"

"Yes, they were there. Three of them were killed, though, in the accident. It's so sad."

"We know, Tim told us. But there is one friend, Hannah Wicker, whom he mentioned survived. Do you know where she is?"

"No, I don't."

"Was she close to Fiona?"

"Not as close as the others, but in the group. She came over our house a lot. She was a great rider and she used to exercise Paladin, my mom's horse."

Mary thought a minute. "Allegra, let me switch gears for a minute and ask you something. Who are you close to at home?"

"Nobody, really."

Mary couldn't even imagine what that felt like. "Who's in the house on a regular basis, including staff? Is Janet Wolsey there?"

"Yes. How do you know about Janet?"

"Tim told us. How do you get along with her?"

"Great, she's wonderful." Allegra smiled. "She's so nice and she practically raised me, after Fiona died. She really loved Fiona, too, and I guess I'm close to Alasdair, too."

"Who's that?"

"Alasdair Leahy, our caretaker."

"Do you know where he lives?"

"Sure, in a house on the property. He's been with us for a long time, too, since I was little. He used to drive me to school and stuff, if my mom was drinking." Allegra flushed again. "I feel bad, telling you about that. Don't tell anybody, okay?"

"Of course."

"Alasdair is great. He does the stables and takes care of the roses, too. He knows everything about horses. He's super handy, though now that he's older, his back hurts."

"And how about Janet? Where does she live?"

"She has a room in her own quarters in the house."

Mary got an idea. "Let me ask you something. Was Alasdair or Janet at the opening party, by any chance, the night Fiona was killed?"

"Yes, they were both there. They're like family."

Mary made a mental note, and she knew Judy would, too. "Let's switch gears a minute. How about down at the cottage? How does that work? Who's there?"

"About six people, like secretaries and stuff. The main secretary, I guess she is like an office administrator, is Millie Marco. She's been there a long time, too."

"Was Millie at the party, the night Fiona was killed?"

"I don't remember, but she would've been there. I'm not as close to the people in the cottage. Fiona used to work there after school, doing filing and stuff, but I was too little. My uncles sometimes come over and work in the cottage, when they don't need to go into town. They don't like the drive and it's easier."

"Tim Gage told us that, at the time Fiona was murdered, she was working on a big project for your uncle Richard, and that he's really nice. Can you tell me anything about that?"

Allegra shook her head. "No, I don't know what she was working on when she was down there. Just knew she worked there, and my dad always paid her, which she liked."

"When she was working down there, would you be at the house?"

"Yes, before I went to boarding school."

"Who babysat for you, during those times?"

"Janet."

"Hold on, let me show you something." Mary slipped a hand into her purse, pulled out the scrap of paper with the handwriting, and showed it to Allegra. "We found this in our car, which is how we knew you were here. Do you know who wrote this? Do you recognize the handwriting?"

"Yes, totally. Alasdair wrote that."

"Aha! Mystery solved. You're sure?"

"Totally." Allegra moved her index finger back and forth over the paper. "Alasdair wrote this. He's English. My mom used to go over there on riding vacations with Fiona, and that's where she met Alasdair."

"Do you ride?"

"No, I'm allergic."

Mary noticed that outside the door, the escort was standing up and stretching. "Do you know why Alasdair would tell us where you were, when your parents wouldn't?"

"He loves me."

"Your parents love you, too, sweetie."

"Oh, right." Allegra permitted herself a sardonic smile. "I keep forgetting."

Mary felt her pain. She couldn't blame Allegra and she didn't want to judge her. "How did Alasdair know where you are? Would your parents tell him?"

"My mom would have, when she used to ride. He would tack Paladin up for her and they would ride together. But she hasn't ridden since Fiona."

"So how did he know?"

"He's in the house all the time. He could have heard them talking."

"How come you didn't hear them talking?" Mary noticed the escort outside the door, motioning to her through the window, then pointing at his wristwatch.

"I was outside a lot. I was actually avoiding them, after I hired you. My dad was pissed."

"Okay, I think our time is up." Mary gestured outside the door, then stood up, and so did Judy. "I don't want to get you in trouble. We better say good-bye, and we'll be in touch with you tomorrow. I assume that's within the rules."

"They gave me a phone in my room, but we're not allowed to use cell phones and they restrict our email and online. You have to call the main number and connect to me." Allegra rose, her forehead collapsing into a new frown. "This sucks, I hate to see you guys go. Do I really have to stay?"

"Yes, honey, for the time being." Mary opened her arms and gave Allegra a final hug, feeling the young girl squeeze her tight. "Don't worry, you're going to be all right."

"Would you visit me? Can you stop by tomorrow?" Allegra sprang out of Mary's arms, alarmed. "Oh my God, I almost forgot to ask you. Can you help me out with something really important?"

"Sure, what?"

"My bees are coming in the mail, and they'll be at the post office tomorrow morning. If you don't pick them up, they'll die."

"*Live bees?*" Mary recoiled. "What, do they come in a box?"

"Yes, with screens for air. They're Italian bees, very docile, and I even got an Italian Queen."

"Is this a joke? I *am* an Italian Queen, and I don't know what to do with live bees."

"You have to get them when the post office opens or they'll die, and please mist them, first thing when you pick them up. They'll be thirsty."

"Bees drink?"

Allegra smiled. "Everything drinks."

"What if I get stung?"

"Are you allergic?"

"No."

"Then you have nothing to be afraid of." Allegra smiled in a way that was supposed to be reassuring, but didn't succeed. "I order from an apiary that sells bees to people who want to get stung."

"They *want* to?" Mary never understood people's sex lives. She was Catholic.

"It's a holistic remedy that helps a lot of people. It's called apitherapy, and you can even buy bee venom in a bottle." Allegra brightened. "I rubbed propolis on my zits and it helped."

"I'll remember that." Mary opened the door. "Just tell me what to do with the bees. Let them out, right?"

"No, then they *will* sting you."

"So what do I do?"

"Bring them to Alasdair. He'll help you. He knows a bit about how to install them."

"A bit?" Mary asked, aghast. "Does he know or not?"

"He's never done it by himself, but he's a sweetheart and he'll help you. He can show you how the smoker works and he knows where my outfit and veil are. Wear them and you'll be fine. You can install the bees with his help."

"I can install software, but bees?" Mary said, dismayed, as the escort approached them. They were out of time, and somehow she was getting stuck babysitting bees, or beesitting. "Can't I just let them die?"

"No, please," Allegra wailed. "Please don't."

"Allegra," Judy chirped up, and they passed through the door. "Does Alasdair have a cell phone?"

"Sure, I'll give you the number." Allegra brightened. "He doesn't email or text, and don't call him this late, okay? He'll be at work at six o'clock in the morning."

Judy turned to wink at Mary. "Think, girl. The bees will help with our next step."

"Great," Mary said, but the only next step she saw was a trip to the emergency room.

Chapter Twenty-five

Mary and Judy left the Pavilion, walking down the long flagstone path to the visitors' parking lot. The night air felt cool and the breeze velvet-soft on Mary's face, and there were no lights this far out in the country. She looked up at the starry bower of night sky, wishing she knew some constellations, and breathed in the loamy smell of fresh crops, but when she exhaled, it sounded like a sigh. "I feel bad leaving her here, all by herself," Mary said, folding her arms across her chest.

"I know you do, but I think it was the best thing for her." Judy walked slightly ahead, her leggy stride characteristically longer, her head bent over her BlackBerry. "God, I have a ton of email."

"She's right, it does suck."

"We could never have gone to court on these facts, and she's smart enough to understand that." Judy scrolled through her email and stepped off the flagstone, taking the most direct path over the grass, though Mary would've stayed on the path. She was a color-within-the-lines kind of girl.

"Can you imagine what it's like to live in a family and not feel close to a single one of them?"

"No." Judy looked up from her BlackBerry and led them through the parking lot, which was empty except for the blue BMW. Circles of light shone on the black asphalt, like hazy halos cast from mercury vapor lamps. "Allegra Gardner is your basic poor little rich girl."

Mary thought it sounded harsh. "She's such a sweet kid, though. She's smart and funny, and she has an open heart."

"I didn't say she didn't." Judy halted at the car and gestured wearily at the door. "You want to unlock it?"

"Sure." Mary dug in her purse for her keys, chirped the door unlocked, and they both got in. "So what's your idea about the bees?" she asked, plugging the key into the ignition, starting the engine, and reversing out of the spot. "And did you follow what she told us later, about misting them and making sure they had enough syrup?"

"No. The bees are a complete nuisance, but they make a perfect excuse to get back on the property."

"True, but *live bees*? Sheesh." Mary steered out of the lot and onto the road that led from the Churchill campus. She switched on her high beams because the darkness was so complete, and her headlights illuminated underbrush, tree trunks, and moths flying this way and that, in random fashion. "I figure we go out to the post office in the morning, after we pick up the plant mister she was telling us about. I assume it's the same thing I use on my fig trees. Maybe I'll bring one from home."

"Let me stop you right there, though. We need to talk about something more important."

"More important than fig trees and bees?" Mary was making a joke, but when she glanced over, Judy wasn't smiling, in the reflected glow of the dashboard lights. "What's up?"

"I'm more worried about this case than I was before, even after today at the farm."

"Why? I feel better about it. We actually have a lead, in Alasdair, and if that note means anything, he might be on our side."

"True, but that's not what I'm talking about. I'm worried about you and Fiona. The stuff I was telling you about before, but more so."

"Like what?" Mary steered through the darkness, trying not to be spooked by the bugs flying into her high beams. They were traveling on another endless country road that she prayed would eventually lead to civilization, or failing that, Philadelphia.

"You were calling her 'sweetie' and 'honey,' and you hugged her."

"So? I do that."

"I know, but even though you do that with a lot of people, she doesn't."

Mary didn't get it. "She needed a hug, and I gave her one."

"Or three."

"What difference does that make?" Mary felt herself on edge, between trying to understand what Judy was saying while worrying if a deer was going to jump out in front of the car, or maybe even a bear or a dragon.

"I just don't think it's such a good idea, and you see that she's already beginning to identify you as her big sister, as Fiona." Judy's tone sounded concerned. "Plus she asked you to visit her, and now you're running around getting her bees, and me, too. I didn't go to law school to go fetch bees, and neither of us have the time to visit her, though I note she didn't ask me, only you."

"But we just said, the bees give us an excuse to talk to Alasdair and get information from them. It's not only getting bees, it's getting information on the case."

"I'm not talking about our motives, I'm talking about the effect we're having on her. Allegra is latching on to us, and by us I mean you. That concerns me."

"I'm trying to understand why."

Judy fell silent a minute, and the only sound was the rumbly tackiness of the BMW's dry tires on the road.

Mary hated silence, so she started yapping. "I'm close to all of my clients. I built an entire client base of people from the neighborhood. Relatives, people's parents, and girls from my high school Latin Club. Every one of my business relationships is personal."

"I know that," Judy said, her tone quieter.

"I go to their weddings, funerals, and their baby showers. I'm god-parents to kids from a plumbing company and an auto body shop. I love them all, I do. It's a different business model. You don't have to be distant to be professional. You just have to be smart and work hard. You just have to care."

"I know all that, too."

"So why is this different?"

"It's different because of the nature of the client. The clients you just named, and I've met plenty of them, are normal adults. They're couples or they have families and support systems."

"So? We take our clients as we find them. We don't pick and choose."

"Allegra is none of those things and has none of that."

"So she needs it, even more."

"She's a depressed young girl, who's completely at odds with her family, which by the way, sounds like it was profoundly traumatized by the murder of Fiona."

"Murder is traumatizing. Can you hold that against them? And how can you hold it against Allegra, if she has an emotional illness?"

"I don't hold it against her, and you know me better than that." Judy's tone changed, but Mary felt like they were sliding toward a fight, which she couldn't seem to derail.

"I do, and that's why I'm surprised."

"I just feel that you're going in a direction in this case I'm not sure I approve of, and now we're not getting paid at all." Judy turned to her, shifting position, which made her voice louder, reverberating off the hard surfaces of the car. "And you were right before, you don't have to justify it to Bennie, you have to justify it to yourself. Is this the best use of your time?"

"To me, it is."

"Is it the best use of mine? I'm not sure I think it is."

"It's so unlike you to not be on board in a case."

"Evidently, it happens, and I'm not on board." Judy sounded re-signed and angry. "Allegra confounds me. She thinks Tim Gage was at the party, she thinks Lonnie Stall was at the house. We run around chasing ghosts or keeping her company in the hospital. She doesn't even want any other visitors but us. I'm an appellate lawyer, not a paid friend. And by the way, we're not even paid."

"She said we will be, in the end, and I believe her."

"But she's thirteen, so she doesn't realize the complexities of trust administration or distribution of a trust's assets, which can take years. She thinks you break open a piggybank." Judy paused. "So, no, I'm definitely not on board. I have plenty of cases to work, and they're only piling up. I'm along for the ride, but you're driving the car."

Mary felt stung. "It sounds like you're not even along for the ride."

"And you don't like that, I can tell."

"Of course I don't like that. It's not like us." Mary steered the car straight, but she felt so out of control of everything, suddenly. Of the cases, of Judy, and of their friendship. "I like it the other way, the way it always is. We work a case together, side-by-side, and we figure it out. We win. We do amazing things. We catch the bad guy. We're a team."

"Not this time," Judy said softly, without rancor, and Mary felt hurt and nonplussed.

"So what do we do now?"

"You're the partner. You tell me. Take me off the case if you want."

"Aw, Judy, don't be that way."

"What way? I mean it, no hard feelings. You have the power now. Wield it."

"If you want off, why don't you just ask me?"

"I wouldn't do that, with Bennie. I'd never *ask* to be taken off a case. If she thought it was the right thing, she'd take me off."

"For real, we're having this conversation?" Mary gripped the steering wheel. Her head began to pound, and her contact lenses were sticking to her corneas like adhesive name tags.

"It's your law firm now, and I'm your associate. Maybe it's kind of fun if we drive around together, trying to answer questions that trouble obsessive children, but is it the best use of the firm's re-sources?"

Mary couldn't understand what was going on without being able to look Judy in the eye. They hadn't eaten in hours, and Mary couldn't help but feel that a nice plate of gnocchi would make all of this weirdness go away.

"Mare? Is that what you really need me to be doing, for your law firm?"

Suddenly, Mary's cell phone rang. "Hold on." She tucked her hand into her pocket, and pulled up the ringing phone, showing the screen to Judy. "Do I need to get this?"

"It's Lou. I'll answer, you talk." Judy took the phone, pressed the button, and answered, "Hey, Lou, it's Judy. Mary's driving. I'm putting you on speaker."

"How's my girls tonight?" Lou's gravelly voice emanated from the BlackBerry and echoed throughout the car.

Mary answered, "We're great. How are you?"

"Okay. Where are you guys? Why aren't you home?"

"It's a long story, but we'll see you first thing in the morning. Got good news for us?"

"Good news and bad news. Which one you want first?"

"The good."

"I'm emailing you the guest list from the party. Another buddy of mine from Blackmore slipped it to me, without his boss knowing."

"Whoa. Nice move." Mary smiled at Judy, but she was looking away, out the window. "Does it show Tim Gage?"

"Lemme check, it's alphabetical."

Mary felt her heart rate quicken, waiting.

"No Tim Gage or any Gage on the list."

"So he wasn't invited, but it doesn't mean he didn't show up." Mary felt more confused than ever. "Allegra says he was there, but he says he wasn't. Can we persuade your buddy to let us have a video-tape?"

"No way. They gave up the guest list only because it's fairly predictable: the Mayor, the Philly Chamber of Commerce, and all the rich people that show up at every benefit. I know from reading the society pages. I'm not sure Lou The Jew would be especially welcome."

Mary smiled. "So I guess we get busy, Lou. I'd ask everybody on the list if they saw anything odd or unusual that night, and also if Tim Gage was there. You can print his picture off his Facebook page."

"They're not gonna talk to me if they're friends of the Gardners, you have to know that. Lemme think if that's the best way to go about it, Mare."

"Okay, we'll talk about it in the morning. I do have a lead I'd like you to get started on."

"Your wish is my command."

"There's a caretaker at the Gardner residence named Alasdair Leahy, he's English. I'd like to find out about him before I meet him tomorrow. Where exactly he lives, anything you can learn."

"I'll start in the morning."

"Lou, I might need it by the morning. I have to go out to the property early, to deal with something, and I'd like it before then." Mary omitted the part about the bee retrieval, avoiding Judy's eye. "There's also a young girl named Hannah Wicker, a classmate of Fiona's at Shipwyn. She's the sole survivor of a horrible car accident that killed Fiona's three other friends, and they'd been drinking. I'm betting she's on Facebook, and Alasdair isn't. I'll take her."

"That damn Facebook's gonna put detectives out of business."

"Ha, not you, Lou."

Lou hesitated. "Mare, you don't sound good. You okay?"

"I'm fine." Mary wasn't inclined to elaborate.

"Judy, what's the matter with our bride? She should be on top of the world."

Judy paused. "She'll be okay, I'll take care of her. Good night, Lou. Thanks for your hard work. Get some sleep."

"You, too," Lou answered, then hung up.

"Well?" Judy hung up the phone. "Am I off the case?"

Mary glanced over at Judy, whose face was illuminated from below by the glowing screen of the BlackBerry, which made her look like a spooky version of herself. "I have a more important question. Are we still best friends?"

"Forever." Judy set the BlackBerry on the console, so even her spooky face was no longer visible. "Now, am I off the case?"

"Yes," Mary answered after a moment, steering into the darkness.

Chapter Twenty-six

Mary locked the front door behind her and let herself into a house that was quiet and still. It was past midnight, so Anthony had already gone to bed, and she set down her purse on the small ladder-back chair in the hallway, oddly relieved not to see him. Maybe because it had taken her almost half an hour to find a parking spot, driving around the block until she was dizzy.

"I want my own parking space," Mary said aloud, to no fiancé in particular. Still, she felt touched to see the bills, mail, and catalogs arranged in neat piles on the console table, sorted into His, Hers, and Theirs, and he'd left the lamp on for her, another thoughtful touch. It was as if she was happy to see the evidence of him, but didn't mind missing him in person. She'd done enough fighting for one night, with Judy, and it left her feeling disoriented and empty.

You have a question to answer, partner.

Mary kicked off her pumps and padded down the hallway, past the darkened living room and into the kitchen, on autopilot. The amber fixture hung over the granite island, where Anthony always left her a note when she got home late. This one was written on a piece of legal paper, since they always had so many canary yellow pads laying around, and it lay next to a ballpoint pen and a flowery pink birthday card that he must've picked out for his mother's birthday.

Mary went over to the note, which read, *"Honey, will you sign the card to Mom? Love you. Get some sleep!"* She picked up the ballpoint, opened the card, and scanned it like a contract before she signed her name after, *Anthony and,* then set the pen down and padded to the refrigerator, where she consumed approximately half an hour of comfort food, including but not limited to a glass of milk, a brownish avocado, hummus with baby carrots, and the entire container of green Ceregnola olives, which coated her lips with a telltale shine, like lip gloss for Italians.

Am I off the case?

The food gave her a second wind, if little comfort, and she watered her fig tree, then left the kitchen, turned out all the downstairs lights, and tiptoed up to her office, where she sat down at her desk and logged into the Internet, with a sour taste in her mouth that had nothing to do with her snack parade. She saw her philly.com home page pop onto the monitor, without focusing on any of the bold-faced news headlines or the wiggly ads for mortgage rates. She felt so strange without Judy, vaguely rudderless, having no sounding board to bounce ideas off of. She'd have to shift to Plan B, working with Lou, whom she loved, but it wasn't the same as working with her best friend.

Judy, what's the matter with our girl?

Mary navigated to her email and scanned the senders' names, who were all clients, so they read like an endless things-to-do list that she'd rather avoid for now. She bypassed them until she got to Lou's email, with its re line that read Confidential, then she clicked Open. It was characteristically blank, since Lou hated to type, but the attachment with the guest list was there and Mary clicked Print, to read it later.

She navigated to Google and plugged in the names of Fiona's friends, the girls who had died in the car crash, Sue Winston, Mary Weiss, and Honor Jason. A lineup of news stories appeared on the screen and she clicked the first one, which opened under a heartbreaking photo of a red car, with its grille smashed cruelly into its shattered windshield, under a headline, TRAGIC ENDING FOR HIGH-SCHOOL FIELD HOCKEY SEASON.

Mary sighed, skimming the article, which contained no new details, except the age of the girls repeated after each of their names, age sixteen, which struck like a blow each time she read it. They were so young, too young to cope with the horror of losing their friend to such an awful and violent murder, but none of that made its way into the story, where they sounded like a bunch of reckless partiers. The alcohol and toxicology tests were still pending, but the girls had already been pronounced guilty in the newspaper, with none of the nuance of the real-life story.

Mary felt her heart go heavy in her chest, and her gaze wandered back to the wrecked car. She flashed on Mike's hideously warped bicycle, wrenched out of shape by the car that had struck him on his daily ride along the West River Drive. Mary hadn't known it wasn't an accident when it had happened, and it had almost cost her her own life to find out the truth. She'd never get over it, and she could never have handled it at all, at sixteen years old. But for the grace of God, she could have been in a car, drinking and trying to outpace the pain. And she couldn't help but add the deaths of Fiona's girlfriends to Fiona's, because the girls were all victims of the same murder. It made Mary more determined than ever to find the real killer.

She hit Print, then skimmed and printed the next few articles about the car crash for her bulletin board in the war room at work, then she navigated back to the Internet, logged onto Facebook, and searched for Hannah Wicker. There were only a few Hannah Wickers, with just one in the Philly suburbs, in Newtown.

Mary edged forward in her chair and opened Hannah Wicker's page. Hannah's email was listed there, and she tapped out an email asking the girl if she would meet to talk about Fiona's murder. Hannah's response came back almost immediately:

How awful, but yes. Say when.

Chapter Twenty-seven

The next morning, Mary scurried down the street, her pumps clattering on the gum-spattered pavement. It was just before dawn, the sky still a dusty blue over the flat rooftops, though the coming light of day would ghost the stars, hiding them in plain sight. Only the runners were out, trying to get some exercise before work, and lights were barely beginning to go on inside the houses. Mary had showered, put on a suit, and left before Anthony even woke up, because she had to get an early start if she was going to reach Chester Springs by the time the post office opened.

Mary kept up her pace, her purse and messenger bag bumping against her hip. She was already feeling stressed that her day would be cut short for El Virus's birthday party tonight, but she tried to keep her residual resentment at bay, though it wasn't easy. She was only on Delancey Street and she had five blocks to go before she reached the car, since the only parking space she could find last night was nowhere near the house. In fact, it was farther than remote parking at the airport, but there were no shuttle buses for women who didn't have the balls to stand up to their fiancé. Nice girls finished last.

Mary slid out her BlackBerry on-the-fly and scrolled through her email, to see if Lou had been able to find out anything about Alasdair overnight. She still felt funny working without Judy, but she told herself to suck it up and opened the email, which was typically terse:

Alasdair Leahy, born, Manchester, England, May 3, 1960. Graduated high school. Emigrated to U.S. 1980. Became U.S. citizen 2003. No criminal record. Employment, Gardner Group, 1992–present. Horse trainer and horse sales, Hagan, Ltd, Unionville, PA, 1987–1992. Jockey and exercise rider, Delaware Park, 1980–1987. Lives in tenant house on Gardner property, 2 bedroom, 1½ bath. Wife Maeve, no children. And he's not on Facebook and her settings are private. LOL!

Mary hit Reply and took a right on Twenty-second Street, then hustled down toward Walnut. She wrote, **thanks and see you at the office around noon xo,** thumbing the keys and trying not to collide with a fire hydrant, vaguely aware that the sidewalk was busier here, with other overachievers doing the same thing, texting their way into high blood pressure heaven, followed by an early grave. She checked her watch, and it was 5:45, too early to call Alasdair yet. She slid her BlackBerry back into her pocket and reached the end of the block where she had parked the car, but halted, confused. Her car was gone.

Mary double-checked the street sign, but she was on the right street. She looked around at the surrounding shops and remembered that she had parked in front of a soft yogurt shop, which was right behind her. Her car should've been at the end of the block, but there was only an empty space. Her first thought was that her car had been stolen, but her gaze found the NO PARKING—TOW ZONE sign that she must have missed last night, maybe because she was exhausted or cranky that she had to park in Timbuktu.

"Damn!" Mary said, but nobody looked over because they were on their BlackBerrys. If her car had been towed, it would have to stay where it was for now. She had to get on the road right away or she'd be responsible for the death of six thousand bees, which was more guilt than even a Catholic could take.

She needed a car and she needed it fast. She thought about using Mike's old BMW, but it was parked ten blocks in the other direction and she couldn't risk its not starting, since it hadn't been driven in months. She could wake Anthony up and borrow his car, which would serve him right, but he needed it. She could ask Judy, but she didn't want to bother her and/or admit that she was wrong. There was only one person left, who was awake at this hour and who could help, and would even be happy to be asked.

Mary reached for her BlackBerry and pressed P, for POP. She waited while the call connected, thanking God for the umpteenth time that her father was still alive, not only because she adored him, but because he was her own personal 911. The phone rang and rang, because even though he was awake, he wouldn't hear the ringer until her mother, who was probably getting dressed for Mass, told him so. The phone stopped ringing but no voicemail came on, because her father didn't know how to set it, so Mary pressed P again, let it ring, and the call was answered on the third time.

"MARE, HOW YOU DOIN'? YOUR MOTHER SAYS HI."

"Say hi for me. So Dad, you're awake?"

"SURE."

"Thank God." Mary felt lucky all over again, that her father rose at the crack of dawn even though he had no job to go to anymore. "Can I borrow your car?"

"SURE. WHEN YOU NEED IT?"

"Right now. Sorry about the short notice." Mary stepped to the curb to hail a cab to go to South Philly. There was only light traffic on Walnut Street, with the SEPTA bus heading toward the bus stop. "I don't see a cab yet, but there'll be one along any minute."

"DON'T TAKE A CAB, MARE. I'LL PICK YOU UP."

"Aw, you don't have to do that."

"I WANT TO. THE CAR'S RIGHT OUT FRONT. I WAS ABOUT TO GO TO THE DINER, BUT I DON'T HAFTA."

"Wait, the diner?" Mary blinked. "You meeting The Tonys?"

"YEAH."

"Perfect!" Mary said, getting an idea.

An hour later, she was steering her father's massive Buick Electra along the expressway, trying mightily to hold it steady despite the softness of its aged tires and the shimmy in a steering wheel the size of the equator. The car was thirty years old, but white as a set of new dentures, with a black interior that must've looked badass in the eighties. It had only twelve thousand miles, since her parents never left the kitchen, and the air conditioning blew a filmy soot, albeit weakly. They drove with the windows half-open, which not only added humidity to the cigar-and-mothballs smells, but rendered it impossible to hear each other. Mary didn't bother playing the radio, which boasted not only AM but FM, and even at speed, the constant chatter of the three Tonys surrounded her on all sides. Her father sat in the passenger seat, and Tony-From-Down-The-Block, Pigeon Tony, and Feet rode in the backseat, jazzed to be on an adventure.

Feet was saying, "Jesus, Mare, how far out is this place? We been in the car forever."

"We're almost there." Mary glanced at the rearview mirror and caught his eye behind his Mr. Potatohead bifocals.

"What?" Feet shouted, his few wisps of frizzy gray hair blowing in the wind. He had on a white short-sleeved shirt and brown pants, and his skinny frame looked swallowed up by the big bench backseat, his narrow shoulders caving in on themselves, as if he were folded in half cross-wise, like an origami octogenarian.

"It won't be long now, Feet," Mary shouted back, loud enough to be heard. The traffic was moving quickly out of the city, since the rush-hour commuters were going the other way. The top speed of the Buick was fifty miles an hour, and at this rate they'd be at the post office by the time the bees were writing their wills. "I'd say an hour more, at most."

"An hour?" Feet groaned. "Can we stop again?"

"Do you really need to? We just stopped."

"I do." Feet shrugged with regret. "What can I tell you?"

"I GOTTA STOP, TOO, MARE." Her father looked over, his lower lip puckering. "SORRY. BETWEEN US, WE ONLY GOT A PROSTATE AND A HALF."

Mary nodded. "It's okay, Pop. Next stop, you got it."

Feet craned his neck toward the front seat. "We must be in Camden by now. Mare, we in Camden yet?"

"No, Camden is in the other direction."

"What did you say, Mare?" Feet frowned.

"We're going the opposite direction, toward Delaware."

"I can't hear you!" Feet shouted.

"We'll be in Camden soon!" Mary shouted back.

Tony-From-Down-The-Block leaned over, peering past Pigeon Tony to scowl at Feet. "What's'a matter with you? Don't you know anything? We're going southwest."

"Get offa my back." Feet glared back at him. "I got a bad sense of direction, is all."

"Camden's *north*, Feet. You don't know that? Who don't know that?"

"Awright awready. Don't make a federal case."

"I wasn't making a federal case. I'm just saying. You're acting like a *cafone*."

Up front, Mary worried that the kids in the backseat needed to be separated. *Cafone* was Italian for country bumpkin, or in the modern vernacular, redneck. "What's the matter with you two, lately? You seem to be fussing a lot."

Tony-From-Down-The-Block turned away, looking out the window on the right. "He's got a problem with me."

Feet turned the other way, looking out the window on the left. "I got no problem with him. He's got a problem with *me*."

Mary was about to follow-up when her father nudged her arm. She glanced over to see him flaring his milky brown eyes at her, which was his version of a Meaningful Look. Her mother was the master of Meaningful Looks, able to convey don't-be-fresh, put-that-down, or lower-your-voice merely by subtle changes in her eyebrows. Her father was an amateur by comparison, but Mary got the gist, so she went to safer ground. "You guys are gonna love it. We're going to the country, the rolling hills of Pennsylvania. It's beautiful."

Feet brightened. "Like Rolling Rock, from the rolling hills of Latrobe, Pennsylvania? Like on the commercial?"

Mary had no idea what he was talking about. "Right, exactly."

Tony-From-Down-The-Block shook his head. "Me, I only drink Heineken. It's *imported.*"

Feet scoffed. "Big deal. It's named after heinies."

Mary decided to change tacks. There was a purpose to this field trip, and one of The Tonys was about to prove indispensible. "So Pigeon Tony, do you know what to do with the bees?"

"*Che?*" Pigeon Tony cupped a gnarled hand to his ear. His thin lips curved into their omnipresent smile, though he sat in the crossfire between Tony-From-Down-The-Block and Feet.

"You know what to do with the bees?" Mary asked, louder. She eyeballed Pigeon Tony, who was about five feet tall, and would fit easily into Allegra's beekeeper outfit. "You know how to get them into the beehives?"

"*Si, si, certo.*" Pigeon Tony nodded, his bald head as hard and brown as a filbert. He had a faded red handkerchief tied around his scrawny neck, which managed to look jaunty with his white shirt and baggy jeans. In his lap sat a wrinkled old paper bag that held the bee mister and other supplies. "I do alla, I take care, you see, *Maria,* I do."

"Good, thanks," Mary said, vaguely reassured. She wanted to touch base with Alasdair, so she slid her BlackBerry from her pocket, scrolled to the email she had sent herself last night, and highlighted his phone number.

Her father gasped in alarm. "DON'T DO THAT WHILE YOUR DRIVIN', HONEY! THAT'S NOT SAFE!"

"Pop, I'm sorry, it will just take a minute. It's really important."

"NO, STOP! THAT'S DANGEROUS! MARE, PULL OVER!"

"I can't pull over, I'm in the fast lane." Mary pressed Call before he made a move to stop her. Her father wasn't angry with her, just terrified for her, and he'd never yelled at her as long as she'd known him, except for the fact that he yelled all the time because he couldn't hear anything. "It's a really important business call, about what we're doing this morning with the bees. I waited all night to make this call. Don't worry, I'll be safe."

"THEN WAIT 'TIL WE STOP." Her father's tone softened. "MARE, GOD FORBID ANYTHING HAPPENED TO YOU! YOUR MOTHER WOULD KILL US BOTH!"

In the backseat, Feet frowned in disapproval. "Mary, you're not supposed to talk on the phone while you're driving. You could die. We could all die. Didn't you see the commercial?"

Mary began to wonder if all of Feet's information came from commercials, and in that case, he was fairly well-informed. "I'll make it fast, Feet, don't worry."

Tony-From-Down-The-Block craned his neck, scowling. "Mare, that's the only thing he's been right about all year. You're not supposed to talk on the phone and drive."

Mary heard the phone ringing, or at least she thought she did, over her father's yelling, The Tonys' clucking, and the wind noise. She would've pulled over, but that was even more dangerous than talking on the phone or driving around with the crazy Tonys. "Okay, everybody, tell you what. I'll put it on speaker, then I can drive."

"NO YOU CAN'T."

"Please?" Mary couldn't believe that she had just become a partner, but she still had to ask her father's permission to make a business phone call. "The call's about to connect, I swear, I'll be one second."

"THEN I'LL HOLD THE WHEEL." Her father plunked a hammy hand on the steering wheel. "YOU TALK."

"Thank you." Mary held the phone to her ear, but there was no answer and it went to voicemail. She was about to leave a message, but a mechanical voice came on saying that the mailbox was full. She pressed End Call in frustration.

"YOU OKAY?" her father asked, his hand on the wheel.

"No answer. Thanks for the help, Pop." Mary slipped the Black-Berry back into her pocket, as her father relaxed back in his seat with a sigh. She remembered that Alasdair didn't text, so she'd have to go to Plan B. "Okay, now I have to tell you guys the plan."

"WHAT PLAN?"

"That's what I'm going to tell you, Pop. What we're going to do after we get the bees." Mary checked the windblown Tonys in the backseat. "Pigeon Tony, can you hear me?"

"*Che?*"

"WHAT?"

"Huh?" said Tony-From-Down-The-Block.

"Wasn't that the rest stop, Mare?" Feet asked, pointing out the window.

Chapter Twenty-eight

Mary pressed the buzzer at the gate, her heart pounding. She'd called Alasdair again from the post office, but he hadn't picked up, so she didn't know what she was in for, and it worried her. She'd been with Judy the last time she'd been at the Gardners' farm, but her only hope for today was her father. Otherwise she felt like the harried mother to the superannuated children fighting in the back-seat, as well as the six thousand live bees buzzing angrily in the trunk. Pigeon Tony had been surprisingly adept at retrieving them while everybody else stood aside, but Mary knew the big test was yet to come, which was getting past John Gardner, making contact with Alasdair, and installing the bees without being stung to death or, worse, getting arrested and thrown in a jail cell with three Tonys and one toilet.

Feet squinted up at the **Houyhnhnm Farm** sign behind his Mr. Potatohead glasses. "Is that even a word, Mare? Hownym Farm? Hunyim Farm? How do you say that word?"

Tony-From-Down-The-Block snorted. "You pronounce it heinie, like the beer. It's Heinie Farm."

"THIS IS SO SWANKY, HONEY! WHERE'S THE HOUSE?"

"Over to the right, wait'll you see." Mary waited for the response to the buzzer and told herself to remain calm. She'd have to deal with whatever happened on her own. The farm seemed sunny, quiet, and still, but she couldn't see anything through the ivy climbing the gate. "Pop, can you imagine growing up here?"

"NO. I DON'T THINK THE KID IS CRAZY. I LIKED HER."

"Me, too." Mary had told him a little about the case on the way over, omitting the part about the police.

"I'D GO CRAZY IF I LIVED OUT HERE, TOO! IT'S TOO QUIET."

"I could get used to it."

"NAH, YOU'RE TOO ANTSY TO LIKE IT OUT HERE, AND ANTHONY WOULD HATE IT."

"That's true." Mary realized that she hadn't spoken to Anthony or gotten a text from him this morning, though they usually exchanged one after they were both at work. "Tonight is Elvira's birthday party. You guys are going to be there, right?"

"SURE." Her father patted her arm again. "DON'T WORRY, HONEY. EVERYTHING'S GONNA BE ALL RIGHT."

"Thanks, Pop." Mary would never get too old to take comfort in those words, and she sensed that her father knew exactly what she was worried about, and it wasn't only getting past the gate. She was about to press the buzzer again when her BlackBerry rang. "Hold on a sec."

"IT'S OKAY, WE'RE STOPPED."

Mary cranked up the window in case anyone in the house was listening, slipped a hand into her pocket, and pulled out her phone. The screen read Lou Jacobs, and she pressed Answer. "Hi, Lou, what's up?"

"Mary, here's a news flash. Tim Gage was definitely at the party the night Fiona was murdered."

"How do you know?" Mary said, astonished. "Did you use the guest lists?"

"No, long story short, I went on Gage's Facebook page and saw some photos of a car he's mighty proud of, a vintage Jag, an XKE, the maroon. I figured if he went to the party, he had to drive there, and that's not the kind of car people forget, especially not a parking valet."

"Okay." Mary felt intrigued. It was an angle she never would have thought of.

"The top-of-the-line valet company in the city is Burgerhof, so I figured that's who the Gardner Group used. I printed a picture of the car and Gage, went over to Burgerhof, and started asking around. Bottom line, one of the valets remembers the car and the kid."

"You're a genius!" Mary's heart soared. Allegra had been right. "How does the valet remember, from six years ago?"

"Mostly the car. Like I said, it's a classic. Once-in-a-lifetime. You're not a car person, are you?"

Mary eyed the Buick. "No."

"Also it didn't hurt that Gage tipped a hundred-dollar bill to leave the car out front because he said he wouldn't be long."

"And he came about the time of the murder?"

"Yes, and left right before. The valet said, not ten minutes later, they found the body and all hell broke loose. And according to the valet, Gage left the party upset. Buzzed, too."

Mary's thoughts raced ahead. "Did the valet see any blood on Tim, or any cuts or other injuries?"

"I asked him, but he said no. It's possible that Gage hid his hand in his pocket, if that's what got cut. It usually is."

"But the valet gave him the keys even though he was buzzed?"

"Yes, it happens, Rebecca of Sunnybrook Farm."

Mary got only half of Lou's references, but loved them anyway. "Did the police interview the valets or the company, when they got there, or even later?"

"No."

"Did the valet call the cops and tell them about Gage, after it came to light there was a murder that night?"

"No, why would he?"

"He might think it was strange that on the night of a murder, Gage came out upset, then a body was found."

Lou snorted. "Mare, the cops arrested Stall at the scene. They weren't lookin' for anybody else, nobody was, and I'm sure the valet didn't relate the two at all. Plus he was a young kid at the time. What do you expect, Columbo?"

"Good point, thanks. See you back at the office."

"You okay? You need me?"

"No thanks." Mary pressed End and put the phone away, her sense of purpose renewed. Gage was looking more like a viable suspect, if only because he'd lied about being at the party.

"GOOD NEWS?"

"Thank God." Mary rolled down the car window and pressed the buzzer again. "This is Mary DiNunzio, here to deliver Allegra's bees, at her request. I have my father and some friends with me who will help install them. May I come in?" There was no reply, but suddenly the gates parted and swung wide open, and Mary took heart.

"Maybe we caught a break," she said, hoping against hope that John wasn't home, which was why she hadn't called to say she was coming. She hit the gas and drove through the gate, bracing herself for battle. It was a surprise attack, DiNunzio-style, an '86 Buick full of cranky bees and even crankier senior citizens.

"SO FAR, SO GOOD, HONEY."

"Wow!" Feet looked out the window, his round brown eyes popping. "The gate opens all by itself!"

"Don't be ignorant." Tony-From-Down-The-Block ran a liver-spotted hand over his orange hair. "It's automatic, like the Acme."

"Gentlemen, play nice or I'll turn this car around." Mary pulled into the driveway, parked, and cut the ignition. The Buick's massive engine rattled into silence, but no one came running with lawyers or handcuffs. "Okay, everybody out of the pool. If we get started, it will be harder to throw us out."

"HERE GOES NUTHIN.'" Her father eased himself from the

seat, and Mary got out of the car, went around the back, and opened the trunk, recoiling from the large wooden box which had two screened sides. It was labeled LIVE BEES for people who didn't believe their eyes, since the bees were clearly visible through the screen, buzzing angrily and swarming frantic inside the box. Mary had never been this close to so many creepy-crawlies.

"Pigeon Tony?" she called out, nervous. "Please. Hurry."

"*Si, si, Maria.*" Pigeon Tony scurried over with his bag, vaguely bandy-legged, gesturing her aside. "You no worry, I do alla, I take care alla."

"IS THAT THE MOM?"

"Pop, please, shh." Mary looked over the trunk lid to see Jane Gardner striding toward them, slim and curvy in a pink Pulitzer sundress, next to a wiry middle-aged man in a white polo shirt and tan britches, who fit the description of Alasdair that Lou had given her.

Feet punched up his glasses. "Wow! She's a looker."

"I'll say." Tony-From-Down-The Block was about to relight his soggy cigar stub, but he slid it back into his shirt pocket, where it made an attractive stain.

"Guys, stay here and say nothing." Mary walked forward to meet them, waving hello in a friendly way. "Hello, sorry to bother you. I'm just bringing Allegra's bees."

"Hello, Mary," Jane called back, her tone formal, but not hostile. "Unfortunately, my husband is in the city today. It's too bad that you didn't let us know you were coming."

"I'm sorry, I didn't know myself, until very late last night." Mary didn't mention that she'd seen Allegra, so she could keep the emotional temperature under the boiling point. She gestured at her father and The Tonys, hoping that would set a peaceful tone and avoid another round of driveway litigation. "This is my father, Matty DiNunzio, and his friends Tony Pensiera, Tony LoMonaco, and Tony Lucia."

"They're all named Tony?"

"Yes, makes it easy to remember." Mary could tell that Jane wanted to ask, *are you serious,* but was too polite.

Tony-From-Down-The-Block stepped forward, picked up Jane's hand, bent over stiffly, and kissed it with a flourish. "Lovely to make your acquaintance, Jane. Thank you for having us to your very beautiful home and lovely grounds."

"Oh. My." Jane withdrew her hand with a half smile.

"Excuse me." Mary stepped in front of him, mortified. She turned to Alasdair, extending a hand, as if she had no idea who he was and only half-cared. "I'm sorry, I didn't get your name."

"Alasdair Leahy. I'm the property manager here." Alasdair nodded, shaking her hand. He spoke with a cool accent, and his bright blue eyes flashed with a wryness indigenous to the British. His unruly blond hair was thinning to a soft gray, and his nose oddly flattened, as if it had been broken. He was built like a former jockey, five feet of sinew and swagger. "Pleased to meet you, Mary."

"You, too." Mary cued Pigeon Tony like a jittery stage manager, and he came forward with the boxes of bees, carrying them as matter-of-factly as canned soda. "His nickname is Pigeon Tony because he races pigeons, but he also knows a lot about bees. He'd be happy to install them in the hives, which shouldn't take too long, then we'll be on our way."

"Alasdair can do that himself," Jane said, her smile fading, but Alasdair hesitated, looking from Mary to Jane.

"Truly, Jane, I could use the help. I've only seen Allegra do it once, and it can be dangerous."

"*Ecco!*" Pigeon Tony yelped, spotting the beehives across the pasture. "*Andiamo,* alla, go!" He took off bandy-legged with the box, in his own little Pigeon Tony world.

"Excuse me, sir, Tony, wait!" Jane turned to go after him, but Mary waved her off.

"I got it, he doesn't speak English. But can Alasdair come with us and get Pigeon Tony a beekeeper's outfit? I wouldn't want him to get stung."

Suddenly, from the driveway, Feet called out, "Miss, is there a bathroom I can use? We were in the car a long, long time."

"I COULD USE A REST STOP, TOO," her father chimed in. "IF YA DON'T MIND."

"Oh, um, certainly." Jane stopped in her tracks, caught betwixt and between the two groups, and it couldn't have gone any better if Mary had planned it, so she exploited the situation.

"Jane," Mary called over her shoulder, "would you please take my father and the others to the house and let them use the bathroom? I'd appreciate it so much." She headed after Alasdair and Pigeon Tony. "I'll go down with Pigeon Tony and make sure he doesn't get hurt."

"Why, yes, okay, sure." Jane gestured, confused, to Alasdair, who was already in motion. "Alasdair, take him down and give him Allegra's gear? You know where her smoker is, don't you?"

"Surely, Jane." Alasdair caught up with Mary, falling into step with her and looking over with a sly smile. "Well done."

"Thanks," Mary said, sensing a secret weapon.

Chapter Twenty-nine

Mary and Alasdair stood a safe distance away from the hives, but only Mary was wearing the beekeeper's jumpsuit, gloves, and veil, because she wasn't taking any chances. It fit like a white burqa and felt hot and clammy inside, but she wasn't a lawyer for nothing. They both watched while Pigeon Tony smoked the screened box with the buzzing bees using Allegra's smoker, which looked like a tin funnel tacked onto some kind of bellows-type hand pump. It emitted a faint grayish smoke that smelled funny, but Pigeon Tony didn't appear to notice, humming to himself and wearing nothing for protection except his red bandanna tied around his bald head.

Mary called to him, "Pigeon Tony, you sure you don't want to wear the outfit?"

"*No!*"

"Why not? We have another one."

"I no like!"

"How about the veil? The hat? It will protect your head."

"*No, grazie, Maria!*"

Mary let it go and looked over, eyeing Alasdair through the black grid of the veil. "So you were the one who wrote the note about where Allegra was?"

"Yes." Alasdair frowned slightly, his deep crow's-feet wrinkling. "You'll keep that to yourself, won't you?"

"Of course. Why did you do it?"

"I'd like not to say more than necessary." Alasdair bit a parched lower lip. "My loyalty is to the family and will forever be. Particularly to Jane, who's elevated me to this position. I was her barn manger and now run this place. Lots of people would have hired somebody over my head when the former man left, but not her. I'm well-paid, and my wife and I live rent-free behind the cottage, in a carriage house. You must understand that."

"I do." Mary noticed that Pigeon Tony was setting the smoker down, so she assumed the bees were calm, if they hadn't taken up cigarettes.

"I decided to help you because I've known Allegra her entire life, before Fiona's murder and after, and she isn't quite as ill as her father thinks. I overheard you and the other lawyer on your previous visit, and I know you're acting in her best interests." Alasdair meet her gaze directly. "Do you think you can get her out of Churchill? She hardly needs residential care."

"Not yet, but let me ask you a question or two about Fiona and her murder. That's what Allegra hired me to do." Mary needed to get to the point, because she didn't know how much time they'd have before everyone returned. In the meantime, Pigeon Tony took an old pair of pliers from his wrinkled sack, went back to the screened box, and turned it around on top of the empty hive, which still looked to Mary like a nightstand. "Alasdair, do you remember Fiona's boyfriend, named Tim Gage?"

"Of course. Tim and Fiona were going steady."

"Was he here often?"

"All the time. He was besotted with her, as anybody would be." Alasdair's tone softened, almost paternally. "Fiona was a lovely girl, and a lovely rider. I've never seen anybody with such a natural manner around horses." Alasdair gestured at Pigeon Tony. "Like your friend, over there. It's his calm demeanor that makes the bees calm. Tony has a very easy way of going, as did Fiona. Allegra has it too."

"Fiona broke up with Tim. Do you know why?" Mary saw Pigeon Tony begin to pry off the front of the wood frame with the pliers, and it cracked as if he were breaking it off, so she took a step back, in case the bees were pissed.

"No, I don't know why they split. But I know he wasn't happy about it."

"What makes you say that?"

"He used to call her afterwards, on her mobile. We'd be on a trail ride, cooling the horses out, and he would call and call. When she answered, it always made her nervous, and she told me once that he said the meanest things to her. I told her not to take his calls, and after a while she stopped, but the calls kept coming."

"I've learned that Tim was at the party the night that Fiona was murdered, that he left upset and had been drinking. Did you know any of that?"

"No, not at all." Alasdair frowned, which turned his eyes narrow and flinty. "How do you know?"

"It doesn't matter. But you didn't see Tim at the party?"

"No, not at all. I know that he was expressly *not* invited. Fiona didn't want him there."

"Was she afraid of him?" Mary was dying to know the answer, but got distracted by Pigeon Tony, who was holding the screen on the box aside so the bees could get out. She jumped back, reflexively putting up her hands in the heavy gloves. "Pigeon Tony, you gonna let them out? Just like that?"

Alasdair edged away. "Not much warning, eh?"

Pigeon Tony didn't reply except to smile happily, as bees swarmed from the opening and flew in all directions, buzzing around the box and setting the air vibrating with their loud droning and collective beating of their wings. The ones who weren't flying clung to the screen, walked all over the hive, or landed on Pigeon Tony's arms, shirt, even his cheek.

"My God!" Mary gasped, afraid for him, but he seemed completely unworried.

"Quite a sight." Alasdair's eyes widened. "He could get badly stung, if he's not careful."

"Is this the worst hobby in the world, or what?"

Alasdair smiled. "Allegra enjoys it, and she makes wonderful honey. Maeve and I use it all the time."

"For what?"

"Tea."

Mary let it go, watching with admiration as Pigeon Tony slowly turned the open box on its side, gave it a gentle shake over the open slats of the hive, and let a living ball of bees tumble inside. Others crawled all over the screen, and Pigeon Tony held the open box upside down until they found their way into the hive, then he set the box aside.

"Now, he'll have to get the queen from the box," Alasdair said, then returned his attention to Mary. "Where did we leave off?"

"Yes, well." Mary got her bearings, but there were still bees on Pigeon Tony's face, so she averted her eyes. "I was asking you if Fiona was afraid of Tim."

"I don't think so. Fiona wanted the relationship to be over, and Tim didn't."

"I understand they broke up approximately two weeks before the party. Does that square with what you know?"

"I don't recall exactly, but it was around then."

"Let me float you a theory, because I'm trying to figure it out." Mary needed a sounding board, and Alasdair knew the players. "My guess is that if Tim didn't want to break up with her, maybe he went to the party to see if she was dating anybody new. In other words, he wanted to see if she had brought a guy to the party, other than her girlfriends. Does that make sense to you?"

"Yes, that would be so like him." Alasdair rubbed his face, his tanned skin shifting back and forth. "I never liked him, not one bit. He's a fraud, that boy. Too posh for his own good."

"How much interaction did you have with Tim?"

"Enough. Fiona tried to teach him to ride, gave him one or two lessons, so she had me hang around the arena, for his safety. He tried to canter right away, before he'd even trotted." Alasdair harrumphed. "You know, I come from a society that some say is classist, but America has its classes, too. The Gardners never act that way, especially Jane, but Tim did. He treated me differently than he treated Fiona, and he treated me differently *around* Fiona. He was polite to me, only for show. Not because it was genuine."

Mary thought of Tim, helping the little boy at the frat house with his hamster syndicate, and she saw him with new eyes. In the background, Pigeon Tony was lifting an unmarked aluminum can out of the empty box, setting it aside, and withdrawing a tiny screened box on a cotton string, which presumably held the queen bee.

"Tim was expecting everything to come to him quickly. The second lesson, he pulled so hard on Paladin's mouth, I had him dismount."

Mary knew she had heard that name before. "Paladin is Jane's horse, correct?"

"Yes, her mare." Alasdair's expression darkened. "Jane hasn't ridden since Fiona's murder. Her heart is simply broken. I'm keeping her mare in work, hoping she'll come back again someday."

Mary checked Pigeon Tony, relieved to see that the bees weren't walking on him anymore, though many flew around the hive, which buzzed noisily. "Around the time of her murder, Fiona was working at the cottage after school, is that right?"

"Yes, on the Meyers acquisition. That's another thing, because Tim resented that time she had to spend."

"What do you mean?"

"I heard her on the phone, explaining that she had to work, that her uncles needed her. It was a big deal, very important to the family business, and she was proud to be earning her own money, even if it was clerical work."

"Why was it a big deal?" Mary's forehead was starting to sweat under the veil, but she wasn't about to take it off. Bees flew everywhere. "I understand she was working with her Uncle Richard."

"That's right. It was about the acquisition of condominiums in Delaware, and it kept the staff at the cottage busy all that month, including Richard, Neil, and his staff. You remember them, from your previous visit. They behaved badly that day, but they're not bad men. Neil, in particular. He's simply protective of the family, like me."

Mary kept her own counsel. She glanced over as Pigeon Tony turned the tiny box on its side and took the string, which had a nail on it, using it to pry out some sort of cork stopper. "You were saying, about Fiona."

"Yes, Fiona did more than her part on the Meyers acquisition. She had many privileges, but she was smart and able, being groomed to take her place in the family business. Tim resented that."

Mary wanted to switch gears. "Allegra told me that Fiona was dating Lonnie Stall, the waiter who was eventually convicted of her murder. Allegra said that Lonnie used to come over when Fiona was babysitting Allegra. Do you know anything about that?"

Alasdair's eyes rounded in obvious surprise. "Fiona, seeing the *kill*er? Lonnie Stall? That would be news to me. I don't know anything about that."

"Did Fiona ever babysit Allegra, that you know? Allegra says yes, but John says no." Mary couldn't completely ignore Pigeon Tony, who had moved back to the open slat of the hive and affixed the tiny box inside, with the queen.

"I don't know if Fiona babysat. I'm not privy to everything that goes on in the house. My main work is on the grounds and at the stables. So it's conceivable Allegra could have been babysat by Fiona."

"Is it also conceivable that Fiona was dating Lonnie Stall?"

"Yes, perhaps," Alasdair answered, ducking an errant bee.

"Would you know Lonnie if you met him? He was one of the waiters employed by the catering service that the Gardners used."

"Yes, I would know him. We try to avoid those parties, though

I'm welcome, as is Maeve, my wife. We lead a quiet life, and I rise early to exercise the horses before it gets hot."

"You went to the party the night Fiona was murdered, didn't you?"

"Yes, we were both invited, and it was a very special night, until it took such an awful turn."

"Were you with Fiona that night, at all?"

"Yes, both Maeve and I were, at around eight o'clock. She came by to give us a hug, to make sure we had what we needed, make us feel included." Alasdair's eyes shone, and he looked away a minute. "Only an hour later, she was gone."

"Was she alone?"

"Yes."

"Did you see Lonnie Stall that night?"

"Yes, when he was serving."

"What about around the time of the murder?"

"No. We saw nothing. We were dancing when Fiona was found."

"Did you know any of the girls she brought that night?"

"Yes, they were always at the house. A great group of girls." Alasdair's face fell. "Another tragedy, all of it, one leading to the next, such a sad, awful waste."

"Hannah Wicker survived the crash." Mary noticed that Pigeon Tony was placing a wooden frame inside the open slat, as if he were sliding in a bureau drawer, then slowly covering the beehive with a lid that had a hole in the top, careful not to squash any of the bees.

"Yes, she did, Thank Jesus."

"Did you know Hannah at all?"

"None more than the others. She rode, though. She and Fiona used to ride out, and she was here often, when she was younger and they were in Pony Club."

"What's she like?"

"A nice girl."

Mary could see that Pigeon Tony was finishing up, putting another lid on top of the one with the hole. The base of the hive had an opening about a half an inch long, and it appeared to be the bees' entrance, because they were already flying in and out. "Did you keep track of Hannah?"

"No."

"Hear anything about her?"

"No."

Mary didn't want to tell him what she'd learned about Hannah last night, so she kept it to herself. "Did the police or D.A. interview you or talk with you?"

"No." Alasdair turned away, to the driveway. "Oh look, they're back."

"Perfect timing. I have only a few more questions." Mary glanced over to see Jane crossing the lawn toward them with her father and Tony-From-Down-The-Block. She glanced at Pigeon Tony. "You finished?"

"*Moment, Maria!*" Pigeon Tony called back, cleaning up the mess, but Alasdair waved him off.

"Leave the box, Tony. I'll take care of it. Good job! *Bravo!*"

"*Grazie!*" Pigeon Tony nodded, leaned over, and spoke to the bees, then scurried after Mary, who gave him a hug in the clunky bee suit.

"Thank you so much! You were awesome!"

"*Prego, Maria!*" Pigeon Tony blushed as red as his bandanna under his leathery tan. "*Andiamo a casa!*"

"You got it!" Mary started walking with Alasdair. "Did any part of you suspect Tim of killing Fiona?"

"Honestly, no. I thought he wasn't there. I assumed he was well out of her life."

"Does it seem out of character to you, for him to have done it?"

"No."

"You're saying that he's capable of murder."

"I'm aware, but there's cruelty in Tim. He yanked so hard on Paladin's mouth, she almost reared." Alasdair eyed the approaching group, his expression growing guarded. "Can we end this interview? I'm an awful liar."

"Sure I called you today, to give you the heads-up, but there was no answer. Is there a way we could meet or talk at more length, if I have other questions?"

"I'm afraid it would be difficult to talk again, with my living here, and frankly, even this conversation makes me uncomfortable. Apologies, I saw someone called, but I was with Jane, so I didn't pick up."

"Understood, thanks for your time today." Mary saw her father laughing as he grew closer.

"MARE! YOU READY FOR HALLOWEEN!"

"Oops!" Mary had forgotten she was wearing the beekeeper's get-up. She popped the veil off her head, inhaled a lungful of fresh air, and fluffed up her hair, since she had veil head.

"I'll take the veil." Alasdair held out a calloused hand.

"Thanks." Mary gave it to him, then slid off the gloves and bee-keeper's jumpsuit, turning to her father. "Pop, we can go now. Where's Feet? In the car?"

"NO." Her father stopped short, blinking. "HEY, WAIT, WHERE'S FEET?"

Jane frowned, looking over. "Oh no, he's not here."

Tony-From-Down-the-Block grinned. "I got no problem with that."

Chapter Thirty

Mary took her father's arm, and Tony-From-Down-The-Block took Jane's arm, and the four of them headed toward the house like the most awkward double date in history. Pigeon Tony scurried ahead of them with Alasdair, whose demeanor had turned newly official. Their group's pace was slow, by necessity, and this was the most exercise her father had gotten in ages. Mary worried it might be too much, and even if it wasn't, that they wouldn't get to the house until Friday.

"Pop, do you and the guys want to wait here or in the car?" she asked, looking over. "We can get Feet and bring him back."

"NO, MARE, I'M FINE."

"Me, too." Tony-From-Down-The-Block winked at Jane. "How often do I get to be in the company of such beautiful women?"

"*Che bella giorno!*" Pigeon Tony exclaimed, throwing up his arms with a grin, and he didn't require translating. The grounds were sunny and beautiful, with a gentle breeze rustling through magnolia trees, climbing roses, and other flora and fauna that Mary couldn't identify, but it wasn't what interested her. She wasn't a botanist, but an amateur sleuth, and she was dying to get inside the Gardners' house and snoop around, like Nancy Drew with a J.D.

Alasdair asked Jane, "Where was Feet the last time you saw him?"

"In the house." Jane scanned left and right for Feet, as they walked along. "He had to use the bathroom right away, because he said his prostate had been so bad lately. Poor man. He didn't think the Flomax was doing any good at all."

Tony-From-Down-The-Block clucked, and his dentures made a dry sound. "It's fake Flomax, that's why. He gets it from China. You know what they put in that stuff? Mouse hair. Rat feet."

"IT'S LIKE HOT DOGS."

Tony-From-Down-The-Block shook his head. "No, it's worse. At least with hot dogs, you got the FDA. The Chinese, they got no FDA. They do anything they want. They got no laws over there, only people. Tons of people, and only one law."

"You mean that they're allowed only one child per family?" Jane asked, her tone so polite that Mary couldn't tell if she was trying to make conversation or was actually interested, in which case she was making a major mistake.

Tony-From-Down-The-Block shook his head again. "No, the law that you have to wear the same clothes. Ever see that? They all got the same brown outfit on, with the hat."

Mary wanted to get things back on track. "Jane, you were explaining about what happened with Feet."

"Yes, well, I put him in the powder room, but then your father said that he couldn't wait, so I showed him to the bathroom in the family room. Then Tony here"—Jane gestured to Tony-From-Down-The-Block, clinging to her like a barnacle with a comb-over—"needed to use a bathroom as well because Feet was taking such a long time, so I showed him to the powder room near the mud room, just off the garage, and I waited for him, because sometimes the cat scratches at the door, since her litter box is in there . . ."

Mary's head exploded, but she didn't interrupt. They passed the aviary on the right and the stables on the left, but nobody noticed the scenery except Pigeon Tony, who swiveled his birdlike head this way and that, his red bandanna and beaky nose making him look like a redheaded woodpecker.

218 | Lisa Scottoline

"... then when he was finished, we collected your father and left the house, but I was yakking away with Tony, and somehow, we must have forgotten all about Feet. Our housekeeper has a dentist appointment this morning, and she would've helped me keep better track of everyone. I've made a hash of it on my own."

Mary got the gist, mortified. "Jane, I'm sorry this ended up being trouble for you."

"No worries, I understand completely." Jane smiled in a genuinely warm way. "I took care of my father for long time. He had Alzheimer's and he lived with us for a decade, almost to the very end of his life."

"My deepest condolences about your father," said Tony-From-Down-The-Block.

"MINE, TOO. YOU'RE A CLASS ACT, MRS. G," her father said, and Mary thought that summed it up perfectly. She was really starting to like Jane, who seemed kind, gentle, and low-key, nothing like her husband. Alasdair had been right in his loyalty to her, and she seemed to embody the strength and practicality of a horsewoman as well as the fragility and sorrow of a mother who had buried a child. Mary was dying to tell her her suspicions about Tim Gage, but this wasn't the time or the place. She couldn't bring up Allegra either, though she sensed that mother and daughter needed each other, more than they knew.

"Yes, thank you, Jane," Tony-From-Down-The Block said, then he scowled. "You know, this is all Feet's fault. He wanders off, all the time. He's too old to hang with us."

"DON'T SAY THAT, TONY. THAT'S WHAT GOT YOU IN TROUBLE WITH HIM."

"Why? It's the truth!"

"WE'RE ALL OLD."

"He acts it. I don't."

"Gentlemen." Mary thanked God that they were only steps away from the front of the house. "Let's not have this discussion now. Tony-From-Down-The-Block, I think you should say you're sorry to Feet, because you hurt his feelings. Now, let's all go inside and find him."

"FEET PROLLY LOCKED HIMSELF IN THE BATHROOM."

"You're probably right," said Tony-From-Down-The-Block, as Alasdair led them onto the flagstone porch under the portico, opened the front door, and held it to the side for everyone.

"LADIES FIRST." Mary's father stood aside and so did Pigeon Tony and Tony-From-Down-The-Block.

"Why, thank you." Jane entered the house, and Mary went in behind her, looking around secretively, like a neighbor at a Realtor's open house. It was new construction, and the layout of the home was clear from the entrance hall, which was generous enough to hold two cherrywood benches. To the left was a formal living room with chintz-covered chairs and couches in fresh green hues, and to the right was an open doorway that led to a formal dining room, with a glistening mahogany table the length of an airport runway. Oriental rugs carpeted the hardwood floors, and tasteful landscapes covered the walls, but what intrigued Mary was the array of silver-framed photographs blanketing a matching sideboard, though they were too far away to see.

"This is the powder room he used." Jane opened a door in the entrance hall, but it was empty. "He's not here, so he must be in the family room."

"I'll go with you and check the garage." Alasdair headed down the hall in that direction, with Jane at his heels.

"We'll be right back," she called over her shoulder. "Everyone, please make yourself comfortable."

"I'll lend a hand!" Tony-From-Down-The-Block chugged behind her like a lovesick caboose.

"I NEED TO TAKE A LOAD OFF." Mary's father plopped down on the cherrywood bench, and so did Pigeon Tony, who took off his red bandanna and used it to wipe his forehead.

Mary seized the moment to sneak into the dining room and peek at the photographs. There was a professional wedding photograph of Jane and John, but all of the others were snapshots of Fiona and Allegra, together through the years; the sisters as babies in bassinets, then Fiona wearing a big sister T-shirt holding Allegra, Allegra dressed as a pony for Halloween with a pig-tailed Fiona in jodhpurs, and Fiona holding a long red ribbon with Allegra in starter glasses, sitting on top of a horse. The photos went on and on, and in almost every one, Allegra was looking up at Fiona with adoration, so Mary could see, as if it were photographic exhibits in a trial, vivid evidence of the love Allegra had for her only sister. The photos stopped at Fiona's induction into National Honor Society, with a gap-toothed Allegra hugging her around the waist, and after that, there were no more photographs, even of Allegra alone. Mary left the dining room shaken.

"We can't find him anywhere." Alasdair came back into the entrance hall and placed his hands on his slim hips. "I'm wondering if he went back to the car. We came to the house without checking there."

"I CAN GO LOOK." Mary's father began to get up, leaning heavily on his knee, but Alasdair waved him back into his seat.

"Please, no. You stay here, and I'll go check at the car."

"Thanks so much." Mary held open the door for Alasdair, who left the house just as Jane returned to the entrance hall, her forehead knit with worry.

"He's not here at all, even in the garage. I'm concerned that he might have gone back outside and lost his way. My father used to all the time, even before his illness progressed."

"THAT SOUNDS LIKE FEET. HE WAS JUST SAYIN' HE HAS A BAD SENSE A DIRECTION."

Tony-From-Down-The-Block opened his palms in appeal. "See, that's what I'm saying. Old! *Old* old."

Mary got an idea. "Jane, I think we should check the cottage. That's right out back, isn't it? Maybe he found his way there, like you said, getting lost."

"You might be right." Jane turned to Mary's father, Pigeon Tony, and Tony-From-Down-The-Block. "Would you three mind staying here, so I know where you are?"

"TALKED ME INTO IT."

"*Mille grazie.*" Pigeon Tony nodded, wide-eyed.

"Can't I go?" Tony-From-Down-The-Block looked heartbroken, but Mary shook her head.

"No, please, stay here. It's a search party, not a field trip. Jane, let's go." Mary headed for the door so Jane wouldn't think twice and leave her behind, too. She didn't want to miss a chance to get inside the cottage, which was the suburban headquarters of the Gardner Group. In fact, she was praying that if Feet had fallen, he fell inside the cottage.

"It's this way." Jane hustled out the front door, and Mary fell into step beside her, excited about the potential for information at the cottage. Maybe there would be an employee who could tell her more about Tim Gage, like the way he interacted with Fiona.

"How many employees do you have down at the cottage?" Mary asked, trying to keep her tone casual. They were walking down a gravel path toward a tan fieldstone house that looked like a smaller version of the main house, except that it had a large parking lot to the right, which was almost empty.

"Our main headquarters is in town, as you know, and we have a hundred there. There's only five here, including the lawyers you met the other day, Neil and his staff."

Mary was wondering if any of the employees had spotted Lonnie Stall at the house one of the times that Fiona was babysitting Allegra. She didn't think Allegra was wrong about the babysitting, especially since she hadn't been wrong about Tim's being at the party. "The cottage must be a great place to work, in such a lovely setting. A lot more relaxing than Center City."

"Yes, that's what John likes about it, and he never complains about the commute." Jane smiled, even though her eyes kept scanning the area. Rosebushes in a variety of pink hues lined the gravel walkway, and they passed a row of evergreens that had been planted in front of the cottage and around the parking lot, presumably to screen the business traffic from view. To the far right, beyond the cottage, stood a smaller fieldstone house with a white picket fence mounded with climbing roses, overlooking a wooded countryside.

"That little house is so charming, and what a view of the woods!" Mary pointed as they walked along. "Is that where Alasdair lives? He mentioned that he and his wife live on the property."

"Yes, and the woods belong to us as well, and John's brothers own the neighboring farms, on the other side of the treeline." Jane cocked her head. "So, Mary, you're from South Philly, born and bred?"

"Yes, can you tell by my accent?"

"It's not so bad."

"Just don't ask me to get my *coat,*" Mary said, accenting the o in the flat, nasal way that Philadelphians did, which was music to her ears.

"I think you were right, asking Tony to apologize." Jane's blue-eye gaze shifted slyly. "Though I know how he feels. I used to think forty was old."

Mary laughed. "You can help me broker a peace between Tony and Feet, and after that we can end world war."

Jane smiled, striding along. "But first we have to find Feet. You don't seem to be too worried."

"I'm not. I've known these guys longer than you, and none of the trouble they get into is very serious. They mean well, despite the hand-kissing and all."

"I can see that, and your father is such a sweet man."

"He really is." Mary hadn't realized the conversation would take such a personal turn, but she wasn't all that surprised, being a woman. She generally knew everyone's life history in the first five minutes after she stepped into a ladies room. "I feel very lucky in both of my parents. I owe them everything."

"I felt the same way. I'm an only child and I was very close with both of my parents. My mother passed only two years before my father, and I counted my blessings in having them for as long as I did." Jane's tone turned tender, and Mary couldn't help but mention the subject they'd both been avoiding.

"Jane, I appreciate your kindness to me today, with what's happening to Allegra, and even though we may disagree on some points, I know you love her and have her interests completely at heart."

"I do." Jane kept her face forward and swallowed visibly. "I love her so much, and I miss her every minute she's not under my roof. Even when she was at boarding school, I missed her, and certainly now, well, it's far worse. I'm just trying to do the best thing for her. I always have."

Mary felt her throat catch. "I know that, and you can see how much family means to me. The day Allegra came into our offices, my heart broke for all of you, including her."

"Thank you for saying that." Jane stopped, turning to Mary, as they reached the door to the cottage. "You know, you've asked me a lot about the property, but you haven't asked me where Allegra is. I just realized that it must mean you already know."

Mary felt nonplussed. She should've thought of that, but hadn't, and she didn't want to confirm or deny for fear of getting Alasdair in trouble.

"You needn't say anything, I know you have client confidentiality and such. But if you happen to see her, please tell her that her mother loves her very much."

"Jane, I know it's not my business, but you have to find your way back to each other."

"I doubt that's possible, any longer. I haven't been the best mother to her, she may have told you." Jane's fair skin flushed pink, and Mary knew she had to be talking about her drinking.

"None of us is perfect, Jane, and any tragedy causes people to act out of character, until they get their bearings back. That's what happened to me, after my husband was killed. I was crazy for years, inside."

Jane's mouth turned down at the corners, and Mary sensed her words had hit home. If she was ever going to make a pitch for Allegra, this was the time.

"Jane, you can still turn it around. I've never been a mother, but

I'm speaking as a daughter. A girl always needs her mother. That, I know from my heart."

Jane's eyebrows lifted, just the slightest. "She has to want it, too."

"She does, she just won't admit it to herself or to you. Call her at the hospital. Tell her you want to see her. Ask her to put you on her visitors' list. You go first. That's why you're the mom."

Jane's eyes shone with sudden tears, and she opened the door to the cottage. "Now. Let's not speak of this again."

Mary followed her into a large reception room with more Shaker furniture, and eggshell-ivory walls covered with business plaques, charitable awards, and corporate portraits of the three Gardner brothers. The family resemblance was remarkable, the same wide-set blue eyes, the small nose and a strong chin, and each was good-looking in his own way. John sat in a thronelike chair wearing a boxy Brooks Brothers suit, and behind him stood his two brothers: one who looked remarkably like him, but was dressed in a hipper, more *GQ*-style suit, and the other looked the youngest, with fewer crow's-feet, longer hair, a relaxed smile, and a work shirt under a corduroy jacket. The caption read JOHN, RICHARD, AND EDWARD GARDNER, which Mary sensed established the pecking order, because so many of the other photographs were only of John, framed with an array of newspaper and magazine articles that featured him.

"Susan's not at her desk." Jane crossed the room to a matching cherrywood desk, which was unoccupied. The nameplate on the desk read SUSAN WEATHERLY, next to a computer monitor, a Phillies cup full of pens, and a plastic cube that held photos of a chubby gray tabby.

"Isn't it lunch time?" Mary checked a fancy wall clock, which read 12:15. The office seemed quiet, almost as if it were empty, so she guessed everyone had gone to lunch.

"Susan?" Jane passed the desk, heading for an open doorway that led down a hallway, and Mary followed her past architectural renderings of apartment buildings, under placards she read on the fly: Jamieson Mews, Canterbury Village, The Presidential Hotel & Condominiums, and Meyers Towers, which she flashed on as the project Fiona was working on.

"Hello? Susan, anybody?" Jane ducked her head in a series of offices off the right side of the hallway. Mary lagged behind, reading the nameplates outside each office and trying to commit them to memory, in case she wanted to investigate the employees later. She would've used her BlackBerry to take photos of the nameplates, but didn't want to get caught.

"Where is everyone? In the backyard?" Jane continued down the hallway, past a file room and a coat closet, then opened the back door of the cottage, when she gasped. "Oh my God!'

"Feet?" Mary said, stricken. She should have realized that something could have actually gone wrong. She raced after Jane and flew out the back door.

Chapter Thirty-one

"Feet!" Mary cried out at the sight. Feet was moaning, his head hanging to the side and his lined face a mask of pain. He lay on the grass next to a picnic table, in the arms of an older woman, with Richard Gardner, Neil Patel, and other Gardner employees clustered around him. Mary rushed to his side on the grass beside him.

"Mary, Mary!" Feet wailed. His Mr. Potatohead glasses lay broken beside him. "Help me, oh, it hurts!"

"Tell me, what happened!" Mary scanned his body frantically, but there was no visible injury. "What is it? Are you having a heart attack?"

"Please, Mary, I'm in so much pain!" Feet wailed louder. "I'm in agony, such agony!"

"Where? Is it your chest, your left arm?"

Jane looked up, equally panicky from his other side. "It could be his shoulder, too. You can feel a heart attack in your shoulder."

"Jane, relax." Neil was calmly sliding out his BlackBerry. "He twisted his ankle."

"No, I broke it! Oooh! It hurts! I bet the bone popped out of the skin! Oooh! It hurts so much!"

"Oh, thank God." Mary felt a wave of relief wash over her, and Jane exhaled, relaxing back on her haunches.

"Right, it's not as bad as it looks."

"What do you mean!" Feet yelped. "My ankle's broken and maybe my foot, too! I never felt pain like this in my life! I might even be paralyzed!"

Mary patted his arm, to comfort him. "I know you're in pain, and I'm sorry. I didn't mean it was nothing. I just meant it isn't life-threatening. I was scared."

Jane patted his other arm. "So was I. I saw you lying there, and I thought the worst had happened."

Neil tapped the keys of his BlackBerry. "Sir, if you feel pain, you're not paralyzed. I don't know who you are or how you got here, but if you're planning a lawsuit, you're mistaken. You're not a business invitee on this property, but a mere trespasser, and there's been no negligence whatsoever on the part of the Gardner Group."

"Neil, I'll leave this matter in your capable hands." Richard straightened up, brushing down his silk tie over a fitted white shirt, which he had on with suit pants. "I have to get back to work. Thanks, everyone."

Suddenly the back door opened, and Alasdair hustled into the backyard with Edward Gardner, who had the same curly hair, bright blue eyes, and a work shirt similar to the one in his portrait in the reception area.

"Oh no!" Alasdair looked appalled at Feet, then at Neil. "Neil, I just got your call. What happened? Is he okay?"

Beside him, Edward looked shocked, his mouth partly open. "I was just coming over with the tomatoes. My truck's right out front. I could bring it around, and we can have him at the ER in no time."

Neil waved him off. "Thanks, but there is no need. It's better to call an ambulance. We don't want to be in a position of providing medical care to trespassers."

Mary looked from Edward to Neil. "Neil, I should be the one to take him to the hospital. You don't need to call an ambulance."

Neil raised a palm to her like a stop sign. "No, we'll handle this by the book, and you, of all people, should understand why. Do you know this man? How did he get here? What's his name?"

"Ooooh, my foot! My foot!"

Mary was beginning to think that Feet was a bit of a drama queen, and The Tonys couldn't have caused more trouble today if they'd tried. "His name is Feet."

"This is no time for joking, Counselor." Neil held the phone to his ear. "I'm calling 911. I'd like to provide them his proper name."

"Tony Pensiera," Mary answered. "His nickname is Tony Two Feet and his nickname's nickname is Feet. He came with me and he's a friend of my father's."

"Susan, do you know what happened?" Jane asked the heavyset woman, who was cradling Feet against her bosom like the Pieta.

"I have no idea," Susan answered, mystified. She had a sweet and caring smile, red-framed glasses, and a halo of prematurely white-gray hair. "We were in the cottage working when we heard a scream in the yard, ran outside, and found this man here, on the ground."

"Ooooh, oooh!" Feet groaned, rubbing his face with his hand. "My foot, my foot!"

"Feet, let me check you." Mary reached over, pulled up each of his baggy pant legs, and tugged down his black socks. She examined each ankle carefully, running her fingers over his bulging veins and ingrown leg hair. Neither looked swollen, much less broken. On the contrary, it looked as if the walk had done him good, and she could swear he had sprouted new calf muscles.

"Oooh! No, it hurts! Eeeh! Did you see, Mary? Is the ankle bone sticking out? I can't move it!"

"Feet, it's fine." Mary could see he was more scared than injured. "It's not broken, not that I can tell. You twisted it, or maybe you sprained it, but we're going to take good care of you. What were you doing back here, anyway?"

"Oooh! When I got out of the bathroom, nobody was around. Oooh! I went out of the house. Ouch! Eeeh! I thought I was going to the car but I ended up here. I fell down on the stones."

"Sir, there's nothing wrong with those flagstones." Neil lifted an eyebrow. "They're not even slippery, and it's a completely dry day.

There are no divots or holes in the lawn, or anything else that would cause you to fall."

"Neil, please." Jane moved closer to Feet. "I'm so sorry this happened to you. I shouldn't have let you alone."

Neil whirled around, BlackBerry to his ear. "Jane, this isn't your fault, it's his. You weren't anywhere near here. There's no need for apologies."

Jane ignored him, eyeing Feet with concern. "Do you think you can sit up? Maybe we can get you to the table, or inside the cottage, where you'll be more comfortable?"

Neil turned again, covering the BlackBerry with his hand. "Jane, please don't move him. Leave him exactly where he fell, allegedly. I've already photographed the scene for the file."

Alasdair leaned down on his haunches, eye-level with Feet. "Hang in there, Feet. Would you like a glass of water or anything?"

Neil stepped away, saying into the phone, "Hello, emergency? We have a slip and fall of a trespasser on the grounds of the Gardner Group . . ."

Edward bent over next to Feet, kneeling on one leg, his forehead creased with sympathy. "I bet that hurts a lot. A twisted ankle can feel broken, I know. Sometimes soft tissue injuries are the worst."

"Ooooh! That's what it is, if it's not broken! It's my soft tissue! It's too soft!"

Mary spied Richard heading for the back door of the cottage and sensed a golden opportunity slipping away. If he had been in charge of the Meyers project, on which Fiona worked, he could have information about Tim Gage, like things he had seen, overheard, or that Fiona had told him herself. Mary knew she had to take a chance because she wouldn't get another shot. Feet was getting plenty of attention from Jane, Alasdair, and Edward, and Neil and the rest of the staff were otherwise occupied.

"Jane, Alasdair," Mary said, rising quickly and edging backwards, "I want to go check on my father and the others, and fill them in about Tony. Be right back," she called over her shoulder, running inside the cottage. She hustled down the hall looking for Richard and spotted him as he turned into an office to the right, so she hurried after him. "Excuse me, Richard, may I speak with you for a second?"

"What? Me?" Richard looked up from his desk, frowning under the expensive layers of his haircut. His blue eyes were as piercing as his brothers', but a shade closer to Arctic. "Neil's perfectly capable of handling a slip and fall. He's one of the best corporate lawyers in the business."

"I'm not here about the slip and fall. Let me introduce myself—"

"I know exactly who you are," Richard interrupted her. There was a mullioned window to the right of his desk, and sunlight streamed through its panes, reflecting off the neat stacks of white papers. "We're a family company, don't you think we talk to each other? You're Mary DiNunzio, a new partner at Rosato & Associates and you represent Allegra in a suit against my brother and sister-in-law. Given those circumstances, what makes you think that I would talk to you?"

"No, that's not the case—"

"If it's not, it's close enough." Richard checked his stainless steel Rolex with a scowl. "Excuse me, I have a meeting shortly and I have to prepare for it."

"I'm not here about Allegra, I'm here about Fiona." Mary knew she had about thirty seconds to spit it out, so she stepped over to his desk. "I have information that leads me to believe that Lonnie Stall did not kill Fiona. I think he was wrongly convicted and I'm trying to get the case reopened. I believe that Tim Gage killed Fiona because she broke up with him."

"Tim?" Richard recoiled. "Your facts are completely wrong. You don't know what you're talking about. The police caught Stall fleeing the scene, with my niece's blood all over him. The blood of a beautiful young girl, an innocent young girl."

"I understand that but—"

"You don't understand anything. The jury convicted him, and

they were right to do so. I sat in the trial every day, and I listened to every word of testimony. So did Edward, all of us. It was a horror. Tim wasn't even at the party that night."

"Yes, he was."

"No, he wasn't."

"I have proof."

"What proof?" Richard asked, in disbelief.

"One of the parking valets remembers him, and his fancy car." Mary didn't know if she should be telling him, but it was time for a full-court press. Richard was in no mood to listen now, but he could come around later.

"Everybody at that party has a fancy car."

"Not like Tim's, a vintage Jaguar."

Richard hesitated. "Car or no car, I'm not surprised you can get some valet to come forward. This is a chance to make a few bucks and get your name in the paper. He wants to be some kind of hero, have his fifteen minutes of fame. I heard the testimony, and it was a fair jury."

"If you would just keep an open mind—"

"Who are you to say that to me? I've never heard anything like this. A lawyer who would represent a daughter, suing her own mother and father? Over a tragic murder that almost blew our family to bits?" Richard's tone was angry, yet controlled, and underneath Mary could hear his anguish.

"Think of it this way. I was hired by Allegra. She's in your family, too, isn't she?"

"Way to miss the point. You entertained Allegra's crazy notions. Look where she is now, because of you. My brother's right, you should be ashamed of yourself." Richard flushed under his smooth shave. "What are you in this for? Your fifteen minutes of fame, too? I've heard of Bennie Rosato, but I've never heard of you, and she's not exactly averse to headlines, either."

Mary got to the point. "I'd like to know if you saw any instances in which Tim was angry or abusive with Fiona. I'm asking because I know that he was resentful of the time she spent working for you on the Meyers project. I'm hoping that maybe you heard something, her talking or fighting with him on the phone, or maybe you saw them quarrel."

"No, of course not."

"Or maybe you saw Tim and Fiona fighting in the house, when you were working here, in the cottage." Mary found herself gesturing toward the house. "You can see a little through the evergreens. Just think about it, is all I'm asking."

"You have no right to ask me anything." Richard rose behind his desk, against a backdrop of corporate awards and framed photographs of buildings. "I don't know what scam you're pulling with that man out there, or why my sister-in-law admitted you to the farm, but your actions can't be ethical. I should have Neil bring you up on charges. Do they have charges for attorneys? Or is there no shame?"

"Nothing I'm doing is unethical, and there's no scam." Mary stood her ground. "If I didn't think Tim Gage was a credible suspect, I wouldn't have gone this far, but he lied to you, me, and everybody else about where he was that night, and he had motive to kill Fiona. Motive and opportunity is a case, Richard."

"The case is over, and Stall should rot in jail forever. He's still breathing every day, which is not something I can say for my niece." Richard walked stiffly around the side of the desk, strode toward Mary, and pointed into the hallway. "If you don't leave now, I'm calling 911."

"Okay, fine." Mary edged backwards out the door. "If you have any second thoughts, or anything occurs to you, even the smallest thing, please call me. Even the smallest bit of evidence could tip the scales. It might not seem significant—"

"Out!" Richard raised his voice, pointing.

"Thank you for your time." Mary left the office, getting out while the getting was good.

Chapter Thirty-two

Mary sat in a blue bucket seat in the ER waiting room, at the head of a forlorn little row that included her father, Tony-From-Down-The-Block, and Pigeon Tony. The air smelled like Febreeze and stale coffee. They were in a small rural hospital, remarkably new and modern, if barely used. They'd been sitting here an hour, and in that time, only one other patient had come in, a man who'd fallen off the tractor and broken his arm. Mary knew it would have been a different scene in a Philadelphia hospital, but out here in the country, the only things that got shot were deer.

Sunlight flooded the small waiting room, which was empty, with fresh magazines on the end tables and a flat screen television playing the afternoon soaps on mute. Pigeon Tony was glued to the television, and she suspected he was a closet fan of *The Young and The Restless,* though he was neither young nor restless.

"HE'S GOTTA BE OUT SOON," her father said, with a worried sigh. His soft shoulders sagged, and he held his hands linked in his lap, which rounded his shape to a human meatball. He had made the trip in the ambulance with Feet, since Pigeon Tony didn't speak any English and Mary had worried that if she put Tony-From-Down-The-Block in the ambulance with Feet, only one octogenarian would've gotten out alive.

"I'm sure he'll be out soon." Mary checked the wall clock, which read 2:06. She had used the time to answer email from her other clients and the text from Anthony, asking how she was doing. She answered fine, because no text could begin to describe the situation, and she noted that Allegra had called her three times, a number that seemed a tad excessive. Mary hadn't called back yet because there were signs everywhere forbidding cell-phone use. She could still be on time for her meeting with Hannah Wicker, if they left within half an hour, but she was here for the duration. Feet took top priority, and Mary was already feeling responsible for getting him in this fix in the first place.

Tony-From-Down-The-Block nodded. "Matty, it's good you called his son. That's the only family he has, right?"

"No," her father answered quietly. "He has us."

Touched, Mary looked over at her father. His head was tilted slightly downward, and he was rubbing one battered thumb over the top of the other. His hands were beat up from a lifetime spent setting tile, and he used to say his grout was like sugar. To look at her father's hands was to see his life story, and she realized that he and his friends experienced a hospital emergency room in a very different way than she did. She wondered if her father were thinking about life and death right now. Her throat caught, and she reached out for his arm and gave it a warm squeeze.

Suddenly, a pretty young nurse in blue scrubs appeared at the doorway, pushing a wheelchair that held Feet. His Mr. Potatohead glasses had been repaired with a piece of Scotch tape at the bridge, so now he had two pieces of tape, and he was wearing a wan smile and a heavy plastic boot on his right foot. "Here we go, gang," she said with a grin. "He's all yours, but we'll miss him. He sang Frank Sinatra to us."

"Dean Martin," Feet corrected her, glancing up.

"Hi, Feet!" Mary rose quickly, and the others less so, though they clustered around him, even Tony-From-Down-The-Block.

"Welcome back, Feet," he said, gesturing at the wheelchair. "Hey, you got yourself a convertible and a pretty girl. Nice work if you can get it."

"HEY, PAL! HOW'D YA MAKE OUT!"

"Tony, *come stai*?"

"So what's the diagnosis?" Mary asked the nurse, who handed her a flurry of papers stapled together.

"Not too serious. A mild sprain, if that."

"Yay!" Mary couldn't have taken the guilt, if the news had been worse.

"*Bravo!*"

"He was lucky, that's for sure." The nurse patted Feet's shoulder. "The doctor told him, from now on, no more long walks without a cane."

Feet frowned, glancing up again. "I walk to the corner to get the newspaper every day, and I don't need a cane."

"I KNOW YOU DON'T. I DON'T NEED A HEARING AID, EITHER."

Mary assumed her father was kidding, but she could never be sure. "So why does he have the boot?"

"To hold the foot rigid, so the ankle can heal." The nurse pointed to the stapled papers. "Those are his discharge instructions, which show the care he'll need. Will you sign them for me?"

"Sure." Mary reached into her purse, rummaged around for a pen, and signed the papers on the bottom, while the nurse continued.

"He's already taken Advil, and we gave him some to take home. He should stay on that for the next few days, as you'll see in the instructions. He's tired, and I know you have a long drive back to the city, so unless I miss my guess, he'll sleep the whole way."

"I'm not tired," Feet corrected her.

Mary smiled. "It's been a busy morning. I think they're all tired."

"I'M NOT TIRED."

"Me, neither," said Tony-From-Down-The-Block.

"*Che?*"

Mary let it go. "What about the boot?" she asked, handing the nurse the signed forms.

"He's going to be wearing the boot for three weeks, but he'll take it off at night or in the shower. It has to be put on and taken off properly, and I can show you how it works. It can be complicated, and the straps are Velcro. He'll also need cold compresses for the first few days." The nurse eyed the group, bewildered. "Who's going to be helping him with that? He told us he lives alone."

Tony-From-Down-The-Block stepped forward like a soldier reporting for duty. "I'll do it," he said, practically clicking his heels together.

Mary looked over, surprised.

Her father looked back at her, flaring his eyes in another Meaningful Look, which meant did-you-see-this-coming?

Pigeon Tony looked at the television, still young and restless, at heart.

Feet looked up at Tony-From-Down-The-Block, his eyes narrowing in suspicion. "You? You'll probably kill me."

Tony-From-Down-The-Block squared his soft shoulders. "Feet, I'm sorry I hurt your feelings."

Feet leaned back in his wheelchair, dubious. "Did Mary make you apologize?"

"No." Tony-From-Down-The-Block shook his head, with its patch of Elmo-red hair. "She gave me the idea, but what made me do it was when I saw you drivin' away in the ambulance. Life's too short to fight with your friends."

"I thank you," Feet said, nodding in his wheelchair, as magnanimous as a king in a throne.

Mary swallowed the lump in her throat, and the nurse looked choked up, too, because nurses were soft-hearted, by nature.

"YOU TWO KISSED AND MADE UP? THEN LET'S GET OUTTA THIS JOINT! WE'RE TOO YOUNG TO BE INNA HOSPITAL!"

Chapter Thirty-three

Fifteen minutes later, Mary was driving the Buick back to Philadelphia, while her father, Feet, Tony-From-Down-The-Block, and Pigeon Tony fell soundly asleep. She kept the windows closed so they wouldn't wake up, though the afternoon sun heated the car's interior, which was filled with the sound of snoring, a deviated septum, and an incipient allergy to pollen, if not fresh air. They had caused their share of trouble today, but she couldn't have gotten any of the information she had without their shenanigans. It made her want to kiss each of them on the forehead.

She noticed the scenery becoming more suburban, with less open space and more homes, then thought about returning Allegra's call, because her father wasn't awake to nag her about using the cell phone. Still she waited until she stopped at a red light to dial the number, because she was that good a daughter. It took a while to get to Allegra through Churchill's operator, but she finally did. "Allegra?"

"Hi, Mary!" Allegra sounded eager to speak with her. "You called at the perfect time. I just met my team, and they have me scheduled for an individual session in fifteen minutes."

"Good, you sound better than last night," Mary told her, meaning it.

"I slept okay, but I still want to get out of here. Can you get me out of here?"

"Not yet, but I did want to update. We got the bees installed in their hives, and I spoke with Alasdair."

"Oh that's great! You didn't get stung or anything, did you? Did he get stung?"

"No, everybody's fine, and we had some help from some friends of mine."

"Great, I was so worried. Were the bees okay? Was the queen alive? Sometimes they die in the mail."

"She's fine, sitting on her tiny bee throne as we speak."

"Thanks so much for all you and your friends did. Alasdair will take care of the work at the hive from now on, he knows what to do."

Mary hadn't realized there was more work to do, but she was officially out of the bee business.

"That's why I called you so many times, I was hoping nobody ended up in the hospital."

Mary almost told her that they had, but they didn't have much time on the phone, and she felt relieved that Allegra had a good explanation for calling so often. "The headline about this morning is that you were right about Tim Gage. He was at the party the night Fiona was killed, and he left upset, though there were no signs of blood or anything like that on him. Our investigator found a parking valet who gave him the information."

"That's amazing," Allegra said, her tone turning hushed. "So he was there. I knew it, all this time, I knew it."

"Also, Alasdair told me that Tim was really upset that Fiona broke up with him, so we are beginning to get some evidence of motive."

"Oh, wow. I didn't know that. So is Tim your main suspect?"

"Only a working theory, but I have to keep plowing ahead. We're not going to get answers overnight, so I don't want to get you too excited, or to expect that." Mary had misgivings about updating Allegra in any detail, especially in real time, given her mental state. Even though she didn't believe Allegra required residential treatment, she kept hearing Judy's voice in her head, telling her she couldn't be sure. "And before we go any further, I just want you to know that even though I'm updating you, I don't want you to focus too much on this. You hired me to do it, and I will. While you're at Churchill, I want you to focus on yourself and on getting better."

"You sound like you think I need to be here." Allegra emitted a disappointed groan, which Mary recognized as the characteristic whine of the American teenage girl.

"I don't think you need to be there, but that's not the point. It would be upsetting for anybody to be going over the details of her sister's murder, day in and day out. Right now, that's my job. We on the same page?"

"Yes."

"Now, I also went to the cottage, spoke with your Uncle Richard, and asked him if he knew anything about Tim and Fiona's relationship, but let's just say he wasn't inclined to speak with me."

"Did he throw you out of his office?"

"Basically, but I've been thrown out of offices before, so don't take it too much to heart." Mary steered the car onto a two-lane road that she vaguely remembered led to the highway. "I also met your Uncle Edward, but only briefly."

"That must have been fun. He's the baby of the family, my dad says. He doesn't come over to the house much anymore, or the cottage, since he quit the business. My dad's the one who runs the show, but he usually works in town, he's like the big boss. He only works at the cottage when he's feeling lazy or if he has a cold. Or, like, I remember he used to work at the cottage in the morning, if Fiona had a field hockey game in the afternoon. He went to all of her hockey games, we all did."

Mary remembered that Edward had been kind to Feet after he'd fallen, but her attention wandered as she approached a fork in the road, at a John Deere dealership. She tried to remember which way to go, because if she were late, she'd miss the meeting with Hannah. Of course, the Buick didn't have GPS. She was lucky it had an engine.

In the meantime, Allegra didn't need to be prompted to continue talking, her loneliness evident.

"Richard works mainly at the cottage, but he goes in town sometimes. I think a lot of his clients are near us, and I know he's expanding the business in Delaware and Maryland. They always talk about that. Work is all he talks about, ever. They think I'm obsessed, but they are. It may be a family business thing, but whatever. Uncle Edward used to work in the business, but he doesn't anymore, not really. He's a sweetie."

Mary took the left fork, hoping for the best. She didn't see any landmarks, only a few white clapboard Cape Cods that looked remarkably similar, except for a variety of different lawn ornaments. She passed a fake plastic deer, a beaver carved from a tree stump, and finally a statue of the Virgin Mary, which made her feel right at home.

"Edward is an antiques dealer," Allegra was saying. "He's really smart, he went to Yale, and he knows a lot about art and antique furniture and rugs, too. He collects needlepoint samplers, and he sells them for thousands and thousands of dollars. Edward works his farm, it's organic, and he grows corn and soybeans with his wife. Her name is Polly. Polly's pregnant now, three months, but it already shows. It took them a long time and they had a lot of trouble, but I don't know too much about that. Richard has a son, Ryan, he's kinda hot but I hardly know him. He's about Fiona's age and he lives with his mom in San Francisco. Richard's divorced because he's a worse workaholic than my dad, even."

Mary hit the gas, reassured when she saw a Turkey Hill convenience store and a FREE FIREWOOD sign, which looked familiar. "Okay, on a different subject, I'm going to see Hannah Wicker this afternoon and see if she can tell me anything more."

"That's really great. You've made so much progress in such a short time, and I really appreciate it. Thanks a lot, and please thank Judy for me."

Mary hesitated. She hoped Allegra wasn't disappointed when she heard that Judy wasn't working the case anymore, but there wasn't time for that conversation now. "Judy's back at the office, but I'll make sure to tell her, and you're welcome."

"Do you think you'll be able to come visit me later on? Even tonight?"

"I wish I could, honey, but I can't." Mary thought of what Jane had said to her, at the door of the cottage. "Allegra, I want you to know I had a very nice talk with your mother today. She seems like such a nice person."

"Oh. She is, really."

"She told me to tell you, if I saw you, that she loves you and misses you very much."

Allegra fell silent.

"Why don't you give her a call? Or think about adding her to your visitors' list. If not your father, then at least your mother."

"Why?"

"Because they love you. They've made some bad mistakes, I know that, but they're your family."

"Tell *them* that! They tricked me into getting in the car. They lied to me. They put me in a mental hospital. They think I'm crazy. Did anybody ever do anything that bad to you?"

"No, but you have to remember they thought they were doing the right thing. They didn't do it out of malice, they did it out of love."

"So what? They don't understand me. Honestly, they hardly even know me. I haven't lived home in years."

"But now you do, and you have to think ahead. The only way they can begin to know you is if you talk to them." Mary hit the gas, speeding toward the highway. "All I'm saying is, think about it, okay?"

"Okay. You sure you can't come tonight?"

"No, sorry." Mary couldn't ignore the hurt in her voice. "I have to go to a birthday party for my future mother-in-law."

"You're getting married?" Allegra squealed. "That's so cool! Do you have a ring?"

"Yes, didn't I tell you?"

"No! I had no idea!" Allegra paused. "Uh-oh, wait, I better hang up. It's almost time for my stupid session."

"Try to keep an open mind."

"All right, see you," Allegra said, begrudgingly.

"Talk to you later. Take care."

"Bye, love you."

"Love you, too," Mary told her, after a moment.

Chapter Thirty-four

An hour later, Mary emerged from a taxicab in industrial Northern Liberties, the gritty city neighborhood where Hannah Wicker worked. The Tonys had been dropped off at her parents', and Mary had kissed her mother good-bye and parked the Buick in front of their house, the way they did in South Philly, where everybody saved his parking space with a plastic beach chair or galvanized trash can. It was an unwritten law that nobody was allowed to park in your space unless they were mobbed-up, but even that rarely happened, as the Philadelphia mob had seen better days and even they respected the right of a man to park in front of his own house.

Mary found herself on Banner Street, a littered alley behind a row of vacant storefronts, an old-school dry cleaner, and a new vegan restaurant, evidence of a neighborhood that had been on the way to gentrifying until the recession. The street was too narrow for the sun, blocked by the buildings, and Mary could almost feel the filth in the air clogging her pores. She loved her hometown, but not all of it was good for your skin.

She hurried down the dirty pavement past windowless brick buildings with steel front doors, double-locked. Some had name-plates identifying the businesses inside, and she read them as she hurried to the end of the block; Olde City Studios, Craig Restaurant Supply, and finally, Northern Liberties, where Hannah worked. It was a grimy gray door blanketed with graffiti, and Mary pulled on the knob because Hannah had told her it would be unlocked, which it was. She went inside and stopped short, feeling a wave of intense heat and scanning the place in wonder. She had never been in a glassblowing studio before, but she didn't expect it to look and feel like hell itself.

The room was huge and dark, its focal point a massive arched furnace that contained a roaring orange-red conflagration, its flames sputtering, crackling, and throwing off so much heat that Mary guessed it had to be a hundred degrees. Three glassblowers worked in front of the furnace, dressed in loose T-shirts, shorts, workboots, and tattoos. Their faces and heads were covered by helmets shaped like a beekeeper's veil, which made Mary realize there were plenty of jobs and hobbies more dangerous than being a lawyer. She wiped sweat off of her forehead, slid off her blazer, and pulled her shirt away from her body, to which it was already plastered. If her pores were clogged by the soot outside, she was getting an automatic facial inside.

She had no trouble telling which glassblower was Hannah, because only one of the three had breasts, though none of the glassblowers looked up or even appeared to notice Mary standing there. One of the male glassblowers had a long iron stick and he was rolling it expertly in the palms of his large hands, swirling a river of molten yellow glass around its end, then pulling it away, attenuating the glass until it narrowed to a skein of pure liquid gold, then swirling it around the end again. His technique reminded Mary of spaghetti being twirled on a fork, except that glassblowing required creativity, boldness, and biceps, whereas all spaghetti required was an empty stomach.

Hannah and the other glassblower seemed to be assisting him, carrying over a large aluminum container that Mary couldn't identify. In fact, none of the equipment in the studio was like anything she had seen before, from the massive steel drums to a row of iron sticks in a rack, and there wasn't any conventional furniture around at all; no reception desk, chair, television, or even a computer. Mary wouldn't have believed there was electricity but for the caged light bulbs mounted on a grid on its high ceiling, which was crisscrossed with pipe and wiring. The floor was of unforgiving concrete, and it was almost too hot to breathe the air, which smelled like fire and cancer.

Hannah manhandled the heavy aluminum drum, fully as muscular and tattooed as the male glassblowers, and Mary could understand why she'd taken the job here, after three stints in rehab for heroin addiction. She could hide here, and at the same time, she could create herself a new identity. Mary wondered if Hannah was forging a new life for herself, formed in fire like the glass itself, or if it was simply the only job she could get. There had to be a reason someone chose working conditions that were no better than the Industrial Revolution, and you didn't have to be a therapist to know the reason was Fiona's murder, and the subsequent death of Hannah's entire circle of girlfriends.

Hannah looked over once her hands were free, and Mary gave her a little wave, to show she hadn't been barbecued as yet. Hannah pointed toward the door, which told Mary they would talk outside, and she didn't need to be told twice. She turned around, hustled back through the door, and inhaled deep lungfuls of cool air the moment she hit the street. The door opened behind her a moment later, and Hannah emerged, with smiling blue eyes under a short chopped haircut, which had been dyed as bright white as Colgate toothpaste. Silver hoops and studs pierced the lobes and cartilage of each ear, and dark green tribal tattoos covered her neck, as well as both arms to the wrist, around which she had an array of leather, beaded, and black rubber bracelets.

"You must be Mary, I'm Hannah," she said with an easy grin, then reached into the back pocket of her jeans shorts, pulled out a cigarette, and plugged it between her Cupid's bow lips.

"You smoke, after that?" Mary blurted out, then caught herself. "Sorry, I mean, it's so hot in there, I don't know how you can take it."

"You get used to it." Hannah pulled out a pink plastic Bic lighter, lit her cigarette, and blew out a cone of smoke. "You don't mind if I smoke, do you?"

"No," Mary answered, like she always did. She hated the smell of cigarette smoke, but she had her own share of bad habits, including an addiction to chocolate chip cannolis. "Thanks for meeting me on such short notice. I can see you're busy, blowing glass, or making glass things, or whatever it's called, it's cool."

"Thank you." Hannah laughed, throwing back her head, and little puffs of smoke came from her mouth. She sat down on the front steps. "I gather you haven't been in a hot glass studio before."

"No, never." Mary sat down beside her. "It looks like an interesting thing to do, like an art form, right?"

"Yes, you could call it that. It's a lot of things wrapped up into one. I'm still apprenticing, but I love it. I'm just learning to start to make my own designs, which is fun. You start to develop a style of your own." Hannah's eyes lit up when she talked about glassblowing, and Mary could see, underneath all her countercultural gear, the upbeat young girl who used to party, play field hockey, and ride horses.

"I think that's true of lots of things, don't you?" Mary was thinking aloud because Hannah was easy to talk to, with an open and relaxed manner, and also she wanted to ease her into the heartbreaking subject of Fiona. "For example, I just made partner at my law firm, and I have to find my own way to be a partner. I can't lawyer the way my partner does, or even the way my best friend does."

Hannah nodded. "Totally, I get that. It's like finding your own voice."

"Right, well said. Well, I hate to bring this up, because I know it's so difficult for you, so the first thing I have to say is, please accept my condolences on the loss of Fiona, Sue, Mary, and Honor."

"Thank you." Hannah's expression darkened, and she took a long drag on her cigarette, sucking in her cheeks. She paused to collect herself, pursing her lips together and letting the smoke flow from her nostrils. "I'm still processing it, even though it's so long after."

"Six years isn't so long, really," Mary said, gently.

"I know, but still." Hannah's gaze shifted away, then back again. "It's just weird to be the only one, you know, that's left. It's like every memory I have my whole life, except my parents, is with those girls. It's hard to deal with that. For a long time, like, I basically wished I didn't have a life before, the memories hurt too much."

"I understand that." Mary's heart went out to her, and even though she knew firsthand how awful and strange the aftermath of murder could be, it was hard to see such a young girl so torn up inside and working so hard to get herself back together.

"I'm over a year clean and sober, and I really feel good, well, not good, but like I can go on, just one more day." Hannah waved her hand with the cigarette, clearing the air, both literally and figuratively. "Anyway, you didn't come here to hear my sad junkie story. Let's talk about Fiona."

"Okay," Mary agreed, if only because she could see that Hannah wanted to move on. "Allegra hired my law firm because she doesn't believe that the man convicted, Lonnie Stall, is the real killer, and she wanted us to find out who is. Is it okay if I ask if you a few questions?"

"Sure, go ahead."

"Do you know if Fiona had any kind of relationship with Lonnie? He was one of the waiters at the catering company her parents used, and he was working the party that night."

"You mean did she date *Lonnie*? The guy that's in jail?"

"Yes."

Hannah frowned. "No I don't know anything about that. The only person she ever dated was Tim Gage. He was her high-school boyfriend."

"Before we talk more about him, let me ask you another question. Do you know if Fiona ever did any babysitting for Allegra?"

Hannah shook her head. "No, I don't know anything about that, either."

"If she had been doing either of those things, would you have known about it, or would one of the other girls?"

"I was closest to her when we were younger because we were both in Pony Club. Typical girls, crazy about horses, you know."

Mary nodded, though she didn't. When she was little, she was crazy about saints, studying their stories and their suffering, which was probably why she'd grown into such a carefree and well-balanced adult.

"We'd been friends for so long, the four of us, that I think our alliances shifted a whole bunch of times over the years, you know how girls are, especially growing up."

"Please, we've all been there."

"But the thing is, none of us were good at keeping secrets, especially each other's, so we all knew everything about the other. We were a bunch of blabbermouths. If Fiona told any one of us about a fight with Tim, we all knew about it by the end of the day." Hannah smiled briefly, but somehow it looked like she was wincing. "So, to answer your question, I don't remember anybody's saying anything about her dating a waiter, and that's juicy stuff. We all would've known about that. As for the babysitting, it doesn't make sense to me, because they had Janet and also because Fiona was mad busy with practice, homework, and working for her family."

Mary made a mental note that it was just what Allegra and Alasdair had said. "Let me ask you a hypothetical. Let's assume that the killer wasn't Lonnie Stall, but was someone else, whether they were at the party or not. Just right off the top of your head, who would you suspect, if anyone?"

"That's easy. Tim."

"Really." Mary hid her surprise because she didn't want to taint Hannah's answers. "What makes you say that?"

"Because he's a jealous and abusive jerk, and he was furious that she broke up with him. We all wanted her to dump him for a long time, but she didn't. He's just a bully."

Mary couldn't process the information fast enough. "How do you know that? Would she tell you guys about fights they had?"

Hannah shook her head, gritting her teeth. "In the beginning, she did, then when we started to rag on him, she shut up. It was like she was protecting him."

"Nobody wants to hear bad things about her boyfriend, especially when they're true."

"Right. And we were young, we didn't really know about abusive boyfriends or domestic violence, and all that. Our families might suck in various ways, but nobody gets beat up, at least not that I know." Hannah hesitated, then bit her lip.

"What? Spit it out. We're brainstorming, and this is really helping."

"This is going to sound weird, especially since I just trashed him, but, after it all went down, I guess I started seeing Tim. Romantically."

Mary hid her surprise again, hoping she was getting better with practice. "How did that come about?"

"Oh boy." Hannah raked her funky haircut with grimy hands and exhaled. "After everyone was gone, we started hanging out to console each other. One thing led to another, and it made me feel closer to Fiona to still have him, because he was such a part of her life. He felt the same way, too, he told me. It was good between us, in the beginning. We really helped each other through a hard time, an impossible time."

"Then what happened?" Mary asked, but she had a few guesses.

"He became jealous of everyone I talked to, boys, girls, even my shrink. He didn't like that I spent time doing anything but being with him." Hannah's blue eyes glittered with fresh anger. "I'm not blaming him, and I take full responsibility, but I think I started using to get away from him. I needed to escape, and after I started using, I fell in with another whole crowd and finally, he ditched me."

Mary was trying not to leap to conclusions, but Hannah was sketching in the details she needed to flesh out Tim's personality. But what she didn't have was proof. "What if I told you that he was at the party that night?"

"Tim?" Hannah's mouth dropped open. "He was? You're sure? We didn't see him, none of us did. One of us would have told the other if we had."

"You weren't with her every minute, were you? Where were you around nine o'clock? Were you in the library with her?"

"No, no. We had been without her for about half an hour. I remember that."

"How?"

"The band was actually decent. We were dancing. We assumed Fiona was with her family, making the rounds with her parents."

"Tim was there, Hannah. I have proof."

"My God." Hannah's face went almost as white as her toothpaste hair. "Then I would say he did it. He killed Fiona."

"You sound so sure. Why?"

"Because I remember something he said, one night. It was early on, before we were hooking up, and he was talking about how much he loved Fiona and how much it hurt when she broke up with him." Hannah looked away, shaking her head at some faraway memory. "He told me that if he ever saw her with another guy, he didn't know what he'd do."

Mary felt a chill, even though she was still sweating.

"I thought it was such a scary thing to say, because we both knew that he meant some sort of violence. When he said it, it was the last thing I ever figured him for. Then, when I started dating him myself, I used to think back to that night and what he said, and realize that not only did he mean it, he would do it. He would go through with it." Hannah swung her head back to Mary, and the two women locked eyes. "I know Tim, and I knew Fiona, and I can tell you that if he was at the party that night, he was there to see if she was dating someone new. And if he believed she was, I don't think he could control his anger. Tim Gage may not look it, but he's capable of murder."

Chapter Thirty-five

Mary stepped off the elevator into a sunny Rosato & Associates reception area. A vase of fresh flowers sat on the end table, which meant Bennie and Anne had won their trial. All lawyers had victory rituals, and the women of Rosato were no different: Bennie always bought flowers, Judy threw a tequila party, and Anne got a mani/pedi. Mary never got mani/pedis because she felt sorry for the manicurists at her local salon, who emigrated from Bulgaria with a Ph.D. in astrophysics but couldn't get jobs here, so her victory ritual was going out to dinner. Some lawyers had defeat rituals, too, and Mary hated the defeat ritual at her old firm, Stalling & Webb, where the men dumped their used socks on your desk if you lost, so you could smell defeat. The lawyers at Rosato & Associates didn't have a defeat ritual, because they were women and knew better.

"Hi, Mary!" Marshall called out with a smile, her usually cheery self even at the end of the day. "Hey, where's your ring?"

"Getting resized."

"Gonna make it smaller?"

"Yes."

"I meant the stone."

"Very funny." Mary reached the reception desk, checking the

clock. It was 4:50, which gave her just enough time to meet with Lou, then get back to South Philly for El Virus's birthday party. "How was today? Busy?"

"Not too. Here's your mail." Marshall handed her a thick packet of letters and professional magazines. "Bennie and Anne won, and you missed the pizza party."

"Rats. Where's Judy?" Mary asked reflexively, then realized it wasn't supposed to matter where Judy was.

"She's at a client's. She had four pieces of pizza. A new world record."

Mary smiled. Judy's carbohydrate intake was a matter of legend. "Her brain burns calories."

"She said she's not on Gardner anymore, but didn't say why. What happened?"

"Nothing. We decided the case didn't require the both of us."

Marshall leaned over the desk. "Between us, she seems bummed."

"Really." Mary felt a guilty pang. "Thanks for letting me know. So where's everybody else?"

"Bennie's in her office, Anne's at a deposition, Lou's waiting for you in the conference room, and I'm almost out of here. Good night."

"Thanks for everything. Good night." Mary headed for the conference room glancing through her mail. It could all wait until tomorrow, mainly because it would have to. She stopped into her office, dumped her mail, keys, purse, and messenger bag on the chair, then went back out and hurried down the hall to the conference room, where Lou was talking to Bennie, both of whom fell silent when she appeared. They looked over, Lou wearily but Bennie revitalized, undoubtedly because of her victory. Mary would've hugged her, but Bennie wasn't the huggy type. "Hi, gang. Bennie, congratulations on your win. Way to go!"

"Thanks." Bennie beamed, hoisting her purse and a black nylon gym bag to her shoulder. "It was awesome. Sorry you missed the party. Carrier wrapped up some leftover pizza for you. It's in the refrigerator."

Mary felt another guilty pang, probably her three hundredth of the day, and she still was under quota. "You must be exhausted."

"No, not at all. I'm happy to have my life back. I'm about to go rowing." Bennie gestured at Lou. "We're just getting up to speed on Gardner. Looks like you have a theory."

"More than that, a suspect." Mary came into the cluttered conference room, sat down next to Lou, and got them quickly up to speed, and they both listened silently, saying nothing, even when Mary mentioned Allegra's involuntary commitment. "So you see, it makes absolute sense that Tim Gage is the killer. The only problem is proving it."

Bennie folded her arms, planting her two strong legs. "Understood. That's exactly the problem. It's really a shame that we weren't defense counsel. This kind of evidence would have been a home run at the time of trial. I would've gone in and raised reasonable doubt about Lonnie Stall. We would've gotten an acquittal."

"I know." Mary felt her heart sink, because Bennie was right. It was the classic third-man defense that she had explained to Stall's lawyer, but the jury never got to hear it.

"But at this point, it comes too late. It's just not legally sufficient."

Mary sighed inwardly. "We have an innocent man behind bars, but we can't prove it, as a matter of law or procedure. Don't you hate it when law gets in the way of justice? They're supposed to be on a first-name basis, aren't they?"

Bennie smiled, without mirth. "It's not the first time and it won't be the last. The days of Perry Mason are over."

"We've only begun to fight." Mary was trying to rally. "We learned a lot in a short time, we just have to go after Gage in greater depth."

Lou cocked his frizzy gray head. "That's the spirit. I've already been digging into his family background, but there's nothing that leapt out at me, and he doesn't have a criminal record. I'm also making inquiries to see if he was ever disciplined in that ritzy school, but so far I'm coming up empty."

"So what's your next step?" Bennie asked Mary.

"I was thinking about it on the way back, and I know what we should do next. We just learned that Tim Gage is abusive and controlling, and we know that that kind of guy doesn't change. He didn't, from Fiona to Hannah."

Lou nodded. "I'm following you."

"The murder was six years ago, and my guess is, Tim Gage has been abusive since then, or maybe even violent. I don't think these guys get better, they get worse." Mary was thinking out loud, and the more she said it, the better it sounded. "I'm wondering if we could figure out, maybe from Tim's Facebook page, who he's been dating, go talk to those girls, and see if he's been violent with any of them. Or maybe he's even talked about Fiona and said something more pointed than what he told Hannah."

"Good thinking," Lou said, gravely. "These guys like to do a little bragging, too, and I had a case once where someone drank too much and spilled the beans to his wife about a home invasion. I'll get on it right away, too."

Bennie walked to the doorway, where she turned. "You've got a tough row to hoe, partner. But you know what they say about when the going gets tough."

"The tough get going to the office refrigerator?"

Bennie laughed, rapping the door trim with her knuckles, which was Rosatospeak for hello and good-bye. "By the way, what happened with Carrier? She told us at the party that you two decided you should work the case alone, but she didn't say why."

Lou looked over, shifting upward in his seat, and Mary realized that was probably what they'd been talking about when she came in.

"That's it, basically." Mary didn't want to say anything that would make Judy look bad. "It doesn't require two lawyers, and Lou and I can get it done together."

Bennie smiled, and if she suspected there was more to the story, she kept her cross-examination to herself. "Good for you. It's a prudent decision, considering that we're working pro bono."

Mary blinked, because Bennie didn't seem angry. It couldn't have been the post-coital bliss of her trial victory, because that would evaporate when it came to fees. "Sorry, I owe you an explanation, and—"

"Stop right there." Bennie waved her off. "You don't owe me an explanation at all. You're a partner now and you run your case. You decide the staffing, as you have, and you account to yourself for the resources it uses or brings in, at the end of the quarter. It's on you. Welcome to my world."

Mary didn't know how to react, for a moment. She felt strange without a boss to persuade, be afraid of, hide things from, bitch about, or blame. "But the other day, you said that we should get out of the case fast, and that it shouldn't be a priority for the firm."

"That's right, and like I told you, I was wrong. Remember?" Bennie smiled, her expression softening. "Because the other day, *you* told *me* that you were a partner and you would make your own decisions about the case and the firm's priorities."

"Oh. Right. I forgot." Mary suppressed a smile.

"Look, DiNunzio, Mary, whatever your name is, it's going to take us both some time to figure out our respective roles in this brave new world. We'll get it straight, sooner or later." Bennie rapped the doorjamb again. "I'm out of here. Have fun, you two."

"Bye," Mary and Lou said in unison, then, when they were both sure Bennie had gone and the elevator had pinged, Mary smiled. "Looks like I'm wearing the big girl panties now."

Lou burst into merry laughter. "It's a trip, watching the two of you. I think it's actually going to work, as a partnership. You and Bennie are really different, but you get each other."

"Maybe that's true," Mary brightened, reassured. "I hope so."

"I know so," Lou said warmly. "I've been at this firm from the day you joined it, and I've watched you go from associate to partner. You're ready for this, and so is she."

"Aw, thanks." Mary felt a rush of affection for him, but she was too tired to get up and give him a hug. "You should have been at the first meeting we had with Allegra."

"Why?"

"Allegra told us that you can't have two queen bees in the same hive. Looks like maybe you can, right?"

Lou lifted a graying eyebrow. "No, not really. Any man will tell you that. You can't have two queens in the same hive."

Mary didn't get it. "But you just said, Bennie and I are getting along great. There's no power struggle between us. We're going to work out just fine."

"I wasn't talking about you and Bennie." Lou's smile faded. "I was talking about you and Judy."

Chapter Thirty-six

Mary set next to her mother and father on one side of the small dining table, and El Virus sat at the head, with Anthony, his brother Dom, and his mother's best friend Bernice Foglia on the other. Half glasses of chianti, leftover cheese ravioli, broccoli rabe glistening with olive oil, and a few pieces of sweet sausage with anise seed remained as evidence of a delicious and festive dinner. A bouquet of pink flowers, which Mary had bought on the way over, sat at the far end of the table, their refrigerated fragrance mingling with the scents of coffee and Polident. They were about to have dessert, and a buttercream birthday cake from Melrose Diner awaited, in its cardboard box in the kitchen.

"WHAT A MEAL, ELVIRA!" her father said, leaning back in his chair.

Her mother dabbed at her mouth with a crumpled napkin. "*Si,* Elvira, the gravy, so good! What you put in?"

"You gotta put pork. *That's* the difference."

"*E vero?*"

"Yes, absolutely." El Virus smiled, sweetly. "You don't put pork in your gravy, I know, but I do."

Mary tried not to notice that her mother's face fell. She rose and waved everybody into his seat. "I'll clear the dishes."

"I'll get the coffee." Anthony got up, picked up his plate and silverware with a smile. "Everybody except Dom takes cream and sugar, right?"

"Right." Dom grinned, patting his paunch, which threatened to fill out his Adidas track jacket. He was Anthony's easy-going, if underachieving, younger brother who'd moved out of El Virus's house only last year. "I don't eat sugar. I'm sweet enough."

Anthony rolled his eyes, albeit benevolently. "Every time, Dom? You have to say that every time?"

"IT'S FUNNY," said Mary's father, with an easy grin.

Mary picked up as many plates as she could carry and headed into the kitchen, feeling uneasy and preoccupied. All throughout dinner, she was racking her brain to come up with a next step in the Gardner investigation and she'd flashed alternately on Lonnie Stall, hopeless in his incarceration in Graterford, and Allegra, confined to Churchill against her will. She knew that they weren't the same situations, but she felt weighed upon by both of them in the same way. Bottom line, she was failing at freeing Lonnie or Allegra.

"You having fun, babe?" Anthony asked, coming into the kitchen behind her and setting his plate in the sink. "You're kind of quiet."

"I know, sorry. It's the case." Mary reached into the cabinet and grabbed a bunch of mugs with sayings that seemed to be speaking directly to her. DON'T WORRY, BE HAPPY. WORLD'S BEST MOTHER.

"I get it, and I have papers to grade. We'll open presents and go home." Anthony kissed her quickly on the cheek, then left the kitchen to get more dirty dishes.

The last of the coffee dripped into the glass pot of the Mr. Coffeemaker, and Mary set the mugs in a row on the counter instead of bringing them empty to the table, because it gave her a chance to hide in the kitchen. It was true that she had been quiet during dinner, relieved to sit back, eat a good meal, and let everyone entertain each other. Happy chatter of wedding plans and gallbladder operations had dominated the conversation, and she had chimed in on one of these subjects, namely gallbladder operations. She could barely get a word in edgewise during the discussion of whether a winter wedding was better than a summer wedding, whether a catering hall would make people feel more at home than a ritzy downtown hotel, and how the ziti should not be overcooked, which everybody knew was impossible, as ziti was always overcooked. Mary knew they were just talking, full of excitement and anticipation, and in the end, she and Anthony would make their own decisions.

Mary picked up the coffeepot and began to pour seven mugs of coffee, trying to stretch the pot to make a first round. She found herself wondering what Judy was doing tonight. She had called her on the way over, but Judy hadn't called back. Lou's admonition about the queen bees had stuck in her brain, lodging deep within the Worry Lobe, and she hoped he was wrong. The last thing she wanted was a power struggle with her best friend on the planet.

"Here comes another wave." Anthony entered the kitchen with dirty dishes and put them into the sink. "I say we load them later, at the end of the night."

"That's a plan." Mary grabbed two mugs of coffee, left the kitchen, and set them down in front of El Virus and her mother. "Here we go, ladies."

"*Grazie, Maria.*"

"Thanks, Mare." El Virus grabbed Mary's arm. "Look at this, everybody! This is my new daughter. Finally, I got my own little girl! Better late than never, that's what I say!"

"Me, too." Mary managed a smile.

"Remember how we met, Mary? Remember that, everybody? Mary was my lawyer! She got me that awning out front, all-new, they replaced it when it leaked." Elvira looked up at Mary, her cloudy brown eyes shining behind her bifocals. "I'm proud to call you mine!"

"Thanks." Mary extracted her arm and fled to the kitchen. She picked up two more mugs of coffee and ran them out to Bernice, who thanked her, and Dom.

"Thanks, sis," Dom said, with a laugh. He worked as a mechanic, finally finding some stability after one or two harebrained schemes to make a fast buck, punctuated by DUIs. "You're my sister now, right?"

"Right." Mary forced another smile. Dominic looked like an inflated version of Anthony, except that his brown eyes were duller, his nose was bigger, his cheeks more puffy, and his lips more fleshy. It wasn't his weight she minded, but there was nothing funny about drunk driving, and her parents felt the same way.

"Mary, welcome to the family!" Dom leaned back and grinned up at her. "You're gonna change your name, aren't ya?"

"Uh, no, honestly," Mary answered, caught off-balance.

"But you're one of us now! You're a Rotunno!" Dom threw up his hands, but Mary felt a headache coming on. She loved Anthony, but she never thought that marrying him would make her a Rotunno.

"Dom?" Anthony turned from the kitchen threshold, a stack of dirty plates in his arms. "For real? Of course she's not going to change her name. She's known professionally by DiNunzio. I don't want her to change her name. I didn't ask her to."

"Okay, bro, whatever, it don't matter!" Dom gestured grandly around the table. "Welcome to the DiNunzios, and happy birthday to my mother! I know that my father, God rest his soul, woulda been so happy tonight!"

"MAY HE REST," said Mary's father, and Mary's mother blessed herself.

El Virus didn't react, probably because she'd divorced Anthony's father years before he passed and usually referred to him as Scumbag.

"I'll go get the rest of the coffee." Mary hurried back to the kitchen, in a deeper funk. Her mother always said that when you marry a man, you marry his family, and she began to feel nervous at the prospect of marrying the Rotunnos. She picked up two more coffees, hurried out to the table with them, and set one in front of her father, kissing him on top of his bald head. "Love you, Pop."

"LOVE YOU, TOO, HONEY."

Anthony emerged from the breakfront with a stack of dessert plates and started distributing them around the table. "Mary, you want to get the cake started, and I'll be right in to light the candles?"

"Sure." Mary went back inside the kitchen and grabbed a cake knife from a drawer, coming eye-level with the sign, **A Mother Is Someone You Never Outgrow.** She used to think it was funny, but now she saw it with new eyes. She closed the drawer and looked around, as if seeing the kitchen for the first time.

It was small, neat, and white, like Mary's parents' except for the modern appliances and funny sayings plastered everywhere. The wall calendar read, **Home Is Where Your Mom Is**, next to a placard on the counter, **I Gave Up Drinking But I'm No Quitter.** A sign hanging on the kitchen doorknob read, **Friends Welcome, Relatives By Appointment Only.** Cake knife in hand, she turned to the refrigerator magnets, her eyes darting from one to the next: **I'm Not Stubborn, My Way Is Just Better. Retired and Spending My Kid's Inheritance. Call your Mother. Italian American Princess.** Mary knew the napkin holder in the dining room read, **Bless This House**, and needlepoint pillows in the living room said, **This House Is Clean Enough To Be Healthy and Dirty Enough To Be Happy. If It's Not One Thing, It's Your Mother. What if The Hokey Pokey *Is* What it's All About?**

It struck Mary that the décor had an awful lot to say, though none of this had given her a second thought before. She wasn't usually judgmental about furniture, especially since she barely had any, but tonight, she found herself reading the signs as if they were red flags.

"Mary?" Anthony asked, standing in front of her with the packet of birthday candles and a matchbook. "Did you hear me?"

"No, sorry."

"The natives are restless out there, and you didn't open the cake box." Anthony's expression softened, and he caressed her shoulder. "You okay? You look kind of dazed."

Mary's mouth went dry. "What if the hokey pokey *is* what it's all about?"

"What?" Anthony burst into laughter, set down the birthday candles and matchbook, and put his arms around her. "It's my brother, isn't it? You know he's an idiot, you don't need to listen to him. I never expected you to change your name and I don't want you to. You're Mary DiNunzio, and you always will be, forever and ever and ever. I love you."

"I love you, too." Mary buried herself in his embrace, trying to clear her head.

"You've got a lot going on lately, and you haven't slept decently in a while. And how can you function, if your sexual needs aren't being met? You're a young woman."

Mary smiled, and Anthony released her gently, smiling down at her.

"Mary, why don't you go out there, sit down, and relax while I bring the cake out? Go, now."

"You sure?"

"Yes, see you, bye." Anthony took her by her shoulders, marched her to the door, then swatted her on the butt, which propelled her into the dining room. She went to her chair, sat down, took a sip of water, and watched the rest of the birthday celebration in a blur, as Anthony brought out the cake, glowing with candles, which were blown out, then cake was eaten and coffee drunk, presents were opened and hugs dispensed all around, then El Virus stood up, with a teary smile.

"I just want to thank all of you for making this such a special birthday. But I have a surprise, a birthday present to myself that's just between Mary and me."

Mary set down her coffee, worried. She hadn't gotten Elvira anything for her birthday, except the flowers and half of the silver frame.

"Mary, I know you're looking forward to shopping for a wedding dress. I know how important that is to every girl."

Suddenly Mary realized what El Virus has been talking about, since Anthony had prepped her the other night. "You're right, Elvira. I really am looking forward to getting a wedding dress, and I would love it if you would come with my mother and me when we go shopping."

"Thank you, but that's not the surprise. Wait a minute." Elvira walked to the threshold of the dining room, where there was a coat closet. She opened the door, reached inside, and pulled out a long, white garment bag.

"Lemme help, Ma." Dom rose heavily, as if on cue, then held up the garment bag by the hanger, unzipped it, and together they extracted an ancient wedding dress, which he turned front and back, to display in all its grandeur.

El Virus beamed, wet-eyed, as she turned to Mary. "Mary, I would be so happy if you would wear my wedding dress on your wedding day, as a special birthday present from a new daughter to a new mother."

Mary's mouth went dry. She didn't know why El Virus wanted her to wear Scumbag's dress, but she wasn't about to ask. The dress wasn't merely outdated, but simply the ugliest wedding dress Mary had ever seen, no matter what the era. It looked like South Philly meets *Gone with the Wind,* with an immensely puffy skirt with equally poufy sleeves and a bodice of heavily beaded white lace, so bright it could illuminate the dining room, if not the tri-state area. Massively ruffled chiffon flowers ringed the scoop neckline, like a series of timed chemical explosions. A thick band of beads at the waistline guaranteed a dangerously diminished oxygen supply, and a billowing bustle in back looked like a second derriere. Hanging behind the dress was a beaded lace train long enough to be Amtrak's Acela from Washington, D.C., to Boston.

Anthony's mouth dropped open. "Mom, that's very nice of you, but Mary might want to pick out her own dress. She'd be happy if you went with them, though. Wouldn't that be fun? You girls can make a day of it, maybe have lunch?"

El Virus dismissed him with a wave. "But a dress like that wouldn't have any sentimental meaning. This dress has sentimental meaning between me and Mary."

Dom nodded, eyeing the dress in wonderment. "I totally agree with Ma. This dress, it's got a lot of meaning. Plus it's so beautiful. Look at alla these flowers and everything. It's got things going on, everywhere you look. You couldn't buy a dress like this today, even if you tried." Dom faced Mary. "You know what I'm sayin', Mare?"

"Yes." Mary nodded slowly, entering a fashion coma. "There's no way you could buy a dress like that today."

"They don't make them like they used to," Elvira jumped in, like a tag team. "Anthony, you shouldn't answer for Mary, just because you're going to be her husband. She's a modern woman, a career girl, a *lawyer*. That's why she's going to keep her own name. So let her speak for herself."

Mary swallowed hard, dumbfounded. She didn't want to crush Elvira on her birthday or she would have simply answered no. In fact, there were so many ways to say no that she didn't know where to begin. She could simply vomit, but that wasn't a realistic option. She was about to speak when El Virus held up her index finger.

"Wait, no, Mare. Don't say nothin' 'til you see the headpiece."

"*Headpiece?*" Mary asked, in horror.

Chapter Thirty-seven

"What was I supposed to say?" Mary said later, turning to Anthony in the car. They'd just left El Virus's house and the wedding dress debacle. "I couldn't say yes, but I said no in the nicest way possible."

"You could have said no. Just, no." The Prius was dark in the interior, but Mary could see his handsome profile in the lights from the dashboard. She knew by the press of his lips that he was upset, and so was she.

"I *did* say no."

"No, you didn't, not exactly. You said 'no, but I'll keep an open mind.'"

"That's exactly what I said. So, I said no."

"That is not exactly no."

"Yes, it is."

"No. It's 'no, but.'" Anthony steered the car expertly through the warren of one-way streets of the neighborhood, and Mary felt grateful every time they drove home that she didn't have to direct him.

"Saying that I'll keep an open mind doesn't negate the 'no.' The 'no' still stands, so I said 'no.'"

"You're talking like a lawyer."

"Can you blame me?" Mary shot back, more sharply than she intended, and Anthony looked over, stung, at the stop sign.

"Honey, I'm really sorry that happened. I had no idea she was going to ask you that. I told you before, I thought she was going to ask you to go dress shopping."

"I know, and I didn't mean to snap at you." Mary couldn't tell if they were in a fight or not, but the conversation felt like just another wedding headache. She was dying to talk this over with Judy, but her best friend still hadn't called back and Mary wondered if they were in a fight, too.

"I tried running interference for you, that's why I jumped in."

"I realize that, and I appreciate it." Mary glanced out the window, and the street was dark, illuminated only by the flickering TV sets in everyone's front window, like South Philly lightning.

"You're allowed to say 'no, thank you.'"

"I didn't think I could say no in that situation. It's her dress, it was her birthday, and it's your mother, for God's sake."

"I understand, and that's why I know with her you have to say no. No. No. No." Anthony hit the gas, his tone exasperated. "With her, if there's any opening at all, she drives the wedge. Dom and I talk about the wedge all the time."

"What's the wedge?" Mary would've laughed, under other circumstances.

"The wedge is wiggle room. The wedge is uncertainty. The wedge is possibility."

"I didn't know about the wedge. How could I have known about the wedge?"

"You couldn't, but I'm telling you now, for the future." Anthony's tone wasn't angry, just exasperated. "Most people, if you said to them, 'no, but I'll keep an open mind,' they hear that you really don't want to do something and they let it go. That's how you are."

Mary nodded. She wondered if that's how Anthony was, too. Then she wondered if that was what she had really meant to say to his marriage proposal. *No, but I'll keep an open mind.*

"If you give my mother the wedge, she drives it in with a sledge-hammer. She takes it as a yes." Anthony steered the car north on Broad Street toward Center City, and the round yellow clock atop City Hall glowed like a full moon.

"You think she thinks I'm wearing the dress?"

"I think she's going to work on you and try to make you wear the dress. She thinks it's just a matter of time until you say yes."

Mary moaned, and just then her BlackBerry started ringing. She slid it from her blazer pocket and checked the lighted screen, hoping it was Judy, but it was her father. She pressed Answer. "Hi, Pop."

"HOW YOU DOIN'?"

"Fine. Did you have fun at dinner? I think Elvira really liked that bowl you guys got her."

"YES, BUT THAT'S NOT WHY I'M CALLING," her father said, and Mary could hear her mother was speaking Italian in the background, which she only did when she was upset.

"Pop, what's up?"

"YOUR MOTHER DOESN'T THINK YOU SHOULD WEAR ELVIRA'S WEDDING DRESS IF YOU DON'T WANT TO."

Mary switched the phone to her right ear quickly, but she knew Anthony could still hear. Every call from her father sounded like it was on speaker. In fact, she was pretty sure they could hear every word in Camden.

"SHE DOESN'T THINK ELVIRA SHOULD TELL YOU TO WEAR HER DRESS. I AGREE WITH YOUR MOTHER."

"Thanks." Mary felt a rush of love for both of them, but didn't want this fiasco to become their problem. "Anthony and I were just talking about it, and we'll handle it from here."

"YOUR MOTHER THINKS YOU SHOULDA JUST SAID NO."

Mary sighed. "I understand that now, but I was trying to be nice."

"YOU'RE TOO NICE, MARE. YOU KNOW HOW ELVIRA IS. SHE'S A GOOD LADY BUT SHE CAN BE BOSSY."

Mary glanced over to see if Anthony was offended, but he was nodding.

"Your father is exactly right," he said under his breath, chuckling.

"YOUR MOTHER DOESN'T WANT YOU TO GET TALKED INTO WEARING THAT DRESS, EVEN THOUGH IT WAS BEAUTIFUL."

Mary smiled. "Don't worry, I won't."

"YOUR MOTHER THINKS ELVIRA IS GOING TO TALK YOU INTO IT."

"She won't, Pop. Don't worry."

"SHE BETTER NOT. IT'S NOT HER PLACE. BECAUSE YOUR MOTHER WANTS YOU TO WEAR HER DRESS AT YOUR WEDDING."

Mary blanched. "What?"

"SHE WAS GONNA TELL YOU BUT ELVIRA BEAT HER TO THE PUNCH. SHE WANTS YOU TO WEAR HER DRESS. THE ONE SHE MARRIED ME IN."

Mary had no idea what to do or say. *No, but I'll keep an open mind?*

"YOUR MOTHER'S DRESS IS EVEN MORE BEAUTIFUL THAN ELVIRA'S. YOU KNOW. YOU SEEN IT IN OUR WEDDING PICTURE ON TOP A THE TV."

Mary closed her eyes, and a vision of her mother's wedding dress materialized like a ghost. The dress was a satin version of a nun's habit, with severe lines, a narrow waistband, and a collar so high and thick it could've been a neck brace.

Anthony looked over, with a smile. "Now this is getting interesting."

"Pop, tell Ma I love her and let's talk about this another time. I have a lot on my mind right now, we don't have to think about dresses. It's late, so go to bed, and we'll talk about this another day, okay? Tell Ma I love her, but we have to go, good-bye."

"Okay, good night, Mare, we love you."

"Bye," Mary said hanging up, and rubbing her face.

"Oh man, what happens now? Mother or mother-in-law? It's no-win." Anthony chuckled, but he wasn't the one who had to choose between dresses, or mothers.

"Honestly, I really don't want to deal with it now."

"You seem so bothered. What's going on?"

Mary thought of her car, still at the impound lot. "My car got towed because I couldn't find a legal space last night."

"Oh no." Anthony cringed. "Sorry. You're mad."

"No, just bugged."

"I'll take you tomorrow, I only have class until three, then we meet everybody for drinks, remember?"

"Oh, right." Mary rubbed her forehead. She had forgotten.

"You can still go, right?"

"Yes, I can."

"I appreciate it."

Mary felt guilty for being annoyed about going. "I can, it's just that we're at the lowest point in this case yet."

"How so?" Anthony glanced over, his tone softening, and they stopped at a traffic light on Lombard Street, almost home. "Tell me what's going on in your case. I can understand it, and it might help to talk about it."

Mary suppressed a sigh as the car cruised ahead and she knew they'd be orbiting the block to find an empty parking space. "There's too many details."

"So give me the gist. It helps me to understand what you do, and you never really talk about your work, not in specifics."

Mary reflected that he was probably right, but the last thing she wanted to do after a long day of disappointment was to talk about disappointment. "Lou and I have been working on it, but I don't think we have enough to get the investigation reopened and I'm not sure what to do next."

"Do you believe it should be reopened?"

"Yes, absolutely." Mary felt a stirring in her gut at the notion that Lonnie Stall was behind bars, while Tim Gage was driving around in a Jaguar. "I think an injustice was committed, and it's driving me crazy."

"How does an investigation get reopened? Do you have to file a brief with the court or make a motion?"

"No, you go to the district attorney and ask them to reopen it."

"You just ask, person-to-person?"

"Yes. You make your case." Mary realized that it was unusual, in a profession layered with needless paperwork, procedural rules, and technical complexity.

"So why don't you just go and ask?"

"I can't do that."

"Why not?" Anthony looked over, braking at the next traffic light. "If you believe it that strongly, you can convince them. You're very convincing when you want to be."

"But I don't have all my ducks in a row. I'm not ready yet."

"If you wait until you're ready, you might lose your chance." Anthony turned to her calmly, and suddenly Mary wondered if they were talking about the case anymore. Or maybe he was, but she wasn't.

"You know, you might be right," Mary said, after a moment. She'd never done anything like it before, especially not on her own, without Judy. But she was a partner now, and it wasn't about her, at all. It was about Lonnie Stall, unjustly accused, and Fiona Gardner, whose murderer had gone free. "If I work all night, I bet I can get my act together. Would you mind dropping me off at the office?"

"Now? Aren't you tired?"

"Not anymore," Mary answered, pretty sure she wasn't using work as an excuse.

Chapter Thirty-eight

The next morning, Mary sat across from the empty desk of Chief of the Homicide Division, trying not to be intimidated while she waited for the Chief herself. There were three hundred lawyers in the Office of the District Attorney of Philadelphia, and they hired only the best and the brightest. The cream of the crop worked in the homicide division, twenty-five of them, and they all reported to the *capo di tuttl capi,* Chief Gloria Weber. Weber was renowned for her judgment, fairness, and intelligence, and her name appeared in the newspaper headlines only when necessary. Mary knew if she had a shot with anyone, it would be Gloria Weber, and the proof was that the Chief had agreed to take the meeting when Mary had called and begged her this morning.

Mary looked around at the large corner office with windows on two sides, showing a southeastern view that was the sunniest. On the wall to the right was a lineup of diplomas and certificates of admission, as well as civic awards. The desk was a modern L shape, of a dark indeterminate wood, and there was a black leather sectional couch to the left, across from a standard-issue row of battered tan file cabinets. A bookshelf held a variety of photos of Weber's three young sons, as well as law books, the Pennsylvania Crimes Code, and notebooks labeled SENTENCING GUIDELINES.

"Good morning, Mary." Weber breezed in with a Starbucks vente and a winning smile, and her appearance took Mary aback. Gloria Weber was almost a dead-ringer for Julia Roberts, tall and slim in a black turtleneck, black slacks, and low heels. Her red-brown hair was pulled back in a knot, and a warmth and humor played around her eyes, with crow's-feet just beginning to show.

"Thanks so much for seeing me on such short notice."

"You lucked out. I'm not in court today and I took pity on you." Weber strode around the desk, smiling at her in wry amusement. "I thought you were going to cry if I said no."

"You could tell?" Mary burst into laughter, feeling at ease, and she understood instantly why Weber was such a successful trial lawyer, because she was completely charming.

"This office is always happy to help an outstanding member of the defense bar, such as Rosato & Associates." Weber set her Starbucks on the desk and sat down, swiveling in her chair in a way that suggested she was having fun. "So go back and tell Bennie I'm not the enemy."

"Will do." Mary smiled. "So you know why I'm here. I've been investigating the Lonnie Stall case. I want to try and persuade you to reopen the investigation."

"Persuade away." Weber opened her palms, then folded her arms across her chest, and her expression grew serious. "Tell me what you got."

"I think that Fiona Gardner was killed by her boyfriend, whose name is Tim Gage. He was a high-school boyfriend, and she broke up with him two weeks before the murder. For that reason he wasn't invited to the party during which Fiona was killed. But when I interviewed him, he lied and said he wasn't there. My investigator found a parking valet who remembers him and his car and can place him at the party that night."

"At the time of the murder?"

"Yes, and he left shortly after he got there."

"Go on." Weber tented her slim fingers.

"I also spoke with Fiona's best friend, Hannah Wicker, who was at the party that night and who dated Tim Gage after Fiona was killed. She said that Tim was abusive, controlling, and obsessed with Fiona, and that he told her that if he had found out that Fiona was dating somebody else after him, that he didn't know what he would have done. The clear implication was that it would've been something violent."

"What else you got?"

"Honestly, nothing more, not yet, anyway."

"What is it you want me to do?"

Mary swallowed hard. "I want you to reopen the investigation."

"And what is it you expect to learn, specifically?"

"Before I answer, let me back up a minute, so I understand your procedures correctly." Mary edged forward on the seat. "When a body is found, the coroner's office goes out with mobile crime techs and they collect trace evidence from a body, such as skin, hair, blood and the like. Is that correct?"

"Basically, that's correct."

"In this case, everybody was pretty sure that Stall was the killer that night, and for good reason, because of his actions in fleeing the scene. He was arrested and charged fairly quickly."

"Yes, there what we would consider 'emergent circumstances.'"

"Right, so then I assume that the coroner and mobile crime techs find trace evidence from Lonnie Stall, bag it, mark it, and that's what the D.A. used to support his case."

"Yes, that's correct, too." Weber's eyes strayed to her desk clock, and Mary knew she'd better get to the point.

"I'm assuming there's lots of trace evidence on the body that was collected but that wasn't part of the Commonwealth investigation, and as such, wasn't used or tested, since it didn't relate to Lonnie Stall. You think that's a correct assumption?"

"Yes, I do." Weber nodded. "There would be a wealth of trace evidence that wasn't relevant to the trial, and that evidence be would be in the evidence lock-up in City Hall or in the police warehouse on Erie Avenue."

"But only the D.A. can get that evidence."

"True."

"Not even a party can get that."

"Right."

"So, in answer to your question, if I could get that evidence, I would specifically like to know if any of it is skin cells, hairs, saliva, DNA, or blood from Tim Gage. If so, that would contradict his story and link him to the murder. Am I right?"

"Yes, completely."

"So what do you think?"

Weber thought a moment, cocking her head. "If this Tim Gage was the victim's boyfriend, then she could have any of that evidence on her."

"No, but they had broken up two weeks prior. He hadn't seen her in two weeks. That kind of evidence doesn't hang around that long, does it? It can't." Mary was thinking out loud, but she had to go with her gut. "Fiona was a teenage girl. If she was like me, she took showers all the time and would've changed into a nice new party dress."

Weber arched an eyebrow. "Can you establish that she hadn't seen Gage in two weeks?"

"Yes." Mary could go back to Hannah Wicker to get the information, or if she had to, go to the Gardners.

"Well, that's interesting, but it's only a good start. It's not enough to reopen the investigation in this case."

"Can you tell me why?" Mary's heart sank, but she didn't let it show.

"You have a two-pronged problem on your hands. First prong. To reopen an investigation, you would need to show me some significant physical evidence, or some very compelling other kind of evidence. Hard evidence."

"I can't get the evidence, if I can't get the record, and I don't have the power to subpoena samples from Tim Gage." Mary thought a minute. "What happens in all those cases where someone is trying to prove actual innocence? Those guys get the record and retest everything."

"That's called being granted access to the original sample, and those 'guys,' as you call them, have more compelling physical evidence to offer."

"What about the fact that Gage lied about being there?"

"It's useless. He didn't lie at trial. I didn't have him on the stand. It wasn't sworn testimony, or even in an affidavit." Weber shook her head. "If he had been called at trial, maybe, but he wasn't. Trial counsel should've dug a little deeper."

"What if you got Gage in here and talked to him?" Mary asked, though she knew the answer.

"It doesn't work that way, we don't reopen piecemeal. You need more on him before we can begin to talk about my bringing him in here."

"Right now, I have an investigator looking into recent girlfriends to see if he was violent with them, or maybe even mentioned something about killing Fiona, like if he was drinking."

"Follow up on that. I'm no social scientist, but in my experience, that kind of doer is arrogant. They love the feeling of power and superiority. Generally, that type of criminal wants people to know how smart he is. Sooner or later, they start talking and slip up."

"What about if I could find him on surveillance tapes, getting into the building? They don't have tapes of the murder scene, because it was a new building."

"That would help, too, so we didn't have to rely solely on the valet's memory, which could be stale at this point. But wait." Weber raised a finger. "I told you there are two prongs to your case, and you have a second problem that's even bigger. The guilty plea. Your client pled guilty. Why?"

"He didn't at the beginning of trial, and he didn't take the deal that was offered, but he changed his mind later on the advice of his trial counsel, who was a nice guy but not experienced in murder cases." Mary hadn't mentioned to Weber that she wasn't technically representing Stall, because the Chief probably wouldn't have agreed to see her at all.

"So why did Stall change his mind?"

"Because he thought he was going to be found guilty and the case wasn't going very well."

"The guilty plea is the second problem you have to overcome." Weber leaned back in her chair, folding her arms again. "The guilty plea matters because it is an admission by the defendant himself and evidence of his accepting responsibility for the crime. And it's a serious crime, the most serious crime there is."

Mary nodded.

"It also matters because of the integrity of the process. The guilty plea gives the victim's family closure and certainty that this matter has been put to rest. That is not something that I or this office takes lightly."

Again, Mary didn't interrupt her to mention that she was representing a member of the victim's family.

"I can see that you feel very strongly about this case, and you might be right about it. But I have to tell you, I hear this all the time."

"Really?"

"*All the time.* From defense counsel like yourself, or friends of the defendant. Everybody and his mother has a theory about why somebody's actually innocent. We couldn't begin to reopen all the cases that we've closed, especially the ones where the defendant put himself in jail by pleading guilty. You can understand that, can't you?"

"Yes," Mary answered, albeit reluctantly.

"I agreed to see you today, not only because you were so persuasive on the telephone, but also because this office really does care." Weber leaned over her desk, looking Mary directly in the eye. "Listen, I know how prosecutors look on TV and the movies, but the fact is we're people who are really trying to do justice."

Mary could hear the strength in her voice and it rang true.

"I care very much, as a personal matter, about the quality of justice in the Commonwealth, and on my watch, I don't want any mistakes, not a single one. Because a single one is a person, a man's or woman's life, and I don't want to make any mistakes when the cost is that high."

"I understand." Mary couldn't resist a final appeal. "So I still have a chance, if I can bring you more compelling evidence and undermine his guilty plea."

"That's what I'm telling you. Hone in on Gage and deal with that guilty plea."

"Thanks," Mary rose. "I appreciate your hearing me out."

"No sweat, and keep digging." Weber grinned. "Bring me back a scalp, and take another shot."

Mary thanked her and left her office, reenergized by the conversation. Her step quickened as she walked along the wall of a large room that held a warren of beige cubicles for secretaries and other staff, its perimeter ringed by offices of the assistant district attorneys. She wished she could share her excitement with Judy, but Judy still hadn't called back. She didn't want the rift between them to get any wider, so she slid her BlackBerry from her pocket, scrolled to the text function, and texted Judy, **call me when you can, okay?** She hit the escalator to the lobby and went out to the street.

Mary found herself pausing on the pavement outside the Widener Building, and lawyers hurried to and from the Court of Common Pleas, bearing thick brown accordion files. Cabs and cars rushed around the shadowy side of City Hall Plaza, but Mary wasn't focused on them. She realized the next stop she needed to make, if she was going to bring back the scalp of Tim Gage.

She turned on her heel and started walking, then picked up her pace.

She didn't feel ready, but she was going anyway, full steam ahead.

Chapter Thirty-nine

THE GARDNER GROUP, read the gleaming metal sign on the ultra-modern company headquarters, a glass cube that reflected the storm-clouds just beginning to cover the sky, and Mary hurried into the building, past two security guards in gray uniforms, and crossed a vast open space to a long, mirrored reception bank, behind which sat a middle-aged security guard and a pretty young receptionist, her blonde hair in a trendy asymmetrical cut.

"Hello," Mary said, flashing a smile that projected more confidence then she really felt. She tried not to think about Lou's information from his friends at Blackmore Security, that anyone from Rosato & Associates was persona non grata on Gardner Group property. "I'm Mary DiNunzio, here to see John Gardner."

"Do you have an appointment?" the receptionist asked, pleasantly.

"No, but it's extremely important that I see him. If you tell him I'm here, I'm sure he'll see me." Mary wanted John to know that her investigation was ramping up, so she added, "And please, could you also tell him that I've just come from a meeting at the District Attorney's Office?"

"Certainly, please take a seat." The receptionist picked up the telephone at her desk and gestured across the room at some high-end microsuede sectionals the same pewter color as the carpet, grouped into a large rectangle around a mirrored coffee table.

"Thank you." Mary went over, sat down, and caught sight of a large open stairway around the corner, across from the elevator bank. The stairway had to lead upstairs to the small conference room where Fiona had been murdered, and she realized that that there had to be a corresponding stairwell at the other end of the building, where the company kitchen must be located, and that on that side was the staircase that Lonnie Stall had used to get upstairs. She would have loved to go snooping, but she didn't want to take the chance with security around.

The receptionist hung up the telephone, and motioned Mary over to the desk. "He's in a meeting, but he says he'll squeeze you in if he can. Would you like to wait?"

"Yes, thank you."

"Great, then would you mind giving Nate your photo ID, please?" The receptionist gestured to the security guard to her left, and if he recognized Mary or her name, it wasn't apparent from his steely blue gaze, behind wire-rimmed glasses.

"May I have your photo ID, please?" the guard asked, holding out a large palm, and Mary extracted her wallet from her purse, pulled out her ID, and handed it over. The guard examined it, logged into the computer, and printed out a visitor's badge, which he handed to her with a professional smile. "Here you are. Please take a seat."

"Thanks." Mary was about to go back and sit down, but wandered idly to the long lineup of building photographs mounted on the wall above the furniture, showing completed construction projects built in California, New York, Washington, Texas, and Atlanta. She was surprised to learn that the Gardner Group had a national reach. Next to the photos were an array of glistening crystal awards and prizes for various projects, then she noticed that the one at the end was for these very offices, which made the cottage in Townsend look like the kiddie table. She walked over, eyeing the pedestal that displayed the glass award, and on the wall behind it hung a framed reproduction of the blueprints for the corporate headquarters.

Mary scanned the drawings to understand the layout of the building. As she had expected, the first three floors contained the employee, staff, and accounting offices, and the fourth floor was the executive floor, with the showplace conference room and executive offices that overlooked the Delaware River. Her attention went instantly to the second floor, and she could see the stairs at either end, and in between a variety of square boxes that read offices, then the small conference room at the head of the back stairwell, where Fiona had been murdered. There were two exits on the back of the building, one which led from the employee parking lot to the reception area, and the other off the kitchen and lunchroom, which was next to a loading dock.

Mary's thoughts raced ahead. She could assume that the parking valets would park the cars behind the building in the employee lot, and that must've been where Tim Gage had dropped his car. She tried to imagine how he got inside the party without checking in at the front desk, and it didn't take long for her to figure it out. He could have dropped off his car with the valet, and once he had done that, he could easily avoid the front entrance and head for the back one, toward the loading dock. He could have entered the building, seen Fiona, and taken her up the back stairs to the second-floor conference room, knowing that all the activity would be on the ground floor and the executive floor. Perhaps they'd fought or he had made advances on her, but that was something Mary would never know until they locked him up. For now, she satisfied herself that in the hubbub of a party, Tim Gage had a way to sneak in, kill Fiona, and sneak out again.

"Miss?" said a voice, and Mary turned around, startled to see two uniformed security guards standing behind her, their expressions businesslike.

"Oh, no. Am I getting thrown out?"

"We'll be happy to escort you upstairs to see Mr. Gardner. Step with us to the elevator, please."

Chapter Forty

Mary was shown into a small vacant office on the third floor, and John Gardner stood behind an empty wooden desk, next to Neil Patel, who held a legal pad. The security guards closed the door behind her, and John gestured her into one of two patterned chairs across the desk.

"Please, Mary, sit down," he said, unsmiling, as he took a seat in the desk chair, and Neil settled onto a window ledge, in the foreground of a spectacular view overlooking the Delaware River, winding its way between Pennsylvania and New Jersey like a snake.

"Thank you for seeing me." Mary sat down. "I want to meet with you to tell you—"

"Excuse me," John interrupted, his tone stern. "I took this meeting only to tell you that you must cease and desist this harassment of my family and my employees or we will file a restraining order against you and your law firm."

"Can I please just tell you—"

"I asked you to leave my family alone, yet you came to my farm yesterday, with a group of your friends who managed to injure themselves."

Neil, who started taking rapid notes, interjected, "If Mr. Pensiera attempts to file any kind of negligence action, you can rest assured that we will file charges of criminal trespassing with the Townsend police. Mr. Pensiera's actions in wandering around the property clearly exceeded the scope of any implied permission he was given when he was admitted to the property with you."

Mary suppressed an eye roll. "No one's filing any lawsuit. I'm here to tell you that—"

John cut her off. "You may have ingratiated yourself with my wife, but I'm not so easily fooled. Allegra is in an institution and she's evidently still not safe from your influence. This is your last warning, which Neil tells me is required, though God knows why. Consider yourself warned."

"Okay, I'm hereby warned. Can you just give me three minutes to tell you why I'm here today?"

"I know why you're here. You're here because Allegra has unfortunate and horrific fantasies about what happened to Fiona, and you're both intent on setting someone you see as innocent free."

"No," Mary shot back, taking a different tack. "I'm here because I want justice for Fiona, and I think Tim Gage killed her."

"That's just what you told Richard, and he threw you out, as he should have."

"So you spoke to him. Weren't you surprised that Tim Gage was at the party, when he wasn't invited? Wouldn't you be surprised that he was abusive to Fiona? And wouldn't you be surprised that he was abusive to her friend Hannah and told her that he didn't know what he would do if he found out that Fiona was dating someone after him? John, doesn't any of that make you wonder if he did it? It may not be enough yet for a court or district attorney, but isn't it enough for a *father*?" Mary found herself on her feet and she couldn't stop now, because she knew she wouldn't get another chance. This was her closing argument, to the toughest judge ever. "I'm not here for Lonnie Stall or Allegra. I'm here for Fiona. I know you won't talk to me about Tim Gage, and I don't need anything from you but the surveillance tapes. I think I figured out how Tim Gage came in the back door, by the loading dock, and went upstairs through the back stair to the second-floor conference room, either with Fiona or without her, and killed her."

John blinked, evidently absorbing the information, but he didn't interrupt, and Neil kept taking notes, so Mary continued.

"The valet told us that Tim came back for his car shortly after he'd gone inside, upset and drunk. If you give me the surveillance tapes, I have to believe that they would show the back of the building, and that we can see Tim Gage enter, go up the stairs, and come back down." Mary modulated her voice because she could see that she might finally be getting through to him. "I know the police have a copy of the tapes, but I bet you kept the original. I can't get the file, tapes, or original samples of skin cells, hair, or DNA from the District Attorney unless they reopen the case, and I need the surveillance film to convince them. Please, let me see the tapes. Or just make me a copy of them. That's all I'm asking."

"No." John rose slowly, placing a manicured hand on the desk. "Here's what I'll do. I'll examine the tapes myself. I'll look for Tim."

"Thank you." Mary hadn't gotten what she wanted, but she could tell by the determination in his eyes that he would look at the tapes, which was second best.

"Now, please leave our offices and don't bother my wife or Allegra again."

"I won't leave Allegra alone because she's my client, and you should know she was the one who remembered that Tim was at the party that night. And she was completely right."

John pursed his lips. "You're still working for Allegra, even if she's not paying you?"

"Yes."

"What does your boss have to say about that?"

"*I'm* the boss," Mary said, turning away and leaving the office.

Chapter Forty-one

Mary got a telephone call almost as soon as she got a cab, leaving the Society Hill section of the city. She took out her BlackBerry, expecting Judy, but the screen read POP, so she pressed Answer. "Hi, Pop, what's up? How's Feet?"

"HE'S GOOD, BUT YOUR MOTHER'S AT CHURCH SAYIN' NOVENAS THAT YOU PICK HER DRESS. SHE DOESN'T KNOW I'M CALLING. YOU GOTTA CALL HER."

"Pop, I love you, but I'm in a really bad position here," Mary said, miserably. The cab bobbled over the colonial cobblestones past the Sheraton Hotel, rattling her brain, though it could have been the conversation. "It never occurred to me that she wanted me to wear her dress, much less that Elvira did."

"IT WAS GONNA BE A SURPRISE. NOW SHE'S ALL UP-SET THAT ELVIRA RUINED HER SURPRISE. YOU GOTTA TELL HER YOU WANT HER DRESS."

"I thought I was going to pick out my own dress."

"YOU CAN MAKE IT YOUR OWN DRESS. SHE UNNER-STANS YOU MIGHT WANT TO FIX IT UP, PUT ON A RIB-BON OR A COUPLA FLOWERS, BUT SHE CAN DO THAT. SHE'S A MASTER SEAMSTRESS."

"I know." Mary felt a wave of guilt, even though she doubted there was such a term, like a master plumber.

"YOU GOTTA PICK HER. WE KNOW YOU LIKE ELVIRA, BUT YOUR MOTHER IS STILL YOUR MOTHER."

"I know that, believe me."

"NOBODY LOVES YOU THE WAY SHE DOES, 'CEPT ME. SHE'S YOUR MOTHER, MARY."

"I know, I know," Mary said, but it came out like a moan.

"SHE CARRIED YOU FOR NINE MONTHS, YOU AND YOUR SISTER. SHE WAS BIG AS A HOUSE! SO YOU GOTTA FACTOR THAT IN, TOO."

"There's no comparison, Pop. I know that. You don't have to make a case for her. I know what you're saying is true. Let me try and figure it out." Suddenly, Mary heard a beep on the phone that signaled she was getting another call, which she was sure would be Judy. "Pop, can we talk about this later? I'm getting another call and I should take it."

"SURE. LOVE YOU, BYE!"

"Love you, too." Mary pressed the button to take the new call, answering without checking the screen, "Jude?"

"No, it's Allegra, how are you?"

"Hi, fine." Mary switched mental gears. "How are you doing?"

"I'm okay, but I really want to get out of here. Can I get out yet?"

"No, honey, not yet." Mary didn't want to update her on the meeting with her father, since there was nothing new to report and she didn't want Allegra to keep obsessing. "Tell me what they have you doing?"

"It's so dumb. I have a therapist I'm supposed to meet with three times a week, and she's nice enough, but I really don't think I need it. There's a lot of nurses and they're supernice too, but I don't see the point. They also got me started in this tutoring program that's supposed to keep me on track with school, but I know it all already and hello, it's summer anyway. In a couple of minutes I have to go down and finger-paint, because they love art therapy here, and after that we play badminton."

"That sounds like fun."

"For kindergartners, maybe. I want to know how the bees are. Did you hear anything about them?"

"No, but I can check."

"They're starting me on Prozac, for depression and obsessive-compulsive disorder. They don't believe me when I tell them I'm not depressed, and if I bring up Fiona, they tell me that that's a symptom called constant ruminations. It's enough to make you crazy, if you weren't already."

"Hang in there, okay?" Mary felt sorry for her.

"I don't care what they say, I'm not taking the stupid pills."

"Why not?" Mary asked, dismayed. She doubted Allegra needed Prozac, but she wasn't a psychiatrist and she didn't like the idea of Allegra going against doctor's orders.

"I read online that the side effects are restlessness and anxiety, and some kids can even develop suicidal ideation."

"Really?" Mary could tell from her fancy terminology and authoritative tone that Allegra had done a lot of reading on the subject.

"How ironic is that? The pill that's supposed to cure you of being suicidal makes you suicidal. Is that even legal?"

Mary let it go. "Allegra, I understand what you're saying, but you need to follow your doctor's orders."

"No, I don't. One of the other girls told me how to cheek the pill."

"What's that mean?"

"She pretends to swallow it, but she keeps it in her cheek until she spits it out."

"Oh no."

"She also told me that if you lick your palm before the nurse gives you the pill, then the pill will stick to your hand. Then you drink your juice and throw the pill away later. That's what I'm going to do when they start my prescription today."

"Allegra, don't do that. Please do what they tell you to do. If they want you on Prozac, take it. You're very smart, but you're not a trained and experienced psychiatrist." Mary tried a different tack, as the cab traveled uptown. "Did you think about what I said, about calling your mother?"

"I thought about it and I talked to my therapist, but I'll keep thinking about it." Allegra snorted. "Hey, wouldn't that be constant ruminations, too? You think they'll give me a pill to stop that, too?"

"Allegra, please think about calling your mom." Mary realized she sounded exactly like her father, telling her to call her mother, but she stopped short of reminding Allegra that her mother had carried her for nine months. "She loves you and cares about you, even if she hasn't been great about showing it in the past."

"Okay, I hear you. I have to go now. I'm supposed to be in the art studio in two minutes."

"Take care."

"Love you."

"Love you, too," Mary said, pressing End, deeply troubled. It had begun to drizzle, and rain dotted the cab window. She looked outside at the gray city whizzing by, torn between feeling as if Allegra were imprisoned in the mental hospital, and feeling that it was a place that would give her help she needed. She sighed, wondering if Judy had been right, all along. Her thoughts roiled, and by the time the cab pulled up in front of the office, she knew exactly what she was going to do.

If it worked for Tony-From-Down-The-Block, it could work for Mary.

Chapter Forty-two

Mary planted herself in the doorway to Judy's office, which was as messy as hers was neat. "Judy, I'm sorry I hurt your feelings. Life is too short to fight with your friends."

Judy looked up from her laptop, her fingers on the keyboard and her expression pained. "Aw, Mare, I'm sorry, too. You were right. I was too negative."

"No, you were right. I was too positive." Mary dropped her purse on the rug and held out her arms, and Judy got up from the desk and met her in the middle of the office, where they hugged and made girl noises.

"Mare, you were just trying to help Allegra, I know that."

"And you were just trying to help me, I know that, too." Mary felt her heart ease and released Judy from her hug. "I knew we were in a fight when you didn't answer my texts or calls."

"What do you mean?" Judy frowned, puzzled. Rain pelted the large window behind her desk. "I knew we were in a fight when you didn't text or call me. I didn't get anything from you."

"Check." Mary gestured at the BlackBerry on the cluttered desk, but Judy was already in motion, picking up the phone and scrolling with her thumb.

"Oh no, my bad! I had the ringer on silent from last night. I forgot to turn it back on."

"See? I still love you."

"I still love you, too. So sit down." Judy cleared her papers and law books off of the nearer chair and dumped everything on the other one. "So what's been going on? Fill me in."

"I've been dying to talk to you." Mary plopped into the chair the way she always did while Judy went back to her desk, sat down, and passed her half of her Swiss cheese sandwich, sharing her take-out lunch. Mary thanked her, took a bite, and started yapping, bringing Judy up to speed on Tim Gage, Hannah Wicker, Gloria Weber, and John Gardner, in addition to the War of The Wedding Dresses heating up between El Virus and her mother.

"You've been a busy girl, or should I say busy bee." Judy grinned, showing the gap between her front teeth, which looked adorable on her. She had on a tie-dyed T-shirt with black yoga pants, and Mary hoped she wasn't going to court today.

"I know, and I had to do it all without you."

"You did damn well. You should be proud of yourself. Going in to see Gloria Weber? That was a smart move."

"I can't take credit, it was Anthony's idea."

"What's going on with him? Are you guys getting a divorce?"

"No." Mary shot her a dry look, though she knew she and Judy were back on track when they were kidding each other. "We're supposed to get my car from the impound lot then meet his friends for drinks. I'm feeling too guilty about Lonnie and Allegra to celebrate anything."

Judy frowned, in empathy. "You can do it, I'd bet on you. Look at it this way. All you have to do is get the goods on Gage, undermine the guilty plea, and wear your mother's hideous dress."

"I know, I agree." Mary wolfed down the last bite of the deliciously mustardy sandwich, which hit the spot. "I'd rather solve a murder case than deal with El Virus."

"You could always murder El Virus."

Mary smiled, then she could feel it fade. "You know, it's funny, my whole life, I worked hard to never give my mother any worries. She grew up so poor, and her life was always hard enough. I've never driven her to novenas, except when I needed a scholarship for college."

"Mare, your memory is terrible," Judy said, gently.

"What, why?"

"Your mother said a novena when we left Stalling & Webb, and she said one for us to win the Steere case." Judy counted off on her fingers. Behind her, her bookshelf was so stuffed with books, papers, binders, and advance sheets that it threatened to fall off the wall. "She said a novena when the firm almost went into bankruptcy, and another one that you would make partner."

"Jeez, you're right." Mary recoiled, grimacing. "I'm a bad daughter."

"No you're not, you just have a great mom. She prays for you twenty-four/seven, like a convenience store."

Mary didn't reply, thinking of Lonnie Stall, who prayed with his mother every Wednesday at Graterford. Then she thought of what her father had said, about how much her mother loved her. She reached for her BlackBerry. "You mind if I make a quick call?"

"No, why?"

"You're a genius. You just gave me an idea."

"Really? What a friend, huh? I rock!"

"You do!" Mary said, scrolling for the phone number.

Chapter Forty-three

Mary got out of the cab in the driving rain, put up an umbrella, and hurried to the rowhouse. She had texted Anthony, **no time to pick up car but will see you at six for drinks,** so she had plenty of time to meet with Rita Henley, Lonnie Stall's mother. The West Philly block was lined with small, two-story brick rowhouses, like the ones in South Philly, and Mary hurried up the front steps and knocked on the front door, which opened partway, on a taut chain lock.

"Mary DiNunzio? Lord, I must be dreaming!" Rita broke into an astonished grin, and her graying eyebrows flew upward.

"Great to meet you, Rita." Mary had forgotten that criminal defense lawyers were the only lawyers anyone was happy to see, and Rita was beside herself with delight.

"Come in, out of that rain. Leave your umbrella by the door, nobody will take it. This is a good block." Rita took off the chain lock and stepped aside, a tall, thin, African-American woman, middle-aged, with a long oval face and prominent cheekbones. Her short haircut showed a lot of gray, but her rich brown eyes had the same softness as Lonnie's, the family resemblance plain. Rita kept smiling, showing even white teeth. "You sure this isn't some kind of a joke? I called Bob Brandt to see if you were on the up-and-up, but he didn't call me back yet."

"No, it's not a joke." Mary closed her umbrella, leaned it against the house, and ducked into a living room that reminded her of her parents', and was almost equally religious. A large wooden crucifix hung at the center of a grouping of photographs showing Lonnie and his mother, pictured alone and as part of a large extended clan, and a yellowed copy of the Lord's Prayer hung in a frame by the TV, which was turned off. "Thank you so much for meeting with me."

"My, my, I can't believe this is really happening! Please, Mary, make yourself comfortable." Rita shut the door against the rain, replaced the chain lock, and gestured, still flustered, to a worn green couch, which was flanked by dark wooden end tables. She had on flowered scrubs and a laminated hospital ID, on a blue lanyard. "Would you like a cup of coffee or tea, or maybe some water or soda?"

"No, thank you." Mary sat down, got a pen and a small legal pad from her purse, and set it down on the green patterned rug. The lamps were bright, and the walls a soft tan, lending the room a cozy feel.

"If you change your mind, be sure to let me know. My, my, my." Rita eased into a matching green club chair, where she must have been sitting when Mary came in, because a mug with a tea bag and a paperback novel sat on a table by its arm, under a lamp. "I couldn't believe my ears when you called. I apologize for the way I look, my work scrubs, I just got in."

"Oh, what do you do?"

"I'm a full-time per diem nurse at University Hospital."

"Enjoy it?"

"Yes, I surely do." Rita cocked her head, in a skeptical way. "Now are you really here about my son, or are you tryin' to sell me something?"

"I'm really here about Lonnie," Mary answered, launching into an explanation that began with the day Allegra walked into their offices, through her meeting with Bob Brandt, and ended this morning, with John Gardner. Rita listened, wiping away a tear, and clucking under her breath, a reassuring sound that reminded Mary of a mother hen. By the time the story was over, Rita's eyes shone with emotion and she had drained her cup of tea.

"Praise God that you have come to see me today." Rita clapped her long fingers together in joy. "I have to say thank you for working so hard on my son's behalf. It looks like my prayer has been answered, this very day."

"Thank you," Mary said, feeling her face flush. "That's very kind of you, but I don't want to get your hopes up too much. It's very hard to get a case reopened. May I ask you a few questions?"

"Surely, feel free. I hope and pray I can answer them, I hope I can help you and my son. You know he's the light of my life."

"I do. First question. Did Lonnie have a relationship with Fiona Gardner?"

"You mean the young girl? The victim? Oh no, no way." Rita frowned, and up close, Mary could see that her hairline was beginning to thin, like her own mother's.

"Is it possible that he did and you didn't know it?"

"No, I doubt that. He had a girl from our church, United Bible, he saw from time to time, off and on."

"Linda Wall?"

"Yes, so I don't know how he'd start seeing Fiona Gardner, though I pray for her soul, and I pray for her family, every day and night. I pray for Lord Jesus to comfort them in their terrible loss, and the Bereavement Ministry prays for them, too."

Mary made notes on her pad. "Well, he could have seen her. He worked the parties at her parents' house, out in Townsend."

"Yes, I know that, but he worked a lot of parties, that was just how he was, he asked for extra hours, he worked hard even while he was in high school and college, all the time for that same catering company, he worked for them, he paid for his own cell phone and even some of his clothes, and he still tithed his 10 percent to our church, and then here we come to trial, and that catering boss turns on him like he never saw him before, ready to believe my son would commit murder." Rita pursed her lips. "I shouldn't say that, but God don't like ugly, and that man, I pray for him, to find goodness and God in his own heart."

Mary couldn't remember if Rita had answered her question. "Would Lonnie have any way to get out to Townsend, that you know of? It's a long drive from the city and I know there is no public transportation."

"We do have a car, I have a nice Altima, and usually Lonnie used to drive me to work because I work the early shift and he picks me up, so he does have access to the car, but I don't know if he was driving out to Townsend."

"So as far as you know, Lonnie didn't have any relationship with Fiona?"

"No, he didn't. He didn't have any relationship with her."

Mary couldn't let it go. If Lonnie had a way to get out to Townsend, which he did, it was possible that he was meeting Fiona, and his mother wouldn't know. "Fiona's sister Allegra, the one I told you about, thinks he used to come over when Fiona was babysitting for her."

"That the little girl? That's crazy, that girl has emotional problems, has mental problems. I hate to say it, and God forgive me because I know it's not Christian, but I'm afraid something's wrong with her head. You have to know that, don't you?" Rita lifted an eyebrow. "She's been writing letters to Lonnie since she was a little girl. She's got my son on the brain, and I've seen those letters, you have to wonder what that little girl could be thinking about, sending him so many letters."

Mary decided it was time to get to the point. "Well, as I said at the outset, I have to attack the guilty plea. I need to understand why he pled guilty, if I want to convince the district attorney to reopen his case."

"It's not his fault, it's his lawyer told him to do it, and he didn't plead guilty when they first asked him, you know."

"I do know that, but can you take me through it? Don't leave anything out, because we don't know which details will be legally significant."

"Okay." Rita nodded. "I remember it very well, even though it was so long ago, I go over and over it in my head, asking myself what did we do wrong. Lonnie is my only child and we're very close, always have been. It was just him and me almost as soon as he was born, until I met Gerold, but I guess he told you that."

Mary nodded, but Rita didn't need any encouragement to continue. Oddly, Rita reminded her of Allegra, the two of them bereft without the people they loved, torn apart by the same crime, on different sides of the same coin.

"We've been through some very hard times together, life's ups and downs, you know that it wasn't easy, after his father left, Lonnie was only six months old, but we survived, with the help of the Lord, you know. Lonnie was a good baby, a good boy with a good heart, I s'pose every mother says this, but it was true from the beginning, except when he got colic he cried, but otherwise no, he has a sweet nature, that boy."

Mary listened to her talk, feeling her pain and seeing her loneliness.

"Lonnie really is a good boy, I know you hear that, you see that on the news, but it is the heartbreak of my life that he got accused of that murder, and you know he didn't kill that girl, he would never do anything like that." Rita swallowed hard, and her dark eyes shone with a wetness that she blinked quickly away. "I lay my head on my pillow every night, and he's the last thing I think about right before I sleep, and you know half the nights I can't sleep. Half the nights I'm up, wondering if he's scared, thinking about him behind those big walls, trapped inside with all those killers and gangbangers and such."

"I know."

"He was a fine student in school all the way through, always rather be reading than even playing basketball, though he was good at that too, and you know his coaches, they tried to get him to play. Tried to recruit him, even though they knew that system would just chew him up, use him up like they do. Lonnie's a good ballplayer, but not good enough for the big leagues, not tall enough neither."

Mary didn't want to interrupt her, but she could see that it was going to be tough to bring the conversation back to the guilty plea.

"I believe the only way to get ahead is to get an education, this isn't a family with the TV always on or the video games and whatnot, John Madden or Kobe or whatever foolishness, like you see nowadays. You can't develop an imagination if that's all you do with your free time, you can't develop your mind. Lonnie was straight A's almost, and he was at Temple University, you know."

"I do."

"He got wonderful grades there, even made the Dean's List and he was competing with kids from a lot better high schools, kids didn't have to go through half of what he went through, and the Lord guided his feet through some of the darkest, times, the darkest times we ever saw."

"I'm sure."

"Right before the end of his freshman year, I find out I have a spot on my liver, cancer. I've been healthy all my life, take good care of myself and him, and boy, that news threw me for a loop. I couldn't have the laparoscopic, I had to have what they call open, right there in University Hospital, where I worked. All the people I knew, the staff, they came by and saw me, and the Church, and the Nurses Ministry, and the Women's Ministry, they visited me at the hospital and at home, they baked up a storm, and the doctors, they saved my life. Today I'm a survivor, I survived, I had to, for my boy. I always tell him, we're all we have."

"I bet."

"I came through with the help of the good Lord, and everybody in our church, they prayed for me, yes they did. The Lord, he does have his own plan, and I didn't see it at the time, but I came to see His way, that my illness, it came about because the Lord wanted our congregation to come together."

Mary believed in God, but still could never square that something like cancer was God's will. Still, she could see where Lonnie got his belief that it was God's plan for him to accept a prison term that robbed him of the prime of his life. Maybe God worked in mysterious ways, but sometimes Mary could do with a little less mystery. She briefly considered setting Nancy Drew on God himself.

"The church, they tithed for me, everybody committed, and the Tithing Ministry carried me on their shoulders, just as soon as they got wind of the diagnosis. You know how much money it costs, the room itself was $1,800 a day and that wasn't even a private. I lost my good health insurance when my husband died. It cost almost $50,000, but the Tithing Ministry and the Church raised it all, yes they did. James, he talked about it every Sunday for a year, and First Lady Donna, his wife, she kep' it going, every Sunday, people made their offerings, they tithed." Rita shook her graying head. "That was a dark time, a very dark time, like rolling the dice with your life and Lonnie in jail, waitin' on his trial, but God had a plan, and United Bible lifted me up, and here I am."

Mary seized her chance. "Now to get back to the guilty plea."

"Yes, well, I remember the day Bob Brandt came here about it, Bob really did want Lonnie to take the deal. He went to the jailhouse to tell him about it, but Lonnie said no. I wasn't there, but Bob came over that very night, sat right where you are, and told me all about the deal. He said it was a very good deal and it would save Lonnie from a lifetime in prison, but Lonnie didn't want to take it."

"Why?"

"Because like you say, he didn't do the murder. He wasn't guilty. He didn't want to say he was guilty when he wasn't, and that was how I raised him. It was a lie, and it was a disgrace. Like I told you, I'm old-school, and everybody in our church thinks the same way I do. We think these gangbangers are a disgrace. Why, I marched in the street when they started that 'don't snitch' nonsense. I believe you should snitch, you must snitch, if you see something, say something, that's what I think."

"And about the plea," Mary prompted her.

"Anyway, Bob kept saying he should take the deal, pressuring him really, I know he thought he was doing the right thing, and maybe he was. Lonnie really wanted to get on the stand and tell what happened, and Bob said no, but then Bob gave in and they called Lonnie in that big courtroom, and you could see that he got flustered as soon as he sat down, and the district attorney, he was slick, and Lonnie's smart, but he didn't have all the cards, you know the district attorney has all the cards. He knows what questions he's going to ask."

"So it didn't go well."

"No, it went terrible, just terrible. I tell you, I watched that, my own son up there in that new suit we bought him, and everybody from Church in the courtroom, we were watching, none of us could believe it. I know he didn't do the murder, I know he didn't, but to see him up there, even I woulda said he was guilty. He got so nervous, and everybody could tell, his mouth went dry and his lips caught on his teeth, just like they did on his first solos, you know in Sanctuary Choir and One Voice, he got jittery in the beginning, but he got used to it. But when he was on that witness stand, he shifted around, and his eyes started looking to the right and to the left, like a baby doll or something, it was a nightmare, I tell you."

Mary remembered reading Lonnie's testimony, and the black-and-white lines in the transcript would tell only half the story. If Lonnie got flustered, it meant he acted guilty, which would condemn him.

"That day, we met after his testimony, in a room in the Justice Center, Bob said they should call it the Injustice Center." Rita wiped a new tear from her eye with a balled-up Kleenex. "Bob said, I'm going to see if we can still get us that deal, if they'll go for it, and I was afraid they wouldn't, but they did and he got it. They did it only because they wanted the bird in the hand, no appeals, a done deal, he told us, and he was right."

"Then what happened?"

"We prayed and prayed on it, me and Lonnie, asking the Lord for guidance, hoping He'd show us the way, and Linda helped, too. Lonnie talked to Linda after me."

Mary hadn't heard that before. "Were you there when Lonnie talked to Linda?"

"No, she wanted a moment alone, and I understand that, she always cared for him, so much, and I knew they were saying good-bye."

"But you don't know what they said, do you? You couldn't hear?"

"No, I stepped outside, and they were together a time, then she came and got us both and we went back in, and Lonnie said he would take the deal. Lonnie was crying, and I was crying. It broke my heart, and it broke Lonnie's, too, but he said yes, and he took the deal."

Mary wondered if somehow something that Linda had said had influenced Lonnie, and if that could help undermine the plea. "Where's Linda Wall these days? Do you have her phone number or know where she lives?"

"Yes, of course. Excuse me one moment, I need to see the time." Rita checked her watch. "Oh, my, I've been talking so much, I almost made myself late. I have to go up and change, then I have to get over to the church, we're having our Family Fun Day tomorrow, our first picnic of the summer. I'm the worst cook in the Culinary Ministry, so Sister Faye said to me, 'Sister Rita, you bring the trays and platters, but we'll take care of the food.'" Rita smiled. "Anyway, I'm sorry, I was saying, I can give you Linda's contact information, though if you want to speak with her tonight, you can come along with me, right after I change out of these hospital clothes. She'll be at church tonight, helping out."

"That would be great," Mary said, brightening. She slid her pen and pad back into her purse.

"Then come along, and I'll introduce you. She's very active and very responsible, and she's a very nice girl, I always liked her, she comes from a very good family, and her mother is a Deaconess. She was very serious about Lonnie. Do you think that you'll be able to get Lonnie free and back home, where he belongs?"

Mary didn't want to give her any false hope. "So far, not yet, but I'm going to keep trying."

Chapter Forty-four

The stormy sky had gone prematurely dark, and Mary eyed the church through the rain-dotted window of Rita's older brown Altima. **United Bible Church, Founded 1947, Reverend James White, Pastor,** read a plastic banner on its brick façade, and a tiny peaked roof covered its entrance, bright white double doors, each with a cross made of windows. Its red trim looked freshly painted and its brick newly repointed, but Mary was surprised by the church's relatively small size. United Bible occupied a double-wide converted rowhouse, wedged between a vacant storefront on one side and rowhouse on the other.

"Rita, how big is the congregation at United Bible?"

"We think it's the perfect size, and there's plenty of room in God's house to fit all of us." Rita kept her eyes on the street, driving slowly, and the windshield wipers flapped madly to keep up with the storm. "We'll be there in force tonight, and Sister Julie says that with the Lord's blessing, one hand can do the work of one hundred hands."

"How many parishioners do you have, though? Can you ballpark it?" Mary was thinking of her own parish church, whose numbers were diminishing every day, which was why she'd been so surprised that it was hard to book for the wedding. "My parents' church has about only 150 active members now. Catholicism has fallen on hard times, that's why so many parochial schools are closing."

"Oh, that's about our size, too, you see, younger people aren't coming to worship the way they used to, except on our choirs, or our Music Ministry and our Praise Team Ministry." Rita accelerated slowly in light traffic, scanning the parked cars along the curb.

"Looking for a parking space?"

"I know that's right, and we should start praying, see, we're late, because I took too long to get dressed and ready." Rita winked at her, and Mary laughed.

"Ha! I don't mean to doubt your faith, but I've prayed for a parking space before, and it never works."

"Prayer does work, this I know." Rita smiled in a lighthearted way, nodding as she kept looking. "Your calling me today, that was the power of prayer at work, yes it was."

"Then parking must be the exception, because my car's in the impound lot." Mary didn't believe God's ultimate plan was to enrich the Philadelphia Parking Authority. "I drive around every night, looking for a space in Center City with my fiancé."

"You're getting married?" Rita practically squealed, and Mary could see her mood brighten as they got closer to the church. "Then that's the answer, that's why! If you can't get a parking space, it must be that God wants you to stay in the car and spend some quality time with your young man."

"Ha! You might be right."

"See that lot?" Rita waved at a rubble-strewn vacant lot, through which the back door of the church was visible. "I don't want you to get the idea that we sit on our hands at United Bible, for God helps those who help themselves, yes he surely does. We tithe to the Building Fund, and we're hoping to buy the lot some day, then clean it up and pave it to make a parking lot for church officials, the elderly, and the handicapped."

"Great idea." Mary spotted a space in the middle of the row. "Look, a space. What does that tell you?"

"Our Lord and Savior wants his Pyrex dishes?" Rita burst into unexpectedly girlish laughter, parallel-parking like an expert. She cut the ignition, engaged the brake, and dropped her keys in her purse. "We're going to get very wet. You sure you don't mind helping me with the bags?"

"No, not at all," Mary answered, and the women got busy, unloading the car and carrying shopping bags full of platters and casseroles wrapped in newspaper, so they wouldn't break. They walked through the vacant lot to get to the church office, then down to its basement, struggling in the rain to bring bags back and forth. Mary had spent her childhood doing the same thing for her own church, so she felt at home, even though she was the only white face. Everyone made her feel so welcome, and Rita introduced her all around as a lawyer who was helping Lonnie get out of prison. Mary could hardly wait to meet Linda Wall and ask her about the guilty plea.

"Well, okay Miss Mary, thanks so much for your hard work." Rita brushed rainwater from her teal jersey pantsuit, which she had on with low black heels, now soaked.

"You're very welcome." Mary looked around the basement of a church that was a smaller version of the one in her parish church, with a windowless rectangular meeting room, the width of a city block. Inexpensive panels of fluorescent lights illuminated inspirational posters plastered over scuffed white walls, like, Be Strong and Courageous! Do Not Tremble or Be Dismayed for The Lord your God is with you, Wherever You Go. Joshua 1:9. Beige plastic folding tables had been set up end-to-end on both sides of the room, and they were covered with packaged napkins, plastic cutlery, paper plates, off-brand paper cups, and rows of mustard, ketchup, and relish, next to bulk packages of hamburger and hot dog rolls. Thirty well-dressed women milled around the basement, inventorying and repacking the supplies and food, filling the room with chatter, laughter, and friendship, but none of them was young enough to be Linda Wall.

"Rita," Mary asked her, "is Linda here? Do you see her?"

"Why, no, I don't. Let me just check into that for you." Rita tapped Sister Christina on her padded shoulder. "Sister, have you seen Linda? I was sure she'd be here tonight."

"Oh she will be, the Deaconess just called. She and Linda are on their way back from Belmont Plateau. They had to make sure the permits were all in order."

Rita frowned. "Oh, how late will they be?"

"The Deaconess didn't say, but Lord knows, we have plenty of chores to keep us busy. Excuse me a sec." Sister Christina waved at an older janitor with a sour expression, threading his way through the cheerful women. "Brother Washington, how are we coming with those folding chairs? Did you count 'em up for us?"

"Yes, Sister." The janitor nodded, frowning in a cranky way. "You don't have to tell me twice."

Rita wagged a finger at him. "Now, Brother Washington, please keep a civil tongue. We have a guest here, in Miss Mary DiNunzio, and this is the Lord's sacred house. We're all working just as hard as we can, and we're all in the same boat. Let's make this a joyful celebration, not a pressure cooker."

"All right, all right." Brother Washington turned away and disappeared among the women.

Rita looked at Mary. "Sorry about that, but you know how men can be, so we let him think he's boss."

Sister Christina laughed. "I know that's right!"

Rita smiled. "Mary, I'm sure Linda will be here soon, and if you can wait, we can sure put you to good use."

Sister Christina nodded enthusiastically. "Miss Mary, we could use you to help Brother Washington with those folding chairs."

"I'd be happy to help." Mary checked her watch, and it confirmed her worry. It was after six o'clock, and if she were going to wait for Linda, she'd miss drinks with Anthony and his colleagues. She held up an index finger. "Ladies, just let me make a quick phone call. Please excuse me for just a second."

"Of course," Rita answered, with a grateful smile.

"Be right back." Mary hit A to speed-dial Anthony and walked away from the crowd to the basement door, where there was an anteroom that was being used as a temporary coat room, holding jackets, umbrellas, purses, and other belongings on rolling metal garment racks. She pressed the phone against her ear, barely able to hear it ring for the hubbub coming from the meeting room and the rain pounding against the metal door.

Anthony's voicemail came on, and Mary realized she wasn't sure what message to leave him. She knew he wanted her to go out with his colleagues, but she was on fire to interview Linda Wall. "Babe," she said, after the beep sounded, "I'm so sorry, but I can't make drinks with your colleagues, at least not on time. I'm in West Philly on the Gardner case, and I just can't leave. I'll try my damnedest to get there, I hope you understand. I'm really sorry, and please make apologies for me."

Mary pressed the End button and returned her BlackBerry to her jacket pocket, torn. She left the anteroom, following the noise of the women laughing and talking as they got ready for the picnic, hurrying this way and that with supplies. They made quite a commotion for only thirty women, and Mary watched them for a moment from the threshold of the meeting room, which was when it struck her.

And she got a hunch that she didn't have to wait for Linda Wall.

Chapter Forty-five

Mary waded into the crowd in the meeting room and made a beeline for Rita, who was at the table on the right, packing paper cups. "Rita, let me ask you a question. Remember today, you told me you got cancer and ended up in University Hospital?"

"Yes, I surely do."

"When exactly did that happen? When did you get your diagnosis? You said that you had cancer while Lonnie was in prison."

Rita frowned in thought, cocking her head. "I was diagnosed in May, six years ago, yes, that's right."

Mary's thoughts raced ahead. "And that was almost about the time that Fiona Gardner was murdered. She was killed on May 1, and Lonnie was arrested immediately, that night. Isn't that correct?"

"Yes, that's right." Rita stopped packing cups, evidently picking up on the urgency Mary was feeling. Sister Christina and Sister Helen lingered behind them, fussing with Brother Washington, but Mary screened them out, trying to put two and two together.

"When was the first time that the plea bargain was offered to Lonnie, do you remember?"

"No, not really, but it was fairly soon, I would say sometime in about a month, like maybe in June."

"And that was the one he turned down, correct?"

"Yes that's correct, yes it surely is." Rita's brown eyes flared slightly. "Does this matter? Why are you asking me this? Will it help Lonnie?"

"I'm not sure, let me follow up this train of thought, and you could help me think." Mary paused. "When did the church start tithing, or beginning to raise funds for your operation? You said they had been doing it for a year."

"Almost right away, they started, we all started chipping in, yes we did, and I remembered it was going strong through Christmas, I remember thanking Jesus with all my heart that everyone was so unselfish and loving that they were, when they had their own families to take care of, presents to put under the tree."

"Then, if you follow the chronology, Lonnie's trial starts about nine months after his arrest. In February, if I remember correctly from the transcript."

Rita nodded again. "Yes, it was February, I remember because he was on trial on Valentine's Day, and my heart about broke for him, for Linda, and for all of us, it was the darkest time, the darkest time of all."

Mary became vaguely aware that Sisters Christina and Helen, as well as Brother Washington, were eavesdropping, so she lowered her voice. "Who in the church would know how much money was raised for you, and when? Who kept track of that, back then?"

"I don't know, I don't remember," Rita answered, her voice trailing off, and Sister Christina came over.

"Sister Rita, don't you remember, it was Brother Kelverson. He was in charge of the Treasury Ministry, and the tithing for your fund went through him. That's how I remember it."

Sister Helen nodded, chiming in, "Me, too."

Mary turned to the three of them. "Where is Brother Kelverson now? Can I speak with him?"

Rita shook her head. "No, may God rest his soul, he passed."

Mary couldn't stop now. She was practically tingling, she felt so close to something. "Who's the head of tithing now? Is he or she here?"

Rita pointed to Sister Elizabeth, who was packing hot dog buns into a shopping bag, at the table on the left. "There, Sister Elizabeth does it now. You met her earlier, when she held the door for us, she's a wonderful Christian woman. But why are you asking?"

Mary didn't want to announce it to everyone. "I'm just curious, for the moment. I'll let you know if I find anything out. I'll come back and help you after I go see Sister Elizabeth, is that okay with you ladies?"

"Of course," Rita answered, nodding excitedly. "If it helps Lonnie, please, Mary, do what you need to do, and go with God's graces and the power and glory of God, working for you and through you."

Mary put a hand on her shoulder instinctively, hoping it would calm her down. "You ladies keep up the good work, and I'll be right back. Thank you very much."

"Harrumph!" Brother Washington muttered under his breath. "I *know* I'm not carryin' those chairs hither and yon, all by myself."

"Mary, go, don't worry about him." Rita squeezed her arm, and Mary took off, wending her way through the crowd to Sister Elizabeth, who was short and heavyset, with big round eyes, pleasantly chubby cheeks, and a broad, omnipresent smile. Sister Elizabeth looked up at Mary, which meant she was only five feet tall.

"Sister Elizabeth, remember we met earlier? I'm Mary, the lawyer trying to help Lonnie Stall."

"Yes, of course."

"They tell me you're in charge of tithing, and I have a question or two about the way funds were raised for Sister Rita's operation, for cancer, about six years ago. You weren't in charge of tithing then, Brother Kelverson was, but I'm wondering if you know where those records are kept."

"What records?" Sister Elizabeth's eyes blinked up and down, like a plastic doll.

"You know, records like who contributed how much."

"Most of it was cash, in the basket on Sunday."

"But some had to be in checks." Mary had put checks in the collection plate herself, when she was short on cash, and so had her parents. "And those checks had to be recorded somewhere, didn't they? In a ledger or in a computer?"

Sister Elizabeth curled her upper lip, in doubt. "I'm not one to speak ill, but Brother Kelverson wasn't known for his record-keeping abilities. Our ministries are volunteer positions, and we don't have any kind of accounting training, or record-keeping on financial things. I'm a dental hygienist, and I do the best I can, like with my own checkbook at home. I use the computer, Quicken and Excel. He didn't even do that."

Mary felt momentarily stumped. "Here's what I'm trying to understand, and I'm going to lay it out for you. Sister Rita told me that the congregation raised $50,000 for her operation, and that doesn't make sense to me, now that I see how small the congregation really is. This isn't a large church, and it seems like it would be too hard for this small a group to raise that much money in such a short time. Can you explain that to me? Where's my reasoning faulty?"

Sister Elizabeth leaned closer, wreathed in a powdery perfume. "I don't know the answer to that question for sure, but I can tell you the rumor. But you have to keep it to yourself."

"I will, I swear." Mary couldn't believe her ears. The last piece of the puzzle was falling into place. Her working theory was that Tim Gage got to Lonnie while he was in prison and made a deal with him to plead guilty to Fiona's murder, in exchange for a large donation to Rita's fund. Lonnie would have sacrificed himself to save his mother's life, because he was devoted to her, and it explained why he took the deal the second time it was offered, but not the first. Evidence of such a deal would be a home run, not only undermining the guilty plea, but nullifying it entirely.

"Sister Rita doesn't know about it, and if she ever caught wind of it, I could get in a heap of trouble with the pastor and the first lady, real trouble."

Mary felt her heartbeat quicken. "I promise I won't tell her, just tell me what you know or what you heard."

"Everybody did commit to tithing, and this congregation always does, whenever any one of us falls ill. Sister Rita is one of our most popular members, and everybody gave just as much as they could. I've heard that they even went to the merchants on Lancaster Avenue and asked them to contribute, and they did. You know, the stores that the church patronizes, like the grocery store where we bought these rolls, for example." Sister Elizabeth gestured at the hot dog rolls.

"That still doesn't add up to $50,000, does it? In less than a year?" Mary became aware that Sisters Helen, Christina, and Rita, along with Brother Washington, were inching their way over, to hear what was going on.

"Well, there was one thing that I should mention, but I don't have any proof of that or anything, either."

"That's okay, this isn't a court. This is just me asking you what you know."

"I heard that there was a single contributor, like that somebody donated a mighty big check, on the condition that it be anonymous."

Mary's mouth went dry. That fit with her theory, too, because Rita would never have accepted the collection money, if she had known that it had cost her son his freedom. No loving mother would let her child sacrifice his life for her own, least of all Rita. "Who was the anonymous donor, and how much was the check for?"

"I don't know the name of the donor, or the amount of the check, but I heard it was the lion's share."

"I thought so! There must be a record of this somewhere. There *has* to be a record of a check that large." Mary was thinking aloud, but even as she said it, she realized that if there had been a payoff, it wouldn't be by a personal check or by any other check that could be traced to the anonymous donor. "Was it a cashier's check? It had to be."

"I think it was, but I still don't know the donor."

"If I say his name, will you recognize it? Is it Tim Gage? He would have been young, like seventeen, and handsome. He drove a Jaguar convertible."

"I don't know, I'm so sorry." Sister Elizabeth shook her head. "I don't know who it was. I never heard a name. I never saw him. I wasn't involved with tithing at all, back then."

"Somebody has to know his name." Mary wasn't about to stop now. She'd ask everybody in the congregation, if she had to. She felt sure it was Tim Gage, but she needed the proof. "Would the Pastor know?"

"I think he might, but I don't know for sure."

Mary looked wildly around the room. "Is he here? Where is he?"

"He's not here. Only the Culinary Ministry is here. The church officials are over at Belmont Plateau, Fairmount Park, setting up for the picnic tomorrow, getting the permits and what not."

Mary's thoughts clicked ahead. "So whoever the donor was, he came here and delivered the check?"

"Yes, that's what I assume happened."

"Who would he have delivered it to? Brother Kelverson?"

"Yes."

"When would he have delivered that, day or night? Do you have any surveillance cameras here, outside, or in the church office? Or a sign-in log?"

Sister Elizabeth laughed, waving her off. "Oh no, we don't have anything like that. But if somebody brought a cashier's check for Sister Rita's operation, he would've done it at night, because Brother Kelverson had a day job at FedEx. He worked at night for the church, and that's when he counted the tithes and did his paperwork."

Mary tried a different tack. "Sister Elizabeth, do you know if the donor was white or black?"

"I heard he was white," Sister Elizabeth answered, lowering her voice. "You know who I think it was? University Hospital. Sister Rita works there, and they love her there, she's been with them for almost twenty years. I figured that they got together and took up a collection for her, and one of the hospital men brought it over."

"No, that's not it." Mary was following her gut. "A group couldn't collect that much money. This donor had to be somebody rich, somebody who could write a big check and not even blink, like this rich kid I'm thinking of, Tim Gage."

"Excuse me," said a voice behind Mary, and she turned around to see Brother Washington scowling at her with dark, glittering eyes, set deep into his gaunt, wrinkled face.

"I'm sorry, Brother Washington." Mary knew she was shirking her assigned chore. "I'll help you with the folding chairs, in just a minute. Can you wait?"

Brother Washington curled his thin lips. "No, not that. Sister Elizabeth is wrong. I was there. I saw the man give the check to Brother Kelverson."

"You *did*?" Mary asked, incredulous.

"I was sweeping the office, and he came in."

Mary gasped. "Was it a young white guy? Good-looking? Was his name Tim Gage?"

"No." Brother Washington shook his graying head, which swiveled on a skinny neck that stuck out of his uniform's collar. "He wasn't white."

"He was black?" Mary's heart sank. Then it couldn't be Tim Gage. It shot her whole theory.

Brother Washington shook his head again. "No. Not white or black. An Indian fella, in a tie and jacket. Brother Kelverson call him Mr. Patel."

Chapter Forty-six

Mary couldn't believe her ears. It didn't make any sense. "Are you sure you heard him right?"

"Sure I'm sure," Brother Washington answered, annoyed. "I may be old but I ain't stupid."

Rita frowned. "Now Brother Washington, please don't talk that way to our guest, in the Lord's House."

Mary didn't mind Brother Washington, who was a piker compared with The Tonys. She was already thinking it couldn't be the same Neil Patel who worked at The Gardner Group, especially because Patel was such a common Indian name. "How old would you say this man was?"

"About forty years old."

Mary didn't understand. Neil Patel of The Gardner Group looked about forty-six years old now, so he would've been forty then. "What did he look like?"

"Tall. Thin. Bald."

Mary thought the description fit Neil. "Did he have glasses?"

"Yes. He look like a lawyer. Act like one, too."

Rita interjected, sternly, "Brother Washington, now that's enough. Mary is a lawyer, and she's here to help Lonnie."

"Hmh!" Brother Washington sniffed.

"Brother Washington, let me show you a picture, and you tell me if this is the man, or not." Mary was already reaching into her pocket for her BlackBerry, logging onto the Internet, and scrolling to the website of The Gardner Group. She enlarged the website with some difficulty, clicked About Us, then Legal, and found a thumbnail of Neil Patel and showed it to Brother Washington. "Is this the man you saw with the check?"

Brother Washington squinted hard at the BlackBerry screen. "How you expect me to see that lil bitty thing?"

Sister Helen took off her hot pink reading glasses and handed them to Brother Washington. "Here, put these on. They'll help you."

"Hmpf! *Pink?* No!"

"Please, Brother Washington." Mary barely kept the impatience from her tone. She was dying to know if it was Neil Patel. "This is very important."

Sister Rita stiffened, angering. "Brother Washington, I *know* you don't want to make me lose my temper, no, you *don't.*"

"Don't need no pink eyeglasses," Brother Washington muttered, but he accepted the glasses, put them on, and peered through them at the BlackBerry screen. "Yes. That him. That the man."

Mary felt thunderstruck. She'd felt so close to solving the crime, but she didn't understand anything, anymore. She had no idea why Neil Patel would be paying Lonnie Stall to plead guilty to Fiona's murder. "You're sure?" Mary asked, incredulous.

"How many times I gotta say?" Brother Washington glared through the glasses, his cloudy brown eyes magnified like brown marbles.

Rita touched Mary's arm. "Tell me, what's going on? Does this make a difference for Lonnie?"

"I don't know yet." Mary's mind was already racing through the possibilities. If Neil wasn't the killer, he had to be protecting whoever was the killer. She put her hands on Rita's soft shoulders. "Don't get your hopes up, okay? I didn't expect his answer, but I don't know if it tells us anything."

"But who is that man?" Rita's face was a mask of confusion. "Who is Neil Patel? What does he mean to you?"

"Let me get all the facts first. I have to get back to my office, as soon as I can." Mary had to talk to Lou and Judy, and process the new information. "What are the chances of my getting a cab outside?"

Rita shook her head. "In this rain, not very good, that's for sure, and the bus doesn't stop near here, either. You can borrow my car if you like. If it helps Lonnie, I'd surely be happy to help."

"I'll take you up on that offer. Thank you." Mary hated to inconvenience anyone, but she didn't want to waste a minute. "Is your purse in the coat room? Let's go get it."

"This way." Rita turned on her heel and hustled through the crowd, saying polite "excuse-me's-please," with Mary at her heels. The two women hurried into the anteroom, where Rita found her purse, extracted her keys, and handed them over, closing her eyes briefly, then opening them. "I just said a prayer to guide your footsteps, and I know He will. Thank you so very much for all you're doing for my son, and the light of God is within you, I can see it plainly, no matter what Brother Washington says about lawyers."

"Thank you so much." Mary gave Rita a big hug, then rummaged around the garment rack for her purse and umbrella. "I should be back later tonight, don't worry. I'll call you as soon as I know what's going on, and get the car back to you. Thanks again."

Mary hurried out the door, opening the umbrella against the driving rain and leaving the church. She hustled back over the vacant lot, avoiding the puddles and watching her step over the shaky rubble footing. She reached Rita's Altima, tucked the stalk of the umbrella under her arm, fumbled for the key fob, and chirped the car unlocked, then jumped inside, closing the umbrella and stowing it on the floor on the passenger side.

She started the ignition, flipped on the windshield wipers, and reversed out of the space, down the street. It was hard to see in the rain, but she cruised to the corner, took a right onto Aston Street, heading for Chestnut Street or one of the other major streets that would lead back to Center City. She couldn't wait to tell Lou about Neil Patel, so she picked up her BlackBerry and pressed L, but didn't hear the call ringing when she held the phone to her ear. She braked at the light and checked the screen, but the battery icon glowed a telltale red. The screen read, INSUFFICIENT BATTERY FOR RADIO USAGE.

"Damn!" Mary reached in the console where she kept her car charger, then she realized she wasn't in her own car. She tossed the BlackBerry aside and looked around for a pay phone, but they were artifacts in most city neighborhoods. She looked out the window but all she could see was the pouring rain, making a blackish-gray haze of the rowhouses and parked cars. Lights shone dimly inside the homes, and pedestrians hurried along the pavement, mere shadows under umbrellas.

She braked at a traffic light, drumming her fingers on the steering wheel, her thoughts going a mile a minute. She couldn't imagine any connection between Neil Patel and Lonnie Stall, so she went backwards in time, trying to piece it together, brainstorming with herself. She'd believed that Tim Gage had paid Lonnie to take the fall for Fiona's murder, so she applied the same reasoning to what she'd just learned about Neil Patel. If her reasoning held true, then Neil would've been paying Lonnie to take the fall for Fiona's murder. The only possible conclusions were that Neil Patel had killed Fiona himself, or that Neil was covering up for someone else who had killed Fiona. And the latter conclusion was unspeakable, because Neil wouldn't cover up for just anybody. He worked for the Gardners, and she didn't even want to think that the killer could be one of the family.

Mary clenched the steering wheel, horrified. Even after the traffic light turned green, she remained stricken, at a standstill. A car honked behind her, and she came out of her reverie and hit the gas. The Altima lurched forward, and she had to brake quickly not to crash into a delivery van in front of her, its red taillights bathing her in crimson. She found herself stuck in an endless line of traffic, two lanes of congestion going both ways, and she'd never get to the office at this rate.

She took a right onto the next cross street, which she seemed to remember was a back way to Center City. She couldn't read the sign for the rain, but she thought it was Huntingdon Avenue. It had to be a main artery because the Altima's tires shimmied as they got caught in the groove of trolley tracks, which crisscrossed West Philly, still used by subway-surface cars. She wasn't as familiar with this section of town, farther southwest than the University of Pennsylvania and her old stomping grounds.

The windows and windshield started to fog up, and she hit a button on the dashboard for the defrost. Air conditioning blew into her face, but the windshield didn't clear and the only thing that got defrosted were her contact lens. The traffic finally started moving, and Mary took the first right she could, then a left, taking the shortcut downtown.

Her thoughts raced ahead, trying to make sense of Neil Patel or someone in the Gardner family as Fiona's murderer. She had no idea what their motive would be, but either would have had ample opportunity to commit the murder. Patel and any family member would have had access anywhere in the new Gardner Group headquarters, including the second-floor conference room, where Fiona had been killed. Mary could imagine Neil or a family member going with the VIP clients who were being shown around, then slipping away from any client group without being noticed.

Mary took a right turn, following the shortcut, preoccupied with the details of how the killer could have committed the crime. She thought back to the layout of the reception area, with the public stairway leading to the second floor, and she could imagine Neil or a family member running up the stairs, going past any cordon or sign without being questioned by security or anyone else. She would bet that the surveillance tapes would show as much, but nobody would think twice if they saw any of them going up and down. Neil or a family member wouldn't have even had to take the stairway by the loading dock and kitchen, where she had thought Tim Gage had sneaked in and which the police believed Lonnie had used.

She took another left turn onto Floodgate Street, relieved to see that she was one of the few cars on the block and that she had escaped the major traffic jam. She wiped a fan in the windshield and noticed that the neighborhood was deteriorating, with fewer lights on inside the houses, some of which appeared to be vacant. She found herself wishing that the car had GPS, but it was too old, or that her BlackBerry still worked, so she could access a map application. Still she stayed the course, because Philadelphia was famously designed on a grid and she refused to get lost in her own hometown.

Mary hit the gas, expecting to see more houses and stores any block now, but her mind was on the murder. Her gut tensed when she started to think of how easily Neil or a family member could have committed the crime. The inner circle would have known that the presentation ceremony would have been at nine o'clock, so everybody would have been busy preparing for the event and security would have been distracted, too. The killer could have lured Fiona upstairs to the second-floor conference room in a number of ways. He could have simply asked her to meet him, at any point in the evening, making up some pretext. He could have told her it was a detail about the presentation ceremony or about anything else, for that matter. If it was a family member, it would have been simple—and appalling.

Mary remembered that Fiona's cell phone was never found, and she felt something click in the back of her brain. Neil and the Gardner family would have known Fiona's cell phone number, so they could even have texted Fiona and told her to come upstairs. Fiona would have run upstairs, leaving her girlfriends behind or maybe even Tim Gage, who was at the party around that time.

The windshield wipers flapped frantically, and Mary kept traveling down the road, sickened by the horrifying scenarios running through her mind. Meantime, the neighborhood was getting worse. There were no people with umbrellas on the sidewalk, and the rowhouses had morphed to vacant lots, cyclone fencing, and empty storefronts. A single car traveled behind her, so at least she wasn't completely alone. She decided to go a few more blocks and if she didn't see more lights or activity, to go the other way. Some sections of West Philly could be as confusing to navigate as the warrens of South Philly, and she must have gotten turned around somehow. Evidently, Feet wasn't the only one with a bad sense of direction.

Mary accelerated despite the weather, her thoughts returning to Fiona's murder, with a powerful sense of dread. The murder weapon had been a common kitchen knife, and the killer could have obtained that anywhere, even from the kitchen in the office that night. He could have been waiting in the conference room and when Fiona entered, he could simply have walked up to her and plunged the knife into her chest.

Mary felt tears come to her eyes, picturing Fiona breathe her last few breaths, shout with pain, shock, and betrayal, then fall backwards on the floor, terror etched forever into her beautiful young face. The killer would have collected the knife and her cell phone, because he would have known they could incriminate him, then he would have left the room quickly and gone downstairs, without an ounce of suspicion.

Mary drove down the dark, deserted blocks, ahead of the other car, trying to figure out the last piece of the puzzle. She remembered that Lonnie had gone upstairs because he'd heard a woman's shout, and she pictured him running up to find Fiona and trying to resuscitate her, just after the killer had left. That would have been consistent with Lonnie's testimony at trial, as well as what he'd told Mary when she'd interviewed him at Graterford Prison.

She cruised ahead in the rain, scanning for a place to turn around, becoming convinced she was heading the wrong way. She wondered if the car behind her was lost, too, because it was still there. Then she had another thought about the case, which struck her as a revelation. If Allegra had been right, that Lonnie knew Fiona and visited her while she was babysitting Allegra, then it was possible that the killer had seen Lonnie at the Gardner house, because Neil and the family worked in the cottage and could have spotted Lonnie on the property, even if the kids had stowed his car in the garage, because the main house was visible from the cottage.

Mary reached the end of the block and took a right turn, putting on her blinker for the car behind her, which seemed to be a dark SUV. She wouldn't mind leaving it behind, because it was beginning to give her the creeps. She cruised down the narrow street, then took another right turn around the block, preoccupied.

She realized that if Neil or the family member had known that Fiona and Lonnie were seeing each other in secret, then he could have guessed that Lonnie's phone number would be in Fiona's cell phone. The killer could have knifed Fiona, picked up her cell phone, and texted Lonnie, telling him to come upstairs and meet her in the second-floor conference room. Lonnie wouldn't have known that the text hadn't come from Fiona and he would've gone upstairs in a flash. He would have tried to resuscitate her, then run out in a panic, as he had, never realizing that he had just been framed for murder.

Mary hit the gas, glancing in the rearview mirror. The big head-lights of the dark SUV popped into view, which seemed strange, unless its driver had gotten lost, too. She hoped she'd get out of the neighborhood soon, and if she'd been driving a nicer car, she would've been worried about getting carjacked. She told herself she was para-noid, undoubtedly because she was envisioning an awful murder.

The more Mary thought about her theory of the crime, the more sense it made, and she felt sick to her stomach as she drove. Neil or a Gardner had set up Lonnie Stall for Fiona's murder, and Lonnie had played into his hands by denying his relationship with Fiona, proba-bly for fear of providing the Commonwealth with a credible motive to murder, which they could use against him. Mary felt the truth of her conclusion with a certainty that resonated within her chest. It wasn't Tim Gage who had paid Lonnie off, it was Neil Patel. The open questions were who had killed Fiona and why, and Mary was determined to find out, but she would have expert help from now on. She had learned enough about the guilty plea for Gloria Weber to reopen the investigation.

"WHAM!"

Suddenly Mary felt a huge jolt from behind, and everything seemed to happen at once. She flew out of her seat but was caught by the shoulder harness. The Altima leapt forward on the slick asphalt, hydroplaning out of control. She screamed in shock and fear. The airbag exploded, shoving her backwards and hitting her in the face.

She slammed on the brakes, struggling to react. The Altima skidded into a telephone pole, striking the front fender on the passenger side. The crash threw her against the door. Her windshield cracked into a million shards. Her brain rattled, her teeth banged together. The airbag deflated into a saggy mess of warm plastic.

Mary tried to collect her thoughts. She had been in an accident, struck by the SUV. She could hear the loud idling of its massive engine. Its high beams blasted the Altima interior with light, blinding her. The SUV must still have been stuck on her bumper. She remembered she didn't have a phone to call 911. She hoped the SUV driver would or already had. Otherwise no one else would call, because the block looked dark and deserted in the rain.

She unfastened her shoulder harness, numb with shock. Her head hurt too much to think. She panted, slumping in the seat. Her mouth was oddly dry. She didn't know if she'd been injured and looked down. She didn't see any blood or broken bones. Her knees hadn't hit the dashboard. Her blazer was covered with whitish powder from the airbag. The windshield had shattered but not fallen apart. She hated that she'd crashed Rita's car. She wondered if the SUV driver was injured. She reached for the door handle, to get out of the Altima and check on him.

"WHAM!"

The SUV crashed into the Altima again. Mary flew forward without the harness. The Altima smashed into a parked car. Her face hit the deflated airbag over the steering wheel. Pain arced like electricity through her nose and mouth. Her thoughts fogged, but she realized it was no accident.

Someone was trying to kill her.

Chapter Forty-seven

Mary glanced in terror at the rearview mirror. The driver's side door of the SUV was opening. A figure got out of the car, a tall, dark shadow in the downpour. She guessed it was Neil Patel but she wasn't waiting around to find out. She had to run for her life.

She yanked the key out of the ignition, hit the panic button on the fob, and clambered over the console to the passenger seat. The car alarm went off and the Altima burst into sound. She grabbed the door handle, shoved open the door, and scrambled out of the car. She hit the street running.

"Help!" Mary screamed, though the rain drowned her out. She raced past a darkened warehouse, as long as a city block. Adrenaline coursed through her system. Rain drenched her face and body. Her breath came in ragged bursts. She prayed somebody would respond to the car alarm, but she knew better. She was on her own.

She slipped on the slick pavement but kept her legs churning. She could barely see a foot in front of her. She glanced over her shoulder.

The shadow was chasing her, raising his right arm in a way that could only mean that he had a gun and was taking aim. A red flare burst from its muzzle.

Mary bolted forward. The crack of a gunshot echoed faintly in the rain. She prayed the bullet wouldn't hit her. He must have missed because she kept running as hard as she could, pumping her arms and legs.

She looked wildly around for a place to hide. There was nothing but the wet brick wall of the warehouse. She didn't dare run across the street, giving him a clear shot. The blare of the car alarm grew more and more distant. No one was coming, no one was around.

"Help!" she screamed, frantic. She raced to the end of the block. Up ahead was another warehouse, but she spotted a light in one of the rowhouses on the cross street. She prayed somebody inside would hear her and call the police. She veered right around the corner and ran flat out for it, screaming at the top of her lungs.

Crack! Another gunshot exploded but she was already on the cross street. She raced to the rowhouse. Rain flew into her eyes. She couldn't see if anybody was home. She couldn't take a chance and slow her pace or stop. Nobody opened the door of the rowhouse. There was no movement or people in the window.

Suddenly she noticed a vacant lot behind the rowhouses. It was her only hope. She glanced behind her. He hadn't turned the corner yet. She stopped screaming so he wouldn't know where she was. If she could reach the lot, she had a chance of hiding. Unless he caught up soon, he wouldn't be able to see her in the rain.

She accelerated, summoning every ounce of strength, ignoring the pain in her lungs and legs. She reached the vacant lot and fell forward onto the rubble, glass, and other trash.

She scrambled to her feet and flattened herself against the wall, gasping for breath. She tried to think through her terror. She squinted in the darkness for anything on the ground that she could defend herself with. It was too dark to see. She threw herself down on all fours, felt around desperately, and came up with a brick.

Crack! sounded another gunshot, so nearby that Mary almost cried out in fright. The sound told her that he was approaching. She couldn't hear his footsteps in the rain, but she spotted his shadow on the pavement, in the light from the rowhouse. His shadow was getting larger, so he was getting closer.

Her heart thundered. She panted in fear and exertion. She couldn't run forever. She couldn't outrace a bullet. She couldn't be defensive. She had to attack. She waited until the shadow loomed impossibly large, then she leapt from behind the wall and swung the brick as hard as she could at his face.

"Arg!" he cried out, in pain and surprise. It was Neil Patel, and the brick had struck only a glancing blow to the back of his head. He staggered backwards, losing his balance. His arms windmilled. He dropped the gun.

"You bastard!" Mary felt a surge of fury and slammed the brick squarely into his nose, hearing it crack.

His hands flew up reflexively. Blood geysered from his nose. He stumbled backwards, collapsed, and fell to the hard pavement, clutching his face.

Mary dropped the brick, picked up the gun, and aimed it at him. Neil was lying on his side in a fetal position. Blood spurted from his wound and ran in watery red rivulets over his face, making a horrifying mask. The gun had a lethal heft, but Mary was a lawyer, not a vigilante, and she needed answers that only Neil had.

"Who killed Fiona and why?" Mary shouted, keeping the muzzle pointed at his temple. "Why did you pay Lonnie to take the fall?"

Suddenly the blare of police sirens cut through the rain. Neil's head turned away from her, and blood ran into his mouth, darkening his teeth. "I want a lawyer," he said weakly, then closed his eyes.

"Neil, tell me!" Mary leaned over him and caught the faint ringing of a cell phone. On impulse, she flipped aside his jacket.

"No!" Neil's arm flailed for the phone, but he was too weak to make contact.

Mary reached into his inside pocket, took his BlackBerry, and looked at its lighted screen, which read, RICHARD GARDNER. She pressed Answer and held the phone to her ear.

"Neil?" Richard asked, his tone tense. "Tell me it's over."

Mary felt heartsick. Richard had to be talking about Neil's killing her. So Richard had to be involved in Fiona's murder, in the slaughter of his own niece. Mary wanted to scream at him in revulsion, but she didn't answer because she didn't want to tip him off. He had the money to flee or even leave the country. So she pressed End and said nothing, but she was dying to say:

It's not Neil, it's Mary. And it's not over. It's just beginning.

Chapter Forty-eight

Mary hurried into the bustling Homicide Squad room at the Round-house, Philly's Police Administration Building, with a uniformed cop who had taken her here from the scene. Her jaw hurt, and she felt shaken and wet, but she wasn't about to delay giving Weber a statement. Neil Patel had been arrested at the scene and taken to the hospital, but Mary had declined treatment, for the time being. She was the only one who knew about Richard Gardner and she'd made sure that the cops bagged Neil's BlackBerry, to use as evidence against him. Tonight's attack had transformed her from lawyer to fact witness, and she prayed that her statement could free Lonnie Stall.

"We should've gone to the hospital first," the cop said, for the umpteenth time. "This isn't procedure."

"I'm fine, I just need to see Chief Weber." Mary scanned the large squad room, where detectives, staff, and uniformed cops hustled this way and that between cluttered metal desks, old desktop computers, and battered file cabinets. She didn't see Weber. "She said she'd meet me here."

"Wait here, I'll find her," the cop said, going ahead just as the door to one of the interview rooms opened and Weber emerged with a cadre of assistant district attorneys, all in suits from work.

"Chief!" Mary hurried after the cop, and Weber turned, her eyes flaring in alarm.

"Mary, My God, look at you!" Chief Weber came forward and gave Mary a brief hug. "You didn't say you were injured, on the phone. You need to be seen."

"I will, after we talk. Where can you take my statement?"

"In the interview room. Let's go."

Later, Chief Weber and two A.D.A.s took rapid notes on their legal pads and laptops while Mary told them in detail what had happened, from how Neil had delivered the check to the church, to how he'd tried to kill her, to what Richard had said to her on Neil's phone. Weber asked her plenty of questions, eliciting the details with concern.

"So, Chief," Mary said, when she was finished, "what happens now and how does it affect Lonnie Stall?"

"First, I'd like to thank you for the doggedness and determination that you showed in pursuing this case." Weber set down her pen in a final way. "I can't say that I expected the day to end this way, after our meeting this morning. You took me seriously, I'll tell you that."

"Thanks."

"You risked your life, and as grateful as I am, please don't do it again."

"Okay." Mary still wanted an answer to her question. All this talking was hurting her jaw, but she wasn't about to stop now. "So what now? Do you go pick up Richard Gardner now and take him in for questioning? Will you offer him a deal to confess or will you offer Patel one, or play one off against the other? And regardless of who killed Fiona, doesn't the fact that the guilty plea was bought and paid for mean that you reopen the Lonnie Stall case?"

"Not so fast." Weber raised a palm. "It doesn't happen that way. This is only the beginning of the investigatory work that has to be done, and it could take time."

"Why?" Mary knew Weber was giving her the party line and didn't understand why an innocent man had to stay in jail a minute longer than necessary. "Whether Neil or Richard killed Fiona, now we know that Lonnie Stall isn't guilty. I don't expect you to unlock Stall's cell tonight, but at least tell me that you'll reopen the investigation."

"I can't discuss with you the next steps we'll take, and I know you will understand that that's confidential."

"Even after tonight?" Mary couldn't help but feel disappointed.

"Unfortunately, yes." Weber's expression softened. "We appreciate all that you did, and don't think we don't. You paid the price, and I promise you, the Commonwealth will reap the benefits of your efforts."

"It's not about me, it's about Lonnie Stall. What benefits will he reap?"

"I understand that, and I'm on the same page. That's all I'll say. Obviously, this is a matter of utmost confidentiality, and since you're not representing Lonnie Stall, don't expect any updates, officially."

Mary blinked in surprise.

"Yes, I know you're not his lawyer. I'm smarter than I look."

"But what about Neil Patel? Are you going to offer him a deal to give evidence against Richard Gardner?" Mary tried to guess their strategy. "I'm not asking as a lawyer, I'm asking as a crime victim. I have a right to know that, don't I?"

"Yes." Weber pursed her lips, their lipstick long gone. "Any deals offered eventually to Neil Patel in return for his testimony will be discussed with you, as his victim, but he isn't talking. However, in connection with his attack on you, we expect to charge him tonight with attempted murder, aggravated assault, assault with a deadly weapon, and firearms offenses."

"Good."

"And it's important you understand that at this point, Neil Patel has not been charged with Fiona Gardner's murder. He is merely a person of interest, and that's what I'm telling the media, when it starts circling. I'm not breathing a word about Richard Gardner, of course, and neither are you." Weber arched an eyebrow. "We're clear on that, correct?"

Suddenly there was a knock on the door, and they all looked over. The door opened, and a detective stuck his head inside the room. "Gloria, you have a phone call."

Weber recoiled with a frown. "Jake, I'm taking a statement here."

"You're gonna wanna take this call. It's from a lawyer."

"Patel's?"

"No." The detective half-smiled. "Richard Gardner's. He wants to come in and talk."

Chapter Forty-nine

Mary sat up on the examining table in the ER bay while the doctor finished typing into a laptop on a plastic standing desk. The hustle and bustle of the busy ER emanated from beyond the patterned curtain, which encased her examining room like a medical cocoon. She'd been so busy with the police and the doctors that she hadn't had a chance to phone anyone. There were so many people to call that she didn't know whom to call first. Her mind flipped through the possibilities. Mary could call Rita first, to tell her that she'd found the real killer, but that the car was an accordian. Or Anthony, to tell him that she had an excellent reason for missing drinks. Or Judy and Lou, to tell them that Neil Patel and Richard Gardner were the bad guys, not Tim Gage. Or her parents, to tell them that they should positively, definitely, not turn on the TV to hear a story about her attempted murder. Or Bennie, to tell her that her new partner had cracked the Gardner case. Or Allegra, to tell her that she wasn't as crazy as everybody thought. Or John and Jane Gardner, to tell them that their legal counsel was also their daughter's killer. Or El Virus, to tell her that she wouldn't be caught dead in that hideous wedding dress, even after a night when she was almost caught dead.

"Okay, Mary," the doctor said, hitting a key on the keyboard. He rolled the standing desk against the wall, walked over to her bedside, and smiled pleasantly down at her. He was about thirty years old, had short, dark hair, and weary blue eyes behind his wire-rimmed glasses. "You're doing fine, but I'd like you to have an MRI and a neck X-ray and I'd like to admit you for observation until tomorrow."

"Okay."

"How's that jaw feel?"

"The Advil helped."

"Good. I'm ordering it for you to keep the swelling down and help you rest tonight. Do you have any other questions?"

"No, but I should probably call someone and let them know I'm here."

"Of course you should." The doctor frowned. "Didn't the triage nurse ask you who you want us to call?"

"I didn't see the triage nurse. The police hustled me in pretty quickly."

"My apologies, then. It's the weekend, so we're busy, but that was an oversight on our part." The doctor slid a ballpoint and a pad from the pocket of his lab coat. "Now, who should I call? I'll do it myself after I admit you and I'll make sure to tell them your room number."

"Can you call more than one person?"

"Big family, eh?" The doctor smiled. "I know how that goes, but we're busy tonight and I usually call one, then they do a daisy chain."

Mary tried to imagine a daisy chain that included both Jane Gardner and El Virus.

"Who's your first call?" the doctor asked, waiting.

Mary thought a minute, and her heart answered for her.

Chapter Fifty

"Hey, honey," Mary said, choking up when Anthony rushed into her hospital room, his dark eyes wide with alarm.

"Babe, what the hell happened?" He hurried over to the bed, sat down heavily, and scooped her up in his arms, rocking her back and forth. "My God, what happened? How did this happen? Who hurt you?"

"Aw." Mary buried herself in the warmth of his neck, blinking away tears that caught her by surprise. The smell of beer and other people's cigarettes clung to his oxford shirt, but she didn't mind. "Were you out? Sorry I couldn't make it."

"Oh my God, who cares?" Anthony held her close to his chest, resting his cheek on her head. "I can't believe this! I thought you were okay!"

"I thought I was, too." Mary sobbed, but she sensed they weren't talking about the same thing. She'd thought she was fine, having been installed in a nice private room after her MRI and X-ray, and she hadn't realized she was upset until she saw him. Maybe that's what love was, after all. It struck her that whoever you cry in front of, that's who you love.

Anthony pulled back, his eyes filming as they searched hers.

"Honey, somebody tried to *kill* you? Are you okay? What the hell is going on?"

"How did you find that out?" Mary wiped her tears, with a final sniffle. "The nurse didn't tell you that, did she?"

"No she just said it was a car accident, not serious, and you'd been admitted. But there's reporters outside, and it's going to be on the news tonight."

"Oh no, my parents." Mary felt stricken. "I don't want them to find out that way. I just got put in this room, and the phone and TV aren't signed up yet. I don't have my phone."

"Don't worry." Anthony caressed her arm, his touch soothing. "I called your parents and told them you were in the hospital, and when I found out what the reporters said, I called them from the lobby and told them that, too. They're up to speed."

"Thank you so much." Mary breathed a relieved sigh.

"They're on their way with my mother and The Tonys, and I also called Bennie and Judy, who called Lou, Anne, and Marshall."

"Thanks so much." Mary realized she did have a daisy chain, after all.

"Now, what happened, and when did it happen? Your message said you were in a church."

"I was." Mary thought of how she wrecked Rita's car and felt teary all over again. "Do you have a cell phone? Lonnie's mother lent me her car and she's expecting me to bring it back, and that's the car I crashed. I have to tell her that she shouldn't worry about the damage. I'll pay for whatever isn't covered."

"Lonnie Stall's mother? What were you doing in her car?" Anthony's expression changed, and he frowned, puckering his lower lip with regret. "Wait, I forgot, your car got towed the other day. Honey, I'm so sorry. I should've gotten a parking space a long time ago. We'll rent a space in the garage from now on, I promise. We'll get two, or maybe five. Whatever you want, you got it."

"It's okay." Mary smiled, touched, as Anthony reached into his back pocket and handed her a cell phone.

"Here, I'm so sorry, really."

"No, I'm sorry, I was so caught up." Mary accepted his BlackBerry, scrolled to the phone function, then realized she didn't remember Rita's cell-phone number, because it was in her phone. "Give me a second, okay?" She called information, got the church's main number, and let it ring before it went to voicemail, when she left a detailed message for Rita and hung up. "I hope she gets that."

"I'm sure she will." Anthony gave her another hug and put out his hand for the cell phone. "You finished with that?"

"Yes." Mary handed it back, then hesitated. "Wait a minute. I'd love to call Weber and see what's going on at the Roundhouse. I have to believe she'll reopen Lonnie Stall's case now, but she wasn't making any promises when she threw me out."

"Really? That's awesome!" Anthony's eyes widened, and he handed her back the phone. "Do it. Make whatever calls you need to."

"Thanks." Mary took the BlackBerry and scrolled to the phone function again, then stopped short, having second thoughts. Weber would have to reopen the case, after what had happened at the Roundhouse tonight, and Mary didn't need a call to confirm what she knew was inevitable. Instead, she looked up at Anthony, and when her eyes met his, an empty space in time was created, one that was filled not by phone calls, but by the depth of their connection and the love she felt for him. And in that moment, Mary eyed his handsome face, with his patient and loving expression, and she learned something she hadn't known before. She set the phone aside, leaned over, and kissed him gently on the lips, then harder, with enough emotion to hurt her bandaged jaw.

"Wow!" Anthony grinned, startled, when the kiss was over. "What was *that* about?"

"Believe it, baby. You just got tongue, in a hospital room."

"I know." Anthony burst into laughter, a deep masculine sound that emanated from his chest, even his heart. "What did I do right?"

"Everything, and when we get home, you might get attempted-murder sex."

"That sounds even better than partnership sex." Anthony laughed again.

"Oh, it is. It involves the element of danger, plus a major felony."

"Yowza!" Anthony lifted an eyebrow.

"Partnership sex is for lawyers. Attempted-murder sex is for badasses."

"Listen to you!" Anthony grinned crookedly, reaching over and moving a strand of hair from her jaw bandage. "You're a badass now?"

"Yes, I am. I hit people in the face with bricks. I'm a changed woman." Mary felt momentarily proud of herself, which was all she was allowed. "At least temporarily."

"I love you, and I love any woman you want to be, even temporarily."

"I love you, too," Mary said simply, and then she found herself adding, "And by the way, where the *hell* is my engagement ring?"

Anthony's happy grin evaporated, and he looked at her with newly serious eyes. "You sure you want that ring? Any idiot can see that you haven't exactly been psyched about getting married."

Mary felt a lump in her throat, pained that she had hurt him. "That was before, but this is after, and after, I know how lucky I am."

"MARY, MY POOR BABY!" came a shout from the doorway, then, "*Maria, cara!*"

"Pop! Ma! Everybody!" Mary called back, as her parents, The Tonys, El Virus, Anthony's brother Dom, Bennie, Judy, Lou, Anne, and Marshall piled into the not-so-private room, filling it with hugs, tears, and contraband baked ziti, until everybody settled down, finding chairs, beds, and window ledges to sit on while Mary told them everything that had happened, editing out the scary parts so she didn't give her favorite senior citizens a collective cardiac arrest.

"MARE, WE'RE SO PROUD A YOU!" her father said when she was finished, hugging her again, and Mary would have thanked him, but everybody talked at once, like an Italian happy ending.

"*Si cara, ti amo!*" her mother said, hugging her next in line.

"Mare, you did a great job!" Feet grinned, from his wheelchair.

"Mary, you're the bee's knees, get it?" said Tony-From-Down-The-Block, but nobody laughed.

"*Maria, che magnifica, bravissima!*" Pigeon Tony blew her a kiss.

"Mary, you're the best daughter-in-law I could ask for!" El Virus said, tears in her eyes, and Dom looked over.

"You mean, 'daughter,' Ma. Mary's a lawyer, and you gotta keep it legal." Dom turned to Mary with a toothy smile. "By the way, great job, Mare. You did the Rotunno name proud."

Her father looked over. "DOM, SHE'S A DINUNZIO! IN THE NEWSPAPERS TOMORROW, IT'LL SAY DINUNZIO!"

"You did an amazing job!" Judy applauded, her face alive with happiness. "Congratulations, and thank God you're okay. Next time, don't get attacked without me!"

"Mary, I got to tell you, you're gonna put me out of a job." Lou smiled at her warmly. "I hardly lifted a finger."

"Mary, way to go!" Marshall grinned.

Anne looked happy, but worried. "Great job, Mary, but no job is worth your life."

Bennie looked askance at Anne, then flashed Mary a thumbs-up, with a sly grin. "Brilliant work. Way to go, partner."

Mary felt happy and excited, despite the undercurrent of warfare between the DiNunzio and Rotunno clans. "Thanks so much, everybody. You're all wonderful to come and see me tonight, and I'm so lucky to have all of you in my life."

Bennie rose, brushing off her khaki suit. "We're lucky, too, especially me. Maybe we should put your name on the letterhead? Rosato & DiNunzio. What do you say?"

"I say yes," Mary answered, with a happy smile.

Chapter Fifty-one

The next morning, Mary got herself discharged from the hospital, left a bewildered Anthony at home, changed into jeans and a cotton sweater, and hit the highway in Mike's old lime-green BMW 2002, which started the moment she twisted on the ignition and still hummed all the way out to Townsend, under clearing skies that she couldn't help but feel were metaphorical.

In time, Mary reached the winding road to Houyhnhnm Farm, braked, and pressed the button on the Gardners' call box. "It's Mary," she said simply, knowing they would see her immediately. The gates opened wide, and she steered through, followed the gravel road to the house, and parked in the family parking lot, where she cut the ignition and got out of the car.

The air was balmy, sweet, and clean, and Mary took a deep breath, inhaling a lungful before she confronted the task at hand. She walked toward the house, surrounded by the green and glorious property, with its bay horses grazing in the pastures and noisy birds chirping in the aviary. Nothing would suggest this was a home in crisis. Perhaps it always had been, but nobody had known it before.

"Mary?" she heard a man's voice ask, and she looked over to see Alasdair striding toward her, dressed in a T-shirt and riding breeches, presumably because thoroughbreds had to be exercised, indictments or no.

"Hey, Alasdair." Mary walked over to him, and they met on the gravel road near the entrance to the house.

"I didn't recognize the car. The police and various lawyers have been coming and going, most of the morning. You threw me off."

"It was my husband's." Mary's chest still tightened when she looked at the car. "It runs a lot better than it looks."

"Oh, I'm sure it does. It's a beauty. I drive a Triumph, the TR6, which was made by British Leyland. I fixed it up myself."

"So I guess you heard."

"Yes, and my wife and I are so sorry about what happened to you." Alasdair touched her arm, frowning with concern. "How are you? Is your jaw injured?"

"No, I'm fine, and it's nothing serious."

"Who knew Richard and Neil would do such a thing?" Alasdair shook his head, his expression pained. "Who knew about any of it?"

"Nobody did, and it's Allegra I'm worried about. I'm going to see her as soon as I finish here."

"Good, give her my love and tell her the bees are doing wonderfully. You think they'll let her come home now?"

"I'm hoping." Mary glanced at the house, bracing herself. "I'd better get going."

"Sure, let me know if you need anything." Alasdair patted her arm again, and Mary took off toward the house, where she was met at the door by the housekeeper, who was short and plump, with a kind smile and halo of gray curls.

"Hello, I'm Janet. You must be Mary. Please, let me show you in."

"Thanks," Mary said, steeling herself.

Chapter Fifty-two

The Gardners had a large country kitchen ringed with raw pine cabinets, rustic tile countertops, and top-of-the-line appliances, and Mary sat across from Jane and John Gardner, downcast in their matching polo shirts and khakis, unsure where to begin. "I guess I should explain what happened with Neil last night, then you can fill me in on why you think it all happened."

"Let me go first." John shook his head, his expression softer then Mary had ever seen before, which she should've expected. "I owe you an apology, that's job one. I'm very sorry for the way I treated you from the outset. I said some awful things to you and your colleague, and I'm very sorry, especially in view of what's come to light now."

"I am, too, very sorry." Next to him, Jane nodded, her hand clutching a fresh Kleenex. "I'm so sorry that you were in danger last night."

"That wasn't your fault."

Jane pursed her lips. "In a way, it was. We thought we were doing what was best for Allegra, but evidently, we weren't. We've made some grave mistakes in this family and frankly, I don't know what I've been thinking, as a mother."

Mary could see how upset she felt. "I'm sorry too, for coming on so strong in the beginning. I could've been gentler."

"Not at all, please." John waved her off. "In any event, to come to the subject, here's exactly what happened last night, and how we found out about Neil and Richard. Jane and I were here in the kitchen, and I was on the laptop when I saw a story online that Neil had been arrested in the attempted murder of one Mary DiNunzio."

Mary tried to get used to herself being referred to in the third person, especially in the same sentence as attempted murder.

"You can imagine, we had no idea what was going on. We couldn't believe our ears. The first thing I did was to call Richard and Edward, and they raced over. We all sat down together, right where we are now." John gestured vaguely to a pitcher of fresh lemonade and a platter of oatmeal cookies that sat untouched in the middle of the lovely cherrywood table. "I said that I couldn't understand why any of this was happening, that it didn't make any sense. Why would Neil try to kill you? Jane felt the same way, we were both of us flabbergasted. Then Richard announced to the room, 'I have something terrible to tell you. I'm going to call a lawyer and turn myself in to the police.'"

"What?" Mary's mouth dropped open, even though Gloria Weber had already given her the gist. But it was one thing to hear it from the Chief, and quite another to hear it from the family.

John swallowed, and his Adam's apple traveled up and down in the open neck of his polo shirt. "By way of background, you know that Fiona had been working on the Meyers acquisition, doing filing and such at the cottage, for him and Neil."

"Yes."

"Richard said that at the time, he and Neil had been embezzling from one of our clients, the construction of Foster Towers in Salisbury, Maryland, and hiding the theft in cost overruns and change orders. They'd managed to keep it secret for almost a year, accumulating about six hundred thousand dollars. But then, on the day our new headquarters in the city were to open, Fiona happened to walk in on him and Neil, when they were having a conversation about some of the funds and bank accounts." John pursed his lips, then continued. "Richard didn't think Fiona overheard anything, but Neil was worried. He knew she was smart and took an avid interest in the business and he was afraid that she'd tell us or the police. Richard calmed him down and believed that he had allayed Neil's anxiety. Evidently, he hadn't, and that night at the party, Neil slipped away and murdered her."

Mary couldn't speak for a minute. She had seen that Neil was a belt-and-suspenders kind of guy, when Feet had fallen. Neil had been so careful to make sure that the company didn't get sued. But she didn't dream that would extend to murder.

John cleared his throat, without success. "Richard had no idea that Neil had done this, and that night, he believed that Lonnie Stall was the guilty party, just as we all did. Now, fast-forward to the present day, when Allegra hired your firm. You entered the picture and started looking into the murder case, and Neil told Richard everything. The two of them decided to stop you from going forward, by any means necessary."

Jane said softly, "It's awful, I'm so sorry."

Mary thought back to what Chief Weber had told her last night. "So Richard came forward, confessed, and implicated Neil, in return for a plea deal."

"Yes. He told us he wanted to take responsibility and spare us all a second trial. He was going to try to convince Neil to do the same, and we hope that he will plead guilty as well."

Mary sighed. "Well, the deal's confession puts the nail in the coffin, as far as reopening Lonnie Stall's case. The prosecution will cover its bases, following up on the payment for the guilty plea and also retesting the original samples of trace evidence, to determine that they are Neil's. But I believe this will set Lonnie Stall free."

"We know." John glanced at Jane and placed his hand over hers. "Obviously, we take some satisfaction in his exoneration, and we're relieved that Richard turned himself in and accepted responsibility for his complicity. But it doesn't do anything to bring Fiona back, which is what we both want, in our heart of hearts."

"I know, and I'm sorry."

"So are we," John said, anguished.

"May I ask a question?" Mary didn't understand something, and neither had Chief Weber. "Why would Richard embezzle money, given his wealth?"

"It wasn't about the money, for him. Unfortunately, we've always had some measure of sibling rivalry, completely on his part, with his feeling that he needs to come out of my shadow."

Mary flashed on the corporate portraits at the cottage, which featured John so prominently among the brothers, and she remembered her sense that the cottage was distinctly junior to the corporate headquarters, in its fancy award-winning building.

"Richard became emotional last night, and he told us that he just wanted to prove to himself that he could do it. That he was smart enough not only to take the money, but to take it from me and hide it from me. So you see, it didn't concern money at all."

Mary eased back in her chair, suddenly exhausted. "I understand the whole picture now, and thanks for taking the time to explain it to me. I know this hasn't been easy for you, either of you. My primary concern, of course, is Allegra."

"Ours, too." Jane sniffled.

"I had intended to see you, then go to Churchill and tell her what happened. I was worried she would find out from TV news or the Internet. More importantly, I thought she should know, amidst all of this pain, that she was right all along, and she deserves to be thanked."

John nodded, and new tears filled Jane's eyes.

"I think she really needs to hear that, but now I understand that she doesn't need to hear it from me. She needs to hear it from you. Both of you."

John blinked, and Jane sniffled, wiping her eyes, leaving pinkish streaks on her fair cheeks.

"So I propose, at this point, that I bow out. Allegra doesn't need a lawyer anymore, if she ever did. What she needs is her mother and her father." Mary could see from their subdued expressions that they were open to hearing her, at long last. "There is no substitute for you both, and you may feel broken and horrible now, but this family can come together. This is the time to start. You may have lost Fiona, but you still have Allegra. As I told you, in my own life, I've lost someone to violent crime, too. And the way to honor Fiona is to embrace Allegra."

Jane rose suddenly. "Mary, I think you're right. We'll leave right now, and I can't wait to see her."

John looked up at his wife in surprise. "But we're not on her visitors' list. She won't see us."

Jane stiffened, squaring her shoulders. "John, I don't go against you often, but this time, I am. Nobody negotiates harder than you do in business, and it's time you put that expertise to work in this family. We're going to Churchill and we're going to sit in that waiting room until she sees us."

John stood up, with a half smile. "Fair enough, we'll give it a try."

Mary got to her feet, feeling a weight lifted. "Good call, John. Your wife is making sense and you need to listen to her."

John grinned, extending a hand. "Thanks. Now, Mary, I know you're the only lawyer in the world who doesn't care about money, but I'll see to it that your fee is paid."

Mary smiled, shaking his hand. "Now that I'm a partner, I appreciate the value of money more than I used to. I'll take you up on that offer. Thank you very much."

"John, well done." Jane brightened, coming around the table. "Mary, I'll walk you out."

"Yes, please do," Mary told her, having an ulterior motive.

Chapter Fifty-three

"Feel better?" Mary asked Jane, as they walked in the warm sun to the car.

"Much." Jane turned to her, with a growing smile. "I'm nervous about dealing with Allegra, but we're going to make it work. We simply have to heal this family."

"Good for you. I'm a big believer in the truth setting you free."

"I think that's right," Jane said softly. "By the way, how's Feet?"

"Wonderful, thanks. If I may, however, there's one last thing I want to mention to you." Mary braced herself to lower the boom. "It's not my business, but I'm on a roll."

"What is it?" Jane asked, mystified.

"If you remember, this all began when Allegra came to us, saying that she knew Lonnie Stall. She told us that she had seen him when Fiona was babysitting her, yet John said that Fiona was never asked to babysit."

Jane's expression darkened, and her pace slowed on the gravel, though she said nothing.

"Jane, I don't think your husband was lying to me when he said that, so the only logical conclusion is that you lied to him. That means that you were having Fiona babysit Allegra without his knowledge, and I can think of only one reason you would do that."

Jane hung her head slightly.

"It doesn't matter to me if you were having an affair." Mary paused, waiting for Jane to tell her to shut up, but it didn't happen. "Again, my concern is Allegra. She knows what she knows. She remembers what she remembers. If she's to have any hope of reclaiming her mental health, somebody has to tell her the truth."

Jane groaned, shaking her head. "I can't do that."

"Why not?"

"Because John doesn't know." Jane kept shaking her head. "What do I do? Tell Allegra not to tell him?"

"No." Mary didn't hesitate. "You need to tell him yourself."

"About the affair?"

"Yes."

Jane's lovely eyes locked with Mary's. "Even if the man I was having an affair with was Richard?"

Mary absorbed the information without showing the dismay she felt. "Even then, and especially then."

"But it's so awful, and of course it ended the night Fiona was killed. It didn't even go on that long. Now I see that Richard never really loved me, he just wanted to best John." Jane closed her eyes. "It's mortifying. It was just Richard proving he was smarter than John. I was a possession to be won."

Mary touched her arm. "Jane, you're a good person, and I'm sure there's a reason why you strayed, but that's between you and John. Allegra's welfare is what matters now, over John's feelings, or yours. She didn't create the problem, and she doesn't deserve to suffer for it."

"I know." Jane nodded, and they both looked over when Alasdair shouted to them, walking over with a grin.

"Jane! I just had an amazing ride, and Paladin's so fit, I swear. You must ride out today. He's keen to go."

Jane quickly put on a smile. "Maybe I will, tomorrow."

"Brilliant!" Alasdair reached them in an effusive good mood, gesturing at the green BMW. "And did you see Mary's car? That's almost as beautiful as a warmblood, at least to my eye."

Jane smiled again. "What is it with men and cars?"

Alasdair laughed, throwing back his head. "What is it with women and horses?"

But Mary was already getting an idea. "Alasdair, you like my car?"

"Love it! Who wouldn't? It's a classic, the BMW 2002. I bet it runs beautifully, doesn't it?"

"Here, see for yourself." Mary fished in her back pocket for the keys and handed them over.

"I can take it out for spin? Awesome!"

"No, I have a better idea." Mary was thinking about what she'd said to the Gardners, which she'd never realized until now. The way to honor Mike was to embrace Anthony. "Give me a ride to the train station, then you can keep it. It's yours, as a gift."

Jane gasped. "How terrific!"

"Are you serious?" Alasdair's eyes popped open. "What are you talking about? I can't accept it, no way!"

"Take it, please." Mary smiled, bittersweet. "I want somebody to give it a good home, and love it as much as my late husband did."

"But why let it go?" Alasdair asked, astounded.

"Because it's time," Mary answered, simply.

Chapter Fifty-four

CONGRATULATIONS, read the banner, and Mary scanned the happy scene in the conference room, amazed that so much had happened in a few short months. Richard Gardner's confession and guilty plea to conspiracy in the attempt to kill Mary, and the statement he gave the authorities about Neil's murder of Fiona had been instrumental in forcing Neil to plead guilty to Fiona's murder, and both were both serving time in Graterford Prison. Richard had been given a twenty-year sentence for third-degree murder, and Neil was serving life without parole. In the aftermath, the Gardners had begun to heal their family. Allegra was happy and healthy in school, seeing her bees every day and her therapist once a week. John and Jane Gardner seemed closer than before, and at the moment, the three Gardners stood together by the baked ziti, engaged in an animated conversation with Rita Henley and Lonnie Stall, who had been released from prison last week, completely exonerated.

Lonnie had been so thankful to Mary and Allegra, and he'd denied having a personal relationship to Fiona because he'd thought it would look like he had a motive for murdering her, or subject him to a charge of statutory rape. He and Fiona had been falling in love, talking on the phone and online, and seeing each other when they could. They'd been planning to go public after The Gardner Group's grand opening party, when her life had been cruelly cut short. Mary felt deeply satisfied that she'd been able to help Lonnie, in addition to proving that the law did lead to justice, however belatedly.

The Tonys were at today's party too, and though Feet's foot had healed, he sat in front of the chocolate chip cannolis, for obvious reasons. Tony-From-Down-The-Block was to his right, chatting up Sister Helen, who had come with Rita and let it be known that she was single. Pigeon Tony was on his third cup of black coffee, speaking caffeinated Italian to Judy, Lou, Anne, and Marshall, who had no idea what he was talking about until it was translated by his grandson, Judy's live-in boyfriend Frank Lucia. Mary felt so happy that all of them were at the party, though there was a hole in her heart, without Angie there. Her twin was still out of the country on her mission, but they'd reached her and she'd promised to be home for Mary's wedding.

Bennie lingered near the head of the conference table, talking with Mary's mother, her father, El Virus, and Dom. Mary watched them with anticipation, knowing that it was time for a surprise announcement, which they'd agreed should come from the senior partner.

"Excuse me, everyone!" Bennie called out after a moment, turning to the crowd with an expectant smile. "If I may have your attention, I'd like to propose a toast to Allegra, for being so smart and brave, and to Lonnie, who has gotten the justice he deserved, however belatedly."

Everyone raised his glass, shouting approval in English and Italian, and Rita called out, "Amen to that! Praise Jesus!" Allegra and Lonnie beamed, standing happily together, one covered with bees and the other with tattoos.

Bennie smiled. "In addition, I have an announcement. All of us at Rosato & DiNunzio are so impressed with Allegra's talents and abilities, and we like her very much. She's been looking for something to do after school, and we've offered her a part-time position as our intern. Welcome on board, Allegra!"

"Yes, welcome!" Mary chimed in.

"Thanks!" Allegra grinned, and Jane gave her a big hug.

"*Bravissima,* Allegra!" shouted Mary's mother.

"ATTA GIRL!" said her father.

"Hear, hear! To my stellar daughter!" John Gardner raised his glass. "And I have an announcement, of my own. I was just speaking with Lonnie, who's been looking for a job, too. I'm happy to report that he'll start on Monday in management training at The Gardner Group, while he returns to classes at Temple."

"Congrats, Lonnie!" Mary called out, applauding.

"Way to go!" Judy nodded.

"Praise Jesus!" Rita clapped.

"Hallelujah!" Sister Helen beamed.

Anthony leaned over and whispered to Mary, "This is your handiwork, isn't it?"

"Shhh." Mary smiled, because he knew her so well. She was lucky to have him, and she remembered it every time she spied her engagement ring sparkling on her finger—though she'd come to think the diamond wasn't all *that* big.

"What a happy, happy day!" Rita beamed. "And congratulations to Mary, too, because she's getting married!"

"Best wishes to the bride!" Sister Helen peered at Mary over her pink glasses. "What kind of dress you gonna get, honey?"

"Uh, I'm not sure." Mary may have become a partner, gotten an innocent man exonerated, and sent a guilty man to jail, but she still hadn't settled the War of the Wedding Dresses.

El Virus chirped up, "She's gonna wear my wedding dress, ain't that nice?"

Her father frowned. "NO, SHE'S GONNA WEAR HER MOTHER'S DRESS."

Mary looked from one mother to the other. She couldn't hurt her mother by choosing Elvira's dress, or hurt El Virus by choosing her mother's, or hurt them both by buying a new dress. In other words, Mary still had her guilt, doubts, and insecurities, which would probably guarantee that she would walk down the aisle completely naked.

Anthony stepped forward, looking sheepish. "Mom, Vita, I have a confession to make. You know I took the dresses to the dry cleaners, to freshen them up, but the cleaners told me he can't find them. They might have lost them."

"Oh no!" Mary couldn't believe her good luck, though she felt a wave of sympathy for her mother and El Virus.

"Ant!" El Virus's eyes flared in outrage. "Ant, where did you take them? That discount place onna corner? I told you not to go there, ever! They lose everything!"

"Sorry, Ma." Anthony puckered his lower lip, with regret. "I'll keep trying with them. They might be able to find them, but we can't take a chance that it's in time for the wedding."

Mary's mother deflated into a chair, and her father frowned. "ANTHONY, I KNOW IT'S NOT YOUR FAULT, BUT WHAT'S MARY GONNA DO FOR A WEDDING DRESS?"

Anthony faced Mary, shrugging unhappily. "Sorry, babe, you'll have to pick out your own dress. The silver lining is that maybe you can take your friends along, and my mom and yours, when you go shopping?"

"Of course," Mary answered, but suddenly caught a suspicious twinkle in Anthony's dark eyes.

And she realized that she had met her perfect match.

Acknowledgments

It feels great to be back with the women of Rosato & Associates, and my first thanks in these acknowledgments go to my editor, Jennifer Enderlin; my agent, Molly Friedrich; and my assistant and bestie, Laura Leonard, who encouraged me to write the Rosato series on a more routine basis, and from now on, there will be a new Rosato every year. Ladies, thank you all so much for your encouragement, faith, and vision.

As for the research aspect of the novel, I'm a former lawyer, but criminal law wasn't my field. I seek out help when I need it because the facts matter, especially where the law is concerned, and I was lucky enough to find some brilliant and kind souls. A huge hug and enormous admiration to Jennifer Creed Selber, Chief of the Homicide Unit of the District Attorney's Office, who gave me her time and expertise in the clutch, and who is so astoundingly impressive that she should be fictional. Thanks, too, to Ed Cameron, also of the D.A.'s Office, who answered all my questions with good humor and kindness. It goes without saying that any and all mistakes herein are mine.

On the defense side, thanks to my legal team of attorneys extraordinaire Glenn Gilman, Esq., now in private practice, and Daniel

Stevenson, Esq., of the Defender Association of Philadelphia, both of whom helped me a great deal with the legalities that I forgot and/or never knew. I adore and admire you both, gentlemen.

Thanks to the folks at SCI-Graterford Prison in Graterford, Pennsylvania, especially Superintendent Mike Wenerowicz, and Wendy Moyer, Sgt. Randall H. Lacey, and C.O. David M. Weaver, as well as Gina, Tracy, Becky, and everybody else in the superintendent's office. Thanks to Peter Zimmerman, architect and beekeeper, who inspired the bees plotline. Someday, I'll get the nerve to get my own hives. For spot-on trusts-and-estates advice, thanks to Margaret Sager, Esq.

Last but far from least, thanks so much to the brilliant and amazing Dr. Sandy Steingard, who's been my bestie since high school and who grew up to be one of the most prominent psychiatrists in the country. Sandy kept me straight on the psychiatric details, and I owe her for that, and for being such a wonderful and loyal friend for so long.

A big thanks to St. Martin's Press, starting with the terrific John Sargent, Sally Richardson, Matthew Shear, Matt Baldacci, Jeanne-Marie Hudson, Steve Kleckner, Brian Heller, Jeff Capshew, Nancy Trypuc, Kim Ludlam, John Murphy, John Karle, Paul Hochman, Stephanie Davis, Sara Goodman, Caitlin Dareff, and all of our wonderful and energetic sales reps. Big thanks to Rob Grom, for designing a wonderful cover to last an entire series. Hugs and kisses to Esther Bochner, Mary Beth Roche, and Laura Wilson, and the great people in Macmillan Audiobooks. I love and appreciate all of you.

Thanks and big love to the amazing Lucy Carson and Molly Schulman.

Finally, love and deepest thanks to my daughter Francesca, my brother Frank, my Mother Mary, and my late father Frank, without whom there would be no DiNunzios, because my family is at the heart of their family.